Third Eye Witness

Kathi Bjorkman

Third Eye Witness
by Kathi Bjorkman

Based on the Experiences of Marilynn Hughes
*Taken from The Mysteries of the Redemption: A Treatise on Out-of-Body Travel and Mysticism, Marilynn Hughes, Chapter Eight, The Out-of-Body Travel Foundation, 2003, SOURCES
The Mysteries of the Redemption: A Treatise on Out-of-Body Travel and Mysticism, Marilynn Hughes, Chapter Eight, The Out-of-Body Travel Foundation, 2003,
Galactica: A Treatise on Death, Dying and the Afterlife, Marilynn Hughes, Chapter Eight, The Out-of-Body Travel Foundation, 2003

Dedication
I dedicate this book to my, late husband Dan, and daughters Sara and Megan, who supported me throughout the many years it took to create my first novel. With their unwavering encouragement, I never gave up on completing Third Eye Witness.

Author of Third Eye Witness published 1/11/11
Finalist in Two 2013 Chanticleer Book Reviews' Blue Ribbon Writing Contests
CLUE Awards 2013 Finalist
Paranormal/Supernatural Awards 2013 Finalist
Author of Third Eye Witness-Bearer of Truth published 4/15/15
Finalist in 2015 Chanticleer Book Reviews' Blue Ribbon Writing Contest
Paranormal/Supernatural Awards 2015 Finalist

Chapter 1

Blinded by beating wipers and heavy Colorado snowfall, Martine struggled to see through the slush-covered windshield into the darkened night. Abrupt and without warning, the long, horizontal-row of yellow-colored tail lights traveling in front of their car disappeared. Visibility was instantly compromised when the semi's rear lights in front of them vanished. Straining to see the driver next to her, she saw horror in her husband's face, like never before.

Paralyzed in fear, Martine watched helplessly as her husband fought to slow their car down on the slick, snow-drenched highway. "James, James," she shouted while the jeep careened sideways on the road. Bracing herself, the out of control jeep took aim towards the upcoming hazard.

Realizing the semi-load of logged trees in front of their vehicle had jack-knifed, Martine's body stiffened like a soldier. "Oh my god," she cried.

"Martine, watch out," James's frantic voice pitched as he pushed her shoulders downward, forcing her to duck until her head hugged her knees.

Shielding her head with both her hands obstructed her vision. Through the corners of her eyes, Martine saw flashes from the trucker's headlights strobe the inside of their jeep as they converged on the moving barricade. Peripheral vision allowed her to focus to the left where she saw her husband's hardened-face contort, as he spirited the car back and forth trying to regain control.

Illumination from the big cab's headlights allowed her to see her husband's face contort in terror as he spun the steering wheel in an effort to evade collision.

"Damn it!" James cursed as his car impacted the heavy trailer.

Crashing sideways into the tractor's platform bed, Martine heard metal sheer and glass smash as the roof of the jeep was guillotined. Martine stayed crunched tight to her thighs as the lower part of the vehicle separated from the top and was allowed to freely travel through the semi-trailer's underbelly. Seconds felt like minutes as the jeep escaped through to the other side of the trailer and came out spinning like a top. Unable to see clearly in the darkened-night sky, she could not distinguish the moist snowfall from bloody injuries as wetness showered on her.

Martine twisted her neck slightly to glance up at her husband as the jeep spun another three-sixty. Fusillade of spitting glass shards had disfigured him when the Jeep's roof was decapitated. Horrified by the sight, she screamed until their car finally made impact with the guardrail. Bashing her head into the remains of their dashboard made her mind black-out.

From the moment she regained consciousness in the hospital and every day afterward, Martine's severe head concussion allowed only the dimmest recollection of that catastrophic night. Dwelling on the brief and painful moments of clarity that followed stunted her recovery process. She continually asked herself why. Why was her husband of twenty-four years slain so gruesomely? Why was she still alive? Why did they take that route? Why did the trucker lose control? Why, why, why?

With James gone, her world was as shattered as their jeep. Growing more and more miserable over the ghastly accident, challenged her identity and purpose for living.

Every day afterward she tried to find reason behind the morbid tragedy. Lacking any motivation to get up each morning, she remained suspended in a depressed state, her life on hold. Existing in survival mode, Martine's instincts kept her alive.

* * *

Seven months have passed since that fateful night. Alone in the kitchen, she switched on her small TV to hear the morning news. Hurricane Katrina's aftermath was still the top story and coverage of the New Orleans devastation dominated the media. Taking her usual seat at the breakfast bar, the newsman droned on about the city that was eighty-percent underwater.

The break to commercial brought on the loud and annoying sound of some new automobile advertisement. Muting the noise with her remote control, she avoided the irritating sound-byte.

Comforted by the tranquil setting of her childhood home, her anchor, she hid herself away from the rest of the world. Except for a few television programs, Martine was disconnected from most of humanity.

Glorious Colorado mountain peaks couldn't block the inevitable rising sun, or another day from starting. Watching the snow covered crests become iridescent from the powerful morning sun captivated her thoughts. Mesmerized, she contemplated how her life had been like the windowpane in front of her, so clear, smooth, and transparent to what the world had to offer, yet so fragile. Like the survivors of the 2005 Tropical Storm that turned into Hurricane Katrina, her life too was shoved off its track.

Expanding rays of light lit up the inside of Martine's private retreat as the glowing sun moved higher. Radiant beams aimed at her face roused her as she studied the migrating deer grazing in the chilly fall weather. Morning coffee was still a work in progress, although she could already smell the effects of espresso French roast.

Seated at her counter, she moved her gaze up at the knotty-pine ceiling and contemplated how today would differ from yesterday. Unable to stay put, now that sunlight was filling her home, she made her way to the abandoned remodeling project her husband James had started in the bathroom a year ago. Refashioning the old family owned ranch house that Martine and her sister Jolene inherited was James' passion. Spending long weekends and holidays at the homestead was tradition for nearly twenty years. After the accident Martine couldn't find the desire to leave the old home and get her legal profession back on track with the FBI in Denver.

Martine missed her husband and the life they had shared. Mending fences, riding horses, gathering cattle, and laughing with friends and family around evening campfires, consumed their time and weaved their lives together. Memories of togetherness were etched in every corner of the ranch, a ranch they frequented at least six times a year.

James' resourcefulness was part drive and part talent. Determined to have the renovations complete by their anticipated retirement, he had milled the lumber and constructed all the woodworking himself as he restored room after room on their conservative budget.

Brushing her teeth was followed by a forced grin in the mirror to examine her work. Fortyish, and well proportioned, she had commanded attention. Considered beautiful and intelligent by her male counterparts, she had flourished in her legal profession. Her Swedish heritage contributed to the perfect complexion, dramatic cheek bones and fair hair that accentuated her once bright smile.

One prescription bottle stood next to her sink. A single anti-depression tablet tumbled around the bottom as Martine shook it. Tossing the container in the garbage after consuming the medication was ceremonial. Today was the last time she would be dependent on the drug that dulled her anxieties after losing her husband.

After the accident, when she started taking meds, she knew they were a temporary solution. Taking the edge off of her emotions was necessary for her survival. Losing another loved one prevented her from performing her job and caused uncontrollable weight loss. Memory failure and constant headaches caused her to confide in her doctor.

When she denied any form of therapeutic help, her physician threatened hospitalization if she refused to follow his medical advice. Martine adhered to her doctor's order, but made it clear that it was against her better judgment. Fearing dependency, she agreed to use prescription anti-depressants for six months. Long term use of mood suppressants was not an option in her mind, neither was years of therapy. Disciplined and determined, Martine was going to get through her crisis within months, not years. After all, she survived the loss of loved ones before in her life and without any medical treatment.

Over the last week she weaned herself off of Valium, Ambien, Tylenol PM, mega doses of Melatonin, and Prozac. Feeling raw and conflicted, she knew staying on the drugs longer was an option, but not the plan. Throwing the last bottle away today was the agreement she made with her doctor and herself.

Before leaving the partly completed bathroom, Martine looked into the mirror at her disheveled blonde tresses and removed the clip that held the length of them. Free from the barrette, her hair cascaded down past her shoulders. She knew her hair was neglected, in need of professional coloring, and way too long. Nothing, including her appearance, seemed important anymore.

While the coffee maker perked, her cell phone startled her with the rambunctious tune from "Bonanza." That was the ring tone she had selected for her sister Jolene who lived hours away in Arizona.

Opening the musical cell phone put a smile on her face. Knowing how much Jolene detested the ranch life, Martine was humored by the western-themed-ring every time Jolene called. Dodging family trips to the ranch was customary for her sister. Wildlife and cattle round-ups did not interest her in the least. Absurd satire caused Martine to select that customized ring years ago when Jolene left home and headed for college. Martine greeted her much younger sister, "Good morning, Jolene."

"Hey, Martine. How you doin' today?"

Walking back towards the kitchen to fetch a fresh cup of coffee, Martine paused in front of the living room window that faced the eastern sunrise. "I'm great."

"Just wanted to return your call before I leave for work. What's up? Anything important?"

Hypnotized by the pulsating sun, Martine replied, "No . . . not really. There's not much going on here at the ranch. You know there never is."

"Yeah, how's it going with Alexa and Eva? I haven't had one single call from your girls."

Smiling at the portrait of her daughters that hung over the fireplace, Martine explained, "Alexa quit her job and is moving in with me today. She says she's only staying a month. Eva doesn't have any college breaks coming up until Thanksgiving. So, if you can get away, you should come visit Alexa and me." Martine finally made it to the coffee maker and poured herself the hot brew while listening to Jolene's reply.

"I can't believe Alexa has quit her job. We just gotta get together. I'll try and plan a long weekend getaway. My job is so demanding, though. I guess you know that, since you helped me get in with the FBI. You could come down here, Martine. I just can't make definite plans. I don't have any vacation time yet."

Sitting down on the cowhide bar stool, Martine said, "Yes, I know we can come down to Arizona, but I don't want to go anywhere right now."

"Martine, you're going to have to get out of that old ranch house you live in. There are people on earth who want to see you again. Don't you miss work? Don't you miss Denver? Transfer to Phoenix if you don't want to go back up there. Have you even talked to the bureau about your job? You just can't stay in Durango. We can talk about that tonight if you want. I need to get going though. Don't want to be late."

"Yeah, yeah. I'll let you go. Miss you. Have a great day."

"Martine, wait. Is there something you're not telling me? Did you have a dream? Do you know something I don't know?"

"No, absolutely not. I haven't had anything like that for months."

"Probably because you're depressed. Who wouldn't be? You're just not around enough people right now. Make that any people."

"Well, sis, you're the detective in the family. I'll let you go till you have more time to talk. Love you. Have a great day at work."

Any conversation about depression drove Martine crazy. Using meds was embarrassing and she avoided the subject with everyone. After all, she was a big girl with grown children.

Left alone with her feelings of failure, she checked to see whose call she missed. Only one showed up on her phone. Her Uncle Michael was probably following up on their lunch plans.

Uncle Michael, or Mike as he preferred to be called, was her father's brother. Martine was her father's namesake, in a manner of speaking. She was expected to be a boy, with a twin brother. Her parents Martin and Joan planned to name the twin boys Martin and Michael.

Shock rang through the hospital when the identical twins turned out to be girls. Being the first born, she was named Martine instead of Martin, and her sister became Michaela instead of Michael.

Martine and Uncle Mike both shared the tragedy of losing a sibling. Uncle Mike was her deceased father's brother and physically resembled him in almost every way. Martine lost both her parents almost twenty years ago. Michaela, Martine's twin sister, met with disaster thirty years ago when they were adolescents. None of these deaths compared to the passing of her beloved husband. James completed her. Lovers, best friends, and confidantes to each other, nothing filled the void she felt inside.

Prompting her voice mail for the new message, she listened to her Uncle Mike, "You better not call me back and cancel our lunch again, Martine. I'll be there early, waitin' on your arrival." Uncle Mike's message ended with instructions on where they were meeting in Durango.

Chapter 2

"Sir, line two is for you," conveyed a pleasant, female voice.

Picking up the portable phone receiver, Director Mahoney answered with his usual commanding voice, "Mahoney, here."

"Hello, sir, this is, Chief Reuben Mayer, with the Holbrook Police Department."

Mahoney settled back in his chair. "Yes, Chief, how are things going?"

"Well, it's been darn quiet up here until now, so, I believe you're the people I should be talking to."

"How can the Arizona FBI help you, Chief Mayer?"

"I suspect you're going to hear about it very soon, thanks to the gung-ho journalists working up here in Holbrook. What they don't know is the connection we believe this latest development has with some other out of state crimes."

Mahoney shifted his weight for comfort, propping his elbow on the chair's armrest. "Chief, what crimes are you referring to? For that matter—what latest development?"

"Sorry, early this morning the body of a missing sixteen-year-old girl was discovered in the desert. She matches the description of a girl, by the name of Lauren, from Southland, Utah. She was reported missing about six months ago. We suspect, from the initial examination, she died within the last month. She also was placed in the desert after she experienced death. We have a very weak crime scene. More to the point, it's more like a dumpsite. The murder couldn't have taken place there."

Standing up, Mahoney turned around to straighten the large framed print of a "roping cowboy" that was heading the horns on a steer. "Hmm, that's unfortunate—what else?"

"You aware of the other missing girls?"

Using his hand, he wiped the dusty framed picture he just balanced on his wall. "I'm not exactly sure what you're referring to."

"We believe that there's an escalating number of missing girls being reported within the Four Corners area. That's what the media doesn't know. We feel the FBI's better qualified to evaluate this speculation, and contain information before it leaks out to more reporters. We don't need public panic, or to jeopardize the victims if they're still alive."

Walking to the side of his office, he looked out over cactus landscaping. "Are you insinuating there's a serial murderer in the Four Corners?"

"Yes, sir, I am. The young detective who was working in Southland before transferring here is the reason we were able to identify the girl at all. Months ago, before transferring here, he was assigned to this young Utah girl's case. He began frequenting a missing person's web site. After his transfer to our department he continued to monitor this web site and observed a significant increase in abductions within the four states. He also noticed the missing girls' ages are between fifteen and twenty. Until now, the detective suspected human trafficking."

Using his free hand again, he tilted the louvers on the miniblind to deflect the bright sun. "Are you saying he doesn't feel that way because a victim was found deceased?"

"Yes, and because of how we found the body."

Mahoney stopped adjusting things and paused for a brief second. "Chief Mayer, what haven't you told me?"

"Sir, you need to see for yourself."

Chapter 3

Zipping her satchel purse closed, Jolene grabbed her coffee cup and finished the last sip. After setting the cup back down next to her sink she walked to her home office, which always appeared organized and meticulous. Jolene was allergic to clutter. Other than her computer, only one barn-wood framed photo of her beloved family adorned her desk.

Martine, her older sister e-mailed the photo memory to update the previous photo by two years. Jolene reproduced the digital photo into an eight-by-ten graphic and framed it. The photo captured Martine and her daughters Alexa and Eva dining in a Durango restaurant—celebrating Eva's twenty-first birthday. Accepting a coveted position with the Arizona Federal Bureau of Investigation prevented her from attending the big event.

Sweeping her shoulder-length blonde hair back, she smiled down at her bouncy cream-colored Pomeranian. The dog could not seem to stop running, spinning, or pouncing on her white cat, Sugar.

Wade, the man she had been dating, made the dog a gift. Accepting the pup from her new boyfriend made her feel like they were creating a family together. Naming her furry-companion, Honey, was an act of spontaneity which was out of character for her.

With regrets, she didn't get to keep the man that delivered the precious pooch to her home. Detective Wade Wagner stopped contacting her and ended their relationship.

Jolene leaned over her desk chair and viewed her incoming e-mails one last time before departing to the Bureau. "Fantastic," she uttered, "They took the bait." She plopped down into her black executive desk chair and scooted herself in front of the computer monitor. After composing an e-mail response in her mind, she pulled out her keyboard and began replying to her long-awaited contact. With swift and effortless strokes she dictated aloud, "Thank You for your interest in Silver Canyon Resorts. The cost for a two-month rental in a Deluxe Casita home is twelve thousand five hundred dollars. A fifty percent deposit is required to guarantee your reservation. Please forward me credit card information for processing."

"Okay," Jolene said aloud, "now I just wait for them to try and pledge fraudulent cashier checks and request lots of cash back when they overpay." Returning her retractable keyboard back under the desktop, she glanced at her watch. Realizing it was time to go, she pushed her chair back in, shut down her computer, and returned to the kitchen to turn off the coffee maker, and feed her fish. Sprinkling multi-colored flakes into the small aquarium spurred the little fish to swoosh to the surface. She admired the beauty of her flashy Betta fish, Patron. The lavender fish with long flowing fuchsia fins was a make-up gift given to her by a Tequila-guzzling source named Paco.

Paco got the wrong impression from Jolene when he discovered her shadowing him while she worked undercover. In order to avoid blowing her investigation, she implied a mutual attraction. After Paco pursued her with unrelenting vigor, she resigned herself to accepting a dinner date at his favorite Mexican restaurant. Avoiding Paco's advances was impossible, but as luck would have it Paco's passion for jumbo gold margaritas caused him to pass out before the date was over. Jolene left him slumped in their corner booth. The next day, while she was still working undercover at the pawn shop, Paco presented the Betta fish to her in a water-filled Patron bottle.

The tequila-night was useful though. Extracting information from Paco propelled the case in a direction that netted her the big catch. Apprehension of an entire theft-ring earned her the status of a true agent and enhanced her credentials overnight. She even accomplished her assignment without anyone knowing it was a date with tequila that provided the valuable leads.

While Patron gulped his food down, Jolene envisioned how her internet fraud case would assure her higher profile projects in the future. Almost thirty years old, Jolene was determined and courageous. Being young and good-looking meant going out of her way to prove her aptitude, and she knew it. She loved her field work and wanted to prove she could be very good at it.

Pirouetting in front of her mirrored-closet doors, Jolene admired her conservative charcoal-pinstriped suit. It looked amazing on her slender, curvy, figure. Likening a thoroughbred, her long trim legs looked remarkable in her designer pant suit.

She spritzed her precision haircut and sprayed Burberry Brit perfume on her wrists and neck.

Feeling a rush of pride, she clipped her FBI badge to her belt, checked her gun, and slid it in her shoulder holster. She was proud to be accepted as a Special Agent with the FBI. The mystique of holding such a prestigious job satisfied her ambitions.

Patting Honey good-bye, Jolene secured all the house doors and departed for her garage. Climbing into her car, she headed to work.

Driving to the bureau with her stereo on low, she reflected on Wade. Charismatic, courageous, and handsome—like James Bond, she wondered what it would be like if they were still seeing each other. For the first time in her life, she met a man that roused her conservative nature. Breaking-up resulted in added hours at the gun range and increased movie rentals. Pride prevented her from sharing her pain with anyone, even her older sister, Martine.

Jolene knew Martine's advice would consist of something like the old Irish blessing they grew up using before meals. Jolene mimicked her sister out-loud, as if she were really sitting next to her,

"Work like you don't need the money. Love like you've never been hurt. Dance like nobody's watching. Sing like nobody's listening. Live like its Heaven on earth." Receiving a pep talk or being psychoana- lyzed did not appeal to Jolene—it never would.

Torturing her heart was unavoidable when playing the CD Wade produced from his over-worked iPod. Self-induced pain seemed to accompany every pop and country tune she listened to on the disc. Turning up the volume, she sang to "Drops of Jupiter." It was their song.

"Tell me, did you fall for a shooting star? One without a permanent scar? And did you miss me while you were looking for yourself out there?" Turning up the volume, Jolene drowned out her own vocals.

Chapter 4

Martine's morning hours were spent cleaning the spare bedroom for her daughter Alexa and getting ready for a luncheon with her Uncle Mike. Putting on makeup, jeans, a suede jacket, and her heeled cowboy boots improved her appearance. Wearing her riding hat solved her hair problem. In Durango she would blend.

Several dramatic mountain passes separated Martine's ranch home from Durango. Residing in this remote region can be a sacrifice, and a blessing.

Outside of town, very few conveniences exist. Likewise, distractions from busy intersections, traffic lights, and fire-engine-red stop signs, were almost unheard of. One modern highway swooped through southwest Colorado, sculpting the dramatic landscape. Flashy fall colors splashed as far as the eye could see. High jagged peaks from the Sharks Tooth and the La Plata Mountains already glowed white from recent snow falls on the thirteen thousand foot points.

Snowmobilers were probably trying out their sleds up there already. Shuttering at the thought, Martine stuffed away the old memories.

Low pasture ground, carpeted in green, blended into the colorful Aspen and Oak tree groves. There was nothing ordinary or common about the endless hues of orange, purple, red, rose, gold, and bronze. Nature's joint venture knitted a colorful and blazing blanket for each mountain side.

Black cows peppered the vast pasture grounds that lay on both sides of the highway system. Border collies rounding up a herd of cattle, seemed to defy gravity as they streaked around the lazy livestock.

Driving into town was always picturesque and therapeutic. Slowing down for the first stop light, Martine shook her head in amazement as she watched kayakers paddle their way down the freezing cold Animas River. Die-hard enthusiasts never missed the moving waters that raged after a rain or snowfall.

Parking on her favorite side street, she deposited quarters into the meter before looking to cross. Passing a tall man with a cowboy hat, plaid shirt, and a worn-out down-filled vest, she returned a friendly greeting when he tipped his hat.

Except for passing an occasional college student, the sidewalks in downtown Durango were desolate. Summer tourists were long gone and the skiers hadn't made their appearance yet. Historic Durango was always a private paradise for the local residents during peak season transitions. With huge retail storefront windows lining both sides of Main Street, stylish western clothing, Indian jewelry, pottery, and cowboy art was always on display.

Pushing on the authentic saloon-style doors for which her favorite café, The Silver Spur, was known, Martine entered the dining area inside a hundred year-old hotel. Aromas from greasy fryers and sizzling grills escaped out of the kitchen, filling Martine's nostrils. Inhaling the scent of freshly baked bread and barbeque beef, awakened her depressed appetite.

A vivacious hostess approached Martine and asked, "How many in your party?"

Pointing to her uncle who was signaling with his hand in the air, Martine replied, "That's my party."

Ushering Martine past the ornate wood carved bar for which the building was originally known, the hostess complimented her, "Your jacket is beautiful. Did you get it in Durango?"

"I did. Thank you." Martine smiled.

Strolling toward the back of the restaurant, Martine admired the rustic décor. Local customers always hung their weathered cowboy hats from time-honored brass hooks mounted at the end of each booth. She loved the warm ambiance it provided.

Seated in the last high-backed-wood cubicle, Uncle Mike flaunted the renowned grin that melted many hearts in his day. Under his cognac-colored leather blazer he wore a button-down denim shirt with a white-band collar. He looked handsome and distinguished with his thick, white, wavy, hair. For an older gent he could still get the ladies' attention.

The hostess handed her a leather tooled menu. Before leaving she said, "Your server will be right with you."

Uncle Mike greeted Martine in typical "good old boy" fashion, "Hey, darlin', good ta see ya. You look fantastic, like a filly I used to chase."

"Hey, Uncle Mike. I see you still think like a *stud*. Or, should I say a *colt*?"

"Thank you very much, young lady, I like the way you make me sound young. Sure been staying to yourself since ya came on down here. I was afraid you'd back out of our little dinner again."

Smiling warmly, Martine explained herself, "No. I wouldn't do that. I just got too busy at the ranch and couldn't break away. I'm here now though. Besides, you said it was important."

Uncle Mike returned her smile and said, "Yep, I did. I think it is darn good news for all of us. So let's talk about that good news after we order. I could eat a steer."

Setting her menu down on the table to signify her readiness to order, Martine agreed, "Me too. I'm ready to order when you are. I know what I want."

Uncle Mike signaled the server while saying, "I've been ready and waiting."

Placing their orders took no time at all and Uncle Mike resumed the conversation like he never stopped, "I got an offer on the five-hundred acres of cow pasture. It is a respectable offer that I want you to consider. We should take this purchase since you don't want to keep cows there. Taxes will go from one-hundred-fifty dollars a year to twelve-thousand dollars when that agricultural classification is gone. You said you don't want to deal with the cattle business. This is a good alternative."

Folding her arms on the table in front of her, Martine leaned forward. "It's not that I have a problem with the cattle business, I just don't have enough help. James and ranch-hand Randy took care of the family land trust, not me. I'm not qualified to do this work without James and you're retired. Who else is there? I'm worried whether I can just give up that place and never go back. I grew up there, and it's been in the family for two generations."

Uncle Mike unfolded his paper napkin and pulled out his pocket pen. Scribbling rectangular squares, he explained, "you won't have to, little darlin'. You can keep the main home on thirty-five acres. When we sell this pasture, you'll keep the homestead and divide the proceeds of the sale with me and Jolene. I'd never make you give up the home you girls inherited from your parents. We just won't be in the cow business anymore, unless one of your daughters would want to be a cattle rancher?"

"Nah. Not much chance of that." Martine shook her head. "Maybe this is the best news I've had in sometime. I thought it would take a lot longer to find a buyer. I didn't know you listed the land already."

Writing a series of numbers on the napkin, Uncle Mike spun it around and slid it in front of Martine for her review. "I didn't. Our neighbor, Rupert, made this offer. Wants our water rights, access to National Forest, ranch hand, mobile home he's in, and BLM land permits. No realtors either. It's a win win."

"Wow! This is amazing." Martine examined the napkin like a legal document. "You mean, after we sell this year's herd, we're done?"

Breezing up to the booth, the college age waitress interrupted the business conversation, "Here's your ice tea, ma'am. More coffee, sir?"

"Absolutely. That's excellent service, missy." Stretching a big grin across his face, Uncle Mike winked with his left eye. Pushing his cup towards her, he added, "Keep it coming." His Scandinavian heritage was undeniable when he flashed his blue eyes and charming smile. Even now as a senior citizen, Uncle Mike had a youthful complexion with healthy tan skin tones.

"Martine, I know I'm no substitute for your parents," her uncle acknowledged, "Or your husband, but I worry about all the unbelievable things you have gone through in your short life. God knows you have been tested like in . . . 'The Book of Job.' You're the daughter, and the son I never had. I'll do whatever I can to get you through this chapter in your life. I believe this sale is a blessing."

"Uncle Mike, have you talked to Jolene about this yet?"

Dumping a packet full of sugar in his cup he replied, "Of course not. Don't ya think she'll want what you want?"

Stirring her ice tea, Martine surmised, "Yeah. You're right. She'll want to know what I think. She also doesn't like 'cow,' unless it is grilled and served in her favorite restaurant."

"Good. And a little fun from you too. That's the Martine we know and love. You always were a witty girl."

"Do you want me to tell Jolene about the offer, or do you want the honors?"

"I think you'd better tell Jolene. We've been in touch on some other stuff. She's busy and preoccupied with her big job at the FBI. It gets harder and harder to tell you two apart. She reminds me of you, all those years ago when you got your big law degree. I gotta tell ya, I've been scratching my head 'bout something that Jolene implied."

Martine scrunched her forehead, "Oh really? What's that?"

Rubbing his chin in contemplation he tipped his head down. "Well, I'm not sure what she meant, but she mentioned you have . . . ah . . . some kinda ESP thing."

"What?" Martine exclaimed as she cocked her head slightly.

Uncle Mike stammered as he glanced down at his black beverage, "Yeah, I think she was just trying to find a way to help me."

"Help you? What's wrong with you? What did she really say? Be more specific."

Uncle Mike struggled to get the words out as he fumbled with his empty sugar packet, "She mentioned how you know things,

things that other people don't know. She kinda mentioned it when I said I was worried about my, my breathing."

"Are you worried about your health? Is something wrong?"

"No . . . no. Just a smoker's cough. I mean an ex-smoker's cough. I should have quit sooner. I just want to know what kinda stuff Jolene's talking about. Like when did this start?"

Martine shifted her weight, leaned forward and lowered her voice, "Well, sometimes I do have some unusual experiences. I guess they started sometime during school. I'm not sure exactly."

"That long ago? Why didn't I know? What about your folks? Did they know?"

"I never said anything to anybody. I guess I thought everyone went through that. Nobody ever talked about their dreams and intuitions, so I didn't think they were important. I didn't think I was different."

"So you say it started in school?"

"Yeah, maybe. Can't say I've really thought about it. Why?" Martine was curious about his reasons for probing into this subject.

"I don't know. But, twins have complex relationships. Jolene thinks that maybe it has something to do with being a twin."

"Uncle Mike, I just don't think about those years. It was a long time ago and I honestly can't remember much."

"Well, your twin sister died in that accident when you were kids. You two were awfully close. That was a very traumatic time. The shock and loss had to be more than a kid could bear."

Large dinner plates full of fries and BBQ sandwiches on Texas-style toast were placed in front of them. The café's sandwich special was a local tradition they shared when meeting for lunch. Dipping a French fry into ketchup, Martine continued, "I can't say I recall too much about her death. I remember the funeral. Nobody talked about Michaela after that. Daddy was so angry."

"Martine, he blamed everything and everyone for that accident, even God." He paused then continued, shaking his head slowly, "There is nothing worse than what your dad and I went through when your sister's snowmobile was buried by that avalanche. We couldn't find her. Time was running out while she was suffocating.

It took hours to locate . . . she had minutes worth of air. I've lost a lot of sleep over that day." Tears rolled out of the corners of Mike's eyes. He pulled a hanky out of his jean pocket and blew his nose. "Excuse me."

Reaching for her uncle's trembling hand, Martine comforted the old man with a tender pat. "I'm sorry she's gone too. I guess it was much worse being out there when it happened. I never thought much about what you and dad went through that day."

"Yeah, it was easier to try and ignore that whole damn day. It wasn't possible to talk to your dad after that. It changed him, and me."

"You know, we shouldn't talk about this anymore. There's nothing that can be done now. Dad, mom, James and Michaela are all gone and it's not our fault." Martine was caught off guard and didn't plan on divulging any more information about her psychic experiences. She wasn't insane and didn't want to defend herself or get into it with anybody. "Tell me what you've been doing with those poker buddies of yours."

Sharing his poker tournament triumphs with her perked up the conversation and made her yearn for the good ole days when she played too. Jovial laughter filled the booth as they reminisced about the local tournament he had just played in. Peeling the wrapper off a restaurant toothpick, Uncle Mike told his latest story, "Only five of us were left and I pulled a queen high flush. Carl didn't just call me. No he went all in. With the king and ace out, I folded. Damned if that rascal wasn't bluffing." Shaking his head, he twirled the tooth-pick that was hanging from the corner of his mouth. "That Carl Jones just keeps winning. He's always in the money and doesn't even have a real job anymore." Uncle Mike chuckled. Dropping his fist on the table, he challenged the odds, "By golly, I'm gonna be the one that beats his lucky streak." Poking the toothpick between a couple teeth, he made his final promise, "He's a bluffer, and I'm not falling for that anymore."

Light hearted and sociable, Uncle Mike could entertain any audience. Satisfied by the big meal and conversation, Martine wrapped-up the luncheon, "I've got to get a move on, Alexa's on her way down from Denver. We'll hook up again while she's here."

"I'd like that. I never see those girls anymore. I'll take you two out for dinner. Maybe we'll celebrate the sale if I can get that darn deal done."

"Super, and thanks for lunch."

Outside the nostalgic café, uncle Mike hugged her tight and kissed her cheek. "I'll call you in a few days. Take care of yourself, Martine. I love ya, little darlin'."

"I love you too," waving goodbye, she headed for her car. The vibrant sun was high in the dark-blue sky as she walked the sidewalks of timeless Durango. Looking like an old west movie set, lit for the next shoot-out scene, Martine reflected on the uniqueness of the town.

Connecting with the warm solar rays, she smiled a big thank you for the possibility of good news. Charging her spirit in the sun, like a solar battery, raised her energy levels as she strolled back to her car. This was her kind of therapy.

Unlocking her car door, Martine remembered her family had been commiserating about her wellbeing. She detested gossip. What good ever came from talking about other's misfortunes? Wasn't that a mortal sin? "He who guards his lips, guards his soul, yeah that's it—Proverbs," Martine said under her breath. She didn't want people suspecting the worse about her character, or abilities. After all, she had very good reasons for guarding her mystical secrets. Enduring the consequences of public awareness had proved to be disastrous in the past.

Chapter 5

Jolene arrived at the Arizona branch office of the FBI prepared to discuss her recent breakthrough on the case she was working on. Unfortunately, she was met with indifference as agents scurried about. Normal early morning routines, salutations, coffee consumption, and personal conversations seemed disrupted. Commotion was centered by Director Mahoney's office.

Pausing in front of forensic accountants Levine and Hess to stuff her sunglasses back into her purse, Jolene overheard Hess, "Two blondes were on opposite sides of the river. One blonde asks the other blonde, 'How do I get to the other side?'"

"Yeah?" said Levine.

"The blonde answers, 'you're on the other side.'" Hess finished with a big laugh as he glanced at Jolene.

Rolling her eyes at the two, Jolene said, "You've got to be kidding."

Jan, the office manager, was moving in their direction. "Don't you boys have something to analyze?" Jan shooed them off with her hands."

"Let's go, Levine, Jan's conducting 'drive-by management'." Laughing at himself again, Hess waved goodbye.

Jan's head bobbled as she acknowledged Jolene with her heavy-southern twang, "Good morning, my dear, do yah know what's going on around here?"

"No, I just got in," Jolene said hesitantly.

Breezing past Jolene, Jan's southern-drawl trailed off, "you'd better find out what's up, sweetie."

Quickening her pace, Jolene navigated herself through a maze of co-workers that surrounded her office space. In the process of setting down her belongings on her desk she noticed her phone's message light blinking. While reaching for her phone, Agent Thad Reese poked his head in her cubicle and interrupted her routine. With a serious expression on his face, he motioned for her attention and said, "Hey rookie, Mahoney wants us in his office—right now."

Without pause, Jolene put the phone receiver down and followed Thad's heels toward Mahoney's door.

Entering her boss's office last, Jolene noticed John Mahoney appeared tense and preoccupied with a phone conversation. Terminating the call, Mahoney motioned to Jolene to close his door. It was apparent that a major announcement was coming.

"Good morning, everyone," he started. "What I'm about to brief you on is for your ears only."

Eleven men, and Jolene, stood in vigil before their boss. Mahoney's concerned expression made it apparent he was about to share sensitive information with his experienced agents. Never before had Jolene been privy to a briefing of this magnitude. Mahoney began pacing behind his desk with his eyes scanning the floor. Looking up at the group, he broke the silence.

"The Holbrook police department contacted me about a young girl's body that was recently discovered. It was an obvious murder. This finding has turned a missing adolescent's case into a homicide. The police have reason to believe that there are other similar incidents that need to be investigated. They're not equipped to perform sophisticated forensics. Because this kidnapping crossed state lines and involves exploitation of a minor it falls within federal jurisdiction. We will be working with the local and state law enforcement agencies. We also will filter leads and false confessions that will without a doubt pour in. Due to the unprecedented violence of this crime we will organize a task force today."

At this juncture, every agent was ready to fire questions at him. Agent Rex Harden spoke-up first, "Has any forensic work been done on the victim or at the scene?"

"Yes. They drew a blank on everything except the victims ID."

Agent Jeff Meyers asked next, "Is this single crime considered big enough for the FBI to take over? Why do we need a whole task force?"

"First of all, the crime already involves two states. Second, a Detective Darin Thom had been monitoring some female abduction cases. It's his theory that a larger-than-usual number of missing girls is being reported in and around the state of Arizona. The statistical evidence, so far, is alarming. The majority of the girls are adolescents. Third, the detective and his agency cannot inspect outside their county's jurisdiction. They are blocked from going forward without us," Mahoney explained.

Agent Ray Edison posed another question, "How many cases of missing girls are we talking about, Chief?"

"On the internet site, they found forty-plus reports, all within a four-state area. We will probably uncover more."

Jolene spoke up next, "Do these qualify as new cases or are they old reports, sir?"

"None of these cases are cold," Mahoney answered solemnly.

Agent Edison asked a second time, "Have any of the other missing girls been found?"

"No," Mahoney answered. "That's why this is an urgent, top-priority investigation. We want to find the rest of the victims alive."

Jim Crane raised his forefinger above his head, signaling his turn to ask a question. "Are there any leads on possible suspects?"

"No, Jim, no leads so far."

After responding to Jim, Mahoney summed it up, "If the perpetrator believes his crimes are under examination, he may flee or eliminate the other victims. Since all the victims are female, they are likely being exploited for the purpose of pornography, human trafficking, or prostitution. The Bureau is being brought in now so we can examine what little evidence exists at the location this victim was found and evaluate the merits of a multi-state abduction operation. Using a Special Task Force, we'll utilize all means available, including covert practices, if necessary. If there's even one thread that links these crimes together, we'll find it. Our profilers and forensic specialists will review all abductions reported in this region."

Jolene flinched when Mahoney's private fax machine turned itself on to receive an incoming document. Watching her boss grab the four-colored fax out of the tray, she studied his stern-faced emotion as he spoke, "Here's the class photo of the young girl that was discovered this morning. We'll alert the local police departments that we are reacting to a rash of abductions and we need their cooperation. Controlling a 'media tsunami' is imperative. It is our job to handle the press."

Speechless as she viewed the class photo of Lauren, Jolene gazed at a beautiful smiling eleventh-grader with perfectly straightened teeth. Her long, wavy, blonde, hair was more than the photographer could capture through his lens. She looked like a precious angel who should've never known the horror of being physically violated and stripped of her will.

From a distance the young girl resembled her own nieces, Eva and Alexa. Jolene made a slight gasp as anger and resentment coursed through her. She detested the criminals who use harmless and innocent victims for their own perverse desires. At that moment, Jolene knew she would heed Mahoney's words, "We'll utilize all means available, including covert practices." Jolene envisioned herself being the agent who discovered the whereabouts of each missing girl.

With her minds-eye, Jolene quizzed herself. Why was she in this meeting? Being the newest, youngest, and least experienced agent in the room, she knew she hadn't created any adversaries, but she did not yet possess the credentials that the other agents earned. Only recently did she find herself sharing the camaraderie that the other agents had established with each other.

Her thoughts were broken when Mahoney concluded, "A comprehensive briefing is being coordinated for this afternoon with the police detective I mentioned. You will all be notified of the time."

Chapter 6

Stoned and semi-conscious from a night of partying, Peter shuffled his way down the sidewalk to his rental room. It was late and no one was around, not even the neighborhood cats that prowl around the alley's and yards surrounding his seedy housing. High privacy fences with loose boards had lost most of their paint years ago and now they made the area look sinister.

All that Peter had planned at this point was sleep, he just had to make it a little further and he would be there. Alone and barely functioning, he groped around in the dark till he found the door-knob to his tiny apartment. Opening the door wide so he could clear the jams, he stumbled into his meager housing. Tripping over his long pant legs made his entrance even clumsier. Wearing his jeans far below his waist was his style.

With only one operable window in the room he was met by heat—at least 105 degrees. No air conditioning. The vintage-style ceiling fan with three blades accomplished very little and it was already on. October was unusually warm this year.

Stripping his clothes off was customary when faced with hot stagnant air. With his pants half-off anyways, he merely used his feet to pull them all the way down. The baggy t-shirt came over his head with one tug. White boxer shorts were last—too hot for even them. Hellish heat inside his second-story room forced him to lay naked on top of his sheets. Without ever turning on a single light his evening routine was complete.

Falling backwards, he landed on the mattress that came with the flat he called home. Passing out at the moment of impact was predictable. There was nothing left to do after a night like he had just had.

Exposed and comatose in his bed, Peter was unaware of the strange visitor entering his room. Oblivious to her presence he slept while the silhouetted figure of a svelte woman glided up to his slumbering body. Only the half-moon floating in the diamond-studded sky produced any light for the bedroom scene. Approaching his still and peaceful body, the enchantress reached down and stirred him with gentle touches.

* * *

Responding unconsciously to the sensations she instilled, Peter turned his head to the side and took in a deep breath. Magnetized to his seductress he unconsciously breathed in more deeply. Immobilized and semi-asleep, he inhaled a foreign-musty-type fragrance.

Like a stealth craft, she maneuvered herself until she lay on him in a prone position. Feeling the weight of her entire body over his, he instinctively reached around hers for a mutual embrace.

Passionate kissing was instigated by her, provoking his perverted sexual appetite. Salty beads of perspiration spread over his body while she used unique skills to excite him. Experiencing physical sensations he had never enjoyed before, he felt betrayed by the cheap magazines he had been satisfied with.

Peter's blood pulsed off the charts. Without a struggle, he submitted and surrendered. Unable to resist her advances, he groped her with equal desperation. Being "one-with-her" took over his Free-Will. Resisting didn't seem an option and the urge to have more was overpowering. Having all of her, right now, would fulfill all the fantasies he'd been harboring. Consumed by her intoxicating scent, and provocative touch, he participated in the enticing seduction. It didn't matter who she was.

Luring him like a cat in heat, the interlude escalated. Her insistent promptings stimulated him into a wild frenzy. Caught up in the moment, he did what felt natural and pleasurable. Dominated and laying on his back, he relinquished his body to her. Anticipating the consummation of the act, he let her do what she wanted.

Feeling her body straddle him, he started to rouse from his drug-induced sleep to see if she was real. Waist-length, thick, wavy, hair blocked the features of her face. Cloaked in shadows and darkness, he aggressively fondled what he could not see.

Closing his eyes and clenching his teeth, he felt explosive pleasure aching to be released. Rapid breathing was the only sound he heard as their bodies rocked in unison. Experiencing ecstasy, his ability to rationalize who the temptress was, failed. He could do no more than focus on the need to have her.

When climax was accomplished, the young man anticipated feeling satisfaction and relief. However, his long-awaited triumph was met with dangerous and unrelenting stamina on her part. Instead of slowing down, her love-making evolved into an untamed fury that demanded more. Her gentle fingers now felt like claws, her soft skin was rough, and her insides were cold.

Forcing more out of him than was humanly possible, his pulse quickened again. Pinned down by her indescribable weight, he found out it would be over only when she wanted to stop. Even when she changed positions she remained on top of his weakening body.

With malevolent energy, she physically manipulated his body. Paralyzing him with her inexplicable powers, he remained in her control. Having finally had enough, Peter twisted and contorted his body in an effort to roll away.

Refusing to let him be on top, she arched her torso back reveling in contentment. Falling forward again, she repeated her actions.

There was no time to analyze her plan. Her supremacy seemed to be claiming him, body and soul. Only when he surrendered himself, did she lie still and let him rest.

Drifting off to sleep was unavoidable for Peter—when the marathon was over. Leaving his bed in silence, the mysterious lover fled the scene without any need for intimacy after the rigors of multiple orgasms.

* * *

Awaking alone in his bed, before the sun was up, he assumed he must have experienced a horrific drug-induced delusion.

Feeling like road kill, more veracity set in as a slight breeze from the open window caused his body to shiver. Wait, his window was open. Maybe someone had entered while he slept. Now, it was his frightened and confused heart that was racing.

While fumbling for the light switch on his nightstand-lamp, his thigh rolled onto a cool moist area. The brilliant glow from his lamp provided alarming evidence that something unusual had happened. Not only was his bed moist from sweat, but pools of body-fluids were noticeable in several places on his dark-green sheets.

Never before had he wakened at five in the morning, nor in such a deplorable state. Devastated and disheveled, he hastened to the bathroom and vomited. The surreal event made him ill, not fulfilled. Rinsing his mouth and splashing water on his face was followed by a look in the bathroom mirror. Examining his appearance, he wondered what he had just done and with who. Drying off his face with his forearm, he promised himself he would never speak about the details of this night with anyone—it must have been a monumental wet dream.

Bewildered and distraught, Peter made his way back to his bed. Hesitating before throwing himself on the soiled, wet, sheets, he decided not to return to bed yet. Rubbing the matted brown hair on his head, he ambled across his one-room home.

Frustrated, he picked up his cell phone and dialed the number last received. "Jules, hey, man, call me when you get this. What kinda shit did we do last night? What'd you hook me up with?"

Chapter 7

"Alexa, wait, don't go up there. It's too steep a climb. My horse and I aren't in good enough condition for this," Martine's voice shook as her horse pranced-in-place. Adjusting her hat forward, she tightened her stampede string up under her chin while keeping her horse in check.

"Come on, mother, you can do it, or rather your horse can. You've done this trail before," Alexa yelled back as she let her quarter horse bounded up the mountainside like a deer.

If it wasn't for the arduous trail cutting into the steep sides of the mountain, there would be no access for the horses and riders. Towering ponderosa pines, jutting boulders, gnarly scrub oak, and Aspen trees with glowing white bark dominated the landscape with breath-taking grandeur. Only God's gardening expertise could produce something so huge and magnificent. It would be impossible to see the top of the majestic mountaintop without making the monumental ascent on foot or horseback.

With her horse rearing its front legs, Martine pondered options for about five seconds. Staring up the steep canyon wall, Martine muttered, "What happened to the easy October ride in the foothills of the Rocky Mountains?" That thought vanished as Patience, her tall, enthusiastic thoroughbred lunged forward and galloped up the hill. Overtaking Alexa and her powerful sorrel-and-white paint horse, Rocket, was inevitable. Martine's horse was a retired race horse and never came in second.

Letting out a loud, "SH . . . UGAR," Martine and Patience, swept past Alexa and Rocket. When Martine reached the top of the ridge she could barely see the camouflaged river bottom they had stood on just moments earlier. Heaving with deep, quick breaths through flared nostrils, the horses moved next to each other.

"That was awesome, mom. You, and Patience, really blew us away. Did you like it?" Swinging her right leg around the back of the saddle, Alexa kicked her left foot out of the stirrup and slid to the ground.

"That's beside the point, Alexa. You promised a sightseeing ride along the river to check fences. Do you have any self-control? All you want to do is run that horse. I came on this ride to ooh . . . and ah . . . with you over the amazing oak and Aspen colors. I'm not into extreme horseback riding."

Walking Rocket in a circle, Alexa checked his confirmation. "Well, mom, you used to be. Thanks for getting Rocket's shoes on. Matt did a great job keeping his heels up."

Martine's eyes followed Alexa's movements. "You're welcome. Don't change the subject. I haven't ridden like that for years."

"Are you saying you didn't like it?"

Martine agreed as she rubbed her horse's sleek, mahogany-colored neck, "It was exhilarating to be in rhythm with my horse again. I even love the smell of her heated body. She really broke a sweat from that run. After nineteen years together, we still can prove ourselves worthy to ride these canyons."

Alexa pulled a long weed-stalk out of her horse's tail. "You need to get out and ride more. You two are in great shape. You just passed us. After all it was you who broke these horses and taught us all how to ride."

Sliding the glide down on her stampede string, Martine adjusted the hat that was no longer in danger of blowing off. "I know you're right, but I haven't been motivated to do much. It's great that you're here. I'm lucky you quit that job. Plus I'm sure you need lots of my advice." Martine chuckled.

Alexa lifted up Rocket's back-right-hoof and used a stick to pry out a stone wedged in a crevice. "You don't like being alone, do you? You really miss dad, huh?"

Martine reached behind her leg and unbuckled her leather saddlebag. She groped inside for a water bottle. "Of course I do, we were best friends. We spent over twenty years together."

Alexa stroked the wide-blaze on Rocket's head as she reminisced, "It's been months since the funeral. It feels so different without him around. I thought it would be better by now. Dad seemed bigger than life when he was here. After all he thought he was a Viking, didn't he? I guess he did look like one, at least when we were down here working on the ranch." They both laughed.

Tossing her daughter a water bottle, Martine nodded her head and reached back for another one. "You better believe it. He was a huge part of my life. I feel like my arm is missing now."

Alexa rubbed Rocket's chest and asked, "When do you think it will feel normal again?"

"I don't even know what normal is anymore. It's the first time I've lost a husband. They say it takes a village to raise a child—what will it take to fix me?" Martine straightened her horse's black mane as she reflected on her loss.

Alexa moved to Rocket's left side and lifted the stirrup, hooked it on the horn, and checked the tightness of her saddle girth. "Maybe you should go back to work. Have you decided if and when you will?"

Martine looked down at her daughter and watched her as she adjusted more of Rocket's tack. "If I go back to work at the FBI I'll have to return to Denver. The Durango field office isn't big enough for an Investigative Law Unit much less a Criminal Law Unit. Eva's at NAU and you said you'll probably get a job in Arizona. I don't know if I want to go back up there. It made sense when your dad and I both worked in Denver. I haven't even checked to see if they want me back."

Leading Rocket over to Martine, Alexa moved her mother's leg out of the way to check Patience's girth. Gripping the leather-latigo rigging on Martine's saddle, she pulled up and tightened the cinch.

"You knew you'd never get a job like that down here in Durango, maybe you could transfer to Arizona. You know, you seem down today. Are you still on your sad pill?"

Martine moved her leg back in place and returned her foot to the leather-tooled stirrup. "Sorta. I've been cutting way back. I have to be myself sooner or later."

Alexa patted Patience on the withers before tightening the buckle on the horse's breast collar. "I hate seeing you so down. Maybe you need to smoke a joint or something."

Unable to control the water in her mouth, Martine blew it in the air. "Yeah, right, Alexa. Then I can be depressed and stupid. They don't call it 'dope' because it makes you smart—or do you know something I don't know?"

Laughter was shared before Alexa responded, "Great reflexes, and you're supposed to drink the water." Pretending to wipe water off her saddle seat, Alexa continued, "Oh, and that's very funny. I don't smoke the stuff either, but they're trying to legalize it for medical reasons. I thought maybe it would be helpful . . . just kidding."

"Not much chance of that since I oppose it so much."

"Seriously, mom, how have you been doing?"

"Let's just say I don't need to smoke joints to feel lethargic, listless, and apathetic."

"Gee, mom, it's going to get better."

Martine looked southwesterly at the cleverly named, Sleeping Ute Mountain Range. "Yeah, I just don't see that happening."

"How can you say that?" Alexa asked. "You seem fine. What do you think will make you feel better?"

"I don't think anything can, but having you here does help," Martine answered.

Concern spread over Alexa's face, "How do you feel when you're alone?"

Martine closed her eyes and searched for the words, "I feel like I'm riding these mountains without a horse."

"What?" Alexa asked.

"I'm unsteady, tired, and getting nowhere fast." Martine shrugged.

Alexa followed her mother's gaze and tried to change the subject as she crossed the reins over her horse's neck, "Hey, do you remember the legend of the Sleeping Ute? From the top of this canyon I can see all the details, starting from his Indian feather headdress down to his big toe pointing up to the sky. I just can't remember why he is lying there, bigger than a cruise-liner, with his arms folded across his chest."

Dropping the water-bottles back into the buckskin-saddlebag, Martine explained, "I believe the local folklore says the Ute Indian was a warrior who was being defeated by the white man. When he was exhausted from the battle, he lay down to rest and vowed he would rise up and avenge his people. The Sleeping Ute Mountain Range looks magnificent with the sun getting ready to set behind it."

"It's amazing. I wish I had brought my camera. This would be a great screensaver on my computer." Using her cell phone she snapped a picture. "I hope this will be good enough." Alexa mounted her horse and gathered up her reins. Looking at her mother with genuine concern, she changed the subject again, "Can I show you a unique rock formation I found last year when I was helping the neighbors round up stray cattle? There's a Ponderosa pine growing out of the middle of this humongous moss rock. I want to see how tall it is now."

Martine agreed, "Yeah that sounds like a *Ripley's Believe It or Not.*" Revved up and ready to run again, the horses trotted side-by-side to track Alexa's latest curiosity. Keeping a rhythmic pace, Martine and Alexa both fell silent to the click, click of metal horse-shoes striking the graveled logging trail.

Interrupted by the chime of a cell phone, the riders both slowed the horses down to a walk. Reacting to the unwelcomed sound, Alexa and Martine both grabbed for their phones. Before Martine got her cell open, she realized it must be Alexa's. Martine's cell phone had practically gone dormant after she arranged a leave of absence from her job in Denver. Retreating to the cattle ranch, inherited from her parents, was supposed to be a temporary escape.

Alexa checked her phone and peered up over the top of her sunglasses. "It's not my phone, must be yours."

Flipping open her phone, Martine gazed at the incoming caller's name. Puzzled that the call said "restricted," she answered, "Hello?"

"Hello, Martine, it's, Jolene."

"Hey, Jolene, how are you doing?"

"Martine, hey, sorry to bother you but I think I might need you. I could really use your help. Can you come see me?"

Caught off guard by her younger sister's request, Martine replied, "Excuse me?" Before Martine could refuse, the phone broke-up with annoying static mixed in with the garbled voice of her sister. Straining to hear Jolene's less-than-audible words, Martine pulled her horse to a stop.

"Martine, can you come to Arizona? I really need to see you."

"Jolene, is this more boyfriend drama? Alexa is home with me right now. Remember? We're riding horses in Box Canyon. Whose phone is this?"

"This is not a boyfriend issue. There is no boyfriend. Alexa can come too."

"Whoa there, little sister, what in the brown desert could possibly be so important that an FBI agent in Arizona needs me? Is this business or pleasure? You know I'm not into either right now."

Sounding like a diver under water, Jolene's voice became inaudible. Turning her horse in circles, Martine tried to connect with a better signal. Jolene's broken-gurgling words faded. Unable to improve the reception, Martine applied strategic and deliberate leg pressures to her Thoroughbred. Like a competitive reining horse, Patience rotated on her haunches till she faced uphill.

Cantering to the top of the hillside, Martine searched for a visual of the nearest cell phone tower. Losing a call is an ongoing inconvenience shared by everyone living and driving in the mountains. This encumbrance alone may be the reason Southwest Colorado remains primitive and dominated by beef cattle, roping horses, Indian reservations, and leathered cowboys.

"Martine, Martine, can you hear me?"

Martine responded, "Yeah, Jolene, I can hear you now."

"I can't risk telling you anything on the phone. I shouldn't talk here. Suffice it to say you have never been needed more. Don't call me back, just come. Leave tomorrow. Remember where the key is?"

Laying her right rein over her horse's neck, Martine spun Patience left for a stronger cell connection. "Jolene, please tell me what's going on. Jolene? Jolene? Are you there?"

Alexa galloped up the hill and slid to a stop. "You must have lost the signal again," she said.

Scrutinizing the bars on her phone, Martine disagreed, "No, Alexa, I think she might have hung up, or had to go. Jolene needs me, I guess. She wants us to come tomorrow."

"Great, you need to get out of here for awhile. There is way more stuff to do down there."

Excited by the run, the horses chomped on their bits for more. Struggling to control her prancy horse, Martine debated with herself aloud, "I don't know why we're going. Jolene sounded up tight. Why didn't she use her own phone? And why does she want us to come tomorrow?"

"It's okay. I think we better go. How can we not?"

"Yeah, that's what I'm thinking. You can't plow a field by tilling it over in your mind. Let's head back, maybe Jolene will call again. I'd like a reason before I drive all the way down there. My imagination is starting to take over." Martine clucked twice to her horse. Patience eagerly responded and broke into a graceful lope.

Alexa loosened up on her dancing horse and it cantered past Martine. Pointing to her left, she offered directions, "Let's cut through up here to Switchback Trail." Neck-reining Rocket off the logging road, Alexa blazed a new trail east. Using this opportunity to pick up the pace, she cued her horse into a fast canter.

Joining up to the high-ridgeline trail, Alexa and Martine weaved through dense Aspen groves. Only elk and mule deer shared the fairy-like-wonderland. Fallen trees created intermittent obstacles in the trail that the horses jumped over like English steeple chasers.

Alexa stayed in the lead as they traversed down the mountainside into the big private pastures that were full of cattle for the winter. Taking turns, Alexa and Martine opened and closed several rusty barb-wired gates. Walking through large herds of beef cattle cooled the horses down before reaching the barn.

With the sun starting to set, they unsaddled their horses, brushed their backs, turned them out to pasture, and put everything away without saying a word. They both knew it was better to take care of business since very little time was left for packing, dinner, and sleep. They finally broke silence as they walked up to the house and discussed what to do next. Dinner was the decided winner.

Alexa offered a final bit of consolation before departing for bed, "Don't worry about your sister. You're going to dream about it anyway. Maybe by morning you will know more than Jolene does about her problem. Don't forget your prayers," Alexa chuckled. Love you."

Chapter 8

"**H**ey, man," Jules started, "what yah trip'n on? That was some freaky message you left on my phone. Did you get home okay last night or what?"

"I don't know what the hell happened last night. We gotta meet, Jules."

"Sure, man, where?"

"Meet you at the bar on Old Sage Street."

"Yeah, sure, Pete. Give me a couple hours—got some shit to take care of first."

"Sure, bro, I'll be there."

Contemplating all the vague things he could remember, Peter paced in his sanctuary of solitude. Was he hallucinating? Were his thoughts merely distorted, or unprecedented?

Naked from the waist up, Peter's menacing dragon tattoo could be seen on his right shoulder. Neglected brown hair had grown long bangs and curly ends. Facial hair was producing the beginnings of a beard and mustache. Being average in height, his five-foot ten-inch frame was underweight. Lack of appetite and exercise created an inferior slim physic.

Years of pot smoking dulled his personality and stunted his social skills. Lacking purpose to his life he escaped to this low-rent underworld where he worked for his next high. Peter owned a tongue ring, flip-flops, low-riding blue jeans, and a nose piercing.

His favorite boxers were green with Merry Christmas in red letters hanging out the back of his pants. Without a clean shave it was hard to tell if he could look good to the average girl.

Drugs, lack of money, and a grungy wardrobe prevented him from attracting respectable females. His temptation was the next street drug that could turn him on. Dependent on cheap narcotics and lacking confidence, he hadn't yet found his identity in this lifetime.

Suspicious, his eyes snapped side to side as he moved around in his private room. Confusion and fear brought back the nervous cough he couldn't control. The involuntary reflex did nothing to clear his lungs. It was just an impulse that he was unable to stop. There were, however, things he had learned to do that suppressed it. A myriad amount of events led up to the dry cough. Only one other person was aware of what they were and he was dead.

Anxious to get some answers from the guy he was with yesterday, he didn't even bother to eat. Relieved to have pot in his possession, he lit up a small joint. Subdued by the drug, his abnormal cough was squelched. Pulling on a pair of well-worn jeans, he eyed his blue t-shirt and fitted his favorite baseball cap to hide his hair.

Positioning mirrored-sunglasses over his bloodshot eyes, he exited the room in a hurry. Needing to get out of the dismal space, Peter left early to walk to the bar.

Sitting on the barstool farthest away from the door, Peter ordered a shot of Jagermeister and a beer-chaser. Paying the bartender from the wad of money he pulled from his pocket, he said, "Keep the change."

Examining the two dollar tip, the bartender nodded. "Hey, man, thanks."

Watching the entrance for his friend, Peter slammed the shot and worked on his light beer.

Tall with a big frame and brown hair, Jules nonchalantly entered the establishment and sauntered up to Peter. Wearing relaxed-fit blue jeans with a solid wine-colored t-shirt under a black sports jacket, Jules looked like a clothing model inside this local bar. Shoving his car keys in his coat pocket he straddled the stool next to

Peter. With his rugged facial features he looked like a gangster-in-training. Curly hair added more inches to his tall menacing frame.

Jules looked around the empty establishment and acknowledged Peter, "Dude, what's happening? You don't look so hot."

Swiveling his stool to face his cousin, Peter asked, "What went down yesterday? You're not dealing tainted shit again are you?"

Removing his sunglasses, Jules stuffed them in his breast pocket. "Hey, it's cool. You needed money and junk, I got you both. I don't have to deal anymore." Delivering a beer to Jules, the bartender offered to start a tab. "Yeah, dude. Keep'em comin'." Jules laid some cash on the bar.

"Dude? Did you call me dude? I don't see no horse in here." The crusty bartender tapped the bills with his knuckle, "Just keep those dead presidents right where I can see'em."

Making sure his voice was out of range from the departing barkeep, Peter whispered, "I mean what kinda stuff did you hook me up with?"

Lowering his voice too, Jules responded, "Damn. You know. Mescaline and pot. The stuff you like."

"Are you sure it wasn't anything special, like blow? I mean did we do some at the party?"

Using his forearm to lean on the bar, Jules moved his head closer to Peter. "Nope, you need big bucks to do that. Hey, you don't' look so good, little buddy."

Clearing his throat to suppress a round of coughs, Peter took the menu Jules handed him. "Never mind how I look. Not enough sleep. Hey, man, thanks for the cash. I'll pay you back as soon as I get my next check. At least I can pay the rent today, thanks to you."

Studying the cheap-plastic menu, Jules replied, "Yeah, about that, do you really want to wash dishes in that restroom you call a restaurant?"

"Not really, but I gotta do what I can till I pay you back and get another car. At least I have a room near my job. Why would anyone steal that piece-of-junk car I had?"

Waving the bartender over, Jules and Peter ordered burgers with fries. After two more beers were delivered, Jules continued,

"Yeah, tough break. I don't know about that. Doesn't make any sense, does it, dude? Maybe they needed an alias car to score a hit, or rob some bank. Could just be kids doing club initiation. Shit happens down here all the time, remember? It's probably an ammunitions target out in the desert by now."

Feeling the buzz from Jager and beer, Peter was loosening up. "You sound like you know."

"Yeah, probably do. What if I could get you a better job? You could get a new car."

"Duh. Jules, man, I'll never own a new car. Who has one of those?"

"Don't be a buzz kill." Jules sniffed hard. "I will, and I think I'm getting close."

"That's great, man. Wish I had something new."

"Hey, new isn't all that. Ever been to New Mexico? Or read last week's newspaper? How 'bout that New Testament? Those dudes' rode donkeys. Let me see what I can do. My job with my uncle's security company is awesome. I work five nights a week and party two. Most of the time I'm security for fancy hookers. It's alright. Haven't had one shit job yet. Oh, I get tips and

Feeling weirded-out again, Peter jerked his head up. "Prostitutes? You didn't hook me up with a prostitute last night, did you?"

"Hell no, I can't afford shit like that and the smack we did. Plus I don't need to pay for no piece-of-ass. Do you?"

Peter chugged the beer in his bottle. "Heck no. I don't have to pay either. Do you think I can borrow a little more scratch? Maybe I can get some wheels and get a job there too. Right now I can't afford the four-hundred-dollars-a-month for that room."

Jules signaled the bartender for another round of the same.

"Sure, how much do you need?" flaunting his ability to lend money, Jules pulled out his wallet and thumbed-out a couple-hundred dollars.

"I was thinking ten-grand? I can get that great little-blue-sports-number I saw in the used car lot next to this bar."

"Ten-grand?"

"Okay, okay," Peter whispered. "Lower your voice. Don't start trippin' out. How 'bout, two or three?"

Jules handed him the cash and offered a better solution, "I'll try and get my uncle to lend you a few. He's generous when he's not insane. That's how I got this job. I borrowed a couple thousand dollars from him when I worked valet at his Vegas hotel. It led to the biggest legit paying job any dude would die for. Check it out. You saw my wheels."

The bartender interrupted the conversation with burger platters. When he departed, Peter retracted his request, "Dunno, Jules, man, I'll just keep grinding it out where I'm at. I can't ask you to borrow money from your uncle, or find a job for me. You know what? I'm really sorry for asking."

Shaking the empty ketchup bottle, like a can of spray paint, Jules countered, "Chill, bro. It's all good. I'll get back to you in a day or two. I know he wants to expand here, that's why he relocated me to Phoenix. You should see the crib I had in Vegas." Jules nodded approval. "Cha-ching."

Swallowing a big bite of burger, Peter acknowledged the unexpected reunion, "I'm really glad you found me. Feels like old times. You're like a guardian angel or something."

"Yeah, that's me. I feel good I found you too. It's been a long time." Jules patted Peter on the back. "Let's bounce this place." Counting his money for the bartender, Jules threw another twenty in his hand. "Here's a double for your tip."

* * *

After leaving the seedy bar, Jules waved goodbye to Peter as he drove off by himself. Dialing his cell-phone, his uncle and boss, Mr. Osborn, answered. "Hello.

"Uncle, hey, it's, Jules. Plan worked. I found me a partner—Cousin Peter. He needs some wheels and clothes. Actually, I made sure of it. Any thoughts?"

"How do you know he won't bail?"

"He's not going anywhere—he owes me and I know what he likes and what he wants."

"Yeah? What's that?" Osborn replied sarcastically.

Jules sounded cocky, "He wants a blue-sports car."

"Forget that, he needs a van," Osborn snapped impatiently.

"Yes, sir. Ten-grand for one of those blue vans."

"Whatever it takes. Make it white though. Gotta big job for the two of you. We're talking huge money with this gig."

"And the clothes, boss?"

"What's wrong with his clothes?"

"If he wore his pants any lower they'd be socks.
Thought you should know."

"Yada, yada, yada. He needs a security uniform, so do you.
Make it happen."

"Uncle, we're up to the biggest job you got."

"Yeah, you think?"

Chapter 9

Snuggling in a hand-hewn pine bed, Martine felt ready to escape into deep sleep, like she had managed for the last couple months. Tonight, however, there were no prescription drugs, or colossal doses of melatonin. Settling for one sleep aid and her ear plugs, she wondered if sleep was even an option after receiving her sister Jolene's distress call.

Watching television wasn't making her tired. The only ways to bring sleep on was to turn off the TV, switch out the light, ignore all noise, close her eyes and say the only prayer that came to mind. "Angel of God my guardian dear, to whom God's love commits me here. Ever this day be at my side to light and guard, to rule . . . ," was all she murmured before drifting off into a profound slumber.

No time passed while she lay asleep before her spirit transcended time and left her earthly abode for another sphere. With her higher consciousness taking over, her Third Eye Chakra opened wide—allowing expanded and more refined perceptions to operate. With her "higher vision" activated, she had the ability to see into subtle realities that were well beyond the limitations put on her earthly physical existence. Etheric dimensions have substance that is distilled beyond human sight. Only through the use of her higher consciousness would she be able to access these etheric realms.

Though Martine's body was physically sound asleep in her bed, her Third Eye divulged an alternate reality that was even more real than the one she laid sleeping in. Without human limitations, her Third Eye sight was able to expose the vast brilliance of a night's sky that would normally require the use of powerful telescope.

Outside of her grasp, beyond her normal human sight, a spiraling array of orbs descended down from the violet-hued heaven. The strand of twinkling orbs wound around Martine like lights wrapped on a Christmas tree. Pure Energy radiated from the beings of light as they took their positions and hovered in place.

One of the little star-like balls of light began to expand in circumference until it equaled Martine's size. While materializing into a humanistic form, the radiant being began to speak. "Martine," an echoing voice sounded.

Guided by the voice of a woman, Martine strained to identify the emerging being that summoned her. Witnessing the transformation that was taking place with the sphere of light was a new and profound occurrence for Martine. Unfamiliar with such an event, she remained steadfast as an elegantly robed being became clearly visible in the mind's eye of Martine's 3rd eye chakra.

Gracefully clothed in a gown of delicate ivory material, the beautiful feminine life-form resembled a Grecian goddess. An aura of golden light that gently pulsated around her human shape further softened the features of the exquisite guest. A more advanced type of love emanating from the angelic caller squashed Martine's instinctive reaction of fear and doubt. She had no desire to disconnect from the magnificent presence of the strange visitor. Rather she asked, "How do I know you?"

"I am your Guardian Angel. Because the love in your heart is abundant and strong, the pain you endure is greater. I bring you a message from your loved one. Your husband is happy, at peace, and loves you very much. Please don't worry about him." Extending her arms out towards Martine, she went on, "Your pain does not serve you well. Because you have asked for assistance your suffering will end soon."

Martine felt emotions welling though her whole being. Tears formed and began to flow out of control. The tears she had held inside for months could no longer be held back by self determination. Nothing could prevent the watery landslide while embraced by the energy of pure love.

"It is safe for you to see the power of love in all its forms," the being explained. "Spiritual gifts and natural abilities will provide your desired outcome. Trust what you see in your mind's eye as well as your human sight."

Martine did not question the messenger's words while she remained in a euphoric state of consciousness. Her soul could not debate a higher wisdom like her human intellect would have naturally contemplated with limitations and disbelief.

In a rhythmic tone, the angelic-looking goddess decreed a final message;

"Inner strength quickens the pace, love in action leads to grace.
Trust your guides to turn the tide, natures wise no longer hide.
Trust your knowing when fear is showing, intuition always growing.
Reach for the stars wherever you are, heavenly gifts are not afar.
Divine rhythm will play its part, like beating from a human heart."

Martine stayed frozen in her stance. Unaware of what this message could possibly imply, she asked, "Please, what does this mean?"

"Your prayers and questions will be answered by synchronistic events, be open to receiving divine guidance," the voice returned.

"I don't understand," Martine replied. "How can I remember this chant and learns its meaning?"

"These words I speak will be stored in your heart—not in your mind." The angel gestured downward with the sweep of one arm. "Now go and see what should not be."

Repositioned like a pawn on a chess board, Martine regained consciousness in the lower realm she was transported to. Standing like an Indian maiden with her arms folded in front of her chest, she made a startled jerk and scanned the primitive space she now occupied. Disgusted by the surroundings and her scanty clothing that resembled a hospital gown, Martine felt negative feelings of vulnerability and helplessness.

Straining her eyes to focus on the hazy imagery, she observed the desolate conditions of a cold-gray hovel with a dirt floor.

Choosing flight over fight, she tried to evacuate the premises. Why couldn't she move her legs? How had she become barefoot and paralyzed in this dark creepy place? Shaken with fear she tried again to move, but found it impossible to operate her legs.

Disgusting and dirty, the chamber did not bear a resemblance to her peaceful home. Searching the perimeter again, she looked deeper for a way to escape. Her eyes skimmed over a blurry collection of wild animals. In addition to the untamed guests, she picked up on an audible, low-frequency hum that was coming from an invisible source. Confused by the knowledge that animals like this did not belong inside the room, they also didn't cohabitate together, and they most certainly did not befriend humans. Regardless, Martine surmised that she was the uninvited intruder.

It didn't take long and they noticed her. Anticipating aggression on their part, Martine flinched when a ferocious bear growled and stood on his monstrous hind legs, reaching fourteen feet high. Twisting her stationary body sideways she saw a white wolf pace back and forth, fixating its eyes on her. Rotating the other direction, she confronted a mountain lion leaping onto the empty table near her. Looking down she noticed a badger as he passed by. Martine had no choice but to hold her ground. Watching the bear drop down on all four legs, she was relieved to see the lion, bear, and wolf retreat together—fading out of sight.

Smaller animals located in the back of the room came forward and approached Martine. Intuition told her the fox, rats, chipmunks, gophers, raccoons, and squirrels, were organized by a commander, who seemed to be the badger. None the less, they were following orders to attack. Martine was perplexed—this was out of character for these small creatures.

The disconcerted arsenal of animals began using intimidating tactics on Martine. They snarled, hissed, charged at her ankles, and some merely raised the hair on their backs. Tensions were escalating when two skunks walked in and caused the armory of mammals to withdraw out-of-site into a cloud-filled corner of the room.

Walking in tandem towards Martine, the skunks resembled a stream of harmless, wiggling, black and white uniformed stripes. Panicking at the thought of being sprayed, Martine tried to escape. Waddling forward, the skunks remained steady and confrontational. Two skunks, converging on her in chorus, were devastating. A dual attack, at close range, would render her incapacitated.

Aware that the noxious liquid from a skunk assault can cause an internal illness that no amount of fresh air can reverse, Martine grew desperate. Irritation to the eyes from their spew will cause temporary blindness. Recalling her past experience, she knew if she were sprayed, she would be unable to inhale or see. Profuse vomiting would compound her breathing problems, and she would suffer exponentially. She herself had survived a single skunk attack that incapacitated her horse and dog. That was all she needed to know to determine her fate. For these reasons every animal in the forest respects this fluffy, low-to-the-ground varmint.

Closing in on Martine's paralyzed body, the skunks stopped two feet in front of her. Stomping their front feet, hissing, and raising their matching tails, the skunks signaled their intent to spray with a synchronized about-face-maneuver. Anchored in place and unable to run-away, Martine closed her eyes.

Nothing happened for what seemed an immeasurable amount of time. Noisy skunk-chatter ensued, causing Martine to squint her eyes enough to observe the two skunks engaged in some sort of intense disagreement. Taking this opportunity to devise an escape, she peered around the room for a way out.

Through a narrow opening to the cave-like dwelling, she could make out the shape of four deer. Two of them were fawns with more spots than Bambi. Moving cautiously toward the cell that confined Martine, the graceful animals appeared concerned. Perched in the tree adjacent to the deer was a watchful eagle. Glancing back and forth between the skunks and the scene outside, Martine contemplated her options.

When she became more concerned with the conflict resulting between the skunks than her own fate, she regained control of her body. Compassion allowed her to bend down and mediate with the feuding skunks. Seconds earlier the two vermin were comrades, Martine wanted to know what happened in those few moments.

Beginning to be drawn away, Martine watched as the primeval, depressing space she occupied disappeared with her.

Without the desired answers, she was scooped out of the pandemonium and whisked back to her warm, familiar bed. Awake with open eyes, she recalled the detail of the profound debacle that took place in the cramped cell-like room. What possible meaning could be extrapolated from such a vivid animal dream-quest?

Disoriented from the experience, she glanced at her small clock. Blinking to see the familiar display of illuminated green numbers, Martine's faculties returned. The time read 6:04.

Switching on her bed-side lamp, she scribbled down some brief notations in her leather-bound journal, as was her custom when she woke up with what she termed "Impression Dreams."

The incident left her longing for a cup of hot coffee and a sun-filled day. While she made her way to the cheery kitchen that awaited her, Martine observed the sunrise bursting behind the thirteen-thousand-foot Shark's Tooth Mountain. In a few more moments the immense monument of rocky earth would no longer block the sun, and the white snow-tops would be more brilliant than a bride's dress.

Staring out her kitchen window, Martine noticed the abandoned bird feeders. Two weeks ago, the hummingbirds, blue jays, and various song birds had migrated south.

After starting a pot of coffee she headed back to her bedroom. More recall from her dream with the skunks surfaced and she needed to document it quickly.

While brushing her hair, she walked over to her private library of theology texts. Searching for her Native American resource book on Indian totems, she recalled the profound memory of the Medicine Man and his wife that gifted her with the revered text. They had insisted that Martine was connected to the ancient bear clan of their ancestors. If the meaning behind this animal-driven dream did not manifest soon she could perhaps help it along with some good old fashioned American Indian research. As of now it wasn't even a meaningful conversation piece for a therapist to analyze.

Only months ago, James would have been her confidant. He would have given her his undivided attention, while she shared her abstract dream odyssey. James knew how to reassure and build up confidence when she was stuck. He used to say, "It's always darkest before dawn—I mean, before it dawns on you."

With James gone, and life feeling foreign to her, she reverted to sharing herself with no one. As luck, or rather medication, would have it she hadn't had any thought-provoking dreams or daunting mind-rushes for many months. Theorizing that the dreams and psychic visions had stopped because of the sedatives (massive amounts by her standards), she was shocked that they could resume so suddenly. Drug therapy suppressed her extra-sensory activities and she had welcomed the relief.

"Shit," she said out loud. "I don't need this happening already. It was more peaceful and calm with the meds. How can I do this without any help?"

Hopeful that a viable connection would materialize, she documented the animal episode in her journal. Unable to shake the feeling that there was more to her dream that she couldn't recall, she wrote what she remembered. Jolene's appeal for assistance probably triggered the gibberish dream.

At nine AM Martine knew that Alexa was up and at it when the sounds of Keith Urban could be heard blasting from her bedroom stereo. When Eva and Alexa were teenagers, it was customary for them to battle out tunes before leaving for high school. Alexa was country, and Eva was punk or hip-hop. Emerging from her room, Alexa's noisy flip-flops clipped towards Martine's bedroom.

Knocking on the door jamb, Alexa asked, "Hey, mom, are you up?"

Martine looked up to see Alexa walking through the open double doors that divided the bedroom from the rest of the home. "I'm up. I can't believe you're up though."

Alexa yawned and tucked her long, golden hair behind rhinestone-studded ears. "Did you talk to Aunt Jolene?"

Stuffing the Native American book into her purse, Martine replied, "No, no news since yesterday."

Alexa plopped on her mother's bed. "Why don't we e-mail her so she knows we're coming? She didn't say not to e-mail her."

Pulling a suitcase out from under her bed, Martine set it on the antique storage chest positioned at the foot of her bed. "True, sweetie, but let's not till we know more. How much time do you need?"

Unzipping the bag for her mother, Alexa replied with confidence, "I can be dressed, packed, and in the car before you."

Raising her right hand in the air for a high-five, Martine accepted the challenge. "Okay then. We'll see about that. Either way, let's get out of here by eleven. Can you call Randy, and let him know we are leaving, and how to get a hold of us. Tell him I can't help the ranchers gather cows this weekend. Tell him he's in charge. I'll get dressed and packed."

The wardrobe Martine maintained at the ranch was very condensed. Selecting her favorite blue jeans, a teal-colored top, and her roan-colored, ultra-suede jacket, made up the finest of her available duds. After lacing up her distressed-leather riding boots, she removed the spurs. Looking in the mirror, she held up three of her favorite belts and selected the brown one with silver Conchos. Joining the ends of the belt together with a turquoise buckle made it a local fashion statement.

When Alexa returned dressed and packed, Martine announced that she was ready as well, "All right, daughter, let's go."

Placing her hand over her mouth, Alexa tried to suppress a giggle. "Okay, Dr. Quinn, Medicine Woman."

Insulted, Martine put her fist on her hip. "Excuse me? I hope that was a compliment. I haven't dressed up in a long time."

Walking closer, Alexa shook her head. "Really, mom, you need to think about what it means to get dressed-up and leave the ranch. Do you remember where we're going?"

Straightening her wicker cowboy hat, Martine walked over to the antique full-length mirror in the corner of her bedroom. "I know where we're going. And I'm fine with what I'm wearing. I realize I could never look as adorable as you and your sister."

Standing behind her mother, Alexa looked in the mirror and elaborated, "Wrong, you look great, but you look like you're going hunting." Pulling her burgundy hooded-sweatshirt over her designer shirt drowned her words a bit, "I can help you pick something out."

Adjusting the fringe on her jacket, Martine demonstrated her affection for leather. "Well, I don't know. What's the problem with my clothes?"

Alexa critiqued her mother's appearance, "Besides the hat, boots, jeans, leather jacket, and that platter you call a belt buckle, you look great."

"So what's your point, Alexa? Do you want me to lose the hat or all my clothes?"

While Martine contemplated Alexa's diplomacy, her daughter attempted another formable strategy. "Mother, you've told Eva, me, and our boyfriends, to 'dress for the job you want, not the one you got.' Doesn't that apply to you?"

"Yes it does, and I am dressing for the job I want. That job is right here miles and miles away from toxic people, rush-hour traffic, crowded offices, pathological liars, and narcissists."

Enunciating her response as slow and precise as possible, Alexa approached her mother again, "Gee, Indiana Jones, tell me how you really feel? Isn't there any room for compromise?"

Martine frowned. "Maybe."

Lifting the hat off of her mother's head, Alexa offered a resolution. "You've just been here too long. Alright, at least lose the big belt buckle and the hat."

"Fine." Taking the hat back from Alexa, she flung it next to her suitcase. "I'm bringing them both with though. You go pick out a belt." Martine conceded this time. She was a nonconformist that would never consider adapting her values to what is simply popular to everyone else. However, keeping peace was better this time.

"Daughter, it's time to get on the road. I'm driving." No sooner had that been decided than Eva's custom ring tone came out loud and clear from Alexa's cell.

Before Martine could hide her hands in her pockets, or escape, Alexa handed the phone over to her and said, "You talk to her. I don't even know what to tell her. She'll be pissed that we're going to Aunt Jolene's without her."

Accepting the cell phone, Martine cleared her throat and swallowed hard—like a nervous witness being cross-examined in court. "Oh boy, this isn't going to be good. Opening the phone she said, "Hey, Eva, how are classes going?"

"Hey, mom, classes are all right. They're sort of boring. So, what are you guys doing? Is Alexa up yet? I bet she sleeps till noon. What are you doing with her phone?"

Glancing over at Alexa's apprehensive expression, Martine replied, "Actually, Alexa's, busy loading up the car for a little road trip. It's more like a business trip."

Eva's voice rose in volume, "What? Where are you going?"

Cringing at the inevitable, Martine remained nonchalant, "Jolene kinda needs me right now. She called yesterday afternoon and begged me to come."

"What's wrong? Does she need me too?"

Moving next to her mother, Alexa patted her shoulder with a yeah-sure-you-bet-she'll-fall-for-this. "No, no! She doesn't need you. I don't think it's personal. Probably work. You know how she over analyzes everything. Don't worry about it."

"Boy, I'd give anything to go with you guys." Eva's voice dropped an octave. "I know you're more like a mother to her. I mean, she's like my big sister. I should help too, if there's a problem."

Martine bit her bottom lip. Eva was right. Jolene was fourteen years younger than Martine and more like a daughter than a sister. Their parents were taken in a tragic car accident when Martine was only twenty-four years old—Jolene ten. Jolene came to live with Martine, James and Alexa. Martine had been pregnant with Eva.

Jolene, Alexa, and Eva were more like sisters. Serious dating was rare among the three girls and boyfriends were scarce. Martine wasn't sure if they were fussy or too busy to date. She just knew they stuck together.

Only two years ago, Martine had reassured the three girls, when they all expressed how discouraged they were with dating, "There are more thorns than roses in the garden. The roses stand out though, so keep looking."

Martine tried to hand the phone to Alexa, but Alexa pushed her hand away. Having no choice but to calm Eva, she answered, "Eva, it doesn't make sense for you to come. You've got school. We don't even know how long we'll be there. I'll call you later tonight."

"I suppose you're right, but it doesn't feel okay. Don't forget to call me. Love you."

"Love you too. We'll talk later."

Sliding into the driver's seat, Martine advised her daughter to buckle up.

Chapter 10

Driving from Southwest Colorado to Arizona has never taken Martine more than seven hours. It's an uncomplicated route. Few towns interrupt the steady flow of traffic. Long stretches of highway score undeveloped naturally preserved Indian reservation land and massive animal pastures. The Wild West has been ingrained in the history of this land as well as the genetics of the inhabitants. Legends of mystery and misfortune have thrived in the Four Corners region for eons. Steeped in centuries of historical accounts, these rare places can haunt the visitor for years.

Before seeing even one Saguaro cactus, they would pass by rock formations that were forced out of the underworld by earth-forming events. The ominous rocks resembled skyscrapers erected in the middle of the flattened deserts of New Mexico.

After passing through Shiprock, New Mexico, Martine had the notion to peruse the Native American Totem book she had brought with.

Glancing sideways, Martine addressed her daughter, "I think the dreams are coming back already. I'm not taking enough sedatives to drown them out anymore."

Alexa turned her head towards Martine and quizzed her, "What went on in your dream last night? I knew you would start getting dreams again soon."

"In my dream there was a crappy room full of animals that acted aggressive. Well, maybe not all of them. I think it was the little animals that were trying to scare me off, or get rid of me. It made no sense whatsoever. There were skunks—just two of them."

Shrugging her shoulders, Alexa said, "Give me some more details, maybe I can help."

Martine repeated the whole dream sequence to her daughter, and paused for her reaction.

Shaking her head, Alexa said, "Nope, I can't possibly tell you what the weird dream meant—or what it had to do with Jolene." Acting disenchanted, Alexa pushed another CD in the player and turned the volume up.

Martine raised her voice to speak over Alexa's blaring music, "Alexa, please reach behind my car seat and grab the book out of my purse."

Rummaging through Martine's purse, Alexa pulled out the book and read its title, "Sacred Animal Totems." Using her thumb she fanned the bound pages and continued, "Do you think there will be some answers in here? That's actually pretty cool that you thought of the totems," Alexa shouted.

With the music level adjusted lowered, Martine searched her mental library. "Look up skunk."

Twisting open the top of a water bottle, Alexa shivered. "That is probably the animal that scares me the most. Remember what happened when our cat got sprayed? If you wouldn't have found him he would have died outside in the weeds. I still can't believe he begged you to bath him so he could get better. That was pretty cool of you. We just locked him out of our rooms."

"Yeah, he was a neat cat."

"Yeah . . . right, except when he ratted on us. I can't believe he was a spy for you. I mean he was just a cat. How did he know we were doing something we shouldn't be doing?" Alexa sipped on her water and cracked open a bottle for Martine.

"If you girls got in trouble it was your fault, not the cats. He was a truly psychic cat. He would find me and stare me down until I would pay attention to him. I can't explain it, I just understood him. You're getting off the subject. Just look up skunk."

Martine shook her head in amazement as she took the opened bottle from her daughter. It was true, and a guarded secret, until it slipped out one day when Eva got busted for sneaking out of the house late at night. It was their cat Pandora that woke Martine up to tell her Eva was gone. Is that what they mean when they say, "Don't let the cat out of the bag?" Martine's mind stopped wandering when Alexa interpreted the skunk totem.

"Skunks are slow moving solitary animals that spend most of the daylight hours underground or in the dark. They like to take over abandoned homes that belonged to other creatures. Throughout history they have carried a reputation that is respected as well as feared. They spray their victims to blind and incapacitate them. A skunk totem indicates imminent danger or caution. The stripe running from the head to the tail is linked to the creative life force within. Those with this medicine need to look beyond this world to see what is really important. Unbalanced skunk people have a habit of tooting their own horn for recognition. Those with this totem are either liked or disliked."

Martine pulled the visor down to block the blazing hot sun out of her eyes. "That's interesting. Can you look up chipmunk?"

Turning the pages back, Alexa read on, *"They have no fear of people and are found in rural areas.* That's cute, mom, is chipmunk one of your totems?"

"Very funny, Alexa. I think not. Can you just focus on chipmunk?"

"Okay. Eeeoouu, they don't sound very organized. Listen to this. *They scamper to and fro always in a hurry to get somewhere. They go in circles and end up where they started. They have an air of independence and they will go where they should not. They can be constructive or destructive. If you have this totem you may not be in charge of your life.* Mom, you definitely do not have chipmunk on your totem." Alexa affirmed with a nod.

Martine felt a new connection with her daughter and couldn't help but smile. Alexa was always so quiet and reserved around the rest of the family. She liked her daughter's sense of humor, when she used it. "This is really odd, I'm sensing a pattern. Can you look up gopher?"

"Uh huh, these are kinda interesting. I'm gonna look up my totems when we're done. I hope you brought the medicine cards too?"

"No, I'm afraid I didn't," Martine replied.

Paging ahead in the book, Alexa continued, "Okay, *gophers live their lives underground in complex tunnels. They are part of the underworld. They uncover hidden truths. Because they tunnel in gardens they pull large numbers of plants down into their burrows. They are blamed for destroying crops.*"

"Yikes. Well that doesn't sound too great either. Will you look at Rat?" Martine shook her head in disgust.

Alexa thumbed ahead in the book and summarized the long dissertation on rat, "*Rats are survivors, and humans have eliminated most of their predators. Pack Rats are famous for collecting items that are valuable, but not theirs. They hoard what they want because they fear they won't get enough. They're greedy and will fight aggressively for what they want.*"

Martine adjusted the cars thermostat to handle the warmer temperature outside. "Dang that feels better. Let's do a couple more. Check fox."

Removing her sweatshirt for better comfort, Alexa reassured her mother, "No problem, as long as I don't have to read all two-hundred pages." Alexa tossed the hooded cover-up into the back-seat and read, "Alright, fox, *extremely clever and cunning. Likes the arts of camouflage, invisibility, and shape-shifting. Skilled and unpredictable. They work at night.*"

"Hum." Martine pondered her next inquiry. "Look up Ricky Raccoon."

Alexa frowned at her mother's attempt towards humor, "*Raccoon is nocturnal, and travels in small groups. They are curious and like to explore new things, but when they do not use caution their curiosity leads to trouble. They are thieves.*"

"Well, this next one ought to be good. Please look up squirrel."

Checking the signal strength on both their phones, Alexa sighed. "We only have one bar. Nobody can call us for awhile. No wonder mine isn't ringing." Scanning for missed text-messages, she repeated her mother's latest request, "Squirrel." Flipping to the new page she went on, *"They have an endless supply of energy. Quick and agile. Constantly preparing for the future. Tendency to forget where things are. They prepare for survival."* Laughing out loud, Alexa changed the subject, "Remember when dad was re-modeling the laundry room a few years ago? He pulled the old venting out and fifty pounds of dog food fell into the room." Alexa roared even harder, "Those squirrels must have been preparing for Armageddon."

"Pu . . . leeze, how could I forget?" Joining her daughter in the jovial moment, Martine reminisced with her, "That was hilarious. I can't believe how long it took to get all that dog food out of the wall."

"Or the laundry room," Alexa added.

Positioning her pillow up against the car door, Alexa prepared for a little nap in the sun, "I'll do one more, and then I think I'll be passing out. The last two days of driving and riding has finally caught up."

"I bet you will. Look up lion."

Alexa scanned the lion totem and asked for clarification, "Male or female?"

"Uh . . . it was a male."

"Lion is linked to power. They are fearless. They look regal, and are called kings. Lions do not fight for the sake of fighting. They just look like powerful commanders."

"Well, that was interesting. I'll have to think on it for awhile. Can you put one of your new country CD's on for me?" Martine straightened her back for the long journey ahead.

"Here's one you'll like. It's Eva's favorite," Alexa yawned through her words. Slouching back on her pillow, she closed her eyes.

Transitioning from the barren lands in New Mexico to the wooded forests of Arizona was a sacred experience to Martine. Uneven topography between Holbrook and Payson looked similar to their surroundings in Southwest Colorado. Tall pines started to take over the terrain, and pastures disappeared as they climbed higher up into the Arizona White Mountain communities.

* * *

Martine drove hours while Alexa slept. Without much warning, Martine had to brake suddenly when she met up with a small herd of elk crossing the road.

Alexa reacted to the abrupt stop and sat up in surprise. "What's wrong?" she blurted.

"Elk. Everything's fine," Martine informed her daughter. "Alexa, I better fill-up the car now. This is a good time to grab something to eat and drink."

While topping-off her gas tank, Martine noticed Arizona license plates dominated the gas station and roadways. That mere fact proved the tourists were gone for the season.

Sprinting out of the convenience store with drinks and chips, Alexa returned to Martine before the gas tank was full. "We're almost there. Do you want me to drive, mom?"

"No, I wouldn't mind you looking-up a few more totems for me while we still have daylight." Placing the gasoline nozzle back in its holster, Martine added, "I'm running to the restroom, I'll be right back."

Back on the road and heading east, Martine said, "I thought of some other totems to check out. The lion, bear, wolf, and badger were in the room first and then retreated immediately. After thinking about it, they were not aggressive towards me. Let's see . . . look up 'wolf' for me, please."

Flipping the pages to the totem for wolf, Alexa read aloud, "*A wolf totem is a transformative totem for people with leadership qualities. It is 'teacher' medicine that is used to learn how to trust insights and inner knowing. Wolf is highly misunderstood. In reality they are friendly and social. They are the epitome of the wild spirit. They are balanced, loyal, faithful, and intuitive. People with wolf in their totem have keen senses, a strong bond with family, and great inner strength."* Alexa paused and looked at Martine. "That's pretty deep. Here listen to this, it says, *slow and steady gets the prize, but wolf people have the ability to speed it up. If wolf appears in your life examine where you need to develop more confidence."*

Martine pondered the information and its meaning. "Can you see if badger is in that book? That seems like an odd totem to have."

Alexa replied, "Why wouldn't it be in here?"

"Not every animal is a totem-animal."

"Well, it's here. Eeeoouu . . . *badger is a member of the weasel family. Family members mark each other with scent for recognition. Badger is associated with illusion. What you see is not necessarily what you get. They are organized, and fastidious about their sur-roundings. Remarkable diggers, these loners live below the surface. This ability ties the badger to the mysteries of the underworld, where the magic of life and creation is stored. That sounds really icky."* Alexa cringed. "Oh, listen to this, *badger people are not balanced. When they are out of control they are feared and hated. They are dictators. They have no concern for others. They aggressively seek revenge. There is no mercy in badger people for they care for no one except themselves. Badger is the power of monger—the control freak. Badger is the mark of aggressiveness carried to the extreme."*

"Yeah. The badger may have been in control. Let's look at bear," Martine suggested.

"Hey, mom, bear is one of your Indian totems. You've got the page marked." Alexa fell silent as she read the long dissertation on the bear. "Okay, this is interesting. *They are considered to be a highly desired ally and spirit helper because of their fearless power. It is believed that the power of the Great Spirit lives through this animal. Bear is the spirit keeper of the west. The gifts that bear offers to those with this totem are strength, introspection, intuition, and knowledge. No other animal totem is active both day and night— only bear. It teaches us how to go within and find the resources nec-essary for our personal survival. When bear shows up in your life pay attention to how you think, act, and interact. Use discernment. Bear will teach you how to make choices from a position of power."* Alexa stopped and looked at Martine. "Boy does that sound like you. I can see how bear was meant to be your totem. You were the one that always saw the bears around the ranch. You even were able to photograph them. It was like they came to see you."

"It's been many years since the Navajo medicine man did my totem. I forgot about all of this till I had that dream last night." Bursting into view was a panoramic sunset that blinded both passengers. "Why don't you put the book away? I really need to focus on this stretch of road, and I can barely see where I'm going."

Descending from the Mongollon Rim area around Payson, into the populated valleys below, Martine was awe struck when they were met by a multihued skyline. Heavenly colors ranged from lavenders to fuchsia. Like sophisticated stage lights, the dreamy sky illuminated gigantic tree-sized Saguaro cactus. Sprouting arms, which curved up in the most distinctive configurations, were characteristic of the thirty-to-fifty-foot cacti. Protruding out of the slopes and flats of the Sonoran desert, the Saguaros loomed throughout the land like soldiers in a battle field. Proudly flaunting the Arizona state-flower, the magnificent specimens dwarfed the passing cars.

Driving fast, seventy-miles-an-hour, down from the high country of Arizona likened a one-hour freefall. Unable to take her eyes off the steep winding highway, Martine sat silent as the enormous spot-light faded out for the night.

Chapter 11

Stiff from the seven-hour journey, Martine was relieved to turn into Jolene's neighborhood and park her car on the street. Toting their suitcases behind them, Martine and Alexa walked up to the porch. Finding all the lights-off inside the home, Martine located the familiar cactus garden that housed the entry key. Lifting the ceramic coyote, which sat amongst a plethora of cacti, she recovered the house key from under the terracotta figurine.

Using the key, they entered through the front door into the welcoming spins of Jolene's dog, Honey.

Martine and Alexa were taken aback when Jolene walked out of her bedroom staring at her portable phone with a perplexed expression.

Startling one another, Martine sprang-up with the gyrating Pomeranian in her arms. "Hi, you're home."

Jolene gasped, "Wow, you scared me. I didn't hear your car. What a great surprise. I've sure missed you both." Her odd reaction was followed by a stiff hug.

Oblivious to the awkward moment, Alexa ran to the sleeping cat, Sugar, calling out, "Litter critter."

Noticing that Jolene was acting abnormal, Martine played along using succinct enunciations in her words, "Jolene, it's—great—to—see—you—too." Rubbing Honey's extra-fluffy-coat, she continued, "Are—we—too—late—for—dinner?"

"Good one. Still making fun of my culinary skills aren't you, Martine?"

"Not at all. You don't have any culinary skills, remember, sis? Is there anything you want to talk to me about before . . . ?"

"Oh that. Not to worry I think everything is fine now. I misunderstood someone at work. It's all good, and you both came. I'm just so happy you dropped in. I hope you'll still stay for awhile?"

Martine and Alexa both looked at each other and said in unison. "What?"

Still acting suspicious, Jolene explained, "Yeah, I guess there really wasn't a problem after all."

Martine petted the jazzed-up dog while it sniffed her long-hair and leather-jacket, "Well, Jolene, tell me what happened."

Fidgeting with the portable phone, Jolene replied, "It's embarrassing. I need the right time to get into it. I think it's best if we talk later."

Irritated by demands and secrecy, Martine probed further, "Are you sure you don't want to talk about it now? I thought it was an emergency."

Reaching for the panting dog being coddled by Martine, Jolene excused herself, "No, get yourselves unpacked. I'll take care of dinner."

Reluctant about the weird reception, Martine retreated to the guest bedroom. In the process of unpacking her suitcase, Eva called. A cheery greeting got her attention back on track.

"Hey, mom, is everything okay?"

Holding up a wrinkled blouse, Martine did her best to answer, "Great, I think."

"Are you with Jolene?"

"Yep, we're getting ready for dinner."

"Well, I got good news. I'm coming."

Dropping the shirt, Martine exclaimed, "What?"

"Yeah, I tested out of the math class early, thanks to the summer class I audited. Thinking of you all together motivated me to go for the test early. When I explained the family emergency my teacher agreed. I'm driving down from Flag in a couple days."

Martine took a seat on the bed and debated with her daughter, "Eva, I don't even know what I'm doing here. Jolene says everything's fine now. There's no emergency."

"That's great. I'm really coming for the pool and food. Just kidding. She probably tricked you so you'd get out of Durango. Hey, someone's calling me, I'll see you soon. Love you."

"Eva, wait . . . do you know something? Eva . . . are you there?" Hearing nothing—Martine hung-up. After terminating the conversation with Eva, she joined Jolene and Alexa in the kitchen.

Biting into a crispy egg roll, Alexa mumbled, "Dinner smells awesome. I'm starving."

Giggling with a playful expression, Martine couldn't pass up the opportunity for a sisterly-jab, "Hey, Jolene, dinner looks—ethnic? I see you outdid yourself."

"Yes I did. I slaved for hours over Chang's takeout menu. Any objections, counselor?"

"No, your honor. It's perfect. We concur."

Dinner conversation was steady but vague. Martine took Jolene's cue to not pry until after dinner. Excusing herself to go call her friend, Alexa left Martine and Jolene in the dirty kitchen.

Shoving Styrofoam containers into the trash receptacle, Martine attempted to meddle again, "Okay, Jolene, what do you want to do now? I guess Alexa's in her room talking to Heather."

Jolene pushed the dishwasher door closed, and faced her sister. "Actually, I'm in the mood for the hot-tub. How' bout you?"

Caught off-guard again, Martine pressed her lips together and countered Jolene's proposal, "What? I didn't bring a suit. How' bout we play a slow game of scrabble?"

"I've got suits, and I'd rather do the hot tub after a long day. Wouldn't you like to relax with the jets on your sore joints? I know you went for a ride with Alexa yesterday. I can only imagine how that went."

Popping the cork out of the bottle of Chardonnay, Martine looked into the dark sky outside. "No, I'd rather sit over there at the game table with you. Let's get caught up, and drink this bottle of wine."

"Fine. Let's do both." Jolene motioned to her beautiful wooden scrabble game, which held a pious position on its' own table. "I'll be over there—getting the game ready."

Because Jolene's exquisite game board was left in the same condition as the last time it was played, a maze of metallic-gold letters needed to be cleared and shaken up in a burgundy-velvet bag. While Martine was pouring the chardonnay, Jolene took a seat at the table and pushed the heavy tiles into a mound.

Glancing over towards the scrabble table, Martine noticed that Jolene was still fumbling with the letters, so she excused herself, "Hey I'm going to check out your restroom. I'll be right back."

When Martine returned she seated herself across the table from Jolene. Anxious to start a fresh game of scrabble, she swiveled the wooden-board game on its turntable till it faced her.

When Martine lifted the burgundy-bag to pull a starting letter, she noticed most of them were arranged in a strange configuration on the board. Words that should intersect each other vertically and horizontally weren't present. Instead the letters formed a sentence on the board that read.

SOMEONE MAY BE
LISTENING AND
WATCHING US
LETS GO OUT TO
THE JACUZI

Shocked, Martine jerked her head up and looked at Jolene. "Let's use the hot tub first, I've changed my mind."

Chapter 12

Flopping back on his mattress, Peter let his new drugs take effect while his stereo played heavy metal music. Relishing the high like a bear with honey, he laid on his back with a perpetual grin. Barely able to function, he kicked off his sneakers, and wiggled out of his jeans.

His mind started to soar with promising ideas. He felt on top of the world as his drugs worked their magic. Taking more than one narcotic amplified Peter's euphoric experience, causing him to believe he was invincible. With his hazy eyes, he reached over for his light switch and turned it off.

Still smiling, he shut his eyes and reminisced how he use to get off on smelling gas. Only eight years old when he first did it, he never stopped trying to find that type of pleasure. Ready to sink into a night-long stupor, he let his mind go and the demons take over. Alone in the dark, he drummed the erratic beat on his thighs as he rocked-out to the angry-sounding music. Fantasizing about the possibility of getting a new job with real money, he felt on top of the world for the first time. He knew he just needed a break, and he was due for one.

Entering again as she had before, the sumptuous woman with an intoxicating scent descended on him and fondled his groin. Dazed from his drugs, and out of touch with reality, he participated more freely in her sexual advances. Thinking he was a king and she a queen, he accepted his lover like he deserved her.

When she finally wore him down to total unconsciousness, he dozed off and remembered it like it was all a dream.

Chapter 13

Once in the gurgling-whirlpool Jolene reverted to her old self and confided in her sister, like a neurotic with a psychiatrist, "I'm sorry, Martine. It just hit me when I was sitting alone at the table that something is really wrong. I think I had a panic attack."

"Jolene, what's going on? You've had me in suspense for over twenty-four hours. We dropped everything and drove all the way down here. I felt like an overreacting fool when you implied nothing was wrong. Now you 'scrabble' me that someone is watching you. Give. What's wrong, and why are we here?"

Adjusting the water temperature to high, Jolene explained, "Well, I think it has to do with a big case we're working on. That's why I needed you."

"Me?"

"Martine, I was hoping you'd get one of your feelings if you were here. Everyone is clueless, and there may be a leak at the Bureau. Names are getting out to the media and suspects are invisible to us."

"Jolene, it doesn't work like that. I'm not a human lie detector. I may get a strong impression, or warning, but it'll be cryptic and take awhile. It's typical for clues to unfold over time, not overnight. This is very controversial. You've always insisted I keep this to myself. You're a doubter, remember?"

"You're right. I'm not comfortable with it. No one needs to know about your abilities. Plus for your own safety, and Alexa's, it's imperative that you appear to be consulting. Your reason for being at the Bureau will be for providing legal advice and guidance concerning the lawful jurisdictions, and of course profiling."

"Profiling? Who? How? When? I work in the legal department, remember?"

Jolene rambled undeterred, "I've arranged for your clearance with the consent of the Director. I'm the only person that knows why you're really here."

"Your boss has agreed to this?"

"He has. He'll be hiring you as a Special Consultant. Since you already have security clearance with the Colorado FBI he retained you as a consultant without any red tape. Of course, he doesn't know about your intuitions."

"Really, when did this happen?"

"Today."

Tipping her head forward, Martine narrowed her eyes on Jolene. "I need details on why you think you're under surveillance, and why we couldn't talk about it."

"We knew that someone was getting information and that could mean cell phone tampering. I didn't want your number to become compromised—at all. I'd be communicating sensitive information that was under a 'code of silence' that we all had to adhere to."

"You are all operating in silence?" Martine questioned.

"Yes, I thought I was going crazy. When I came home from work yesterday afternoon, Honey was locked outside in the backyard and my keyboard was pulled all the way out. Oh, my desk chair was cockeyed—not pushed in tight like I leave it. My computer was on. I never leave it on during the day."

Moving her head back-and-forth doubtfully, Martine interrupted, "Okay. I give, Jolene, how does that prove someone is monitoring you?"

"It doesn't prove that, but I never leave my keyboard pulled out because the cat sleeps on it and messes up my functions. I've always left my dog in the house when I leave. Somebody must have come in the house through the garage, using the back door. That door leads to-and-from my private yard. Because of my high concrete privacy fence no one can see in or out of my yard. The dog would run outside, if she could, and hide in the oleander bushes to get away from a stranger. Honey would be trapped in the yard after they left. That door would've been easy to pick and relock. No dead bolt. That's when I called you from my neighbor's phone. I couldn't talk in front of them."

"Oh . . . that's why I didn't recognize the number."

"Right. They kept trying to listen to me. I couldn't let her hear anything about my job either."

"Seriously, couldn't you call the police for that? Shouldn't you call the police?"

"How would they help me? How would that look at work?"

"You have a small point."

"Oh, and I noticed my car seat had been moved from its normal position. The car is always unlocked when it's inside my not-so-secure garage. When I pushed my setting control the seat automatically moved forward about ten-inches and the back adjusted even more. I know someone else had to have been in my car."

Inhaling the aroma inside her wine glass while she swirled it around, Martine complimented her sister, "Good work, Watson."

"I guess I put it all together when I came home tonight and discovered my portable phones where switched around. I have the ringer off on the bedroom phone—annoyance calls wake me up. Someone called right before you arrived and it rang in the bedroom. This was probably done yesterday too. That made me realize I may be bugged. Who would enter my house, let the dog out, not take anything, but move my phones, keyboard, and car seat?"

"Have you performed a sweep for bugs?"

"No—not yet. I just figured this out. If there are audio transmitters around, I don't want to tip anyone off right now. I don't want them to know that we're on to them. As soon as we move or disturb even one device they will know their surveillance has been compromised and they'd probably come back.

"You could be right," Martine nodded thoughtfully.

"We know from past experience that water features like Jacuzzi's and radios prevent conversations from being audible. I feel safe right now. Plus it is just a theory."

Martine swallowed a sip of wine. "I hope you don't feel safe just because I'm here. I'm not qualified to protect you. I don't even pack a gun."

"I know that, I feel we're safe and will be left alone because the intruder believes I'm being adequately monitored. The big question is who would want to get information from me? Does it have to do with the big case I'm involved with, or something else?"

Watching her sister reach for the wine bottle, Martine replied, "You know, sis, I think you better tell me about the case now."

Martine gave her undivided attention to Jolene as the meager findings existing in case file "Tombstone" were summarized.

* * *

Pouring Chardonnay into their empty glasses, Jolene finished her long briefing, "The worst part of this case is the mere fact we can't connect the abductions to any common denominator. We can't prove they're even related, or if there's merely a better engineered street drug luring runaways into prostitution."

Jolene's phone sounded out the Bob Dylan song, "There Must Be Some Way Out Of Here." Knowing Jolene liked quiet and solitude—and would never tolerate a noisy phone ring—Martine was curious to know who it was. Waiting minutes for Jolene to finish reading a long text-message, she asked, "Jolene, who was that? Or should I ask whose ring was that?"

"Just a friend responding to an e-mail. He's a rocker I met at the conference last month. He's a great contact I use on DMV stuff."

Arching her head back to look at the stars, Martine asked, "So it wasn't that guy, Wade, you're dating?"

"No it wasn't, and I wouldn't call it dating. We don't even see each other anymore."

Martine straightened herself back to an upright position. "What! As I recall you were dating. What's wrong? Did you try to arrest him for having bad hair? Honestly, Jolene, you can be so picky."

"That's not funny, and *he* stopped seeing *me*. I guess he didn't think I was funny."

"Funny? Jolene, you're not known for having a sense of humor. Tell details."

"Well, remember when Wade busted that drug dealer? He and his partner received a lot of notoriety. His good looks served him well when the reporters jumped on the story. Wade sure thought he was all that."

"Okay, what went wrong? Don't beat around the bush. I want the short version."

"I'm not sure what happened. He was sort of flirting with girls, and he wouldn't stop bragging about being on that cop show. It seemed like he didn't really want to be with me, but he assumed I wanted to be with him. I had no choice—I had to do something about it."

Adjusting the jet blasting her back, Martine said, "Oh boy, what in the world of emotionally-challenged people did you do?"

"Well, for his thirty-fifth birthday I drew his picture or rather 'likenesses' on a 36"x30" canvas."

Cringing at the thought of her strong-willed sister confronting a defenseless man, Martine probed deeper, "Really? What exactly did you concoct?"

"I drew a portrait of Wade's head. It was very accurate and flattering."

"Right, Jolene. Like why would you draw a portrait of your new boyfriend? I mean you can draw alright, but you draw like Andy Warhol."

"I told you, he was acting arrogant."

"So, you drew this because . . . ?"

"Well, okay. I kinda drew a caricature."

"You've got to be kidding. I've got to see this. Did you take a picture?"

"Yeah, sort of. I took a picture of him holding it at his birthday party—before I knew he was pissed." Picking up her cell phone, Jolene scrolled for the picture display. Handing the phone to Martine she looked away.

Stunned at what she saw, Martine shrieked, "Oh my God! Oh my God! Jolene what were you thinking? I mean *why* weren't you thinking?"

"Is it really that bad?"

"No . . . It's really that good, but I know why he's not calling you." Shocked by the phone-photo, Martine studied the caricature in disbelief. "You must know what you've done."

"I didn't think it was so bad."

"Did you have to add the caption?"

"At the time I did. He was a jerk."

"Whoa, you managed to get right to the point." Shaking her head in disbelief, Martine read the unavoidable bold words, "AC-TUAL SIZE," painted at the bottom of Wade's large facial portrait.

Absorbing the repercussions of Jolene's forwardness over-whelmed Martine. "You know, you managed to get your point across like a blizzard in Phoenix. Your talent may have worked against you though. It's an impressive piece of work, but will it do any good if you're not with him?"

Jolene scrunched her lips together before answering, "Every-one at his birthday party laughed. They said it was funny."

Weighing Jolene's actions, like a criminal investigator, Martine cross-examined her, "Did you really need to kick his butt like that? Have you gone out with him since then?"

"No. I even bought him a little gift the next day when I realized he took my drawing the wrong way."

"I hope you didn't make it worse."

"No. It was a store-bought coffee mug that said, 'It took me thirty-five years to look this good.' That's when he let me know he wasn't the *transparent idiot* I drew. Since that night our relation-ship has been cordial and one-hundred-percent professional. He is without a doubt over me."

"I'd love to see this art project."

"Not much chance of that. I'm sure it's in the nearest landfill."

Martine's maternal instincts kicked-in. "You know, Jolene, you can be a little judgmental when it comes to the imperfections most of us are burdened with. It sounds like you were a little too harsh?"

"No! Just to the point," Jolene said defensively.

Tuning-out her sisters excuses, Martine scolded her, "Yeah, I get that, you're tough and righteous—sometimes to the extreme. It can be irritating. Can't you keep anything to yourself?"

Rolling wine around in the crystal glass, Jolene defended herself, "I realize you're more tolerant, Martine, but you've got the same tendencies. You don't have a problem telling people what they don't want to hear."

"True, but I try to avoid being too condescending. I like to use humor, or analogies, not an audience."

Raking her fingers through dampened hair, Jolene dropped her voice, "You think the sketch was a bad idea. Don't you?"

Stimulated by the wine, Martine spoke candidly, "I bet you went to this extreme because you were thinking more about yourself and didn't give a thought about causing hurt. How do you know that Wade isn't more sensitive and intelligent than you gave him credit for? How can he face you as an equal after you humiliated him—at a party, and in front of his friends—no less?"

Sounding defensive, Jolene turned the thermostat down on the hot-tub and replied, "How would you know? You weren't there. You haven't even met him."

"Jolene, you drove him away. You implied he wasn't good enough for you."

"I only meant to make him laugh and get over himself."

Exasperated and flushed from the hot steam rising around her head, Martine tried to counsel her sister, "Wade is haunting your conscience. That's why your feelings for him are peaked. Don't even try and deny it with me. You have found fault in every guy you dated. And there hasn't been too many of them."

"Darn it, Martine, it's really irritating when I go personal with you. I despise it when you act like you know my thoughts."

Familiar with Jolene's dilemma, Martine wanted to help. "I can't control what you're feeling. I also can't stop your frustration from hitting me. I'm only bringing the obvious facts to your attention. That's what happens when you confide in me."

"Are you being a lawyer, psychologist, or psychic?"

"Probably all of the above. I feel like a baseball-pitcher just threw me a two-hundred-mile-an-hour fastball."

"WOW!" Jolene accentuated the small word. "What are you saying? Or rather what are you feeling?"

Flustered, Martine leaned forward and asked, "Do you want to be a candle without a wick?"

"What-the-hay does that mean? Another one of your cliché's?"

"If you're willing to share your heart with another, and live in a less than perfect home, you'll experience warmth, challenge, and purpose. Alone, you won't be noticed, or loved."

"Is that what you see in your crystal ball?"

Bracing for an argument, Martine got right to the point, "Jolene, be serious, I just want you to know that you can fall in love and be happy with someone that isn't perfect. Together you can bring out the best in each other. Separately, you'll have no one to share burdens or triumphs with. There'll be no surprises to come home to if you're alone. If we were all perfect, we wouldn't need each other."

"Yeah, well I know you're alone, too, Martine."

"I'm not. Losing James isn't a tragedy. The idea of never knowing and loving someone more than myself would be the crime. Got it, Agent Frost?"

"I can't believe it, you're suggesting I'm a cynic and Wade's a victim? He's the one that stopped dating." Covering her ears with both hands, Jolene shook her head pretending not to hear. "I can't listen to this."

"I'm sorry you're not taking this in the spirit it is intended. Telling you how I see it—well that's just the way I'm wired. I think you pushed Wade away."

"It's not that . . . it's just too late."

"It's not too late for you and him," Martine countered with a whimsical smile. "Don't be afraid to go out on a limb, that's where the fruit is."

Jolene smiled weakly. "Did you just make that up?"

"No, Arthur Lenehan said something like that." Martine smiled affectionately.

Jolene's gorgeous, corn-flower-blue eyes, and rosy-complexion never radiated more. Admiring her sister's beauty, she studied how much she resembled their mother at this moment. Attracting guys with her good looks was never the obstacle. Martine felt her sister's vulnerability. Noticing tears swelling up in her eyes she tried to comfort her, "Unless you are physically incapable of crying, it's time you did. Just know I'm here for you."

Martine knew this was the greatest ache she would experience. Pulling the scab off the wound would force her sister to face the pain start dealing with it.

Alexa emerged from the house with Jolene's dog bounding at her heals. Giggling, Alexa threw Honey's squeaky toy and watched her charge the faux-bone. "She's so adorable, I can't resist her."

Nodding at the playful scene, Jolene found her smile again. "Oh, yeah, she's cute as a button, just not quite as smart."

It was a well-timed interruption for Martine. "We've been in here long enough. I'm as hot as a snowball in the desert. Jolene, tell me what I'm doing tomorrow and let's get out."

Chapter 14

Relaxed from the effects of Jolene's hot tub, Martine was ready for a good night's sleep. "Let's wrap it up—I'm calling it a day." Exchanging hugs and giggles before calling it a night, the three of them headed for their own rooms. Swimming in reams of information that Jolene shared in the hot tub would undoubtedly cause some sort of dream experience with more downloads and impressions. Dreading what she would inevitably need to decipher, Martine hesitated before climbing into her bed.

She located her journal and unhooked the leather straps that held it closed. Her journal and pen next to the digital alarm clock would be her only consolation when she tried to make sense of the events she had now been drawn into.

Martine's sleeping body appeared still and tranquil as she was spiritually transported to another space and time. Even though her restful body wasn't moving, in her mind's eye she was catapulted to another dimension that sparked her attention with its stormy atmospheric conditions. Deafening claps of thunder and brilliant lightning phenomenon crescendoed around her, indicating a storm was brewing.

Settling into her latest occurrence, Martine connected with her new reality by focusing on the dramatic lightning show in front of her. Overwhelmed by the brightness generated from the lightning,

Martine realized she had materialized like a time-traveler and was now inside her Colorado home.

Feeling a familiar presence, she recalled how the Thunder Beings announced themselves years ago in this exact scenario. What would the spiritual-messengers from the Native American culture want with her now? Confused, Martine tried to process why she was whisked back to Colorado.

Walking out of an illuminated cloud with dramatic lightning bolts slicing through it, a magnificent Thunder Being approached her. Raising his hand up in a formal Indian-style greeting, he quickened to her his most important position within the Native American heavenly-hierarchy.

Enamored by the majestic angel, Martine studied his appearance. Chiseled facial-features were coated white with a blue-river of paint descending from the corner of his left-eye to the side of his mouth, indicating a giant tear of sorrow being released. Three large eagle feathers pointing up to the sky were affixed to his long, black, wavy hair, symbolizing his position of notability. Adorned in a colorfully woven, red, blue, gold, and turquoise robe of nobility, he indicated with his thoughts that he was sent to provide spiritual guidance. A leather-bound walking-stick decorated with beads and feathers designated his high degree of wisdom and understanding. His rawhide shield was painted with the stars, crosses, bear, eagle, and horse that defined his authority and bravery. Striking his fist on a breast-plate, made from buffalo horn, further signified his place as a warrior for truth and peace.

Historically, Native American shields, faces, clothes, and horses were painted and decorated with symbols that would add power to the wearer. Familiar with their culture, Martine knew that these Indian possessions were designed to confront and frighten off anyone that would do harm.

Before another moment passed she was lifted away with her new advocate, Sky Warrior.

As if zapped by a genie, Martine and the Thunder Being reappeared in a primitive Indian village inhabited by the Hopi. Escorted by Sky Warrior, Martine was led to a ceremonial Kiva that can only be entered through the cribbed wooden roof. Climbing down a wooden ladder, they emerged inside the Kiva. The round, stone structure was a spiritual meeting place for holy rituals. Preparations for a religious gathering were in progress.

Hopi Elders invited Martine and Sky Warrior to join the circle of Indians seated cross legged on the floor. The stone bench that was built into the walls of the Kiva held bundles of sacred relics that each attendee brought with, indicating the commencement of a Sacred Ceremony.

In comparison to Sky Warrior the Hopi Elders wore simple attire. Their deeply-dark complexions were contrasted by white tunics with loose fitting pants. Belted with woven sashes, the multi-colored weavings presented symbolic drawings indicative of each Elder's clan origins. These artful designs displayed unique and meaningful pageantry telling a story of Hopi tradition and creation.

Wondering why she went backwards-in-time to this place, Martine questioned the gallant winged-guide that manifested with her. Aware that his place was high in the chain of command with Great Spirit, she communicated her willingness to understand his mission. Only in this "Etheric Realm" could she comprehend and discern the ancient native-tongue spoken by him and the ancestors of the Great Hopi.

Ushering her to the circle of twelve Elders that were sitting around an open-fire, Sky Warrior explained, "Powerful medicine is needed. You get it here."

Seated among the elders on an earth-packed floor, Martine glimpsed at the preparations that had been made inside the primitive ceremonial site. Atop a brightly woven blanket were ritual objects placed with precision, according to use. Seeing numerous items that she recognized from her interactions with Navajo and Hopi acquaintances, Martine understood their symbolic meanings. Several crystals and stones indigenous to the region were dispersed among the array of ceramic crucibles, pipes, feathers, pouches, shells, beads, and arrow heads. Special objects held a place of honor on woven materials or leather padding. The compilation of colorful religious artifacts signified an important revered ceremony had been arranged.

Chanting a prayer of blessing and guidance, Sky Warrior, and the Hopi Elders, joined together to extend special protection and enlightenment. Raising his head from a downward bent position the Hopi shaman directed his message to Martine, "This is the time to pray to your ancient ancestors, the ones that came before you. The tobacco in the pipe represents the prayers of your heart." Holding up the pipe he presented it to his audience and continued, "This is a time to offer gratitude to Mother Earth and Father Sky for your true gifts." Lowering the pipe the Shaman proceeded to light it and summon the Great Creator Spirit that comprises Mother Earth and Father Sky. "It is time to be resolute in one's desire to live a wholesome life and leave a beautiful path for those yet to come." With slow humble gestures the Shaman picked up a stately-bird-feather and waved it at the pipe smoke. "This is the time to ask for help. If you ask for something through the pipe—the creator will grant it."

Martine, in her "etheric-state" of being, comprehended their native tongue, and listened intently as they projected their powerful medicine into the universe, requesting specific knowing and aptitudes be bestowed on Martine. The key aspect of this Hopi ritual was for her to strengthen her relationship with the Great Creator Spirit.

Calling upon the four cardinal directions of the earth, the Shaman summoned the four animals guarding the north, south, east and west. Representative of each part of the world—lion, bear, badger, and wolf were called upon respectively, and each time the Shaman did so he added a pinch of tobacco to his pipe. Lighting the pipe, the Shaman sent the prayers to Spirit.

When the ceremony concluded Sky Warrior spread his colorful, feathered, wings and reached into a leather-pouch. Pulling out a handful of wood-tiles he shook them like dice, and threw them down on the ground. Martine sounded the letters that tumbled at her feet, "M, T, E, I, L, W, O, H, R, N, A." Looking up at the towering-being, she said, "I don't understand."

- 81 -

Speaking in a commanding tone, Sky Warrior boomed;

"The truth is hidden—the story deep,
It's only there for those who seek,
To pass the test and lessons learned,
Find the meaning in two double-words,
Never forget your guides are near,
There is no need for human fear."

Pausing, Sky Warrior remained stiff-faced as he looked at Martine.

Shaking her head in confusion, Martine said, "What are the words? I only see letters."

"Narrow minded you are not,
Find the things that you forgot,
So much is there for us to show,
With time and wisdom you will know,
Look among the letters sublime,
To see how man offends the divine."

Stopping again, Sky Warrior stepped back and spread his wings to their fullest.

Martine stood tall in front of the winged-warrior and pleaded, "Wait. Please don't go. I need more."

Raising his hand toward heaven, Sky Warrior resounded:

"Lift up your sword to this great calling,
The human race it is falling,
We add these letters to help your mission,
Heaven stands by with your permission."

Anxious for more guidance, Martine shouted, "Yes, Yes, I give heaven my permission. I accept the work that they commission."

Bowing his head in silence, he reached into the bag again and pulled out another handful of tiles. Shaking them as before he threw them down like craps.

"Because your bravery we implore,
Three words are given to explore."

Martine reviewed the throw out-loud, "E, E, E, P, U, T, O, L, V, N, L, S, and W."

Watching the Spirit-guide soar out of sight, Martine awoke with a corresponding quick-breath. Finding herself back in her sister's home she reached for her journal on the night stand, and made a customary connection with the digital clock that Jolene had without a doubt synchronized with her own.

For the second time the illuminated numbers read 6:04. She jotted down every word spoken by her guide, and documented each letter revealed by the throw of his tiles.

Chapter 15

Rolling over on his side, Peter answered his ringing phone, "Yeah."

"Peter, come on, buddy, got a call from the boss. You're in."

"Hey, man, that's awesome."

"Pick you up in an hour. Got some shopping to do."

"Sure." Hanging up the phone, Peter sat up on the side of his bed. Still groggy from the effects of forceful sex, he decided the mystery woman might be a hallucination. Never in his room when he went to sleep, nor present when he woke up, the visitor could arguably be a drug-induced figment of his imagination? Psychologically hooked on his new partner, he didn't mind being exploited in his dreams. Satisfying this mythical female was exhausting and did drain his energy, but the nightly need for his attention expanded his shriveled ego.

Remembering the night of rough sex piqued him and provoked a round of quick coughs. How could she make him feel exhilarated and like a slave at the same time? Sound asleep when she came to him last night, Peter only felt the nakedness of her body and the aggressiveness of her demands. Blind to the details of her face, he imagined she was young and gorgeous, but questioned why she wouldn't show herself.

Natural light lasered through a single window, allowing Peter to locate his discarded pants. Reaching down for the worn-looking jeans, he pulled them up to his lap and scrounged through the pockets for his favorite vice. Freeing a fresh joint from his front pocket, Peter coughed louder as he clicked his lighter for a flame.

Inhaling the drug calmed his cough and mellowed his mind. Savoring the remedy to all his problems, he held his breath as long as he could.

After finishing his morning ritual, Peter laid back down on his bed. That's when he felt the burning sensation from a cut.

Close examination of his naked body revealed deep scratches on his sides. Springing up from the bed he headed for his bathroom mirror where he viewed more scrapes on his lower back. Physical phenomena from his lover made him question if she was real or not. Catching a glimpse of her eyes last night left him with the impression she maybe a mischievous woman, but not necessarily earthly. Cat-like eyes that glowed yellow from the moon's light had put his hair on end.

Condoning the illicit sex seemed to cause more aggression and longer encounters.

For a single moment Peter felt brave, wanting to confront her and see what he couldn't during their evening trysts. "Where are you," he demanded. Met with a deep pervading silence, he questioned the existence of his secret lover. Sitting in the lit room he noticed more damage to his body. Bruises were evident on his arms and neck.

Suspicious of his only lover, he got himself dressed in the usual attire and left the building for a cigarette smoke. Standing in the graveled yard he watched a few people come and go—wondering if she was one of them, or if his cousin Jules set up the rendezvous' as some sorta perverted game.

Curious about the job offer, Peter looked back at the haphazard living arrangements he hoped to leave behind. Working part-time as a dishwasher didn't cover the rent, or the cheap highs he needed on a regular basis. Evening shifts suited him because it prevented him from interacting with real people, and he liked it that way. Living in the seedier part of town, like a hermit, was his choice after his stepdad Dan Avery and his mother Nancy died.

Peter was about eight-years old when his mother informed him that Dan Avery was not his real father. Dan was an out of control alcoholic that began inflicting physical abuse on both of them. Domestic violence was well documented by the local police department and the deaths were recognized as inevitable since his wife would not press charges. Because the murder/suicide deaths of both his mother and stepfather Dan left Peter parentless, he went to live with his surviving relative—Della Avery. At the age of nine, Peter was thrown into a lonely and confusing existence in a remote area near Prescott.

Covering up for her son's shortcomings, Della remained in denial about Dan's compulsion to abuse his wife and stepchild. Lacking any professional counseling during the pivotal adolescent years, Peter's personality and social skills stayed stunted.

Having survived the death of both parents, Peter was considered fragile and alone. Brought to Della's for safekeeping, no one suspected that young Peter had witnessed the actual deaths.

Reared by an abusive man that was not his real father was more damaging than his disposition would allow. Convinced he could no longer love or admire the parents he idolized, Peter was left betrayed and alone. Exploring life on his own, he decided not to trust another adult.

Interests in bizarre comic books, pornography, and Dungeons and Dragons evolved into ways to get high by the age of ten. The much older Jules eagerly introduced him to assorted occult practices that elaborated on the desires the two shared. While other boys where finding odd jobs around the neighborhood, joining sports teams, and performing household chores, Peter and Jules invoked spirits through Ouija board séances after finding some way to get a cheap buzz.

Drifting apart a year after their friend Sharon vanished, the two young men had recently renewed their friendship. Detached from his grandmother and Jules, Peter lived a meaningless existence. Indifferent about his life, he only felt good when he was numbed-up on his favorite street drugs. Insecure and lacking social skills he kept his eyes downcast, screening out the rest of the world.

Functioning in cash-paying, sub-standard jobs, he drifted into this despicable tenement section of town when he found a dealer he liked. He used prepaid cell phones to contact his grandmother with bogus updates on his location, and work status. How else would Jules have located Peter? Unfortunately, Peter was supposed to be cooking in the restaurant, not washing dishes.

To avoid judgments by family and peers, Peter chose isolation. Satisfying his selfish needs and wallowing in self pity opened a doorway that welcomed negative energies and perverse thinking. Calloused and greedy for the easy things in life, he was eager to find out what easy money opportunities Jules had arranged for him.

Older and more promiscuous than Peter, Jules was profane and sadistic. Recognizing how lazy and selfish his cousin was, Peter wondered what had Jules so motivated in this job. Presuming that Jules couldn't be working too hard for the big bucks he had bragged about, Peter imagined that the new job would suit him well too, but would the new beginnings mean leaving this strange relationship behind?

* * *

"Hey, get in," Jules said through the passenger window.

Sliding into the front seat, Peter dragged hard on his cigarette before tossing it out the window. "Is it really noon? I need a burger or something."

"No problem. We'll hit a drive-thru."

"What's the plan?"

Peter's face flashed an expression of alarm when he saw his friend wearing a security uniform that resembled a military officer. Authoritative in dark-blue attire with an official looking patch and a shinny badge, Jules looked like law enforcement. The strapping officers-styled-hat was most impressive. Jules pointed to his black belt with a holster and gun. "What do you think? Is this a trip or what?"

Chapter 16

Alone in his office, John Mahoney drank his first of many cups of coffee. Arriving at the bureau before anyone else gave him time to assess the days' events. Nobody seemed to know much about John except he was brazen, impatient, demanding, and extremely diligent. Good-sized and rugged like John Wayne, he sported a do-it-yourself beard and mustache. Working like a modern day cowboy, John was brave and relentless.

Like any self-respecting-western-lawman, he kept his saddle housed in the corner of his office complete with a worn-out-looking-cowboy-hat, leather chinks, spurs, bridle, breast collar and bucking strap. Sown in the leather were his lessons, and memories. He liked to say, "My tack is a reminder of where I've been and where I'm going." Pessimisms never deterred him. Likening each case to a new challenge that hadn't been realized, he believed God's intervention was directing him in a constant battle between good and evil.

Resenting the red tape that preceded the incarceration of dangerous criminals, John Mahoney knew the law. Disgusted with people that tolerated the obsolete legal system, he pushed hard to get his cases heard. Disagreeing with criminal rights, he never settled for the customary plea bargains. Despising incompetent lawyers and continuances, he worked outside the customary guidelines to obtain hard evidence.

He had brought down his share of criminal activity and experienced the out of balance legal system that could easily reject a lawmen's work. Undeterred and having seen it all, he worked hard to secure the evidence and make sure no criminal was released on a technicality.

John Mahoney hadn't been born cynical. His disposition was hardened and complicated by the loneliness he harbored after the loss of his young wife and child, victims of a robbery gone wrong. Neither mother nor child survived a vicious carjacking.

Twenty years ago, he was a good-looking man, a husband, father, and homicide detective in the state of Texas. Five years later it was all gone—his family murdered. Due to a technicality, the men who massacred his family were released. Embittered by the atrocity, he left his job and ended up on a cattle ranch mending fences and driving cows. That's where his facial-stubble turned into a beard that stayed with him.

Wrangling cattle on the open range for four years was his escape and therapy, until a lifelong friend recruited him to the Arizona FBI. Convinced by his friend that only *he* could fill the position that was immediately available, John took him up on the attractive offer.

Now, with the loss of his loved ones unresolved, he directs all of his energies to fighting crime with the force of a strike-team, even though that means using some unconventional methods.

John has never discussed his personal life in or out of the office. When home alone at night he thrives on the subject of world history.

Staring at his saddle, he contemplated his options on this new case. The special task force he called into action was standing by, or to be more specific, standing still.

"Tombstone" is the case name. In true western tradition, each case in the Arizona branch office is identified with an authentic cowboy theme. Just like families use proper names to personalize their estates such as; Wuthering Heights, Tara, and Shalimar, John does the same for complex cases. His intense thoughts were interrupted by his ringing phone. He picked up the receiver with the greeting he has rehearsed for ten years, "Mahoney."

"Sir, it's, Jolene. Is it a good time?

"Yes, Jolene. When can you be here?"

"About fifteen-minutes."

"I'll see you then."

"Good, sir."

Chapter 17

Commandeering Martine's car for the day was the only viable solution to avoiding a ride in her potentially bugged car. Jolene rationalized that Alexa could stay home and walk to the shopping mall where she planned to meet up with her college friends.

Snapping her cell-phone closed after speaking with her boss, Jolene glanced at her sister who was sitting in the front seat next to her. Trying to envision how Martine, and her reserved employer, would get along, she resigned to the needed debriefing as best she dare. Choosing her words carefully, Jolene started, "Martine, Mr. Mahoney is a really unique man. I love my job and admire him. Hope you'll agree after you meet him today."

"Yeah, I'm looking forward to meeting him. Can't say I know much about him or his background."

"Well, Martine, I think it's best to sorta listen to what he has on his mind before you give him any advice or suggestions. He's not real . . . personable." Jolene couldn't help but caution her sister. She knew Martine preferred to avoid conflict, but if her Swedish temper was provoked there would be enough tension for a ski lift.

"Don't worry. I don't have anything I want to share with anyone at this point. I actually feel out of my element in every way possible. I think you should reconsider involving me. After last night it seems everything I'm experiencing is really jumbled up. I wouldn't want to even discuss it in a church confessional," Martine replied while shoving her journal in her bag.

"Why don't you tell me what you were writing down this morning?"

"Yeah, I have no idea what to do with that information yet. I'll keep you posted when I get something remarkable. For now it's just a dream."

"Martine, you can tell me anything. It's Mr. Mahoney that can't know."

"Sure, I get that. I really don't know what to do with what I've written down so far. Just give me some more time. Okay?" Martine reassured her sister, "I'll figure it out—I always do."

Exiting off the busy highway, Jolene reflected on her sisters circumstances. Was she ready to do this? Aware that Martine could be both creative and blunt when she expressed her opinion worried Jolene. Not being able to perform at all hadn't crossed her mind till now. Acting on impulse, she had highly recommended Martine to her boss.

Had she built up expectations of Martine's talents beyond what she is capable of? Hearing her sister express doubts about herself, she tried to lighten up the low-point they had both reached, "Hey, you're not changing your mind, are you? This is a big opportunity for you to get back into the FBI—I mean the world," Jolene coaxed. "Plus, this is the first time we've ever worked on the same case."

"Do you think that's because I worked in the legal department? In Denver?" Martine joshed.

"That's probably it," Jolene teased back.

While at a stoplight, Jolene began silently theorizing the worst scenarios. If Martine encountered resistance from Mahoney she would carry on without him and find another way to get the job done. She wouldn't try to change him or herself. However, he might feel dispensable when she finally got what she wanted.

Likewise, if her boss did not appreciate Martine's unusual abilities, she would be asked to cooperate or leave. Of course he would do it in the most diplomatic way possible. That just might not be enough for Martine, or even noticed.

Having lost two nights of sleep worrying about how to coach her sister and referee these two well-meaning-alphas, was making her edgy. What had she gotten herself, and her job, into? This was going to be good—good like . . . *Vikings vs. Packers.*

Conscious that Martine would never have accepted the invitation to help if she had been given time to contemplate her boss's disposition, Jolene planned to run interference. Fretful about the magnitude of this case, she felt justified to use Martine's expertise to solve a complicated crime that was evil enough to possibly cause her own privacy to be breached?

Shaking her head as she made a left turn onto the last busy street, Jolene admired her sister's wardrobe. Martine didn't look a lot different than yesterday. In the Arizona field office there wasn't a dress code, due to the fact Mahoney preferred Wranglers to Dockers. Maybe they'll have that in common, Jolene thought to herself. Unwilling to advise her older sister on how to design her wardrobe or style her long hair, Jolene held her comments in check. Martine always looked attractive anyways, regardless of her modest appearance and lack of fashion. She was the opposite of pretentious. Striking in every way, Martine didn't spend much time on grooming, dieting or makeup. Guessing her correct age was impossible.

It was reassuring to have Martine with her and she liked her sister just the way she was—even in metro Phoenix. She tried to shake her feelings of fear. Second guessing herself wasn't an option, it was official—Martine was recruited to the case out of desperation.

Was it instinct or impulse that had caused her to contact her sister? She couldn't decide. Counting on Martine to be discrete and willing to help her was natural. Confidence was restored and her thoughts became clearer.

Chapter 18

Following her sister through the vestibule of the FBI Headquarters, Martine was hit with a huge déjà vu. Her adrenaline surged. Like getting back in the saddle after a big fall, she suddenly felt "on." Extending her arm for a handshake with Jolene's supervisor, felt empowering. Heightened awareness rose through her, causing renewed confidence. Energy was contagious and she caught a mega dose. This sensation had all but disappeared and been forgotten until now.

Blindly keeping pace with Jolene, she entered Mahoney's office. Martine didn't even notice him sitting at his desk as she looked around the large office that resembled a cowboy museum. After moving her attention to him it was obvious they were expected from the nod of his head. Tuning into his presence, Martine heard him explain that little time remained before the department personnel convened in their work stations, and interruptions would be unavoidable.

Appearing awkward and uncomfortable with the females dominating his space, Mahoney knocked over his coffee as he stood to greet them.

Approaching his desk she offered a handshake. "Hello, sir, I'm, Martine."

Reaching his arm out, Mahoney clasped Martine's hand firmly and shook it. "Hi, I'm, John Mahoney, nice to meet you." Exasperated by the watery mess spreading across his desk, he blurted out, "Hell, what am I going to do now?"

Setting her purse down on a dry corner of his desk, Martine dug in her bag for a stash of tissues. Handing Mahoney some of the Kleenex, she continued, "Jolene has given me an extensive briefing on the case."

"Good," Mahoney said with a nod.

"I'm ready to get started right now," Martine finished with a formal smile.

"Uh . . . well, I guess that's fine," he answered.

"When can I see the evidence that you're working with so far?"

Moving a stack of papers from the spill, Mahoney replied, "That'll be today."

Helping dab up brown rivers of coffee on his desk, Martine added, "Will you be sharing all your information with me—or do you departmentalize?"

Moving his day-planner to the credenza, he momentarily turned away displaying a hand tooled brown-leather belt with star-shaped silver conchos. "Yes, I'm willing to share all the files we have accumulated so far."

Knocking on the office doorjamb, Jolene's supervisor, Thad Reese, leaned in the room and interrupted the informal meeting, "Hey, Jolene, can I see you right away. Do you mind, sir?"

"No. Not at all" Mahoney replied.

Jolene glanced at Martine. "Do you mind?"

"Absolutely not, go ahead."

Antsy to get started, Martine continued, "Do you have any theories on this case, Mr. Mahoney?"

"Just the likely-hood that we're dealing with some sort of human-trafficking."

Looking for a way to discard the wet tissues, Martine handed them to Mahoney. "Are there any obvious similarities or patterns evolving in your investigation?"

"Not yet. We have no idea when the various police departments will respond or if there's any information they can supply us with. As of today we're working aggressively with the case files that a

Detective Thom identified from watching a 'missing-persons' website. We're also engaged in our own expanded search."

"Any ideas why someone would want to closely monitor my sister?"

Motioning to the chair in front of his desk, Mahoney offered Martine a seat. "I didn't know somebody might be monitoring Jolene. What would lead you to believe that?"

Returning to the office, Jolene had a seat in the chair next to Martine. "Sorry about that interruption."

Martine quizzed him again, "So, you don't know about it and you're not responsible? Are you?"

"Me? Heck no. What are you suggesting?"

"I just wanted to rule out the possibility that this office would run surveillance on the task force. It's possible on a sensitive case to monitor the working team for their own protection."

Observing Mahoney's confused reaction, Martine turned to her sister. "Jolene, you better fill him in. He needs to know."

"I've had some suspicious things happen that lead me to believe my home was entered and tampered with. I think I may be bugged. If I am it's a very professional job. The hidden-devices are audio—so far as I know. I haven't located any cameras, and I don't want to appear to be looking for them. Right now, they've made the mistaken assumption that I'm oblivious to the surveillance. So, if they think they were successful, and I don't take offensive measures to remove the devices, we could use this to our advantage. We could put a dead-end to their efforts. Even flush them out. What can they possibly gain if we're careful or even misleading?"

Mahoney focused in on his young agent. "Why have you not told me about this before, Jolene?"

Martine answered for her sister, "She just surmised the possibility. She came home the other night and noticed things were out of sorts. Because of my arrival she was distracted. You have a 'code of silence' right now with your agents and their cell phones. According to Jolene, you suspect there may be satellite tracking going on already in this investigation. Sounds like sophisticated criminal activity if you're suggesting the agents can't use their cells.

Anyway, it was under control since Jolene figured it out before I got in town. I think we leave the devices in place so that they don't know we're on to them? We can stay there and maybe set up a trap with false leads or something. We've been taking precautions. They don't know we're on to them."

"You must watch too much TV, Ms. Martine."

"I try not to. It's just an idea. Why don't you think on it? I'd like to get some impressions—I mean information—from the files you have in your staging room."

Mahoney stroked his beard and reflected thoughtfully, "Jolene, weren't you working on a counterfeiting operation before we pulled you for this case?"

"Yes, sir."

Mahoney stood up and jingled loose change in his pocket, "Okay. We leave the monitoring in place—for awhile. It actually could be possible to manipulate the predator."

"Exactly," Jolene replied.

Mahoney proposed an alternative, "You realize it could be a perverted voyeur living on your street. We should do a sweep immediately—forget about setting a trap for some deviant."

"Y-yes, sir," Jolene stammered, her voice catching in her throat.

"Okay. I'll authorize that for you."

"Wait, sir," Jolene interrupted, "isn't that what we're in business for? Isn't it our job to flush out the creeps and crooks? Isn't that what I'm trained for? Well, I like to keep my friends close and my enemies closer. It would be like working under cover, or in disguise, without conducting a tedious three month stakeout . . . in a pawn shop. We do that all the time here. And if it's a pervert from the neighborhood why would he bug my car? He'd bug my bedroom with cameras, not my phone."

"Your car is bugged?"

"Yes, sir, my car. At least I'm pretty sure it is."

"I see your point Jolene, and I like the way you two think. Let me put some thought into your suggestion. I want to consider whether it's safe for you and feasible for us to use some kind of reverse-surveillance for arresting your criminal. We can sweep the car immediately and get a confirmation on the device without tipping anyone off. They probably have a tracking device on it too. I'll order it directly."

"Great, sir, the car is at my house though. We weren't sure if I'm under surveillance because I work here, or if the undercover case I was working on was checking me out."

"I see. You definitely shutdown any chance of contaminating your sting operation."

"Yes, sir."

Injecting herself back into the head turning conversation, Martine suggested, "I have an idea, Jolene could use a different vehicle during the day if she leaves the bureau. Driving the car between work and home won't raise any flags if she parks across the street. Plus my car will hopefully not meet with the same fate."

"I see." Mahoney looked thoughtful.

"You wouldn't want her car to go anywhere that would be of interest to whoever is monitoring her," Martine surmised. "And, we can't share a vehicle." Elaborating on the proposed plot, Martine continued, "I was involved in a case something like this and we put our own visual surveillance around the neighborhood to try and find out who improperly entered our building and breached our security. We were able to identify all the vehicles coming and going. We used really high-tech cameras for the night photos. Even though there is no street lighting in Jolene's residential neighborhood it is possible to use infrared cameras. Can we do something like that?"

"Good suggestion. I'll requisition my best electronic technicians to handle this operation. The least we can do is minimize your exposure, and increase your security. Let's find out what's in your home and car. We'll get a good idea what we're up against when we have those details."

Martine asked, "Who'll I report my findings to, and how often?"

"How 'bout you report to me for now. Things are a little disorganized on this subject. I'll be available to meet with you at anytime. I'll also have a desk available for you by tomorrow."

"It's okay if I work outside of the office—isn't it?" Martine tipped her chin slightly.

"Where?" Mahoney asked.

"I like to do my own investigating. Can we arrange for secure-communication with phones?" Martine opened her cell to add his contact number.

"What do you mean? Are you going to be in the field? Your sister led me to believe you're a respected expert. According to her, and your colleagues, you are an accomplished lawyer, criminologist, and the author of *Blessed are the Guilty*."

"Yes, I wrote that book. Have you read it?"

"No, but Jolene tells me it has revolutionized the psychology used to extract confessions from criminals. That's what I need."

"Yes, I do have credentials in criminology, however, I really like to work from a fresh prospective."

"I thought you would be a coordinator and profiler here in the office. We'll bring the suspects to you," Mahoney planned aloud.

"How 'bout I do both," Martine compromised.

"I was under the impression you would facilitate the inevitable legal ramifications we encounter when working with multiple jurisdictions. We already have three states involved," Mahoney countered.

Holding her ground, Martine continued, "Naturally, I'll advise you on those issues as they arise. I just want to do everything I can within my capacity to help solve your case."

"I'm not sure how that'll work here. I hired you because you were available immediately. I haven't even decided if I can use your help and now I find out you're not planning to be in the office . . . much? How can you help lead this investigation if you're out and about? Where are you going to go that we wouldn't investigate first?"

"Mr. Mahoney, you don't understand, I intend to help, however I want field privileges and credentials from your office. Introduce me to as much information as you have, including any new break-throughs your task force makes, and I will be as productive as your most experienced agent. I want to be able to look in directions that haven't been explored. Trust me I won't duplicate efforts," Martine ended with a convincing smile.

Mahoney's brow line narrowed as he nodded slowly. "Well, Jolene did say you were unconventional but very effective on some big cases that we're all familiar with. Let's give it a try and see how it goes. We've already sent through the request for your usual compensation," Mahoney conceded as he came from behind his desk. Escorting her and Jolene to his door, he added, "This is growing into a huge case. Let's not turn a blind eye on anything you notice in a file or interview. Even the Governor's office called. They're concerned that this will be spun into 'Political Malpractice' by the media."

Noticing Mahoney's formal mannerisms, Martine wondered if he was ever this ceremonial with the other agents. It pained Martine to know that Mahoney had no idea what techniques she would be relying on to help move this case forward. Anxious to see the files on hand, Martine turned to leave his office. It was better to get on with some tasks, and avoid discussing details.

Guarded about sharing her gifts of intuition and knowing, Martine's unorthodox-talents would remain secret.

Guided by Jolene, Martine was introduced to all the agents and the staging room named, "Tombstone". Boxes of files relating to missing girls and local suspects consumed Martine's entire day. Accumulating volumes of information was inevitable when the FBI involvement was announced to regional law enforcement. Heading-up the growing case load was Mahoney's right-hand-man, Agent Ken Harmon.

Chapter 19

"911, what is your emergency?"

"I need help. I have an emergency," the hysterical voice reverberated into Sandra's headset.

Experienced as the lead 911 operator, Sandra reacted in an attentive and calm voice, "Ma'am, please slow down and give me your name and address." Hearing no reply, Sandra repeated her request, "Ma'am, are you there? Can you please give me your name and location?"

There was a loud sob followed by uncontrollable gasps for air. Realizing the caller was losing her composure; Sandra was about to repeat her question. Before she repeated her standard verbiage the caller stammered a breathy reply.

"I-I think my daughter is in trouble. She called me from her cell phone and something went wrong. She stayed after school for volleyball practice and called to tell me something. I was just asking her where she was, and . . . and it sounded like her phone fell."

"Ma'am, can you give me your name?"

"Janelle Danielson, my name is, Janelle. My daughter is, Maria Danielson."

"What is your location, Mrs. Danielson? Can I get your full address?"

"My address is 14260 North Canyon Rd. Scottsdale, Arizona. That's my home address. Maria was at school—she called me from

Garner High School. We only live about a mile west of the high school. I would drive to the school, but I'm confined to a wheelchair. I just had surgery. I just know something has happened to her."

Sandra continued guiding Janelle, "My name is Sandra. I'm going to stay on the phone with you. Please don't hang up."

"Can somebody please help me look for my daughter? It's already getting dark outside. Maria should be home by now even if . . ."

Sandra broke in, "Thank you, Janelle. That is enough information for me to pass along. Somebody will be at your house shortly. Can you tell me if anyone else is with you?"

"No. No. I'm the only one here. I'm a single parent. You've got to find her," Janelle pleaded to Sandra.

"Are you in any danger yourself?"

"No! I'm only worried about Maria."

"Yes, Mrs. Danielson, the police are on their way to the school right now. Can you give me a description of your daughter?"

"Maria is seventeen years old. She has long blonde hair and blue eyes. She's tall and thin, about Five-foot-eight and one-hundred and twenty-pounds. She's probably wearing her gym clothes . . . Ummm—she has a black messenger-style school bag. Let me think . . . what else?"

"The officers should be there any minute. Please stay on the phone a little bit longer, Janelle. Can you think of anything your daughter said?"

"No—not really. Something went wrong as soon as she called me."

"Janelle, if she's not at school, where else might she be?"

"My daughter would be a few blocks from school by now, if she was walking. I have a feeling she was hurt though. I just know something is wrong. We have to help her," Mrs. Danielson's fearful voice sounded in Sandra's earpiece.

"Janelle, explain to me why you believe her safety is in jeopardy."

"Well, I guess, when she called me from her cell phone something went wrong as soon as I answered. I heard her say, 'Mom,' and then nothing. That has never happened before. It sounded like her phone crashed to the ground. I think I'm still connected to her cell—but she's not answering me. Something cut us off. When I call her phone I get her voice mail. I've called and called and called. I'm going crazy. I think she might've been hit. Please, you've got to help her."

Sandra kept Janelle on the line while she relayed all the information to the local police via her computer terminal. The response time was immediate due to Sandra's competent handling of the call.

* * *

Uniformed Officers Kate Casey and Tristan Lovell were patrolling in their squad car only three miles from Garner High School when they received the dispatcher's alert. Without hesitation they turned their vehicle around, and moved out with their deafening siren blaring and blue and white halogen lights flashing. Several other squad cars assisted in patrolling the school parking areas and surrounding neighborhoods adjacent to the school. Casey and Lovell were then dispatched to the Danielson's residence.

After formal introductions were finished, Officer Casey advised Janelle she could terminate her phone conversation with Sandra. Entering the Danielson's home, the two officers couldn't help but notice the spicy aromas of cooking. In late October the skies were dark by six. They knew the urgency of conducting a thorough search of the area and requested a few items: names of friends, a recent photo, Maria's cell phone number, a detailed description of her attire, and an account of the possessions she carried.

Officer Kate Casey exhibited tact and grace by kneeling down in front of Janelle's wheelchair before proceeding with her questioning, "Mrs. Danielson, would it be possible to obtain a recently worn article of Maria's? I can go to Maria's room for you and get something."

"Why do you need her clothing?" Janelle asked while struggling not to cry.

"It's standard procedure, Ma'am. We secure clothing, or even recently worn shoes for 'scent articles' that our canines use in helping us find missing persons," answered Officer Lovell. "We're calling out a canine unit right now."

"How do you know she's a missing person? She's probably hurt."

"Yes, ma'am, it'll also help us locate her if she is lost or hurt."

"Follow me to her room. We can find plenty of 'scent articles' in there." Janelle tried to conceal her anguish and regain her composure as she moved her wheelchair into Maria's creatively decorated bedroom.

Propped up against the window wall inside Maria's room was a classical guitar housed inside a black-hard-cover case. Sheet music strewn on her bed proved she planned to practice. Purses, hats, and clothes hung from a brass coat rack. Books and figurines lined all her shelves till no more space was possible. Lively posters of theatrical plays papered her violet painted walls—advertising her love and involvement in acting.

Gesturing to the floor in Maria's walk-in closet, Janelle said, "Take what you want." The five-foot-by-seven-foot space was colorfully carpeted with discarded garments. Janelle attempted to explain her embarrassment, "These are the clothes that need to be laundered. I haven't been able to pick them up for a week now. Maria and I have a good reason for not being great housekeepers."

Officer Lovell concluded the brief encounter, "I'll take this shirt and the brown shoe. That should do it, Mrs. Danielson. We're going to be leaving right now. A detective will be assigned to meet with you if we don't locate your daughter soon." Janelle escorted Officers Lovell and Casey back to the front door.

Officer Lovell instructed Janelle to stay put and wait for her daughter.

Outside, police and canines congregated for instructions. It was customary to wait for the first responding officers to update them.

Casey and Lovell directed the law enforcement personnel to retrace Maria's possible paths. The canines were given her scent and her photo was passed around. Several squad cars left the Danielson's home, and headed slowly down the darkening roads that lay out like a matrix of perfect squares.

Within an hour a loud voice broke over the police radios, "This is Sergeant Byron. I found a cell phone. It matches the description of the 'victim's—pink-and-blue rhinestone decorations.' There's no sign of the girl. Phones in the open position. I've secured the site at Raven Street and Dodge Boulevard."

Casey inquired without hesitation, "Sergeant, is the phone operational?"

"No, Casey. Appears the phone was dropped like a hockey puck on ice."

Chapter 20

Inhaling pizza like football players, Martine grinned as she watched Jolene and Alexa divide the last slice. Speechless for the first time in hours she was relieved to be at Jolene's for some decompression time. Martine didn't have anything profound to share and was famished when they sat down at 8:00 pm to eat dinner. The massive downloading she took-on today caused extreme exhaustion. Finally food tasted good to her and had a purpose.

"I'm positively beyond tired. I'm going to my room to read before I fall asleep. I'll see you both in the morning. Love ya." Martine waved goodnight to Alexa and Jolene.

Layering pillows to the desired height was necessary before Martine could climb in bed with her journal. Finessing her mind with the numerous entries, would be essential in her evening rituals. However, like saying prayers before bed, she never could finish before nodding off. With just enough energy to touch the lamp on her nightstand, all earthly lights went out.

Etherically soaring through a heavenly passage, Martine glided down to the hazy formation of a peaceful countryside community. Like focusing a 35mm camera, her vision sharpened until she clearly observed the obscure rural surroundings, which dated back to the early nineteen-hundreds. Barren roads, lined by fields and livestock indicated she was visiting a primitive peaceful rural area. Straining to hear anything, she remained clueless as to her exact whereabouts, or the purpose of this visit.

A man leapt towards Martine in urgency, and for the first time she heard noise, "Move . . . Move out of the way—they're coming— make way for the soldiers."

Jolted energetically by the interruption, Martine turned to see an army of uniformed men converging on her position. Materializing into the psychic realm, the military unit appeared stiff and unyielding to her presence. Etherically, she sensed they were responding to orders, and a mission they were committed to. "Stop," Martine stepped out in front of the oncoming parade of army forces.

Armed and unaware of her existence they marched through her invisible body. They were blind to everything except their mission, causing Martine worry. Left to follow the rows of soldiers marching down the road, she spied a large gated monastery. Clanging sounds from a huge bell mounted high in the building's steeple sounded loudly as they all approached. By the time the bell rang out six times, thirty-five soldiers lined up in front of the monastery's big iron-gate.

"Yes, can I help you?" inquired a meek sounding nun.

"Open the gates, sister," The officer demanded.

Facial features hidden by a large black-veiled habit with accents of white clearly implied an older order of nuns. "What are your orders, sir?"

"We need to take over your premises for our purposes."

Martine saw about five nuns with rosaries in hand milling together in the courtyard. Prayers were being chanted in earnest.

"Open the gate, sister, or we'll break it down and arrest all of you."

Yanking open the steel gate, the sister let the soldiers in. Praying nuns were no match for this horde of aggressive men, observed Martine.

Every soldier participated in the frenzied inspection. Deep in the shadows of the huge nearly abandoned monastery, Martine could see the murky figure of the evil leader who instigated the invasion.

Curious, Martine took precautions and snuck into the desolate caverns of the Monastery. Not sure if she would remain invisible to the soldiers, she crept around where they had not gone.

Finding her way down into an underground crypt, she heard muffled sounds, "SHHHH . . . SHHHH."

Familiar impressions processed through Martine, like a software program. Spinning to her right, she saw a shadowy outline of people crouched together. Separated by floor-to-ceiling wrought-iron bars, she could not get any closer to the group of young people hiding from the army rampaging through the massive monastery. The whole experience appeared more and more like the motion picture *Sound of Music*. Compelled by this coincidence, Martine moved toward the group of scared adolescents and noticed that there were forty or more girls gathered around a girl they addressed as Maria. Watching closely as Mother Superior beckoned Maria—Martine noticed she was holding a large skeleton key and a rosary.

Alone, Maria began to approach Mother Superior. Stopping briefly, Maria grabbed a large silver candlestick holder and lit the candle with the matches that lay next to it. Illuminated by the glowing flame, Maria was no longer invisible when she continued toward the dividing-bars that separated her from the Mother Superior.

Martine watched in silence as Maria stopped again by a table loaded with books and documents. Maria selected a book and an official looking document before proceeding to the nun. When Maria was as close as she could get to the Mother Superior, she handed her the two items through the steel bars. Martine identified one item as a bible.

Everyone inside the chamber remained silent in anticipation as Mother Superior delicately unrolled the second item. Mother Superior's somber expression was radiated by the voluminous candle flame as she read the contents of the parchment document. Appearing shocked by the contents, Mother Superior dropped the bible and scroll of paper to the floor. She handed Maria the key and rosary before she backed away.

Martine hurried over to grab the antique-looking note. Noticing the bible had fallen open to the book of Genesis, she found it futile and irrelevant to read all the fine type. Unable to physically grasp the article, she squinted with all her might to read the contents. Able to see only the top of the page, Martine saw her reaching hand start to dissipate.

Glancing back at the frightened group of girls, Martine heard an accented voice, "Adieu, mademoiselle."

Instantaneously zapped back into her sleeping body, Martine could not reply.

Back in her body, Martine began to awaken from her dream state. Before her surroundings came into focus, writing from the parchment document flashed brightly in her mind. Dumbfounded by what she remembered, she wrote down the four letters before they escaped from her mind. Recognizing them as the documents' title, Marine was perplexed by its significance. The four letters, separated by periods, was definitely from the papered-message that Mother Superior received from Maria.

"F.U.C.K.?" She said out loud. "Damn. I can't even repeat that pathetic word. There must be more."

Knowing she had to be alert and productive by the time she arrived at the Bureau, Martine had no time to contemplate this clue.

"Crap," she said to herself. "I need something better than this or I'm going to be in the way of this investigation." Struggling, Martine questioned how any one of her dreams could lead to missing girls? She felt so discouraged.

Chapter 21

Pasty-faced from the depressing dream, Martine tried to shake it off as she made her way to the kitchen for a cup of Jolene's fresh ground coffee.

Finding Alexa sitting at the kitchen table reading a book, she joined her for the sake of confiding in someone.

"Morning, Alexa."

"Morning, mom. How'd you sleep last night?"

"Okay, I guess." Knowing she couldn't speak freely in Jolene's home, she invited Alexa outside, "Let's sit on the patio and check-out Jolene's cactus. I need some fresh air to wake-up."

Looking perplexed, Alexa accepted, "Sure I'll get some cool morning air."

Outside, Martine wrapped her robe tight and shivered. "How would you like to help me with a little research?"

"Yeah. Of course. What do you have in mind?"

"Remember my Indian totem book? I'd like you to finish looking up some more totems." Setting the book down next to Alexa, she placed the list of animal totems to research inside the cover. "I also had another dream that makes no sense, but is riddled with clues. If I give you some of my notes maybe you can look for meanings. I just don't have time to study this stuff when I'm with Jolene all day."

"Sure, mom, of course I will." Alexa reached for the book. "Can I use Jolene's computer too?"

"Definitely not." Martine shook her head. "Stick with your laptop."

"Tell me about the dream you had while it's fresh in your mind."

After relaying the dream about the Thunder Being and Hopi Elders she handed her daughter the worn-journal. "Can you try and make words out of these letters?"

"Yah, sure, I can look up totems and make words from these letters I guess. I'm sure I won't know what any of it will mean. This seems really far out there."

Sounding discouraged, Martine agreed, "I know. I don't know how you'll figure this out or what I'll do with them if you do."

"Oh, I got an idea how I can do it." Alexa's face lit up.

Warming up from the hot coffee, Martine gulped, "Already?"

"Oh yeah." Pointing through the patio doors toward the game table, Alexa said, "I can use those letters and move them around to find words. I'll get this done before you're home tonight. I can't beat you or Jolene in Scrabble, but I can do this."

Excusing herself to get dressed for work, Martine looked back at her daughter. "Call me if you get anything solid."

Admiring Alexa's Scandinavian features, Martine saw how she also resembled James the older she got. Alexa's complexion was so perfect that she rarely wore make-up. Her thick long hair didn't require styling for volume. Alexa rarely decked-out, mostly because she didn't need to and partly because she didn't lack confidence like the rest of the world. Tall and bold like a model—Alexa appeared poised in every situation. Nothing seemed to rock her boat. Martine wished for some of that.

Passing Jolene in the hallway, Martine noticed a towel wrapped around her head and the cell-phone tight to her ear. Waving at Martine as she walked by, Jolene signaled she was deep in conversation with the caller. Without a reason to delay the inevitable, Martine surveyed the scant amount of clothing she brought.

While styling her hair at the bathroom mirror, Martine was interrupted by Alexa, "Hey, mom, can you help me outside? I want to move the table into the sun."

Martine took Alexa's plea for assistance as code for "Let's talk." Joining her daughter outside, Martine teased, "Alexa, did you not see the hair emergency I have going on here?"

"I've got one, mom. It's weird. But it works. I got, 'Woman Hitler.' Does that mean anything to you?"

"Heck no. it makes about as much sense as trimming that rose bush with a machete. Any progress on the other group of letters?"

"Haven't tried yet. I'll work on them while you're gone. Eva's already on her way. She can help when she gets here. I'll tell her everything when were outside. I promise we will be so careful. First I'm gonna make you guys breakfast though. I know you'll eat if I cook for you."

"This is excellent, Alexa. Remember that the next thirteen letters will spell three words, not two."

Alexa shrugged. "Three words? I wonder if that makes it harder or easier."

Returning to the bathroom mirror, Martine resumed combing through her hair, clipping it to the back of her head, and touching it up with hairspray. Minutes later, she had artfully applied her standard make-up. Like breathing air in and out, her morning routine was on autopilot while her mind pondered the bizarre clues from last night. Questioning her psychic experiences, Martine looked in the mirror that reflected her doubts. Expressing her dismay with a quick frown, she turned off the light.

Aromas from Alexa's cooking infused the air. As a result, Martine's hunger pangs resonated from her stomach. Craving the eggs and toast, she hurried the final chore of making her bed. Certain she was dressed and ready before Jolene—she walked to the scrabble table to examine Alexa's work.

Rearranging the tiles while Alexa slaved away in Jolene's kitchen consumed Martine's thoughts. Haunted by the notion that finding the meaning behind the mysterious words may be the real dilemma, Martine moved the letters around in haste. Unclear what Alexa's puzzle-word could mean, she tried to make something else out of the letters. Unexpectedly her scrabble skills kicked-in and she jockeyed the letters around until she created two new words.

"Mother In-Law," she said slowly to herself. Stumped, she looked at her journal notes and read, "*To pass the test and lessons learned, find the meaning in two double-words.*" "Two double words," she said under her breath.

Determining the exact meaning behind these clues meant identifying the last three words. Frustrated with her lack of understanding, Martine stared out the window.

"Breakfast is ready," hollered Alexa like a cook in a greasy diner.

"Great. I'm coming." Lifting her empty coffee cup from the game table Martine moved to the kitchen.

"Nice. This looks fantastic, daughter. I'm impressed."

Chapter 22

Gagging from the urge to vomit, Maria rolled over on her side and up-chucked on the floor. Hanging her head over the side of the cot, like a sick dog, she panted for air. Heat rushed through her body as consciousness returned.

Waking up in a concrete-block room, she found herself alone and caged like a cat at the zoo. Groggy and ill-feeling she struggled to get to her feet. Seeing a door in the barely lit room, Maria made her way to it and pleaded, "Help! Help! Is someone there?" Pounding on the only door, she sounded panicked as she screamed louder, "Please, is someone there? I'm locked in here. Let me out! Let me out!"

Muffled, but near, she heard a thumping sound in answer to her cry. Listening intently she heard it again and surmised she was not the only occupant. Tears were her response when she couldn't hear anyone come to her rescue.

Disgusted by her accommodations, she glared at the military-sized cot housed in the corner of her compartment. Resembling a jail cell, Maria's new home grossed her out in every way as she focused-in on the dirty toilet that didn't even have a seat. Knowing how desperate she was to use the restroom, she closed her eyes and cringed as she sat on it.

Hungry and missing her own home, she laid her ear up against the door and strained to hear any noise outside her prison. Faint thumping from further away gave her hope. Unable to hear a voice she pounded back and yelled, "Help! Let me out!" Dizzy and weak Maria sank to the floor and whimpered like an abandoned baby.

Chapter 23

Eva and Alexa were still giggling over their reunion when a noisy truck back-fired outside.

Posing as maintenance and landscape contractors, FBI Agents Rodriguez and Romero parked their old-white-flat-bed truck in front of Jolene's home. Dressed like Mexican immigrants, they wore ragged clothes to hide their true identities.

One man donned white overalls that were splashed with multitudes of paint. Resembling a color pallet, he could definitely pass as a painter.

The other worker wore fagged out jeans and a t-shirt with the arms cut off at the shoulder. Sporting a massive tool belt, he passed as a maintenance man. Their big-brimmed hats hid most of their facial features. The two *hombres* looked anything but FBI. Slash from palm, and mesquite trees brimmed over the top of their truck bed, proving they were Hispanic landscapers too.

Entering Jolene's yard through the side gate, Eva watched through the patio door as they proceeded to conduct gardening services while discretely sweeping the property for surveillance equipment. Working together, they surveyed Jolene's tiny backyard in less than fifteen minutes. After completing their inspection they proceeded to install one of their own monitoring devices by her patio gate.

Eva scrutinized, "Alexa, look how easy it is for someone to spy on a girl."

"No kidding, anyone could do that to a neighbor." Pulling her hair back in a ponytail, Alexa shook her head in disbelief.

"This is what it's like having a voyeur spying on us, man is this creepy," Eva replied.

Alexa nodded. "Yah, we're lucky though—we know about this one."

Knocking on the patio door with their hands loaded-up with painting and maintenance supplies, Rodriguez and Romero stayed in character when they were greeted by the girls.

Aware that the inspection process was scheduled, Eva and Alexa acted like willing customers that hired the help.

Romero introduced himself in a very thick Spanish accent, "Hola, Señoritas."

"Buenos dias, Señor," Alexa greeted cheerfully.

Appearing impressed, Romero replied, "Buenos dias', Señoritas."

"Cómo está usted?" Alexa asked.

"Muy Bien," Romero returned.

"Habla inglés?" Alexa asked.

"Muy poquito," Romero replied.

"Come in, por favor." Alexa gestured for the two impersonators to enter the home.

"Gracias," Romero exaggerated his native dialect.

Attempting to engage with the workers herself, Eva commented on Rodriguez's work clothes, "Who faux painted you?"

Nodding at Eva with a sarcastic smile, Rodriguez showed off his accent too, "Hola, Señorita."

Turning on Jolene's stereo system, Eva blasted music from the radio. With the ambient noise playing throughout the home, the agents were able to work discreetly without causing any verbal slip-ups. Recognizing the plan was to act convincing while being monitored, Eva pretended to help without talking. Luckily she didn't speak Spanish and wouldn't be able to engage in conversation like Alexa. Staying in character was like acting on stage.

Following the agents around the home, Eva used sign language to communicate while the speakers sounded loud tunes. Ushering them to Jolene's bedroom, she pointed out the first phone. Finding a device in the mouth-piece, Romero signed with a tug on his ear to indicate a listening device. The rest of the bedroom was clean.

Coming upon a tiny camera hooked on the fireplace screen, Rodriguez pointed to his eyes like a tuning-fork.

Careful to not be detected by the single camera found in the living room, the two men presumed to be working when they passed through its line of sight. Escorting the two agents to Jolene's office, Eva pointed to the computer.

Lastly, Rodriguez visually inspected every inch of Jolene's desktop computer before inserting an anti-virus software disc. Detecting invisible spyware on Jolene's computer the screen flashed WARNING. After downloading the special anti-virus software the final message read "Remote Monitoring Software Disabled." Signing with a thumbs-up, Rodriguez left Jolene's office.

With only one camera and several listening devices still in operation, the agents began installing their own paraphernalia around the doors and windows. Using their maintenance disguise as a cover, they threw a drop-cloth on the fireplace camera so they could move about the home more freely.

"Señoritas, ya terminado," Rodriguez said with a thick accent.

"Gracias, Señor," Alexa responded graciously.

Eva looked at Alexa questioningly. "What did he say?"

Winking at the agent, Alexa explained to her sister, "He said he's finished."

Escorting the ethnic agents to the door, Alexa said, "Adios."

"Si, Señorita, adiós."

Outside in the driveway, agents Johnson, and Davis pulled into the driveway and set up a ladder to install a new TV-dish satellite on Jolene's roof. Cameras mounted on the dish surveyed her entrance and both directions of her street.

Passing vehicles as well as parked ones could be monitored and identified twenty-four hours a day. Suspicious activity would be acted on in moments—not hours. Breaking into the home would trigger the most deplorable alarm mounted behind the dish. The trap was set.

Chapter 24

"**O**ver forty young victims—all Caucasian, female, all abducted. All single, roughly taken in one week intervals." Running his fingers through his hair, Agent Reese briefly hesitated, "ages fifteen to thirty. All different types of families and social groups. No relation to schools or clubs. No common pattern or connection. No witnesses. Yet to determine how they are selected—no common theme there either. That's what we know," Thad Reese concluded his debriefing.

Martine sat quietly in the packed room as each investigator got their chance to contribute to the meeting. Studying the wall, plastered with faces of young girls, she wished for a smoking gun.

Ken Harmon, Mahoney's lead investigator added, "Based on the abduction dates you see on our map, the pattern has been as unpredictable as a scud missile. The areas are so broad there is no specific type of neighborhood we can protect. Preliminary screening indicates the girls don't have anything in common. Not school, sports, gyms, shopping centers, restaurants, or interests." Rubbing his head, he went on, "We're stumped so far."

"Processing leads will be handled by agents Crane, Anderson, Harden and Dwyer. Expect leads to go up exponentially when this goes public," Reese told the agents.

"We're going to get a break here soon, so let's just make sure we're ready and we're doing it by the book," said Mahoney.

"There is no shortage of theories, sir." Standing up, Jeff Meyers passed a rap sheet out. "This is Juan. He's a likely suspect wanted for selling prostitutes. Maybe business is so good he stopped recruiting and started taking." Jeff tacked his poster up on the wanted board. "We've lost touch with him and he has a bad reputation with the lady's. He's hooked-up with sex rings."

"What do you mean you've lost touch with him?" Dan Dwyer asked.

"Don't know where he's operating. He's been underground so damn long, the worms can't find him," Jeff stated in dejectedly.

"The police and detectives I've spoken with are sending us the files on suspects they've considered within their jurisdictions," said Rex Harden. "They're also re-examining all their missing persons, especially the ones they wrote off as runaways."

"I've canvassed a few of the stripper joints looking for these faces—nada so far." Rick Helm peered at the wall of forty-plus. "I didn't see anyone resembling these girls."

"C'mon now," Mahoney objected. "We need better than this."

"Sir," Dan Dwyer cut in, "There hasn't been one thing to go on. No ransom notes, no demands, not even a note left behind by one of these victims." Rapping his knuckle on the table, Dwyer went on, "There is just no clear picture. We may need the media."

"Jeez, Dan, it's too soon," Mahoney rebuffed. "You know what will happen then. You think this is unmanageable now, wait till you're investigating every teenage girl on a date."

"Hmmm," Dan mused, "the net is going to come down on us. Probably sooner than you'd like."

Hearing the tensions rise in their voices, Martine searched her mind for something to say. Dumbfounded, she tuned into her own method of deductive reasoning.

"Excuse me," Martine interrupted, "well . . . maybe we're looking in the wrong place—because there has to be some sort of pattern if these are related."

Dan shook his head in bewilderment. "We've looked at this in every way possible. We've run these cases through computer profiling programs. There's nothing. I'm saying, maybe the pattern *isn't* there this time," concluded Dan Dwyer.

Martine pushed the agent harder, "There has to be a coincidence somewhere." Like any marriage, her psychic "knowing" and their forensic science was in contention. Needing both to make her investigative abilities work, she relied on these agents to trigger something for her.

"There isn't even a latent print for us to work off of," Dan defended his position. "We can go on the usual premise that there are always sex offenders in the area, and crimes with these types of victims are sexually motivated. Oh, we can also expect a mountain of bogus leads."

Rex interrupted the debate and supported the agent's conjectures, "Dan's right, we're just as busy disproving false leads as we are investigating the victim's background information."

Emotions were spiking in the tight group. Martine tried again, "Ummm . . . was there ever evidence of a struggle? Did these girls make enemies?"

"Nope," Dan was adamant.

Martine deduced her own theory, "That tells me there easily could be an organized effort in operation that targets a certain type of girl, selects them, and then waits for the perfect time to abduct them. No witnesses, no crime-scene forensics, no chance to get away. Not even one near miss. Totally premeditated." All eyes watched Martine. "So, we can at least start with that and the fact that their families do not believe they were runaways. Which again could mean, they were probably targeted."

"Have we ruled out crimes of passion in every case here?" Jim Crane questioned his colleagues.

"These girls are too young, and spread out," Jolene explained. Directing her answer to Jim she continued, "no way is some Romeo, or john responsible for all this. There's not enough time in-between abductions for one individual to keep it together. A serial-killer—maybe." Jolene added, "It would take a lot of street drugs to manage all these girls at once."

Agent Ray Edison reflected, "This could be the case of the century."

Administrator Chuck Emery came in the room. "Here are more cases. Yavapai County just forwarded us ten unsolved abduction cases." Looking distraught he said, "I don't think they're going to stop coming in—this makes about fifty."

Agent Don Clems started hanging more photos on the wall-sized bulletin board. "What are we going to do? We might as well be wallpaper hangers."

Martine's dream from the night before had a girl named Maria hiding with forty-to-fifty girls. Deducting that her dreams were connected to this case encouraged her to keep moving forward with her own intuitions.

Agent Romero strutted in the big room with Rodriguez following. Announcing himself, he used his biggest accent, "Mexican Maintenance." Clowning around the two agents looked like hotshots in their semi-casual office attire. Romero nodded at Jolene as he walked past her to the front of the room. "Well maybe we got something now."

"Did you find what you were looking for?" Director Mahoney asked.

"Oh, yeah," Romero nodded

"Amateur job?" Reese asked.

"I don't think so," Romero's accent rang out.

Rodriguez added, "Phones were bugged, computer was monitored, camera and mic mounted in main part of house. Good stuff."

"What was on the computer?" Reese asked.

"Definitely some kinda 'Advanced Invisibility Technology.' Set-up for some intense remote viewing. Same stuff the National Security Agencies use. Sophisticated—not detectable."

"Good job," Mahoney said.

"Not to worry, Jolene, you and your girls are covered now. If anyone does anything to get in your home, every neighbor's going to know. It's loud," Romero stated with confidence.

Chapter 25

Peter woke up to the sound of his ringing cell phone. Groggy from another late night, he groped the side of his mattress till he located the noisy gadget. Clearing his voice, he answered, "Yeah."

"Peter, its Jules."

"Yeah, man. What time is it," Peter muttered.

"Time to get up. It's almost 2:00 in the afternoon," Jules chuckled.

"I thought we weren't working today," Peter mumbled.

"Think again. You did great yesterday. We got another target to move in on."

"Jules, man, what did you do with that girl we took yesterday?"

"No worries, Peter. You don't need to know. We got paid, didn't we?"

"Yeah, that was awesome." Peter sat up. "Is she okay? Where did you take her?"

"Hey," Jules reminded him, "I already told you—we are getting her back to her real family. All we do is just deliver her to a safe area. I don't know where the hell they took her. I gotta new name for us. Let's get going before they give the job to one of those other goons out there."

Scratching his head, Peter tried to sober-up. "Sure."

Dazed from drugs and lack of sleep, Peter got up and dressed himself as fast as he could. Skeptical about the events that transpired the day before, he chose to accept Jules' explanation and the financial success they were both enjoying.

Finding it impossible to resist the supply of drugs and money that came with the new job, Peter didn't even contemplate whether he might be breaking the law.

Chapter 26

Joining the task force that was gathering in the staging room, Martine sat at the table with three other members. Lunch was brief for all of them since much more information needed discussing after the long morning victim debriefing. Handing Martine a few files, Ken Harmon the lead investigator said, "I need someone to check out the suspects I received from Nevada. They're close enough to be in striking distance even though we haven't requested a search for missing girls in that state. Do you mind?"

"Of course not," Martine obliged.

Answering his cell, Ken turned away to take the call. Cupping the phone for privacy he turned back to Martine, Ray, and Jeff. "Give me a few minutes before we start."

Within five-minutes Ken resumed the afternoon meeting. "Alright, folks, that was Bill Raines . . . our expert profiler won't be with us today. Let's see how much we have to look at so far. We can't wait another day." Seriousness etched in his face, Ken pointed to the agent closest to him. "Let's start with you, Ray. Tell us about the suspect profiles you put at the top of your Utah group," Ken's mild-mannered voice matched his professionalism.

Revved up like a race car engine, Ray snapped to attention. "I've got rap sheets on several guys." Spreading the folders out like a fan, he continued, "There's about twenty-five Utah suspects handed over to us at this time. Not familiar with most of them." Enthusiastic to share his stash of knowledge, the eager-beaver with a New York accent, exuded confidence and combat readiness. Youngest in the room, Martine guessed him to be in his late thirties.

"What do you have, Jeff?" Ken questioned the next agent.

Pensive with a slower disposition, Jeff clicked his pen and pointed with it. "I got a long list from our own Arizona state. Not a surprise." Adjusting his thick-rimmed eyeglasses, Jeff momentarily set the pen on his stack of files. "I'd say there's at least fifty." Showing the premature grey of a man in his mid-forties, Jeff's starched white shirt and pinstriped tie were out of fashion along with his tan dress-pants that didn't coordinate with anything.

"Alright, this case isn't going to get solved anytime soon without great investigative work," Ken warned. Walking up to the white-board, he drew three columns. "One is for common denominators connecting these crimes. Two is for names of our favorite suspects without solid alibis. Three is for a list of possible methods of abduction, based on the files we're working with and historical information. We're going to start with a little deductive reasoning until we hit on some characters we like."

Holding up an artist's sketch, Ray said, "This is *Rambo*. He's a nasty guy with the young girls. Suspected molester from the Utah area. He's evaded capture and DNA testing. Haven't seen him for over five years."

"We can't use that sketch. That's how I drew in fifth-grade," Ken complained. "Get to work on a three-dimensional sketch. Add some age enhancement. Don't hang anything in here that looks like it came from a grade school drawing contest."

"Yes, sir," said Ray. "This guy *Rambo* has lots of warrants for his arrest. We just need to find him."

"What's he wanted for?" Jeff asked, squinting at the ridiculous drawing.

"He's got more skeletons in his closet than Arlington Cemetery."

"Meaning?" Ken injected.

Skimming through the filed reports, Ray reviewed, "Professional hit man, bank robbery, prostitution ring, molestation, ties to a couple gangs . . . oh, and kidnapping."

"Why can't they find this guy?" Ken asked.

"I don't think they're looking," Ray returned, slapping the file down like fly-swatter.

"I like *this* guy." Jeff presented his favorite mug-shot. "He's out on parole. On the street they call him *Crazy Con*. He gets his girls young and drugged. They usually turn 'snitch' on him," Jeff concluded.

"Why's that?" Ken's green-marker added *Crazy Con* to the board.

"I guess he offers them great sounding employment with full dental and medical, and then hands them a toothbrush and a hotel-room key." Repugnance on his face, Jeff added, "They never get what they're promised . . . according to the ones still on the street."

"Where's he now?" Ken rapped his knuckle on the white-board.

"Nobody knows." Thumbing through the notes, Jeff refined his answer, "Supposedly he's had more work done on his face than the space shuttle. They can't find him."

"I got a background on a guy that named himself *Robin Steal*." Ray presented again, "he's bad—not normal in the head."

"What do you mean he's not normal?" Ken asked for clarification, "Does he lick windows? Or talk to himself?"

"No, he doesn't do that," corrected Jeff. "He's disturbed, but it's worse. He uses the dark corners of the internet to seduce and lure girls of all ages. He's a sexual predator of the lowest degree. He's probably changed his MO with all the heat on his type of internet practices. He's also never been caught or prosecuted. This guy's cyber business has eluded everyone so far." Jeff elaborated, "And no art on him."

Following Ken's erratic handwriting, Martine saw *Rambo, Crazy Con,* and *Robin Steal,* posted to the board.

"This guy, *Crack Hoe*, has the conscience of Meteor Rock." Jeff clutched a thick file. "He's a Mafia type and a German Nationalist. No luck finding him. He's been under the radar for the last year. Not hopeful we can shadow him either."

"What's he wanted for?" Ken probed.

"LAPD named him *Crack Hoe* because of all the crack whores he's suspected of running. Big time prostitution rings. Probably more than one state by now. Last known whereabouts was here." Jeff proceeded to report on the thick file. "He's one of my picks because he wants big business and has stayed in operation as far as we know. If he wants to expand here he needs a fresh harem that he can get hooked on drugs."

"I got my eye on this guy they call *Matchmaker*. He's another electronic predator, and dirty like a toilet." Ray shook his head shamefully. "He's a real POS. Lures them from the web-sites and chat rooms, especially the private teen ones. Then he hooks them up with electronic reservations on buses, trains, and planes. Before we know it, the victims are vapor. He's the 'Kingpin' of child pornography and abduction. We've suspected his victims don't stay in the country. He believes he's their savior and uses a psychologically advanced 'love language' to manipulate them into leaving home. The problem seems to be he likes them younger. This would be a change in his MO."

"What else do they know about him?" Ken probed further, "Have they tried to track him down with IP addresses?"

"Yeah, they tried, but you know the IP's track computers not people. When they performed the reverse IP's, they found the computers in coffee shops and libraries. He uses lots of methods to dodge his true identity," Ray explained.

"How does he lure these girls out of their homes?" Ken wrote *Matchmaker* on the board.

"We're not sure about that," Ray admitted.

"Can I take a look at that?" Martine offered.

"Sure." Handing her the file, Ray addressed Ken, "Let's circle his name."

"Yeah, definitely," Martine injected. Skimming through the file she added, "Its rather genius, and he could easily be foreign. He befriends the young teens who hate their home life and tells them that they should leave and start over with him. One of his rescued victims said he told her that 'those who can do—and those who can't . . . complain.'"

"Okay, we'll keep him towards the top," Ken complied.

Martine addressed the file that bothered her, "This is a report filed by Special Agent Sparks with the Nevada FBI." She turned another page and continued, "He's an expert in money laundering and extortion." Instilling her own opinion she continued, "Sparks says this guy *Schultzy*, has been linked to German Nationalists and some mysterious disappearances. *Schultzy* probably isn't his real name. They don't rule out his involvement in drug trafficking and prostitution. Even though they can't prove it, they think he's a backer. None of his suspected victims have ever been located. I recommend surveillance. We know where to find him right now."

"What's he doing and where is he?" Ken underscored *Schultzy's* name.

"Nevada. He's a rude, uncouth, ill mannered, professional crime-boss type. It says here he's colder than a Minnesota winter."

"What else you got on him?" Ken questioned.

"He's an enforcer type. He's subtle like a chainsaw trimming a rose bush. He works out in the open. Stays under the radar just enough to not be prosecuted. His name comes up a lot in the Vegas area. Runs his own casino."

"Ray, you're going to get hold of Agent Sparks. Let's get a fresh update on . . . on?" Ken stuttered.

"On, *Schultzy*," Martine filled in the blank.

"It does possibly tie in with the Evidence Response Team that we sent in to reexamine the Holbrook crime scene." Opening the file, Ken summed the findings, "we have some preliminaries after they used the blue light at the crime scene. They confirmed that there are no fibers, or foreign blood present. No body fluids of any sort. Everything went under the microscope. Cleanest crime scene ever. This leads me to believe a very professional cleanup was ordered." Ken directed his attention to Martine. "You might have a point. Our ERT's are Scientists with Badges. They're implying that this is a highly unusual crime scene for around here." Expecting a response, Ken eyed Martine.

Martine caught Ken's look, "I think these particular girls are getting snatched because they are just old enough to be classified as runaways, and then become cold cases within a few months.

They're also young enough to be coerced into working. I think they're alive and I want to pursue the guys that round girls up."

"What kinda work?" Ray asked.

Jeff answered, "Shoplifting, drug trafficking, prostitution, porn, stripping . . . they like'em young so the girls can't be prosecuted if they get picked-up. They also consider them trainable and drugable. And of course they are worth big bucks."

"No," Martine disagreed, "these girls wouldn't be used like that. They'd be picked-up and back with their families by now. There are also a number of missing girls that are in their twenties. We can't rule them out of this equation completely."

"Maybe, but you're not necessarily right either. You know most of these police departments don't share with each other. The johns usually get their girls out so fast they don't sober up in time to talk," Ken debated Martine.

"Yeah," Ray agreed. "It's a pity being corrupt and stupid ain't painful."

Martine leaned back in her chair. "I mean . . . if they're in some third world country, and drugged . . . who are they going to talk to?" Martine pushed, "We need to look for the suspects that are smart . . . too smart. A lot of the guys in my pile here have brains the size of walnuts. They're driving around on three-tires. Don't give me the dolts, I want the ones that are hard to find or impossible to prosecute. Anything else is probably a snitch at the most," Martine was adamant. "Name some crime lord types we can find tomorrow? That's how we find the ones on that white-board."

Ray suggested, "I got a lookout for *Manuel*. He's bad, and very hard to find, but not impossible. It might be good to see who he's working with, and who he's hanging around. He likes contract work."

"How many bosses does he have?" Ken inquired.

"He doesn't commit to anyone or anything. He doesn't even fill his gas tank. He's a tough guy. If he's alive," Ray drummed his fingers.

"Oh, here's a file on *Black Jack*. He's hooked up with casino money and prostitution. Lot's of his girls on the Vegas strip. He doesn't do his own recruiting and has never actually been charged with kidnapping. Did time once. I bet he can't even use a computer," Ray chuckled at the ex-con's supersized afro.

"Is he a professional business-man-type or a convicted crazy?" Ken asked.

Laughing louder, Ray held up his mug shot. "It doesn't say he's a crazy person. I don't know if he's normal though."

"He's not our man. Maybe a snitch. We need our technology to catch-up with the internet crimes and the psychotics that operate them. That's where we should be going with this search," Ken shared his thought out loud.

Walking in the room for an update, John Mahoney caught Ken's attention. "This better not be a contest between these nut jobs. Sounds like we have too many suspects."

"We all know about 'serial killers,' but what do we know about *Serial Abductors*? It's just not likely . . . right?" Ray asked.

"I just got another one delivered. Phoenix Homicide says he's a pompous little ass." Tossing another file on the table, Mahoney looked at the names on the white-board. "Tell me what you're focusing on so far?"

Martine broke the long silence, "These are the guys that are corrupt, high functioning sociopath-types. Something's broken, but they lean toward personality disorder more than psychotic." Martine recapped further, "I mean they may not look like monsters, but there is a serious defect. That means the worse they are the better control they have."

"How'd you come up with that conclusion?" Jeff asked.

"Haven't you read her book?" Ken grinned.

"No. What book?" Ray tuned in.

"It's called *Blessed are the Guilty*," Ken announced.

"Are you serious?" Jeff looked at Martine.

"It's not what you think, Jeff," Martine tried to defend her book's title.

"No, that's not what I mean, I read your book. You're the author?"

"Yep."

"Your book is about reaching the true nature of the criminal. You believe everyone was born with sin, and therefore equally susceptible to being evil."

"Right." Martine replied. "So when does sin constitute a crime? And, why are some capable of facing their guilt and others . . . never?"

"Exactly. You studied the difference between being guilty or damned. You separated them into one of two categories," Jeff resounded. "How'd you do that?"

"I noticed that the 'guilty' personality failed the polygraph every time. And the 'damned' personality beat their raps, and passed a polygraph, all day, every day. There isn't guilt in them and the poly's don't detect any stress in these individuals. They're like mutations in the human race. They're so convinced they're telling the truth, and believing it, they pass with flying colors and walk out of police stations. They usually have terrible personalities, only care about themselves, and love lots of money. Oh, they don't share very well."

"Wow. Ya think that's what we're looking for?" Ray asked.

"If we want to narrow this down and focus on a type—that's my pick." Martine nodded with confidence. "Experts say as far as polygraphs are concerned, you're either telling the truth or not. It's a 'Pure of Heart Test.' If you feel good in your heart and you're being honest, fine. If you're not . . . well, your heart isn't pure, you believe your own lies, and create a false polygraph."

"Well, you sound sure of yourself." Mahoney's eyes left Martine for the whiteboard. "I got some bad news for you four. Our victims are over eighty as of now." Waving a small piece of paper in the air, he added, "Rumor is this young girl went missing in our backyard yesterday." Mahoney let his arm drop. "Today we submit our first Victimology Report. We're including all the possible, potentially dangerous, people of interest. That would include illegal aliens, registered sex-offenders, and the usual suspects." Gesturing towards the white-board, Mahoney added, "I see some new names. Good job. Can you provide me with that, and your shortlist?" Mahoney looked at Ken.

"Absolutely." Ken nodded. "That's what we've been narrowing this group of files down to."

Mahoney continued, "So, I gather, there is no shortage of 'persons of interest' since our region is full of criminals who like young ladies. And in a matter of hours they can be out of the country."

"And we can't rule out the fact that half of these cases probably involve someone in the victim's immediate family circle, relatives, and friends. We know that from pure statistics," Jeff added.

"That's right. Sometimes we look around and sometimes we look within. We'll have to be a filter for each victim's case as well."

"Okay, boss, distinguishing rumor from innuendo is already dragging us down," Ray weighed-in.

"Expect tips to come in at about two-hundred a day," Mahoney warned.

"They'll probably increase if more cases are reported back to us, and we should expect that," Ken contributed.

"I recommend we notify Child Abduction and Serial Murder Investigative Resource Center," Martine suggested. "Let's keep them in the loop. I've seen cases jumpstarted with their assistance."

"We'll hold off as long as we can on that," Mahoney countered. "All we have right now are blanks. They're used to seeing one case at a time, maybe three. This is unknown. I didn't get good at my job by letting someone else do it for me. We're working late today if need be. Let me know if that's a problem for anyone?"

"Well it's obvious if we look hard enough, we'll find fault in anybody. It's our job to stay here till we narrow this down." Ken glanced at the newest member on the team. "Martine, are you okay with this?"

"Of course."

"Do you need to call your husband or something?"

"My husband?" she paused and contemplated the awkward question. "No, he's passed."

"Really—I'm sorry . . . the ring. I saw your wedding ring and assumed you were married."

"No. I'll stay with this till we have it down to something more manageable for the task force."

Chapter 27

Saluting everyone goodnight, Martine retired to her bedroom. Adjusting volumes of pillows for perfect comfort, she propped herself into a reading position. Prepared to highlight certain points of interest in her journal, she found herself speed reading through all her entries. When the summary session was nearly over she dozed off into a dream-state of profound proportion.

* * *

Having crossed what appeared to be death's doorway, an unforeseen force pulled Martine down into a cone-shaped cavern. Descending down towards the center of the earth she journeyed into a mystical episode void of sunlight. Daunted by dismal impressions of damnation, she traveled through an ever-narrowing funnel that resembled "Dante's Inferno Hell." Passing through eight levels, she landed in the last—*Traitors*. Adequate time to process the purpose and develop a plan of action was not allowed. Likewise, rejecting the transcendental state she was plunged into was not an option. Martine surmised it was hell. Internally, she knew logic and compatibility would not be present.

Escaping the grips of the blackish tunnel she stumbled out and saw a desolate land begin to materialize like a mirage in the desert.

Similar to the terrain she recently traveled through during her road trip to Arizona, she likened it to barren Indian reservation land.

Regaining her faculties in the realm she now occupied was complicated by the absence of any habitat or vegetation. Infertile surroundings left Martine standing in a wilderness of sand.

Finding herself dressed in jeans, boots, and chaps, she wondered what kind of a ride she was in for. Seeing her long blonde hair move from a micro-burst of air, she realized it was hanging free like it did when she was a child. Curious about her circumstances, she felt the top of her head and found her hat was in place with the stampede string pulled tight.

Hearing a rumble in the sky followed by another puff of air, Martine turned to the unearthly horizon where a massive storm cloud began to form. Escalating quickly, the ominous weather cell rolled through the sky—building momentum. As fast as her mind could travel, she watched the wall-cloud turn into a rotating monster. Spinning clockwise, like a corkscrew, the classic super-cell morphed into a roaring tornado.

Appearing to be more than an apparition, she witnessed the dark tunnel-cloud form over the waste land—her eyes' following its descent down to earth. Twisted to a narrow point, the blackish-cone moved towards her spraying brush and sand each time the tip dipped down and cut into the earth.

Observing that the trajectory of the violent wind-funnel was aimed in her direction, Martine used her hands as a dust shield to scan the horizon for shelter. Off to her right was indication of a rural farm house with out-buildings.

Stranded in the isolated field at least a mile from the outline of the homestead, Martine searched for a hurried way to reach the sanctuary.

Hearing the loud whinny of a frantic horse, she turned back to the oncoming twister to see a valiant steed galloping towards her. Without hesitation, Martine stepped in front of the panicked animal, spread her arms out like a cross and yelled, "Whoa, Whoa!"

Sliding to a stop at her command, Martine grabbed the frayed lead rope hanging from the halter, steadied the animal, and did what felt natural. Stroking the horse's white neck, she gathered up the thick mane and swung herself onto its bare back. Commanding the horse as if it were her own thoroughbred Patience, she hollered, "Hee-yaw!"

Galloping at full speed they headed for the farmhouse. With the long mane in her hands and the horse running at a 'Derby' speed, they reached the buildings seconds before the fast approaching storm could pelt them with its wrath. Shooing the horse into a sturdy looking barn, she ran to the quaint little house surrounded with a white picket fence.

Finding the windows boarded-up and the doors locked tight, Martine left the front porch to find another way in. Bucking wind that pushed her, she staggered and swayed till she forged her way to the side of the dwelling. With debris beginning to fly and bombard her, Martine hesitated when she located a storm cellar door that lay at an angle next to the homes foundation. Like Dorothy in the *Wizard of Oz*, she lacked the balance necessary to quickly open the door. Distraught and ducking the increase of airborne fragments, she yanked the door handle again until it swung open like a submarine hatch. Blinded by dust and narrowly missing the tyrannical cyclone, she stepped down into the darkened stairwell.

Encountering more gloom with each descent down the flight of steps, Martine used blind faith to enter the belly of the house. Rattled from the harrowing escape, she looked for a beacon of light as darkness consumed her space and presumed to swallow her. Alone and defenseless she felt her way into a primitive tunnel system that resembled an abandoned mine shaft except for the moving glow of some obscure light source, far in the distance. Desperate to see where she was, Martine moved towards the radiant flicker.

Embarking down the cave-like hallway she reluctantly explored the unfamiliar territory as she neared the illuminated space ahead. Hearing lamenting groans, she panicked and backed up against the shadowy passageway wall. Peeking around the corner of the curved wall she observed what could only be described as tormented souls of the damned.

Happening upon the gathering of satanic worshipers, she paused to study their intent. Startled by their grotesque appearance, she lingered until one of the crazed looking demons in the group asked for her participation, "Come here, my beauty, help us burn this holy bible." Yellow-eyed with a goat's face, the deformed being beckoned her again, "Here, you can throw this in the fire."

Observing that they could not put their beastly hands on the holy relic, Martine declined, "No, I must go."

Wandering incognito through the underground cavern, the experience worsened the deeper she went. Reeking of evil energy, fuming with pits of fire, and smelling putrid like rotten eggs, Martine crept by grieving souls and netherworld-habitats.

Realizing she was out of her element, Martine stopped again and pressed her back tight to the rocky wall. Clutching the blessed crucifix that hung around her neck, she closed her eyes and took in several deep breaths. Relying on its protection, she recited a popular prayer used in fighting evil forces, "St. Michael the Archangel, defend me in battle. Be my protection against the wickedness and snares of the Devil. May God rebuke him I humbly pray, and do Thou, O Prince of the Heavenly Hosts, by the power of God, thrust into hell Satan and all the evil Spirits who wander the world for the ruin of souls. Amen."

More empowered than before, Martine forged ahead into the widening recesses that housed horrid, cave-dwelling beings. Unable to completely disguise herself, she left her crucifix exposed in order to ward off any unwanted attachments.

Almost immediately she happened upon a progression of initiation ceremonies that were being conducted by violent, sadistic, sexually deviant antichrists. Observing the chaos, she noticed that void of purpose, most of the Satanists were acting dazed and confused as they searched for a place to belong. Joining together in smaller remote groups, the disorganized souls slinked away when she passed by.

"Who are you?" yelled a tall werewolf-faced monster.

"Come join our group," summoned a robed figure with a badger's head.

"We have room for your soul here," offered a zombie with a snake's body.

Ogres the size of grizzly bears tried to follow her, but couldn't snatch her when she narrowly escaped through a small doorway.

Inside this particular chamber the power of light radiating from her essence repelled hordes of entities and caused disruptions in their planned escapades. Inquisitive about their plight and how they could end up in such a place she sought to get closer. Tiptoeing up to a cloistered group she saw they resembled vermin with human shape. The demon figures moaned and scampered away like rodents when her glowing-form got too close.

Suddenly her safety was compromised and location detected. "Stop her," a ferocious voice growled. "Bring her to me."

Watching an army of animal looking demons surround her, she searched for a way to escape. Captured in an enclosed circle by possessed and wailing souls, Martine yelled, "Stop." Holding up her crucifix like an exorcist, she made a three-hundred and sixty degree circle. Projecting the power of God's only begotten Son, Martine recited her Latin catechism words, "Deus laudetur, God be praised."

Backing down from her command, the army-of-evil looked less intimidating, so she quickly thanked God using the power of Latin words, "Deo gratias." Chanting like a Catholic Monk, Martine spouted praise be to God, "Laus deo." After replicating the Holy words three times she found herself spaced safely from the throngs of demons.

Summoning for her presence, the entity claiming dominion over the dark kingdom stood up from his throne and used another approach, "Come forward. Let me see you." Ghoulish bat-faced beings left his side and skulked closer to Martine. Ordering his gargoyles to stop, the commanding creature addressed Martine, "You can come here."

Disgusted by the condition of his chamber and unable to see him clearly, Martine rejected the notion of accepting an audience with him, "No, I will not come into your room."

"Really," his guttural voice boomed. "We'll see about that." Standing up from his throne, the dragon shaped beast towered over his subordinates. "If you follow me to my room of riches I will give you what you seek."

"I will never follow you." Fearless and unwilling to accept his bold invitation, Martine stood her ground while the beast approached her. "Stay back," she commanded. Knowing her real power came from her faith in God, she relied on more pious words, "Get behind me in the name of Jesus Christ."

Mocking her in a child-like tone, the serpent replied, "I will never follow you. Stay back, Get behind me." Letting out a loud roar that silenced his subjects, the reptilian beast, barked louder, "Then I will have you brought to me."

"That is not possible," Martine replied. "You can speak with me out here." Refusing to move from her position she heard the angry beast growl as he sat back down in the darkest corner of his room.

Flinging a bible at her, the Beast retaliated. "Take that, you zealot."

Ducking from the attack, Martine yelled back, "What are you doing calling me a zealot?"

Raging at her with eyes that looked like red-glowing coals, he bellowed back at her, "Everyone here can see you do not belong. We are opposites."

"Yes. Thank God, we are!"

Roaring like a wild lion, he bellowed more, "You, infidel. Do not speak His name. Take your worthless bible that you waste your time with."

"My bible is not worthless."

Seething with a raspy voice, the Satanic Devil argued, "Oh yes it is. You have nothing to show for what you claim it does. There is no salvation for the human race. We'll be in charge soon."

"Really, I can't say I like what you've done with this place. Did I just pass through the abyss you have planned for your followers who are *faithless, lustful, gluttonous, money hungry, wrathful, heretical, violent, and fraudulent*? Is there really a waiting list to get in this club?"

"Blast you to hell." Hissing like a snake the dragon-shaped beast propelled his fiery breath at the bible. Like a flamethrower, the scaly creature tried again to torch it. Unable to even slightly singe the bible, the demon blasphemed her again with a string of threats, "Damn you to hell. I will own your soul. We will persecute you all the days of your life."

"You have no power over me unless I consent to follow." Martine continued her challenge without faltering, "I know how you hide. I see how you operate. You can't fool me. I know what you don't have."

Enraged by her defiance, the Ancient Deceiver stood up and thrashed his tail about as he howled in anger. Leaving his chamber he stomped up to Martine's small human frame. Bending his face down low he used his forked tongue to swipe a taste of her skin. Like a lizard devouring an insect, the giant reptile savored the experience. "Ummm, you are delicious. Now tell me what I don't have."

"You don't have what everyone wants. No one chooses you. You deceive. You mislead. You hide the truth."

"What do you know? What does everyone want? You, human mouse."

"I know how your evil energy manifests in our world. Just like good deeds and positive energy manifest into wonderful creations, you make bad things happen. You want to be invisible so that you won't be blamed. Just because we can't see electricity, doesn't mean it doesn't exist. You hide your hideous identity. Why is that?"

Seething in frustration, he drew back and fixed his beady eyes on her, "What do you seek? I will give it to you."

"Love," Martine demanded. "The one thing you don't have and can't give me." With fight still in her, the evil vortex began to dissipate and she exited the horrendous cavern, returning to a serene-state-of-mind inside her sister's home. Opening her eyes in the cozy bedroom, designed in feminine colors of sea-foam-green and lavender, she noticed her digital clock read 6:04. Making note in her journal of the time and the hellish-dream, she said, "I need a bible."

Chapter 28

Discouraged and impatient on her third day at the bureau, Martine arranged for a private room to review the most recent files that had been provided to the task force. Alone she previewed files on missing persons, suspects, and the initial autopsy performed on Lauren. Feeling obligated to her sister, she was determined to help in any way, but realized this wasn't going to be easy. The only thing she felt certain about was that the professionals involved had been left grounded.

Caught off guard by Jolene's appeal for her services, she instinctively responded though she lacked proper planning. Regretting that both her daughters were here now, she anticipated rebellion. They were very persuasive when they wanted attention and she had promised to spend the afternoon with them.

While preparing a list of questions to be followed up on, Martine felt repulsed by the negative energy from one particular file. Experiencing a queasy stomach she doubled over.

Closing her eyes in the locked-room, Martine regained her composure and meditated with the file in her hands. Vibrating like an electric sander, she slumped back in the chair till she fell unconscious. Feeling her subconscious come to life, she watched a dark figure materialize in the room with her. Walking to a corner table the male-form picked up a white rag. Focusing on details, Martine observed the mysterious visitor pour a potion into the cloth.

Uncertain of the contents being applied to the fabric, she strained to see if there was a label on the red container. After the ghostly guest departed she examined the bottle left behind, and opened the screw-off top. Leaning forward to smell the contents, Martine felt her nostrils begin to burn, and her head spin dizzy—causing a mild vertigo.

Waking up from the sickening experience, her head throbbed and her eyes watered. Regaining her bearings in the small room, she recalled the slurred words that came out of the dark-stranger before she lost consciousness, "It's just a game."

Startled by the noisy ring of her cell phone, Martine realized it must have jolted her out of a trance. Fumbling around a slew of files she located the ringing device. "Martine here."

"Hey, mom, I'm with Alexa and we want to meet you and Jolene for lunch. Don't say no, or that you're too busy. Just tell us where. We're hungry and bored."

"Let me check with Jolene. I'm sure she is ready for a break. I know I am. We'll meet you at the café next door as planned."

* * *

While lunching with Jolene, Alexa and Eva, Martine hoped to discuss the dilemma they all had with surveillance obstacles invading home privacy. "The breach in security at Jolene's house is very real. It makes it impossible to all stay there together," Martine's voice trailed off to silence.

"That's why we want you two to go stay somewhere else," Jolene said in agreement. "Eva, you should go back to school, and Alexa you could go back to Flagg with Eva or go back to the ranch," Jolene suggested as her head vacillated between the two sisters.

"Heck, no!" Eva expelled loudly. "I just got here. We can be careful. Just like you two."

"I'm not leaving right now either," Alexa stated with a frown. "Just tell us what to do."

"Do you understand that Jolene's home was bugged, and now we're bugging the buggers?" Martine summarized.

"Of course we do. We know where everything is," pushed Eva. "We were there when your FBI guys found everything."

"There was only one camera," Alexa said. "It was aimed at the living room and kitchen. No big deal."

"Let me tell you how I think it works." Jolene cleared her throat. "The car had a transponder. That means they could track me with a GPS everywhere I went. The house had mics, probably for when my cell was off. They can use my cell as a GPS device and intercept all my communications when it's on. The mics were probably backup for when it's off or I'm not using it. The computer had software installed that monitored every transmission."

"Wow . . . what do you think that means . . . what could they want?" Alexa pondered, exchanging a glance with her sister.

"It probably means they will try and use your phones next if they see mine is off," cautioned Jolene.

"How did they monitor your cell? How do they track a cell?" Alexa queried.

Jolene answered with a shrug, "There's so much spyware out there now that they probably just needed my number. All cell phones can be tracked using satellite triangulation . . . even yours."

"The only way to stop someone from tracking you with your own cell phone is to turn it off," Martine answered wisely. "You could never do that . . . right?"

"I was working a money laundering case till recently. My cover may be blown. I need to be careful," Jolene shared with a sigh.

"What kind of money-laundering case?" Eva shot back.

"That's classified," Jolene stated.

"Well, we're not leaving today. We already have plans, and they're not at the house." Turning her phone off, Eva braved the circumstances with confidence. "We'll be fine. I don't need this . . . see?" Musical tones rang out as her phone powered down.

"Right," Jolene agreed sarcastically. "For now, no one can ever be alone in the house. When your mom and I are at work you two can go shopping or to the movies, but stay together." Jolene pressed the ground rules, "I mean it . . . this is serious."

"We're planning a little sting. We just need some more time," Martine reassured the girls. "You'll be gone by then."

Enthusiastic to help with the real-life espionage, Eva butted-in, "Awesome. This is going to be like a reality show. Well, I want to help while I'm here. I've got really good instincts too."

Behind the giant menu, Martine joked under her breath, "There is nothing for you to do. You're not trained in anything except hair and make-up."

Reaching across the table, Eva grabbed the menu out of Martine hands. "Very funny, mother, what exactly are you going to do?" Eva challenged.

"Actually, I've got a lead I'm going to check-out after lunch. I'm driving up I-17 towards the Prescott Valley area. I'll be back about dinner time," Martine announced. "I'll need your car. Jolene will be using mine today," explained Martine. "I'll drop you off at that Anthem Outlet Mall."

"You're kidding right?" Eva sputtered. "We had plans with you." Insistent and persuasive, Eva countermanded her mother, "We don't want to be ditched. We want to go with you. We're going to talk about trading my car in, remember? I can't drive this car in the snow. I need four-wheel-drive, and a co-signer."

"We told you not to get that car," Alexa blamed her sister.

"I really need your help," Eva pleaded. "There are tons of dealerships off I-17."

"I need to check-out this hunch, or lead," Martine explained. "Trust me you don't want to go. I probably won't have time to do both," Martine reasoned, looking at her daughter.

"Why can't we help, and get this over with faster. You're the one that always said, 'Two heads are better than one, well, three heads are better than two.' There are three of us here right now! How long can it take to check something out anyway?" Eva rationalized with determination.

"Eva, you two would be as useful as rope licorice. Without any skills you'd be in the way. You know that don't you?" Martine shook her head in disagreement.

Jolene suggested an alternative, "I can pick you up from the mall when I'm done at work."

Breaking into the conversation, Alexa spoke, "Thanks, Jolene, I think we want to ride along with mom. We've been sitting home all morning because she was spending the afternoon with us. Remember?"

Martine looked at Eva, who was nodding her head. "You two will be bored once we get there. I might chat with her for hours. I'm trying to spare you."

Alexa tried again, "I've got an idea. We can interview her while you case the place."

"It's not a crime scene, Alexa," Martine corrected her.

Persistent, Alexa asked, "Alright, why don't you tell us what you're checking out?"

"Well this is a bit of a reach, but I'm going to visit a woman who attempted to anonymously report a missing girl. It was a few years ago. The disappearance became a cold case that showed up in the FBI expanded search today. Little was done on the case back then, not even an interview."

Sitting across the table from Martine, Eva pleaded, "You've got to let us go with you. That's not dangerous, and you're driving almost all the way to Prescott. That means you'll be gone all afternoon. Do you know where she lives exactly?"

"It's somewhere in the Prescott Valley South Wetlands area. I have to go today. The woman works two jobs and this is her one day off."

"Go next week when she has another day off," Eva argued.

"I can't wait that long. I felt dark, cold energy when I read the file. Actually I saw something," Martine explained while looking into her menu again. "I even smelled something. There's definitely a problem with this girl's disappearance."

Eva blurted, "Snap!" Looking at her sister sideways, she exploded, "I knew it. She is on to something that the FBI down here hasn't even checked out."

Flattered by the enthusiastic compliment, Martine relented. "Okay, if you go with me, I need you to help, and look useful. I'll give you each something to do. Alexa you'll take notes, and Eva you'll listen and search for things that seem out of place." Void of a smile she finished, "Let's be efficient and impress Jolene's boss. If you waste time on your cell phones it will be the last time you get to tag along. Agreed?"

"Fine," Eva said. "Let's order."

Chapter 29

Starting to wake up from a deep sleep, Maria tossed and turned on her cot as her reality came back into focus. Barely able to remember her walk from the school to the student parking lot where she was going to catch a ride with a friend, she really had to strain to recall the circumstances that prevented her from getting there.

Realizing she was in a small cell, and very much alone, she looked at the door that locked her in. Maria moved towards the door and found herself staggering as if drugged or drunk. Pressing her ear to the door, she listened for signs of life.

Distant noises echoed back to her as doors opened and closed with a clang. "Help," she shouted. Pounding on the door, she yelled again, "Help, someone." Using both fists, she hit the door twice, "Let me out of here." Hearing no response to her plea, she looked around for something to assist her in escaping.

She saw nothing except a small table with a tray of food. Pangs of hunger enticed her to rush over to the cold meal of bread and cheese. Devouring the food like a caged animal provided relief to her basic instincts, but brought her no closer to gaining her freedom.

When she finished consuming the meager nourishment, she drank the bottle of water that was also provided before throwing the empty plastic container at the closed door. Strengthened by the sustenance, she felt renewed anger surge through her body.

The urge to charge the door and scream at the top of her lungs was instantly compromised by euphoric feelings of relaxation. Feeling her body succumb to the need for sleep, she collapsed on her cot and drifted off into another coma induced slumber.

"They drugged me again," she muttered slowly as she faded off to sleep.

Chapter 30

Martine, with her daughters, departed for Della Avery's residence after lunch. All apprehensions disappeared when she met Della. The old woman was like Aunt Bee from Mayberry RFD.

Surveying Della's surroundings, Martine was saddened by the lonely life the poor woman endured. It was apparent she was anchored in this place and everyone else was a memory. Antiques flourished in the Avery residence. Della looked at home in her vintage domicile, complete with lace curtains, and white picket fence.

"Hello, Mrs. Avery. I'm Martine."

"Hello, Martine, please come in."

"Thank you. Can my two Student Interns accompany me?"

"Certainly. You're all welcome. I don't really get company out here anymore."

As planned, Eva and Alexa remained silent while Martine questioned Della. Martine did her best to avoid sounding and behaving like a lawyer who was interrogating an unwilling witness. Extracting useful information from criminals was an art she was trained in. Authoring a book on the subject made her a celebrity among criminologists. Della, however, did not appear to be a criminal.

Passing through the formal dining room of the old farmhouse, Martine asked, "Della, can you explain to me how you came to know this girl named Sharon?"

Looking at Peter's framed graduation portrait hanging on the wall, Della reminisced, "Peter was Sharon's friend."

Martine glanced at Alexa to make sure she was writing. "Della, I didn't see anywhere in the file that Sharon had a friend named Peter."

Fondling the charm bracelet on her wrist, Della explained, "That's because nobody knew they were friends. Sharon was only fourteen when she and Peter met. The group home she lived in wasn't too far from here. Hanging around with boys wasn't allowed. Any violation meant an automatic termination in the residence. Sharon would be returned to a juvenile facility if she got caught. I know it was wrong, but I felt sorry for her and went along with their secret. I thought Sharon was good for Peter. They both seemed happier together, even though she couldn't spend too much time away from the home."

Consoling Della, Martine nodded in agreement. "I can understand that."

Della moved into the antique-ridden living room and gestured for everyone to take a seat. "Can I get you girls some water to drink?"

Eva offered to assist, "Water would be great. Can I help?"

Della reached for the photo album stored on the coffee table. "Here are some photos of Peter during his high school years." Handing the album to Martine, she asked, "Do you want to take a look? I'll be right back."

Paging through the photos occupied Martine until Della returned. Accepting the glass of water handed her, Martine took a sip and pointed to a photograph of Peter pushing a cute little brunette teenager on a tire swing.

Placing her reading glasses on, Della exclaimed, "That's Sharon. See how adorable they were together. Everything seemed so much better for Peter when she was around. He'd been through so much before and after his parents died."

Turning another page, Martine questioned the large- framed boy standing next to Peter on graduation day.

"That's Jules. He's older than Peter. They liked to hang out to-gether. All three of them were friends. I liked it better when Peter was home with Sharon, and not running around somewhere with Jules. I had no idea what Peter and Jules did when they took off in the car."

After finishing with the album, Martine handed it to Eva and addressed Della, "Why didn't you tell someone all this before? None of this information was recorded in Sharon's file."

"I figured the group home probably reported her as a runaway. When I noticed that Sharon wasn't coming over to the house any-more I asked Peter about it. He said he had no idea where she was. It was Jules who said she ran away. When I asked Peter again about Sharon, he was defensive. I thought she must have broken off the relationship with him and he was hurt or mad."

"Della, what made you contact the police anonymously?"

Wringing her hands like a worried mother, Della described the events, "I found a backpack of Sharon's in our old storage shed out back. It was full of her personal items. The kind of things you take with you if you're going somewhere for awhile."

Sounding as casual as possible, Martine asked, "Do you still have the belongings, Della, or did you give them to the authorities? It might be very helpful to have someone else look through them one more time."

Appearing sincere, Della said, "I do believe I still have them. Be-cause I didn't know if she was missing or merely hiding her things here, I didn't think they were important to anybody else. I really hoped that Sharon would come back and get them."

Letting her breath out, Martine sighed. "You're right, without a doubt you had a good reason to question Sharon's whereabouts. Did you notice anything else that could help us?"

Dabbing the tears that were gathering in the corners of her eyes, Della confessed, "I found Jules's behavior unsettling. They both became withdrawn and reclusive, but Jules was over here more and more and he wouldn't talk about Sharon at all. It was like he wouldn't leave Peter alone."

Curious, Martine probed further, "What do you mean when you say they were reclusive?"

"They spent all their time in that room or dungeon."

"Dungeon? What and where is this dungeon?"

"Peter and Jules wanted to use the basement for privacy. Something about a business, or club. I later discovered that they were really using the abandoned root cellar that was tucked away in the far corner of the basement."

Glancing over at Alexa, Martine verified that she was transcribing the conversation. Noting that Eva was studying the family albums and other framed photos, Martine continued, "What do you mean you discovered the room?"

"One day, while they were at the movies, I was in the basement looking for my Christmas decorations. While I was searching around I noticed the faint outline of a door. I was curious and went to check it out. When I opened the door, I saw a bunch of candles burning in the room. The light from the candles inside the room had created the outline of the doorway, or I wouldn't have remembered it was there. It was the abandoned root cellar. The room looked and smelled so bad that I never went in or asked them what they used it for."

Della had Martine's attention. "Go on, Della."

"Well, Peter was left alone at home most of the time. I worked two jobs. Anyway, he seemed content staying home with Jules. It was better than them running around and getting into drugs and stealing wasn't it?" Della looked down into her lap.

Staying focused, Martine coached her, "And you say there is a room in the basement where he spent a lot of time?"

"Yeah, well, sort of. I don't know what you'd call it. It's a pretty small space. Looked like they put some furniture in it. I guess Jules must have brought it over from his place."

Martine felt Della withdrawing. It was obvious Della didn't want to talk about Peter's activities. Martine was a mother too and sensed Della was convinced Jules might know something about the disappearance of Sharon, but not her grandson.

Martine feared if she didn't do something quickly Della would clam up to protect Peter. Aware of the panic building up in Della, Martine fired off another question before Della stopped cooperating, "Where are Jules and Peter now?"

"They're not friends anymore according to Peter. They both left town after Peter graduated. I have no idea of Jules's whereabouts. I think he went to Vegas. Peter moved down to the valley, and rents a room. He never comes home."

"Great, Della, you've been really helpful. How about we keep this visit private until I talk to the boys myself? I wouldn't want Peter to tip Jules off that we're looking for him. It'll be easier to find Jules without Peter scaring him away. You can understand our need to talk to Jules, right?" Martine was hoping Della would respect her wishes if she appeared to be looking for Jules and not Peter. It seemed to work well enough for the moment.

Smiling at her hostess, Martine phrased her question artfully, "Della, do I need a key to look in the cellar?"

"Oh yes, you need a key to go down into the basement, but you wouldn't want to go down there. It's horrible. In fact the whole basement is. The root cellar is just worse. We stopped using that room when the fruit orchards were sold with the farmland about thirty years ago. This house should be on the historical registry."

"Not to worry, I grew up in an old house too. I'll be fine. Do I need a flashlight?"

Della scurried into her kitchen and returned with a flashlight. Martine flipped it on and discovered the batteries were dead. "We may need to replace the batteries, if you have any?"

Della left for the kitchen again to search for charged batteries.

Martine whispered the next phase of her investigation, "Alexa, Eva, wait here with Della while I check out the cellar?"

Making their intentions known, both girls glared at Martine. Alexa whispered, "I don't think so. We're not going to sit here and visit with her. She'll figure out we're your daughters."

Frowning, Martine suggested, "I think it's best if I go down there and look around myself. You two can take a break."

Alexa stood up. "Mom, I'm going with you."

Twirling her long hair with manicured fingers, Eva joined her. "I'm not letting you go down there without us. No way am I going to get stuck talking to this old lady."

Returning empty handed, Della said, "Sorry, girls. No luck. I have a couple lights down there with pull strings. The lighting isn't good. And I don't think there is a light in the cellar room. I saw inside because of the candles they left burning. The candles are probably still there though. Do you want a lighter?" Della offered.

"Absolutely. Oh, Della, while we take a look at the room would you mind getting Sharon's backpack for me? I think I should inspect it. I'd like to do that when we get back from downstairs. Would you mind showing us the way?"

Della escorted Martine and her daughters outside the home to the basement entrance. Aided by the reading glasses hanging around her neck, Della opened the combination lock that secured the heavy metal door laying at an angle over the underground stairway.

Curious about the unique door's relation to last night's dream, Martine kept the Déjà Vu to herself. Proceeding ahead was the only way to properly connect this experience to a recent dream.

"This is really an odd way to get into a basement," said Eva, wrinkling her nose.

Shaking one end of the chain off of the padlock, Della explained, "Well, that's because back when this house was built, they planned for bomb shelters."

Alexa questioned the concept, "A bomb shelter? How can this protect you from nuclear fallout?"

Pulling the loosed-chain away from the door handle, Della elaborated, "Nuclear bombs weren't around during World War I & II. I didn't say it was 'still' a bomb shelter, honey."

Martine injected, "It was a different world back then."

Martine and Della grabbed the handle together and pulled up and over. With the door hatch swung open like a book, Martine and her daughters peered into the blackening staircase leading down into Della's basement.

Guided by Alexa, Martine descended down the stairs. Adjusting to the darkness inside was almost impossible after standing outside in the blinding sunlight.

Leading Martine and Eva down a flight of concrete steps, Alexa opened another door that led into the underground level of the Avery home. Total darkness surrounded them as the door to the outside stairwell partially shut itself.

Chapter 31

Tasked with the job of reviewing a new slew of files—classified as "missing," kept Jolene working late. Local police listed these girls as being, Unexplained Missing Persons. No hint of a serial predator was suspected. Pondering the daunting files spread on her desk, Jolene glanced at her watch. The whole day had been disappointing and stagnant. Startled by an incoming call, Jolene picked up the hand-set on her desk phone.

"Hello, this is Agent Anderson."

"Hello, Jolene, it's Wade."

"Wade?" Jolene stiffened.

"Hey. Long time no talk. I heard you're involved in the missing girl cases."

"That's privileged information, Wade. How did you hear that?" Relieved he couldn't see her, Jolene gulped from nervousness.

"I spoke with your boss this morning and he told me himself."

"Really?" Jolene sounded surprised. "Is that what you're calling about?"

"Basically," Wade explained, "I've been contacted by my chief to coordinate and share any information our investigators might have with your task force."

Remaining formal, Jolene asked, "Do you have information we haven't seen?"

"I believe we do." Wade's soothing voice went on, "Is there any chance you have time to discuss it?"

"I'm interested in anything that can help move this investigation forward," Jolene replied coolly. "Of course I'll find time."

"Great. When are you available?" he asked.

"I'm good now. Tell me what you've got." Butterflies flitted in her stomach.

"Well, it's pretty late. Let's eat," Wade suggested in his cavalier voice.

"Do you have anything good to share with me?" Jolene's reservations kept her guard-up.

"I think so. You'll be the first to hear all about it," he coaxed. "Ah, I hear we should limit phone activity—I'm on a cell."

"Fine. You're right," Jolene said sharply.

"Hey, c'mon, hostility probably doesn't go with what you're wearing," Wade said facetiously.

Aware that he saw through her, she relented. Maintaining a professional wall of defense, Jolene grabbed a message pad. "Go ahead. Tell me where we're meeting."

"Outside."

"Outside? Where?"

"Outside your building. I'm in the parking lot," Wade ended casually.

His confidence enthralled her, and his boldness always trumped her stubbornness. "Okay," she replied. Straightening-up her posture, Jolene looked down at what she was wearing. "Give me a few minutes. I need to wrap up a report I'm working on."

Speeding to the restroom, Jolene checked her hair and makeup. Flustered at her wardrobe, she unbuttoned her jacket so her lacey-blue camisole top was more exposed. After applying dark-pink lip gloss, Jolene smacked her lips together and faked a smile in the mirror.

Rushed by the unexpected invitation, Jolene quickly shot off a text message to Martine about her dinner plans. Shaking-off the memory of her sister's words of advice, she asked herself, *"How does she do it? How did she know I would be seeing him?"*

Returning to her cubicle, she proceeded to shut everything down for the night.

Stacking the files neatly on her desk she bundled up her personal belongings and left for the parking lot.

Wade's tall handsome figure was standing next to his red Pontiac GTO. Wearing great fitting jeans with a dress shirt and sports coat, he was as dashing as ever. Beneath his great hair was the signature smile that always melted her composure. Irresistible in every way, Jolene knew how she really felt about this man.

"You look fantastic," Wade said, looking Jolene up and down.

"Thanks, Wade."

Opening the car door for Jolene, he asked, "How've you been doing?"

"I'm fine," she lied.

"Oh, good . . . good," he said faintly.

Sliding into the driver's seat and buckling his seat belt, Wade checked Jolene over again. "It's really great to see you."

"Yeah," Jolene said with a timid grin.

Starting up his car he suggested their favorite restaurant, "High Steaks?"

"Absolutely," she replied, knowing they'd be comfortable in a cozy cushioned booth.

Making small talk about work, Wade drove the ten minute route to High Steaks. Parked towards the back of the busy lot, he escorted Jolene into the restaurant like he was on a date. Opening every door and exuding charm, he knew how to magnetize her.

Still angry about the penalty box he put her in—Jolene remained guarded and pious as they settled into the dimly lit booth. Sacrificing many relationships because of her righteous nature, Jolene found herself struggling to be less judgmental. Guilty and embarrassed that she caused their relationship to fizzle, she tried to act indifferent.

"Tell me what ya got," Jolene asked as she glanced at the file he brought in the restaurant. Personal discussions made her uncomfortable. Wanting to hold the file like a security blanket, she reached for it.

"Not so fast," Wade stopped her. "Glass of Chardonnay?"

"If you are," she said.

"Yeah, I'm off duty," Wade justified.

"Is this another missing girl?"

"What else."

"You could've dropped it off for me," Jolene reasoned.

"Yep, however, this just happened."

"You're kidding. When?"

"The other night. We think you better take a look at it."

"Wow, this is new. Tell me you have some leads on this one."

"Nope. Just a police report." Handing Jolene the file, Wade explained more, "Casey and Lovell where the officers. You've met them."

"Yeah, I have."

"Girls name is Maria Danielson. One parent, barely seventeen, blonde, blue eyes, very pretty. I'm the investigator."

Inside the folder, Jolene skimmed the report, "This is shocking," she exclaimed. "Your officers responded immediately. You even know where the abduction took place. It's near the school. How can there be no witnesses?" Jolene summarized the report out loud as she breezed through the papers.

"I'm going to be interviewing everyone that could have seen her that day. I'll keep you posted, unless you want to do it all yourself."

"No, we need help and cooperation from law enforcement."

"How many cases are you guys handling already?"

"Yesterday was forty—something, today before I left, over one-hundred."

"Wow. That's intense."

"I'll say."

"Jolene, I'm sorry I haven't been in touch," Wade sounded sincere as he changed the subject.

"Oh . . . that, don't worry about it. I know we're broke-up." Defused by his noble apology, Jolene blinked to control her sensitive eyes from watering.

Leading the new conversation, Wade lifted his eyebrows, "You surprised me. I didn't know you were such an artist."

"There're a lot of things you don't know about me," sipping her wine, Jolene replied curtly.

"Apparently," Wade agreed. "I want you to know I deserved it. I shouldn't have punished you—I'm the one that had the big head."

Smiling at the pun, Jolene looked down in shame.

"I knew I could get a smile out of you." Reaching for her hand, Wade comforted her.

Caving like a sand castle, Jolene said, "I'm sorry. I wish I hadn't done that to you."

"Hey, it's no big deal."

Thumping inside her chest made her unable to maintain FBI self-control. "What'd you do with it?" her voice crackled a little.

"It's right where it needs to be," Wade answered.

"In the fireplace?" Jolene asked sheepishly.

"No—hanging over the fireplace."

Laughing together, Jolene released the emotions she'd been burying. Relieved by the unexpected outcome, she dropped tears on her cheeks.

He's exactly what I want, Jolene thought, as she giggled with Wade. Renewed sentiments surged inside her as Wade's sincerity melted her defenses. Realizing his sense of humor was more developed than hers, she felt pangs of longing for him. Being close to *him* like this made her crave his companionship even more than before. Wade completed her in every way.

Chapter 32

Moving single file, they were overcome with the pungent odor of a stale basement.

Martine and Eva piled into the back of Alexa like a collapsed accordion when she stopped abruptly. "Sorry, you guys, I can't see in front of my face," complained Alexa.

Without hesitation, Martine offered, "Let me do this. It's not necessary for either of you to go with me. It's only going to get worse."

Eva objected, "We're going to do this together. There's no way we're letting you go alone."

Moving forward, Alexa felt for the string Della had described. Pulling on the cord she let out a loud, "Phew."

With the faint illumination from a dirty forty-watt, bulb, Alexa navigated them through stacks of abandoned boxes, trunks, bags, furniture, appliances, and toys.

Eva clutched the back of Alexa's shirt to steady herself as she shuffled her feet across the cement floor. Irritated by the clutter, she complained, "The Avery's, evidently do not dispose of any-thing. They just relocate their belongings to this crypt when the useful life is expired. This is like a graveyard for crap. I'd like to see somebody 'Flip this House' on TV." Tripping over a crumpled-up rug, she added, "And do it blindfolded."

Alexa cautioned, "It's too dark to see ahead. Can either of you spot the other string?"

Impatient as usual, Eva responded, "Let me go first, I'll find it. We're going to do this as fast as possible. You don't have to be a psychic to know there are spiders and rodents down here with us."

Maneuvering around Alexa, Eva took the lead. Moving her hands back-and-forth in front of her face, like a stranded motorist flagging down a car, Eva groped for the invisible string. "I think I just felt it. Can I have the lighter, mom?"

With the help of the small flame, Eva located the next string and pulled it. "That helps," she remarked.

"Girls, I don't want you to bring anything back that doesn't belong to us," Martine instructed.

"Not much chance of that," Alexa replied.

Eva looked appalled. "You've got to be kidding. Why in this jungle-of-junk would you think that?"

Martine explained, "You wouldn't. I just don't want anything attaching to us that wasn't invited."

"What are you talking about?" Alexa questioned.

"Everybody stop where you are," Martine commanded as she halted the Congo line.

Obeying without argument, the girls stopped. Martine dug in her purse till she found a small-white pouch. "We need all the help we can get, and I brought some," Martine stated with confidence.

Holding Martine's purse like an attending nurse, Alexa inquired, "Is there something wrong down here?"

Eva answered, "Excuse me? It's not obvious?"

Opening the pouch, Martine explained, "Something is draining my energy. I sense heavy, dark entities."

Pinching grains of blessed, exorcised salt between her fingers, she sprinkled white granules on each of them. "Now we can proceed."

Concentrating on the location of the hidden door that lay ahead, Martine prophesized, "This place is dark with or without light."

Disturbed by a loud obnoxious sound, Martine jerked.

Screaming from fright, Eva turned around and hugged her sister.

Frozen in place, Alexa's shaky voice yelled, "What's that sound? What's gurgling?"

"Girls, didn't Della say there was a sump pump down by the cellar-room door?" Martine asked.

"Oh. Yeah. What's a sump pump?" Eva questioned.

"Eva, unless you grew roots, we need to keep moving towards that noise before it stops," Martine ordered.

Holding onto Eva's arm, Alexa complained, "This place is so gross. These guys have got to be weird to have ever hung out down here."

Eva attempted humor in a show of bravery, "Don't try and set us up with these losers, mother."

"Eva, you're amazing as always. How do you do it?" Martine asked.

"Better let me go first," Alexa volunteered as she used her new RAZR cell phone to shed more light into the black recesses ahead. The light from her phone made a soft glow.

Eva copied her and activated her new phone's video-camera light. Together they produced enough illumination to find the concealed opening. Only ten feet in front of them hung a dingy-gray door that was camouflaged into the concrete-block wall.

Pawing at the spider webs clinging to her face, Eva shrieked, "Shit! There's probably a giant spider down here too." Shining her light on more webs, she whined, "You definitely would need to know this was here or you'd never get to it. Nobody normal would go through all this."

Pulling the door open, Martine used her phone to see inside.

Clasping her hand over her mouth, Eva gasped at the site, "Oh my goodness! What did people use root cellars for? This is unbelievable."

Squirming in disgust, Alexa agreed, "Let's light some of those candles and get this over with. We'll drain our batteries if we don't. This is worse than any haunted house I've ever seen."

Proving to be shoddier than the basement, the cellar was confining with a six-foot-high ceiling. Alexa lit a candle that she found on a large log standing on its sawed-off end. "So . . . do I need like sixty of these to make a sixty-watt-bulb?" Shaking her head, Alexa laughed at her own joke. "This is really primitive."

Blackness hid decaying piles of wood that made the room smell dreadful. As the candle flames multiplied, the room began to resemble the "dungeon" that Della had described. Dark-gray concrete walls, spider webs, dirt flooring, and a low timber ceiling made the cellar look like a cave. The suffocating vacuum of stagnant air was dank, and oppressing.

Fearing for their safety, Alexa and Eva complained about the probability of beetles, roaches, spiders and mice.

Eva pointed out an old coffee table with more candles. Igniting the wicks with the lighter, she said, "I've got my candles lit. Look at this crap, these guys sat in here and smoked their brains out. Check-out all the ashtrays." Picking up an empty bottle of Jack Daniels, she added, "Oh, they drank too. I should have known that's all they did in here. Let's go."

Drawn to an ornate candleholder, Martine stopped Eva. "Not so fast. Check-out these candelabrums. Have you ever seen anything like these?"

Backing into a log, Alexa squealed at the sight of a bat hanging from the low ceiling. "What are we looking for, Dracula?"

"Oh, great, it's a bat cave too?" Eva returned.

"Girls, don't get each other started. There is a table here with things on it. Can you bring some candles over?"

Setting her candle down on the table, Alexa inquired, "What is this old stuff?"

"Looks like moldy rubbish," Eva commented as she picked up a framed picture and blew the dust off of it. "This is a really old photo. It's so old it's in black-and-white."

Alexa redirected Martine's attention, "Look at this stuff over here. There are old medals, more candlestick holders, and photo albums. I've never seen . . . make that smelled old stuff like this before."

Peering at the framed photograph with Eva, Martine commented, "Hey, I've seen this guy before."

"What do you mean, you've seen him before—like on *History's Mysteries*?" Eva scowled.

Martine laughed, "You're not far off, and he is ancient." She pointed to the middle of the photo. "I think this guy is Himmler."

Inspecting the condition of a military-looking hat, Eva picked it up and stepped closer to Martine. "Who's Himmler?" she asked.

Studying a box with an ornate war-medal, Martine answered, "Himmler was the top level advisor to Hitler. Obsessed with power, they say he ran the Third Reich."

Contemplating the war decorations on the table, Martine closed her eyes. "I feel uneasy in here." She glanced up at Eva and blurted, "What's in your hand?"

"It's a hat. What do you think? Would it make me look 'Boss' if I got me one of these?"

"That looks like a World War II German captain's hat." Martine grabbed it from Eva and dusted it off.

Alexa added, "Are these Nazi pins then?" Pulling one of them out of the fabric, she peered at it. "There's a bunch of them pinned on this tablecloth."

Martine's line of sight narrowed in concentration as she moved her candle slowly above the surface. "Yes it is and this isn't a tablecloth, it's a Nazi flag."

Lifting up two-corners of the cloth, Eva confirmed, "You're right, mom."

Before Martine could comment further, Alexa opened a drawer in the antique armoire that stood next to the table they were studying.

"Look at this. It's some kind of old Ouija board game. How does this work?" Alexa questioned, as she held up the alphabet-board.

Swinging her head sideways, to verify Alexa's discovery, Martine shouted, "Put that down! Don't touch it."

Stunned, Alexa dropped the old-wooden board like a hot potato and asked, "Why?"

Staring at the seemingly innocent board, Martine explained, "Because it's not of God. It's like a gateway to the astral worlds, the underworld."

"So what, how can it hurt us?" Eva questioned.

Martine answered, "We never learn anything useful by consulting the devil and his demons. Ouija board-devices open doorways to malevolent spirits that deceive. It connects with destructive energies and illusions. You could call it psychic debris. If messages do not originate in our 'inner knowing' their origin is most likely demonic or etheric pollution. It's not a game." Hearing her own words, Martine's mind spun. Just hours ago in a vision, she heard a "Being" tell her . . . "It's just a game."

Martine's head whirled. Glimpses from her recent dreams surfaced, like the cellar-type-room full of animals, and the Nazi invasion on the monastery. This place had the same revolting sense of loathing that she experienced in her sleep. Martine winced at the thought of all the negative vibrations being generated in this focal point. "This is all it takes to create a vortex to the astral world of disqualified human consciousness," Martine uttered.

Unwilling to handle the channeling-tool, Martine breathed deep and asked, "Alexa, whose signature is on that thing?"

Bending over to read the scripted letters, Alexa sounded out the name signed on the bottom of the ancient-looking board, "E.C. Reiche."

Eva scrutinized the board with her sister and added, "The signature is dated October, 15, 1892. This is probably a valuable item, huh?"

Pressing her lips together in repugnance, Martine shivered. "Only, if you want to conjure up the dark-side. What else is in this chest?"

Eva took inventory of the contents. "The drawers are full of clothing and uniforms from the early nineteen-hundreds, I guess. These things look like they were very fancy and expensive back then. There is hand sewing. They're not costumes."

Adjacent to the table, Alexa found an antique trunk. "Look at this," she said, pulling up on the rusty-brass latch. "It's not locked."

Moving the candle over the open trunk she did a quick synopsis, "It's full of old books, dolls and official-looking documents. None of it appears English." Removing an album, she added, "This is a baby book with locks of hair." Dropping the album back in the trunk, Alexa shuddered, "Ish. I wonder if they're still alive."

Skimming through a few items, Alexa updated her findings, "These things are really old and worn. Most of the pages are tattered and ripped. Someone has taped a lot of this stuff back together. Whoever did it was terribly sloppy. If any of this was important they wrecked it. There's still a roll of packaging tape in here."

Alexa wiped the dust off of a leather-bound book, gilded in gold. "This looks authentic—like it belongs in a museum."

Setting down the large candelabrum on the table, Eva lit the nine candles and reiterated, "Don't you think this all belongs in the Museum? Really, mom, I've seen enough. This is the creepiest place I've ever seen. It's like 'Halloween Fifteen' or 'Scary Movie Ten.'"

Absentmindedly, while turning pages in what looked like a diary, Martine supposed, "I do believe we have stumbled upon a lair. We need to figure out who owns this stuff and how it got here."

Confused and unable to digest what any of this could possibly have to do with the case she was working on, Martine formulated a plan. "I need to process these items, Girls. I need some idea of what these things mean."

Repulsed, Eva suggested an emergency exit strategy. "Let's run and get some help, or maybe a dumpster."

Assessing her surroundings, Martine strategized her mission, "No! We're not leaving till I get some evidence."

Alexa corrected her, "You said we don't want to take anything with us, remember?"

Eva grimaced and rubbed her hands on her jeans. "No way are we taking anything out of this dump. Let's get the hell out of here. I need air."

Breasting her concerns, Martine needed to find a solution quick, she knew Eva's attention span was waning, and so was hers.

Solving the problem, Eva dug in her jean pocket. "Let's take pictures," she offered.

Shaking her head, Alexa looked at her sister's phone. "Sweet."

Martine questioned, "We don't have a flashlight much less a digital camera."

Undeterred, Eva countered, "Oh yes we do."

Scoffing at the notion, Martine challenged her, "Where are you going to find a digital camera that will work down here?"

Eva opened her phone. "I bet I can get a shot of that red gas can with this camera."

Turning to face Eva, Martine questioned her, "What red can?"

Pointing to the corner behind the trunk, Eva's cell phone let out a brilliant flash. "That one."

Connecting to her most recent vision, Martine walked over to the corner to shake the canister. Confused, she muttered, "Why is this here?" Unscrewing the top, she sniffed inside. "Damn, that's gas."

Demonstrating her impatience, Eva mimicked Martine, "Why is this here? How would I know? Why is any of this here? Mother, we have got to get out of this dungeon, bat cave, lair, or whatever. Why would you want to photograph this stuff if you could?"

Martine grinned. "Cute, Eva, can you photograph and video?"

Snapping a picture of Martine holding the can, Eva returned, "So, what's the point of doing this?"

Alexa pulled her cell phone out of her pocket and interrupted the sparring match, "It doesn't matter. She'll figure it out later."

Eva hesitated with a blank stare before rolling her eyes. "You've got to be kidding?"

Martine said, "And you two thought these phones were only good for sending each other text messages, boyfriend photos, and party videos. Well it's time you show me what your phones can really do."

Like a disgruntled draftee, Eva conceded, "Okay. Fine. Just tell me why we're doing this. The things in here can't possibly mean anything."

Directing her gaze at Eva, Martine replied, "I don't know yet. I think I have enough confirmations to pursue more information on this place, or these guys. I really could use your help, girls."

Ten minutes later, Eva straightened up and gingerly closed the cover of the ledger she last photographed. "That was disgusting."

"Yes, mission accomplished," Alexa summed-up when her phone went dead.

"More like 'Mission Impossible,'" Eva quipped back.

"Halt," Martine ordered. "We may need some trace evidence to tie this room to a possible crime." Turning in a circle, she surveyed the room like a member of the President's Security Detail.

Eva balked, "Like what? Isn't that what the photos are for?"

Ignoring Eva, Martine justified her decision, "Photos won't be enough. They rarely are. None of us have touched the door to push it open yet. I'm sure we can get prints off of it since no one else has ever been in here, including Della."

Sputtering with frustration, Eva replied, "Finger prints? This ought to be good. How are you going to get prints? I know you don't have a fingerprint kit on you, you don't even own one."

"True," Martine agreed. "But I have the next best thing."

Exhaling loudly, Alexa offered to assist, "Give me your purse. What do you need?"

Martine handed Alexa her purse, "I need my blush compact."

Alexa complied. "Anything else I can get you?"

"Yeah, how about that roll of clear tape you found stashed away in the trunk?"

Martine applied face blush on the surface of the door, where someone would presumably push the door open with their palm or fingers. Assisted by her daughters, she adhered strips of tape over the powdered areas. Working by candlelight, they removed the strips of tape and sealed the contents with a matching clean strip of tape.

Martine took one last glimpse around the room and eyed the large ashtray. Using chunks of tape, she acquired cigarette and marijuana butts from it.

Turning to her daughters, Martine was ready to retreat. "Let's check-out of this joint. Damn, did I really just say that?" Martine smiled in admiration at what she and her daughters had collected.

"Ewww," Eva moaned, as she flicked a crawling bug off her arm. "Well, now that we're done, do you want me to tell you what looks out of place here? I mean, that was my job wasn't it?"

"Yes, of course I do. What is it?"

"Us."

Chapter 33

Martine had found it very easy to converse with Della. Interviewing the elderly woman proved useful. Martine found her sincere and forthright. Her description of her grandson's life had got everyone's attention. According to Della, Peter, her grandson, endured a traumatic childhood that left him without any parents.

Martine's mind processed the encounter with Della while she drove down the long driveway.

"Beep, beep," Martine's cell sounded from an incoming text.

"Here, Eva," Martine said, handing her daughter the cell phone. "Read this to me," she said as she turned her car out of Della's driveway.

"It's from Jolene," Eva read from the passenger seat. "She's going to dinner with some guy."

"Great! That's really great," Martine responded.

"What should we do?" Eva asked.

"I want to hit the library. I got a lot of questions about this stuff we just saw."

Animated, Eva erupted, "No way!" Glaring at her mother, she added, "You've got to be kidding. We've done enough today."

"It'll just take a minute."

"I'm down here to get away from libraries and classrooms." Provoked by what they had just encountered, Eva ranted on, "Look what we just went through. We need showers."

Navigating her car onto the fast highway, Martine compromised. "I promise we'll be quick. I'll take you out to any restaurant you want." Checking the time on her car display, she added, "It's not that late."

"You really are kidding, right?" Eva questioned sarcastically.

Playing into Eva's drama, Alexa chuckled in the backseat, "I think it'll be interesting."

"No it won't."

"Think about it. We'll be helping with research. I'd like a job like that," Alexa defended her mother.

"You two do it then," Eva scoffed.

Passing Eva her CD case, Alexa suggested, "Let's play some music."

"It'll be fun. We'll grab some coffee and hit the library. Dinner by seven," Martine wagered.

"Sounds good," Alexa weighed-in.

"Fine." Eva relented.

"Maybe I better tell you about the dream I had the other night," Martine began, "It meant nothing until I was in Della's root cellar."

Chapter 34

Marching side-by-side through the Library parking lot, Martine detailed her plan, "Anything we saw in Della's basement could really matter. We'll probably need some help if anyone is available."

Her visions were validated today when she recognized how her dreams correlated with Della's disgusting lower level. Deciphering the findings would be challenging though.

"Put your phones on vibrate," Alexa whispered as they were escorted to the inner sanctum of the library.

"Oh . . . Yeah," Martine replied in a hushed voice.

"Here are the older European books I told you about," a librarian said softly, pointing to walls of shelved writings.

"We'll start here." Martine signaled to Eva.

"You can access the microfiche archives over there," the librarian finished with a smile.

Since Della reminded Martine of the Mother Superior associated with her childhood church she felt comfortable keeping Della as an ally that could help if need be. Digging deeper into the meaning behind the unusual findings without her help would keep things kosher with Della.

Moments into the research, Eva tapped Martine on the shoulder. "This stuff is giving me the creeps again. I'm going to look through some books and find pictures of these guys," Eva said as she studied the phone. "There's probably a connection here with that Nazi dream you had."

"That's fine," Martine said.

"Is this Himmler?" Eva asked pointing to the man in the middle.

Martine looked at the photo. "That is definitely Heinrich Himmler."

Delivering a stack of books to Martine, Alexa explained, "These sorta relate to what we saw at Della's."

"Jeez, there's a lot of information to go through," Eva murmured.

"Alexa, I just can't see these photos on your phone good enough to read anything," Martine strained to see more details.

"I've got an idea," Alexa said as she snatched the phone. "I know what to do."

Utilizing the library's media center, Alexa printed out the photos and returned to Martine's table with a great thought, "Let's try and do our own translating."

"Seriously? How?" Eva raised her brows.

Setting down the biggest dictionary Martine had ever seen, she listened as Alexa presented her idea, "I'll look up some key words for you," Alexa finished.

Circling some specific words that looked notable, Martine handed some of the large photocopies back to Alexa.

"Wow!" Alexa snapped to attention. "This is weird." Motioning in silence, she handed Martine the translation.

"What's this?" Martine asked in a hushed voice.

Excited, Alexa answered, "You won't believe what I think this is talking about."

"No! I haven't got any idea what these documents are about," replied Martine.

"Here, look at this. Maybe you can make more sense out of this." Alexa elaborated, "This is about sterilization, slavery and kidnapping."

"Can someone try and find what a ring and sword with the Nazi insignia mean?" Martine asked.

"What did the insignia look like?" Alexa asked.

Martine drew the insignia with three connected strokes, "It resembles a lightning bolt," Martine handed Alexa the diagram.

Alexa squinted at Martine's doodle. "Isn't that what all these guys have on their uniforms?"

"Not exactly," Martine leaned in to suppress her voice.

"Alright, let me give it a try," Alexa whispered back.

Eva tapped her pencil on the dictionary. "That title you wanted is; The Secret Doctrine, by Madame Helena Blavatsky."

"I've heard of her," Martine gasped. "She's a famous psychic from the world war II era."

"Did you know there is an inscription on this candlestick holder? It's in German of course," Eva cautioned.

"Naturally, I hadn't noticed when I was holding the real one," Martine sounded chagrined. "Eva, please try and find an article about this type of candlestick. Start in a book on German antiques."

After finding a picture of an identical candlestick in an English language antiquities book, Eva sparked, "I got it!" Trolling her finger down to the second paragraph, she stopped to read, "Okay, listen to this. The inscription on that candlestick says; *You are only a link in the clan's endless chain.*" Moving away from the table, she announced over her shoulder, "I'm going to make a photo copy of this. I'll be right back."

"Here is the ring," Alexa proclaimed. "It says that the ring belongs to a brotherhood of Teutonic Knights."

"Really?" Martine pondered.

"Yeah, it says the ring and sword invoke the Teutonic heritage and dates back to the middle ages." Alexa added, "The lightning bolt symbol stands for victory."

"Hey I got something," Martine shared. "It's something like a genealogy register It's called a family tree, or tree of life."

"Uh . . . this one is called *The Human Animal,*" Alexa said.

"Who authored it?" Martine inquired.

Alexa searched a moment. "It was written by Gestapo Chief Himmler."

"Let me see that." Martine reached for the book. "This is about Nazi propaganda that promises every German citizen should receive the same things like, a Volkswagen, medical treatment, a house, a job. It's socialism."

"That's socialism?" Alexa asked.

"Yeah, pretty much. It says here that they planned to turn the people into Human Animals." Martine's face expressed disapproval. "That's what Hitler promised he would do for everyone if he was elected. This must be the psychology behind his thinking."

"Sounds generous," Alexa remarked. "What's wrong with it?"

"Everything," Martine responded. "*A government big enough to give you everything you want is strong enough to take everything away—Thomas Jefferson*," Martine said matter-of-factly.

Bustling up to the table, Eva interrupted, "There's a really cute guy using the copy machine. His name is Joseph. He asked me out to dinner."

"Seriously, you met a guy, in a library, by a copy machine, and he asked you on a date?" Alexa summarized sarcastically.

"Yeah. He's really good looking."

"Eva, you get more hits than EBay," teased Martine.

Eva lowered her voice when the table nearby looked her way, "Hey, Joseph said this candlestick represents a gift of honor."

"I think he might be right," Martine agreed. See if you can find something about that Byzantine cross with a swastika in the center?"

"Sure, Joseph's helping me." Eva bolted back to the copy center.

Martine and Alexa resumed searching publications for the authentic framed photo that was stored in Della's root cellar.

"I think the photo originated from a newspaper," Martine said.

"I can see in this magnified photo that Himmler's holding an award with a date inscribed," Alexa replied. "Let's search that date in all the German newspapers. This photo probably ran as propaganda in almost every city."

Huddled around two microfiche screens, Alexa and Martine searched newspapers dated August, 14th 1933.

Immediately Alexa had a hit. "You're right, here it is."

Grinning with satisfaction, Martine ordered, "Print it."

Alexa retrieved the printed copy and summed it up, "Hey, type-set in big bold letters is a headline, *Mutter-Kreuz*, along with an entire front page story and the photo we found."

Exhilarated for the first time in days, Martine said, "Let's go." Glancing at her watch she remembered her promise. "This is a good time to pack it in for the night."

Chapter 35

Relieved to be back at Jolene's after the long day at Della's and then the library, Martine slumped into Jolene's sofa. Eva and Alexa disappeared to make calls to some friends they were starting to miss.

Alone with her sister, Martine initiated a cryptic conversation, "Get any shopping done today?"

Jolene nodded. "Yeah, as a matter of fact."

"Find anything I'd like?" Martine asked.

"Possibly, I'm not sure how it will fit though. I got a new suit for the hot tub. Want to join me?"

"Absolutely." Martine made herself get up. "I'll meet you there in ten minutes."

"Super. I'll tell the girls."

Arriving at the hot tub with wine glasses and a bottle of chardonnay, Martine joined Jolene, Eva and Alexa who were already soaking. Filling the wineglasses, Martine handed everyone a goblet before raising her glass to make a toast, "Here's to life's adventures."

"Cheers," they all chanted.

"Get in. The waters magic," Jolene said.

Sinking into the perfectly temped tub, Martine sighed, "Damn, I needed this."

"Let me just say today was a drag, and I don't mean "Dragnet." Eva laughed at her own joke. "How can you people stand going through somebody else's disgusting crap?" Elaborating more, she continued, "Losers like that need professional help. This is more like it. I need to sterilize my body after what I went through."

"Ok Eva, let's have it," Jolene shook her head sympathetically. "I want to know exactly what you three did today."

"Is it possible for you to tell Jolene what we did without being a *Diva Detective*?" Martine quizzed her daughter.

"Not a chance. If I'm not going to have a good day you guys are gonna know all about it."

"Can you stick to the facts tonight? I really need to fill Jolene in on the important stuff we stumbled on," Martine pleaded.

"Stumbled on? We didn't stumble on that place anymore than submarines fly," Eva smirked. "It was all moms' idea. She deliberately tricked us into going down into this abandoned dungeon." Eva skimmed her audience for effect. "Then she made us swim through spider webs, wade through bugs and rodents, examine drug paraphernalia, and use our cell phones to photograph the stinky stuff. Like we're tourists or something. And then she held us hostage at the library . . . all night," Eva dramatized like an actress.

"Wow! That actually sounds better than my boring day. I'm dying to know what you think you found in the *dungeon*. Any idea how this helps the case Martine? And what is a dungeon?" Jolene questioned her sister.

Eva jumped on the question, "A 'dungeon' is where warlocks hang out."

Martine broke-in, "Eva, quit exaggerating. It wasn't that terrible."

"Speak for yourself," Eva said.

Smiling with a nod, Martine relented, "Okay, it was pretty bad."

"Thank you. That's what I'm talking about. It really was the shits, Jolene, trust me. I'll never go back," Eva reiterated her position.

"Actually, Jolene, they were both amazing today, and invaluable. Eva's proficiency in phone technology and dating saved me hours . . . make that days of investigative work." Martine grinned at her rambunctious daughter.

"It's true. If Eva wasn't so high-maintenance, you guys should hire her at the FBI," Alexa said half-heartedly.

"Seriously, it may be a bit too soon to make any bold assumptions, but there's something about all the things we saw today that make my suspicions grow," Martine tried to justify their adventure. "There're some very interesting findings that will either help incriminate, or eliminate these guys as suspects."

"Like what?" Jolene inquired.

"I feel certain the documents we found may be connected to the case we're on," Martine shrugged her shoulders a bit as she stretched the truth.

"Great, can I see them?"

"Not exactly . . . I couldn't take them with me."

"They're also in German," Alexa clarified.

"German?" Jolene marveled.

"Yeah, but we know what a lot of it means after we went to the library," Eva volunteered.

"Yeah, I know it doesn't sound like much, but it was a lot to digest." Martine added, "I'll need to locate the two guys that used to occupy the old basement. I know that sounds a little vague at this time, but it's all I have for now."

Alexa addressed her mother, "Do you have any idea what those documents are about that we found and researched in the library?"

"Not really," Martine said.

How about we locate someone to translate German for us?" Alexa proposed.

"Actually, I was thinking the same thing," Martine said as she looked at Jolene. "Preliminary research clearly has created more questions, and that means more suspicions as far as I'm concerned." Martine added, "I need an interpreter."

"Hey, Jolene, did you know mom and Alexa found some of the stuff really provocative," Eva spiced up the conversation. "At least it seems to allude to some sort of sexual activity. That's why FBI experts are needed," Eva's inflections had a flirtatious undertone.

"Yeah, Jolene, those guys that were here this morning were cute," Alexa weighed-in. Egging her sister on she added, "and probably single, Eva."

"Right, Alexa, but I know you're interested in the guys that hung out in Della's basement," Eva sneered back.

"Wait, what provocative stuff did you find today Martine?" Jolene pulled the subject back on track.

"That's right, we want to know what kinda sexual activity you are researching," Eva taunted her mother.

"This sounds extremely weird . . . and German?" Jolene sounded disappointed. "How'm I going to get Director Mahoney to help you? To put it delicately he'll think you're nuts." Jolene went on, "he's going to really resist unless you give a better reason. He'll say no."

"Jolene, you gotta ask him," Martine insisted.

"How'm I going to persuade him to allow a detailed translation of German documents in connection with this task force? Isn't there another way to do this?" Jolene debated.

"We need to get these documents and transcripts authenticated and translated. We can't afford to waste time or risk a translation that is not accurate. There are multiple dialects in Germany. We need someone proficient and qualified. I really suspect the content of the documents themselves go back in time quite far," Martine dodged Jolene's excuses.

"Martine, that still makes your request a big stretch," Jolene argued. "Mahoney will think it's irrelevant to what we're working on."

"Logically, it would appear that way. I just can't ignore what I feel and I can't put it into words. I'm certain it's important though. I don't think we're dealing with your average predator—that's all I can say I know as of now," Martine said with certainty.

Jolene bit her bottom lip in contemplation, "Martine, are you going to be that mysterious? You don't want me to get removed from the task force . . . do you? I mean if my boss removes me he's going to remove you."

"Well, I'm out of here," Eva announced as she eased her way into the cooler air. I've got some reading to do. Good luck with this, you two."

"Me too," Alexa said as she joined Eva and grabbed her over-sized towel.

Waving goodnight, Jolene replied, "Thank you, girls. You had a very interesting day."

"Goodnight, girls. See ya in the morning."

A harmonic chime sounded from Jolene's cell phone, breaking the temporary silence.

"Hello."

"Jolene—it's Wade. I just heard from the police that there appears to be another very recent abduction in Tucson. The media's got hold of this one."

"Okay, Wade. Thanks for the 411." Closing her phone, Jolene turned a blank expression to Martine.

"Wade?" Martine's voice lilted.

Chagrinned, Jolene responded, "Oh, yah. We're talking."

"Great. Right?" questioned Martine. "Your text said you had dinner plans. Was it with him?"

"Yeah."

"Is everything okay?"

"I don't know if I can trust a guy like that. He can get any girl he wants . . . and I think he likes all of them all too."

"Jolene, if he didn't like girls, he wouldn't want you?"

"That's not what I mean."

"I know. You just haven't convinced me he is superficial with a cheating heart."

"I want to forget the whole relationship. I want to rewind. I don't want to hold on and fix it. I don't like being hurt. It felt terrible when it fell apart."

"Is it your heart or your mind that doesn't trust him? Which one is afraid? Which one are you protecting?"

"I don't know."

"You have no more control over the loss of a loved one than I did. You can't stop Wade from hurting you, anymore than I can prevent James from dying senselessly."

Jolene argued, "At least you're left with the memory that you were loved. I felt terrible and rejected."

"I hear your pain. It's uncomfortable. Crappy. It rivals every broken-hearted Country song."

"Quit being funny."

"Sorry, no one wants what happened to me either. I can't e-mail, text, or call James . . . just to hear his voice. My heart was ripped out through my big toe."

"I know you're right, but I can't bring myself to trust him not to hurt me again."

"Again? You're not over the first one. This is not again. You're avoiding a relationship because you fear failure. You dread the shame of rejection. You're bitter because you cared so much for him and he broke it off. You're in denial. I'm right—aren't I?"

"I'm not in denial."

"Yes you are. You act like he left you deliberately. It was actually you who drove him away. Well at least what you did at the party."

"Why does love have to hurt so much?" Jolene frowned.

"To feel it. To prove it's fragile. To prove we experienced it. To remember we were loved. So we won't forget it and take it for granted," Martine paused. "Want me to go on?"

"You don't know a way to turn this off so I can forget about this guy do you?"

"Heck, no! I would have done that myself if I could. Blame it on Free-Will. God gave us that so we could willingly choose love— choose Him."

Jolene sniffled through her words, "They say, you can't buy love. Why not the cure though?"

"I told you why."

"Love is such a game." Jolene pressed her lips together in contemplation.

Martine perked up, "What? What did you say?"

"I said . . . it's such a game."

Martine's mind rushed. "My dream . . . the Mother Superior said . . . , 'It's just a game.'"

Chapter 36

Overloaded with information from Della's basement and the library, Martine had questions to match each impression. Reviewing notations written in her journal from the Indian dream, she recalled the promised words, "This is the time to ask for help. If you ask for something through the pipe—the creator will grant it."

Closing her eyes she said a prayer for help, "Dear God, Lord in Heaven, send me the exact assistance I require at this time. Help me know how to find every single one of these missing girls. Keep them safe and protected from any harm or injury." Lying in bed her exhausted mind drifted off to sleep. Leaving her body through a mystical process, she drifted into spirit form.

Slowly entering into a new reality, she witnessed a celestial being start to materialize far away in a distant field. Noticing the apparition resembled a Native American Indian—she felt comfortable enough to approach the solemn spirit that stood afar with its head down. Floating closer towards the stranger, she recognized the importance of his position by his wearing a full headdress of an Indian chief. Knowing that a feathered headdress with trailers touching the ground represented a traditional war bonnet, she theorized the Indian was probably a link to the Navajo Nation.

As she passed by a tribal community, her transparent body took form and settled in front of the Indian leader. Glancing around at the desolate land surrounding the ancient village, Martine used her knowledge of Native American culture to discern who she was with. Assuming she passed by a Navajo or Apache tribe of people, the Indian chief would be standing on the land of a southwestern Indian Reservation.

Raising his head he greeted her in Diné with a magnetic voice that matched his ominous presence, "Ya'ah'eeh shich."

Bowing her head in reverence, Martine returned the magnificent leaders welcome, "Hello, my Chief."

Accepting the greeting in Martine's native tongue, the ancestral Chief of an Indian Nation acknowledged her importance by reverting to her language, "My daughter, we have much work." Eyes piercing hers, he continued, "Do not be afraid—follow me." Extending his arms to the sky he took a step and called upon the heavens, "Come spirits of ma'iitsho, shash, nashdoitsoh." Sparking and arching like an electrical storm the Chiefs outstretched hands ignited the atmosphere. Charging the heavens like a lightning rod, he chanted, "Come Great Spirits."

Becoming visible in the field ahead were the wolf, bear, and lion respectively. Walking up to his side the threesome stopped on his command.

Honored with the vision of another Native American Spirit Guide, Martine bowed her head in acknowledgment. Perceived to endow great achievements in spiritual evolution, Indian Spirit Guides were recognized as wise and advanced. Knowing that assistance from their hierarchy was significant, she eagerly asked for answers, "Tell me what I need to know."

Waving his arm like a wand, the Chief relayed;

"Puzzled woman you are not
Look for land that time forgot
Deep beneath the loamy sand
A hellish realm of corrupted man
Searching far down below
You will find your evil foe
Don't despair of his lair
You will find it with due care

You're the breed we all find rare
A warrior ready—that we've prepared."

Recognizing another Divine rhyme that delivered a higher form of communication, Martine responded, "Please show me more."
The Indian Chief responded to her;

"These powerful spirits will be your protection
Wicked demons fear your reflection
Evil dances under earth
Only you can destroy their mirth
Heavenly Spirits cannot enter
The underworld that is their center
A physical body like yours is needed
To battle the outrage they have seeded
Only you can make them pine
Present now in space and time
In an instant you'll find the key
That saves the lives that are to be."

"Go now. Go together," he said. Dissipating like a whirl of sand in the desert, the Chief was gone.

Glimpsing at her newly appointed guardians, Martine's inner spirit deduced they were further confirmation that the Indian Tribes still had a guiding hand in her journey. With her realization completed she was whizzed away with the three animal spirits.

With the animal-guides accompanying her, Martine was transported to the bottom of a deep ravine. Noticing an opening in the side of the canyon wall, she presumed it was the way out. Once inside the entrance of a dark cave, she and her companions walked slowly into the darkening recesses. Brave in the company of her newly acquired comrades, Martine cautiously lead them down the underground tunnel system into a large chamber.

Stopped inside the rock cavity, Martine instantly experienced a whooshing sound that rushed past her ears as dark-shadowy entities swarmed around a barrage of smaller animals. Increasing in size and numbers, the army of vermin became a colossal threat as the demented ghosts of evil men possessed them.

Growing to the size of large dogs, the arsenal of animal-shaped demons began to wage war on the visitors. Taking up a defensive position, Martine and her three friends stood their ground as the ghetto of demons charged. Intending to instill fear in the innocent, they rushed toward Martine and her animal companions.

Baring their teeth at the armory of angry demonized-animals, the lion, bear and wolf showed their strength and defended Martine. Because these evil manifestations were primarily superstitious and not righteous beings—they scowled and slinked away when Martine stepped forward into their oncoming attack. Braver than before, she "willed" that her protection exceed their cause.

Appearing again were the two skunks. This time Martine understood the disagreement that transpired between them. Arguing over her, one perceived her to be the enemy and wanted to follow the orders of a difficult and controlling leader. The other skunk decided she was a Deity. Blonde haired and a beacon of light, the skunk feared Martine's status and the power she brought. Seeing that her human spirit reigned, she learned its importance in battling the evil she was up against.

Comprehending this important concept, she left another hellish realm. Waking up in her comfortable bed, she laid still while the ceiling fan moved air across her heated body. Looking at the time, the clock read 6:04.

Chapter 37

Smoothing the front of her dark-blue blazer, Jolene rolled her shoulders like a prize fighter entering the boxing ring. Knocking on the door to Director Mahoney's office, Jolene heard, "Who's there?"

"It's, Jolene." Anticipation coursed through her like a fight for the heavy weight championship. As luck would have it, there was an audience observing her every move.

Jolene admired her boss, as everyone did at the bureau. Approaching him on such an off-the-wall request embarrassed her. Martine didn't make anything simple when she was on a mission. Preventing Martine from asking Mahoney was the logical thing to do. Martine was adamant about not wasting any time. Saying no, to her beloved sister, was impossible. Discussing it with her boss was down-right suicide.

After announcing herself, she proceeded to approach him. "Good morning, got a minute?" She worked her way up to Mahoney's desk while making small talk about the case. Appealing to Mahoney's interest in history, she asked, "You mentioned once that you're a history buff of some sort. Ever read anything on these guys?" Jolene handed him the article and stammered nervously, "What do you think this article is about? Have you ever seen it before? I'm wondering if something like this is valuable or rare."

"Heck, I have no idea what this is about. You'll have to ask someone else if there is any value. You can find this stuff on EBay now. This is just a photo copy anyway."

"Yes. I know where the original is though. It's framed and looks important."

"Yes, well it might have been important, but from what I'm looking at . . . that was a long time ago and their legacy failed."

"So you do know who they are? I'm very interested in what these guys are doing together. Actually, I was wondering if there was someone who could translate the article that goes with this photograph."

Staring at the 1933 newspaper article that Jolene presented, Mahoney lifted his puzzled expression, "Jolene, what are you wasting your time on? You're on a Special Task Force or have you forgotten?"

Being a trained professional, she tried to control her body language by sitting down in the chair that faced his desk. "No—sir. I could never forget what I'm working on. I just kinda find this a little intriguing. Don't you?"

Scrutinizing the document, Mahoney raised his voice. "Intriguing? Unless you speak German and can translate a confession out of these guys I don't have time for historical nostalgia."

"Well, I believe that there may be a clue for our case within this article."

Mahoney appeared dumbfounded as he sat back in his office chair and dropped his hands down on the armrests. "You what? You can't be serious, can you? You say there's a clue?"

Crossing her legs, she replied, "Yes. I understand your apprehension, but if you let me explain you might agree. Likewise, it just so happens there doesn't seem to be any breakthroughs. Maybe this could lead us somewhere we're not looking."

"Okay, Ms. Anderson, did you lose a bet? Who is putting you up to this? It's not a good time for any kind of office jokes."

"No, no. I think it's a possible lead, but we need a little help in translating the article I found."

Leaning forward, Mahoney clasped his hands together. "You say . . . we? Who is . . . we? Maybe you better fill me in, since this is so far off from the scope of your assignment."

"Well, my sister, Martine, visited a source regarding the disappearance of a girl from years ago. Her interview led to the discovery of a secret room hidden in the basement where the grandson and his cousin engaged in bizarre cult-like practices. Among the stuff were old German documents, some objects, and this photograph."

"This is from a German newspaper article?" Mahoney questioned.

"You're correct. Martine found the exact same photograph in this newspaper publication at the library. She feels certain that there's a connection, or link of some sort, and would like it translated as soon as possible."

Standing up, his voice seemed to get louder. "You're telling me your sister has connected the photo she found in some hidden room, with a newspaper article dating back to 1930's Germany, and she has a 'feeling' it relates to this case. You know I agreed to use your sister because I was convinced, by you, that she was skilled at investigating and profiling."

Remaining calm and collected, Jolene fought back the urge to bolt. "She is. You wouldn't even be able to use her if she hadn't taken a leave of absence."

"What's she doing now? Profiling these guys?" Mahoney bellowed as he shook the newspaper photo.

Fearful the other agents were now privy to the conversation, she dropped her voice to a whisperer. "I believe she's going to track down the two guys that were harboring these Nazi items."

Noticing the agents outside his office were now looking in his direction he lowered his voice too, "Jolene, I think it's time your sister and I put our heads together. I need to make sense of what she's doing for the case." Sitting back down in his chair, he added, "She may very well be over her head or worse. I don't mean to offend you, but we need to take this case seriously and not waste a moment of time. Is she distracting you? I'll straighten this out if she is. I noticed your sister disappears more than a Klingon Ship. If you can find her, will you arrange a meeting as soon as possible?"

Relieved that she wasn't fired yet, Jolene saluted. "Yes, sir, I'll ask her to come in and meet with you. Meanwhile would you allow us to get this translated today just in case it really does have a clue or two? Martine is smart and efficient—she's not trying to waste time and resources. She has worked on some huge cases, remember?"

Avoiding his gaze, Jolene looked down at the article, "Would that be possible, sir?"

Capitulating faster than Jolene anticipated, Mahoney agreed, "It certainly won't cause any harm I guess. I've got a contact we can use." Mahoney glanced at his desk calendar in front of him and ran his forefinger down the hand-written list of activities for the day. "How about you and Martine meet with me for dinner next door? I don't have any time to meet before six. I should have the translation by then too. I apologize about what I said. I didn't mean to insult you and your sister. Let me buy you both dinner and get to know her better."

Walking with her head down, Jolene exited the office as humiliated as she had expected. She never presumed anyone else would appreciate Martine's request as a valid lead in the crime investigation. Unable to sufficiently explain and defend her sister, Jolene was prepared for the embarrassment that ensued, and it paid off. Getting what they wanted without losing their jobs was a touchdown.

Dinner would be interesting, maybe even exciting, when these two pros rallied together. Jolene was glad she wouldn't miss it.

Chapter 38

Desperate for some solid leads, Ken Harmon had arranged for interviews with several prison inmates. Martine was summoned early in the morning to attend interrogations with Ken because legal representation was deemed pertinent should any negotiations be required. Cutting deals with local, state, or federal prisoners was never taken lightly by the FBI. Standards were upheld and scrutinized when this Federal agency dealt with legal matters. Determining the merits of traded information was rigid when conversing with already convicted criminals.

Replacing the legal counsel already employed at the FBI became necessary when lead counsel called in sick. Flu and cold symptoms caused the man to stay home, leaving the agents stranded without legal counsel. Martine became the emergency back-up.

Dropping a stack of files into his brief case, Ken Harmon hurried her to the car that waited in the parking lot for them. "Here read these on the way. There're three cons to question at this facility. The interviews may lead to more snitches. I'm hoping your legal mumble jumble will get us all the interviews we want. Meyers and Edison are already there coordinating. I expect they will have everything ready for us when we arrive."

* * *

At the prison, Ken quickly briefed Martine on the first convict, "His name is Lamar and he's a mid-level drug dealer. He had a tight group of loyal supporters. No one's been able to crack open his organization, so it won't be easy," Ken paused as his finger skimmed the rap sheet. "He got caught in a sting operation and the net came down on this guy. He's in here on possession, and refuses to turn informant."

Martine listened intently. "Were there any undercover officers involved?"

"No," Ken replied, "he's really guarded and won't even rat on the rival drug gangs that he competed with in his street cocaine business." Ken read from a report, "He believes in a code of honor."

"Yeah," Martine responded. "He sounds like a real boy scout."

Steel doors slammed, echoing throughout the labyrinth of prison cells. Buzzers echoed in the hallways as convicts were ushered in and out of secured areas. Martine sat transfixed in a miniature-sized meeting room, studying the rap sheet of her next interrogation. Talking incessantly on his cell phone, Ken paced back-and-forth behind her.

With the slam of another metal door, prison guards entered the room with an overweight man. Martine noticed the garish-orange jumpsuit fitted the convict like he was two sizes too big for it.

Shackled in cuffs, the five-foot-nine prisoner was seated in a chair across the table from her. "Good morning," Martine formally greeted the scruffy faced man.

Preoccupied with his cell phone call, Ken flashed his FBI badge at the con.

Raising his chained-up hands, the con gave Ken a one fingered salute. "What do want from me? I haven't finished my breakfast coffee."

"We're here to ask some questions, Lamar," Ken answered as he shut his phone.

"I don't answer to you. I don't answer to anyone," the prisoner smarted off.

"You're gonna talk to us, Lamar, unless you want to look like orange fruit forever." Ken narrowed his eyes on the convict. "I hear they have more charges pending from that bust they got you on."

"Okay, I'm scared now. I'll talk," Lamar snickered through his words. "What kinda sound does a pig make?"

"I don't know. What sound does a pig make, Lamar?" Ken played along.

"Freeze, Muthafucka," Lamar laughed at his joke.

"That's funny, Lamar," Martine said. "I see here from your records that when you're not a comedian you've run with this guy Robin Steal. Can you tell us where to find him and about his recent activities?" Martine asked politely.

"I don't dance with that group any more. I got nut 'n, Honey. You can find him yourself."

"Nut-N-Honey is a cereal. Wrong answer," Martine deflected his attitude.

Directing his attention to Martine, he quipped back, "So you think you can get me to talk and rat on just anybody?"

"No. We're just interested in Robin Steal's clan. We heard you're the real muscle in his little club," Martine tried to pump his ego.

"I'm just a human shield for the real bullies in here. I'm not squealing on anyone. You're on your own, bitch," he wisecracked.

"So you're working with some real mercenaries in here, huh?" Martine questioned the bulky man.

"Don't insult my intelligence, lady," Lamar smirked sarcastically.

"How 'bout some names then. You probably made friends in here. Or, maybe you don't know anything anyways," Ken egged the thirty-five year old con.

Lamar grinned, "Oh, I know plenty."

"Good. Why don't you tell us who really is the power here? I heard it's your old friend Hank. Who's he talking to?" Ken moved back and forth like a caged tiger.

"Hank? Hank ain't good for anything. He throws his back out peeling potatoes in the kitchen," Lamar scoffed.

"You really have no choice but to give up some information. It's gonna look bad if everyone thinks you did anyway. You should really get a gift for the hassle. We can deal you something you want."

Lamar shook his head, "It's complicated in here. I don't want anything from you."

"Really." Ken nodded in agreement. "How complicated can life be in an eight-by-five-foot room with a meal plan?" cynicism rang in his voice.

"Really complicated, smart ass," Lamar rebuked.

Martine broke-in, "Actually, we know that. That's why we don't want you to look bad to the other guys. We can let everyone know you didn't talk." Pausing briefly, she finished, "or not."

"Yeah, how yah gonna do that?" Lamar sat back in his chair with a doubting expression.

"Well," Ken aggressively solicited Lamar's cooperation, "let's see, tough guy, we're meeting with a few of your neighbors next. Your file reads like a guest list to a gangster wedding. There're lots of folks to visit with here," Ken antagonized Lamar.

Lamar rocked his chair forward. "You're bluffing."

Ken stopped pacing and leaned into the table, "No, I'm not. Let's just get you back in lock-up so we can talk to the guys listed on your dance card."

"I'll talk to her." Lamar nodded once at Martine. "We need to be alone though. I can't get in the mood with you in here." he winked at Martine.

"You're not in a position to tell me how to take my beer, Lamar," Ken rejected the notion.

"Yes I am. If you want me to talk," Lamar's sinister smile was aimed at Martine.

"Yeah, that's not how it works. I can see you taking the rap for the whole gang you ran with though. Especially if we're not here to help." Ken spurred him like a bronco. "Possession of cocaine that was cut and engineered for profit on the streets carries a heavy sentence. Don't you want to share the blame?"

"Its fine, Ken," Martine permitted the con to take a win. "I think we'll have plenty to talk about." She pulled out two cartons of Marlboro Reds. "I've got twenty questions right here." Opening one end of a box, she pulled a pack out. "One of these should buy me an answer, Lamar."

"You think you can buy me?" Lamar flaunted his integrity with a yellow-stained, toothy, smile. "I don't even smoke those anymore."

"That's right. You can't get'em in here. The only things you're buying are pretend cigarettes." Martine tapped the end of the cigarette pack on the table, "Oh, if you like your current smokes, these will be worth a lot of money when you sell them." Pushing her agenda, Martine added, "They're probably worth more than you. Should keep you safe—if you're scared."

"Scared?" Lamar's voice pitched. "You're the one that should be scared."

"Pu . . . leeze, I've swatted horseflies meaner than you." Signaling Ken to leave the room, she said, "We just need a little privacy. Right, Lamar? Maybe a little help with your parole hearing?" Martine glanced at Ken again.

"I'll go check on that parole hearing for ya, Lamar," Ken announced as he left the room.

Alone with Lamar, Martine wasted no time. "Tell me who's running the distribution ring for Robin Steal?"

"I have no idea," Lamar acted flirty as he evaded her first question.

"Lamar, you haven't been in here long enough to be out of the loop yet. So, I'm going to give that guard standing out there a pack of smokes every time you dodge my question." Martine gave him a stern glare.

"So ya wanta play like that, huh?" Lamar looked irritated.

"Yeah," she said. "Guess so. You're as transparent as my glasses." Martine held her gaze. "When I read your story here, something doesn't smell right."

Lamar glanced at the pack of Red's as he pressed his lips together in contemplation, "Maybe I forgot to take a shower, if you know what I mean."

"Yeah. That's why you get your gifts when I check this stuff out . . . today."

"Fine." Lamar relented.

Questioning Lamar for ten minutes moved her closer to a prisoner that knew more about the female abductions.

"Thanks, Lamar," Martine finished.

"You better not make it worse in here for me, lady."

"Is that really possible? Wouldn't it be better to get out of here and stay out?"

"It's easy for you to be all righteous," Lamar replied.

"You're right. I don't know if you'll even try. But, all the darkness in the world can't put out the light of one candle. Make better choices."

"Choices? What does that have to do with anything?"

"If you don't stand for something, you'll fall for anything. You keep hanging with the wrong folks."

Knocking on the door for assistance, Martine waited for the two guards to enter and take Lamar away.

Ken rejoined Martine in the holding cell. "So," Ken started. "Why this guy? What makes you want to question Lamar's tip?"

Curious about the convict's connections to German friends, Martine tried to justify her decision without revealing the source of her real promptings. "Money. I'm following the money."

Monotonous buzzers sounded as the next prisoner approached. As the guards led the prisoner in the room, Ken introduced Ratchet to Martine.

"Hey, babe, what's up?" Ratchet licked his lips with obscene nuances.

"We've got some questions for you, Ratchet," Ken squared his shoulders at the big thug. "Why don't you sit down?"

"Yeah? Why don't I just sit on you right here, Blondie?" Ratchet humped the chair like a dog.

"Sit down, Ratchet," Ken snapped at the brawny convict.

Curious about Lamar's description of Ratchet, she studied him like a lab smear. Checking the con's left arm for signs of the tattooed insignia of a Nazi rune, Martine could see part of the tattoo was exposed below his orange sleeve. "Actually, we just want to talk to you about some of your friends." Martine motioned to his black-inked tattoo.

"I don't have any friends in here." Ratchet's thin lips stretched slightly as he snickered.

"Not here. The ones on the outside," Ken corrected the brazen con.

"I don't have any friends on the outside either." Ratchet rocked back in his chair and sneered. Nodding his bald scalp, the skinhead's defiant character exuded arrogance.

"Really? Not what I hear. I can't help but notice that you get so many visitors they have to do roll call," Ken chuckled.

"That's funny. I'll listen to your jokes, but that's it," turning his round face sideways, Ratchet huffed.

"What's funny," Ken said, "is your connection to a couple guys named Jacob and Steve. Know where we can find them?"

"Sure, let me take you to them right now," Ratchet retorted sarcastically.

"It doesn't work that way," Ken mimicked the cynical response. "Maybe for the right information we can help arrange a conjugal with your girlfriend."

"I'd rather have one with her." Ratchet gave Martine a creepy smile.

"You'd have better luck trying to get it on with the warden." Martine rolled her eyes up in disgust.

"Thanks for the tip, but he's not my type."

"You have a type?" Martine antagonized the crude bully.

"All right, Ratchet, we came to get some answers. If you don't want to talk we'll make sure everyone knows that all the information we do get today came from your dirty mouth," Ken's voice amplified.

"Nah, the last time I squealed on anyone it was snowing in here," nodding confidently, Ratchet reveled in his haughtiness. "I'm not giving anything up to you pigs." Standing up to leave, the six-foot-three convict towered over Martine.

"Sit down," Ken ordered. "Well, then I guess we came to take and not give."

Setting himself back in his chair, Ratchet said, "That's right. Unless you're giving her away I got no use for any of your shit." While using his tongue to lick his lips, Ratchet made provocative gestures near his groin area with his cuffed hands.

Martine's patience waned. "Listen, buddy, I've about had it with your innuendos. You couldn't turn a nymphomaniac on. You make another pass at me and you'll see some real justice."

"Yeah." He gave her a depraved look. "How's that? I thought you were the good cop. I thought you wanted to show me your goods."

"She's not here to entertain you. She's a lawyer," Ken disclosed. "She's a prosecutor we brought here just in case you wanted to talk. And, this is as good as it gets for you. You can talk to her, or me."

Eyeing the pen Martine had positioned in her hand, Ratchet's ominous voice tried to intimidate Ken, "Are you wearing contacts?"

Ken replied, "Why?"

Reeking of bad breath, Ratchet badgered Ken, "Makes it a little harder to poke your eye out, that's all."

Pissed-off at the sexual insinuations and sweaty predator sitting across the table from her, Martine's corseted anger let loose, "So, if you want to start talking, we can start dealing some favors. Otherwise, you're gonna stay here and rot. Rot like a squid on the beach. Oh, they won't call you Ratchet, they'll call you rat."

Dumfounded, the slack-jawed brute stuttered slightly, "I'm no . . . no rat. You better not set me up. What . . . what privileges?"

Crimson from elevated blood pressure, Martine answered, "How 'bout a legitimate conjugal visit and some legal assistance." Rooting the truth out, Martine continued, "Do you want to get out of here bad enough that you're willing to help us find what we're looking for?" Pausing for his acceptance, Martine waited for a firm nod from the big-framed con. "It could go a long way for you if you lead us to solving a crime or two. We can always use some of your special skills on the inside and outside."

Staring back at Martine, Ratchet looked down at the crucifix she wore around her neck and said, "You pray to your God today?" Scoffing, he continued to mock her, "What you pray for, lady?"

"I prayed for patience." Martine instinctively grasped the gold cross with her left hand. "Lucky for you, Ratchet. Cause if I had prayed for strength you'd have a black eye by now. So, do you want to talk, or not?"

Acting curious, Ratchet nodded in agreement. "Maybe you could use my help. So, you say she can do some negotiating for me?" Ratchet looked at Ken. "It won't be safe in here if I talk."

"Yeah, that's what I mean. First we gotta know what you know."

"Don't trick me, man. I'm not talking unless I get some real legal representation."

"Don't waste any more of our time. It already looks like you've been here too long," Ken warned. "We'll see if you earn any legal advice from us."

Jotting down the number ten, Martine turned her notepad around for Ratchet to view it, "Let's see if we can change this number to a three. That's what we can do for you at your parole hearing." Straight-faced, she stared at convict number 895467.

"You're right." Ratchet's beady eyes focused on Martine. "I don't care enough about these people to even kill them. They've got some really crazy ideas."

"Good, start talking," Ken demanded.

"What do you want to know?"

Ken asked, "Who were you stealing the guns and ammo for?"

"For myself."

"I'm curious about your tattoo." Martine pointed to the black-inked Nazi rune. "Tell me what it means."

"It stands for honor and loyalty." flashing his tattoo, he flaunted his integrity.

"Honor and loyalty to whom?" Ken probed with bolder questions.

"The cause," Ratchet answered proudly.

"Cut to the chase," Ken accelerated the pace. "What cause?"

"An army of select men," Ratchet answered.

Ken fired his next question, "Selected for what?"

"Selected for protecting the world from alien invasions."

"You're a UFO nut?" Ken looked perplexed.

"Oh yeah," Ratchet said sarcastically. "No. Not that kind of alien invasion, you fool."

"Indulge us." Martine tried to look sincere.

Ratchets demeanor stiffened. "From people that don't have any brains. People that want to take what is really ours."

Ken articulated the next question, "Explain what these people you refer to want to accomplish."

"They want a powerful government that will protect our rights. They will give us back 'white power' and remove the alien's."

Ken rubbed his head in confusion, "You're part of a white supremacy movement?"

"No," Ratchet stated defiantly. "We just want what is ours. We just want illegal aliens to give us back what is ours. We want a powerful government that no one will mess with."

Martine shook her head negatively and barged into the conversation, "That's a euphemism for socialism, or a nice way to describe big brother government."

"I've said all I know," Ratchet stopped for a second. "Now you do what you promised."

Ken disagreed, "You haven't given us anything we can use."

Martine added, "We want to know who you were working for."

Belligerent, Ratchet argued, "I told you. I work for myself."

"You're a dealer, Ratchet. You have clients. Or, should I say loyal supporters? You even have a cause," Ken sounded irked.

"Alleged," Ratchet corrected Ken. "I'm an alleged dealer."

"Right. Let's talk about your alleged dealings with drugs and guns." Ken's voice vibrated in the chamber, "For the record, who are you allegedly working for?"

"I don't know what you're talking about. I'm in here because I got busted driving a truckload of guns. That's it," Ratchet started looking more like a colorless corps as the blood drained from his shaved head. "I didn't even know there were guns in the truck."

"Who were you delivering them to?" Ken's forceful voice pushed.

Using psychology, Martine injected her own strategy, "You know what I think? I think you were set-up."

"Yeah," Ratchet focused on her. "I know I was set-up by some cop sting."

"No, Ratchet," she said with confidence. "You were set-up by the guys that you were working for. I bet you already did a lot of dealing for them and they set you up."

Defensive, Ratchet countered, "Why would they do that?"

"Because you're as good as gone now," she paused and gave him a quizzical look. "That is if you're in here for ten years. They probably never even paid you. You kept some secret oath which protected them and let you take the rap."

Dropping his head forward, the big con looked like he lost all the wind in his sail. With his eyes closed he shook his head. "No way. No way."

"Let me articulate," Martine said, "unless you work for free, where's the big money they promised?"

Falling like Goliath, the giant man spilled everything he knew. He finished with, "Robin Steal and Schultzy are probably the same person. Steve and Jacob work for Schultzy. I know they had to report to someone. Too stupid to figure anything out for themselves."

Chapter 39

Confused by the bizarre request Jolene made, Mahoney contemplated how he was going to make good on his promise. How did he get coerced into translating German . . . and taking them out to dinner? Either way, progress was disappointing thus far. Looking at something was better than taking his frustrations out on a young inexperienced agent.

Entrusted with the historic looking photo and article gave him an idea. Dialing his desk phone he let it ring till his buddy Teddy answered. Hearing his friend's voice, Mahoney began, "Hey Teddy, how's it going on your side of the tracks?"

"It's good, Mahoney," came a heavy British accent. "Staying out of trouble?"

"Oh, yeah," returned Mahoney's masculine drawl.

"Do you wish to get in on the Friday poker tournament?" Teddy invited with his formal speech pattern.

"Yeah, I'm thinking about it."

"Counting you in," was Teddy's ridged reply.

"Good. Hey, how are you at translating a little German?"

"German? What kinda German?"

"I'm thinking the 1933 kind of German."

"Yes. I can do that," Teddy replied.

"How 'bout I fax over a rather lengthy article," Mahoney suggested. "You might call this a rush job."

"Then I'll put my teaching assistants on it straight away. They know who needs a little extra credit. Don't worry, Mahoney, I'll check the work myself," came Teddy's stilted answer.

"Need it today . . . is that going to be a problem?"

"I should say not," Teddy clarified with absolute certainty. "What are history professors for?"

Mahoney chuckled at his friend's dry sense of humor, and attempt at humility. Few people knew that Teddy was a working philanthropist. Teaching history was his passion, not his livelihood.

Wealthy beyond his needs, he taught college graduates because he liked choosing his own endowment projects and overseeing the entire program. Teddy only appeared to be stuffy and well-mannered. His Masquerade as a History professor let him blend in anywhere. Appearing more like a pauper than a prince, he protected his wealth and privacy. Unwilling to jeopardize his freedoms he devised a solitary role and played it like an actor.

Without his wealth in jeopardy, Teddy felt safe from shysters' thieves and embezzlers. Eccentric in nature, he lived like a recluse except for his tight circle of buddies.

Teddy and Mahoney enjoyed the intellectual stimulation of shared crime solving challenges and historical debates. Both were brilliant and opinionated men—though loyal to their friendship.

Gravitating to each other was natural after they met four years ago. Seeking advanced knowledge in Forensic Science, they met in New York during a crime solving convention. Equally matched, they were the only two participants that properly identified the perpetrator in a real-life crime scenario.

John Mahoney felt honored to have a male companion like Teddy. Neither had ever made a better friend.

Chapter 40

Curled up on a single-sized mattress, Maria pretended to be asleep when she heard her prison door unlock. Facing the wall, she hid her open eyes from the people that held her captive inside a concrete cell. Ignoring the sound of the creaky door as it opened, she controlled her fear and stayed still.

Hearing the door lock noisily behind them, she played possum as the two men approached her. Feeling their presence next to her body, she closed her eyes and pleaded silently for a miracle.

"Wake up sleeping beauty." Gruff sounding, the younger man poked her in the back with a dull prod, "It's your turn to meet the doctor."

Remaining quiet, Maria searched her mind for a suitable reaction. Frozen in trepidation, she stalled and disregarded the nudge.

"Get up!" he shouted louder, as he jabbed her harder in the back. "We're moving you out of here."

"Du wirst nur bei Lieferung bezahlt," the older man grumbled in a guttural voice.

"Speak English," the younger man ordered. "You're in America now. I know I get paid on delivery, and I delivered her just the way you said."

"Stop, Steve," the foreign man snapped, using a thick European accent. "Put gun away, fool. No bruises. No pay damaged goods."

Pretending to be aroused from a deep sleep, Maria turned over to face the two men. Propping herself on her bent elbow, she yawned nonchalantly, "Where am I?"

"You're not in Kansas anymore, Dorothy," Steve answered. "Now be a good little girl and you won't get hurt," he said smugly.

"Who are you?" Maria demanded. "What do you want with me?"

"You may see, my beauty," Jacob annunciated in broken English. "You be best one," he said with arrogance. "You take meds." Handing Maria some pills, he motioned to her in sign language to gulp them down.

"I'm not taking anything from you," Maria said defiantly. "I don't need meds. Looks like you do though."

Jacob reached his hand to grab her. "Well, I use something stronger then."

"Put your hand down, Jacob." Steve knocked his partner's arm down. "I'll take care of this. Chill."

Maria flinched from the skirmish. "Do I get a phone call in this prison?" Maria fired.

"No." Steve stopped in the middle of his sentence. Taking the meds from Jacob, he swaggered up to Maria. "Phones don't work here and you don't get to e-mail either. How's that, smarty pants?"

Smacking Steve's hand as hard as she could, Maria caused the pills to fly from his hand. "I'm not taking those. I don't care what they're for," Maria rebuffed.

Steve picked the medications off the floor and huffed, "ooooooo-kay, little girl, we'll see about that." Walking up to her, he used his hand to hook the back of her neck and yank her close. "You're going to change your attitude, take these pills, and come with us like a good little girl." Relaxing his grip, he let her pull away.

"The hell I am," Maria snapped. "I'm not going anywhere with you or your warped personality."

"Wie viele hast du haben?" Jacob's angry face stared at Steve.

"English. I said English." Steve snapped his head in disapproval.

Conceding, Jacob slowly repeated his words in English, "I said, how many do you have?"

Looking down at his open hand, Steve answered, "I have three of them. Just like the others had. Is that good enough for you?"

"Nein . . . Nein . . . Nein, she need more."

"Don't say no to me, you slug." Steve exhaled hard. "She'll be just fine. I can handle her all by myself," he replied in a flippant voice. "Give me her new outfit," Steve commanded as he reached his arm back to Jacob.

Pulling a small bundle of clothing from his jacket pocket, Jacob muttered, "Du warst nachlassig."

"What did you say to me?" Steve clenched his lips in disapproval.

"I say you were sloppy," Jacob retorted snidely.

"We'll see about that," Steve said as he shook the crumpled garment out. "Here's a little present for you, princess," Steve said, handing her a hospital gown. "Change into this. Now!"

"No!" Maria yelled. "You can change your attitude and let me out of here."

Jacob's callused voice shot back, "I dress you then."

Sounding amused at her feisty stance, Steve slowly chuckled and tried to push the pills in her mouth. "I'm telling you to take these now, or I'll let Jacob dress you. The Doctor's waiting."

"What are you guys?" Maria tossed her head to the side, avoiding the pills. "Are you terrorists?"

Steve shoved a pill in her mouth, "Swallow you little bitch."

Maria spit it out as hard as she could, hitting him in the eye with it. "Phew," she spat. "You, filthy perverts."

"You'll want these pills. They're your new friends. It will hurt a lot less and go much faster if you take them," Steve cautioned her. "You're going to do what I say or Jacob here is going to help me, and he has something that works every time."

"First tell me what you're going to do to me after I take the pills," Maria negotiated.

"Just a medical exam," Steve answered. "Don't worry, you might even like it."

Threatened by the prospects of strange procedures and scary men, Maria tried to bargain for more time, "I'll take the pills if you let me get dressed in privacy."

"Yes," Jacob nodded, looking at Steve for approval. Unlocking the secured door, Jacob exited the small chamber. "Hau ab!" he ordered.

"What are you saying, you kraut?"

"I say, get out," Jacob bellowed.

Conceding, Steve backed towards the door, "I'll be right back. We'll make sure the doc's ready for you."

"Fine," Maria said sarcastically.

Winking a beady eye, Steve hassled Maria again, "I bet you are fine."

Chapter 41

Entering the restaurant through double-glass doors, Jolene eyed Mahoney seated in a booth on the window-wall.

Sliding out of the booth, Mahoney greeted her and Martine as they approached. Familiar with the restaurant, Jolene felt comfortable in the neutral surroundings. At least as relaxed as was permitted given the circumstances of the dinner meeting.

Nervous and humiliated, she smiled meekly. Martine's request for an expedient interpretation of a German writing came across as extremely presumptuous. Dreading what her boss was going to say, she anticipated being removed from the case that she was so focused on. That wasn't the worst though. How bad would he shame her older sister? Fearing Martine's persecution, she wished she had brought a couple of files they could talk about.

Standing next to the table, Mahoney shook both their hands. "Welcome ladies. I know this isn't the fanciest restaurant, but it's close to the office and serves hot food." Mahoney directed them to sit across from him.

Sliding in first, Jolene allowed her sister the aisle seat. "Thank you, sir. We both could use a little dinner and appreciate the invitation," Jolene said with a cheery grin.

Smiling, Martine added, "Yes, Mr. Mahoney, it's also good to meet again. I've been looking forward to this all afternoon."

Mahoney continued, "This is a bit awkward for me to say. I must admit I was caught off guard and surprised by your recent request. Seemed a little off-the-wall to me."

Without pause, Jolene broke-in, "May we explain, sir? I'm sure we can discuss this and manage to extract the information that Martine felt would be advantageous to the case. We really hope we didn't inconvenience you."

Looking across the table at Jolene, Mahoney sounded a little patronizing, "That's nice, now that I succeeded in getting it done in record time. I want to say that what I've read so far is unorthodox. I guess now you've got my curiosity and I deserve an explanation as to how this has anything to do with Arizona and surrounding areas? Actually, I have more questions than I can count and want to know where you are going with this." Securing a handful of papers from his briefcase, he dramatically dropped them on his placemat. "Here is the English translation you requested." Gesturing with his eyes he signaled Martine for a reaction.

Appearing timid, Martine aimed her eyes back at Mahoney as she eagerly reached for the pile of papers.

Paralyzed by the awkward moment, Jolene observed their every move. Wishing it was possible to disappear—she remained silent, and admired her sister's composure.

Moving the papers close enough to read, Martine asked, "Do you mind if I take a look, Mr. Mahoney?"

Remaining stone-faced, he replied, "No, of course not. Please call me John. May I call you Martine?"

"Yes . . . yes, of course," Martine mumbled.

"Excuse me a moment," Martine said. "I'm going to read this if you two don't mind. You can order me the same thing you're having Jolene. I don't feel like reading a menu at this moment." Handing Jolene her menu, Martine glanced back and forth at them. "Okay?"

"Go right ahead," he said.

Pretending she was hungry, Jolene hid behind her menu.

Introducing herself as Tara, the short twenty-something server approached their table and asked, "Are you ready to order?" Holding her pen in a writing position she waited for a response.

"I'm ready to order when you ladies are," Mahoney answered.

"How's the fish special?" Jolene asked.

Tara smiled politely and said, "The Tilapia is our popular dish. The southwest relish has been written-up in magazines. I can put it on the side if you wish."

"We'll both have the special, please," Jolene said.

"I'll have the prime, medium-rare," Mahoney added.

After Jolene finished ordering the entrees and sides, she discussed her files with Mahoney while her sister finished reading the German newspaper article.

Clearing his throat, Mahoney studied Martine as she set the papers down on her placemat. "Now can you explain the point of this article to us? Oh, and don't leave anything out, including what you've been doing for two days. I just realized you've been a little mysterious and I would appreciate knowing what you know."

"It's not that I know something specific, nor am I withholding information. I do believe there is a suspicious amount of paraphernalia that may provide useful information."

Mahoney leaned forward and whispered, "Tell me everything, from the top."

"Alright then," Martine said cautiously. "Since I just read the article, I can't say for sure what this means. Let me start with what I've been doing. After I reviewed a list of missing persons from case files that were closed, I found one file that was sketchy at best and barely investigated. Reading the report, I found no one ever followed-up with the caller, so I contacted her. When I was interviewing her she disclosed a hidden room her grandson used with his cousin. It appears her grandson had befriended the missing girl. With her permission I inspected the room."

"I'm listening. Did you find some incriminating evidence? I mean besides this photo?" Mahoney asked.

Plunking down a basket of warm dinner rolls, Tara interrupted, "Your meals will be out shortly—can I get you anything else right now?"

"No, we're fine. Thank you," Mahoney dismissed the waitress.

After Tara departed, Martine continued, "Inside the room I noticed they had acquired a multitude of strange possessions. The items that alarmed me the most were displayed around the photo, the same photo found in this article. It is the exact same photo. Naturally I wanted to know more, it could be significant. Because of these unusual items, I felt it was imperative to know why these boys had constructed what looked like a primitive shrine around this photo."

"Hmmm . . ., you have been busy. However, I've read this article and still don't get any connection. Forget that it happened over seventy years ago," he paused and smiled politely before continuing, "I admit, it is a fascinating bit of history I suspect few are aware of, but it hardly seems appropriate for this particular case. I don't feel you're staying focused on why I'm using you. I think it's time we stick to the facts and you start working directly with me," Mahoney rebuffed.

With a thoughtful nod, Martine replied, "Yes. That would be an ideal situation. I suggest it won't be practical to follow me around though."

"Follow you around? Where?" Mahoney questioned.

"I intend to locate these guys and interview them. I find it's better to go alone and appear less intimidating when interviewing suspects. You'd be noticeable and threatening," Martine sounded emphatic.

"Why are you so intent on finding these individuals? I found nothing in this article that could help us," Mahoney responded quickly.

Desperate to help her sister, Jolene shifted her weight on the cushioned seat, controlling the urge to speak-out. Guarding the family secret was a promise Jolene had made to Martine. Aware that sharing this knowledge would work against Martine and her efforts, Jolene stayed quiet. Picking up the basket of fresh rolls, Jolene offered Mahoney and Martine to take their rolls first, "Checkout these rolls, they're fantastic." Passing the basket around, she hoped the distraction would lower the tension that was building.

Jolene feared that when people found out her sister received strong impressions or insights that guided her, they would discredit all her other talents. Jolene felt helpless and wanted to defend her sister's honor even though nothing seemed logical or made any sense at this moment.

"As far as why I am interested in these boys, they are linked to a missing girl. Since no one ever investigated them, it is time we check them out," Martine replied vigorously. "They're clearly unfinished business."

Wishing the meals would arrive, Jolene moved all the papers out of the way and injected herself into the conversation, "We've run a preliminary background check on these two boys, sir, and haven't turned-up anything."

"That doesn't surprise me," Mahoney said.

"I mean it's more like they don't exist," Jolene countered.

Delivering hot plates of food, Tara smiled and stood back. "Can I get you anything else?"

"No, it looks great." Mahoney reviewed his beef entrée.

Shaking her head, Martine added, "No, I'm good."

Surveying her fish special, Jolene said, "I'm good too. Thank you." Jolene watched Tara leave and commented, "Boy does this look great. I bet you're both hungry like me."

Martine was about to take her first bite of food when she posed a question to John Mahoney, "Are you familiar with Adolph Hitler's occult practices?"

"No madam I'm not. Are you saying you are?" Mahoney returned.

Cutting her potato open, Martine replied, "Well, I wasn't there, but I do know he was obsessed with astrology and mystics. Not only Hitler, but his entire inner circle had ties to the occult. As a matter of fact the foundation of his 'new religious order' centered on the lost continent of Atlantis," Martine stated with certainty.

Chewing on a mouthful of medium-rare prime rib, Mahoney offered his observation, "I have a feeling you've studied World War II, Martine. That doesn't interest most people."

"I wouldn't say I've had an interest in Hitler or war, but I do study religion, and World War II was very faith driven. Martine challenged her new boss, "As a matter of fact World War II was the result of a real life drama that started with the book of Genesis. You probably knew that though, didn't you?"

Stabbing another chunk of beef with his fork, Mahoney extended a quizzical glance towards Jolene before replying, "This I didn't know. How 'bout you explain that to us."

Listening like a word receptacle, Jolene finally weighed-in, "Wow, I thought Genesis was written thousands of years ago."

"It was, Jolene, I'd love to hear your sister's explanation though." Pointing his empty fork at Martine, he said, "Please continue."

"In Genesis, the sons of God saw how beautiful the daughters of man were and they took as many as they wanted for their wives. Anyway, they cohabitated, bore sons, and thus were born the heroes of old, giants, and the men of renown. Then when God saw how wicked man became he regretted his creation and sent a flood to wipe them all out," Martine paused to take a bite of her fish.

Chuckling, with his head rocking back-and-forth in amusement, Mahoney exclaimed, "Wow, I didn't really know that was in the Bible, but what does that have to do with Nazi's anyway?"

"Well, Hitler's occult practices were a perversion of ancient pagan world beliefs. Hitler and his followers were convinced that the priests that survived the flood, like Noah did, were descendents of the original race of Aryan God Men. The land that the 'God like men' inhabited was Atlantis."

Mahoney interrupted, "You must believe in Atlantis."

"It doesn't matter if I believe in Atlantis—Hitler did," Martine corrected him.

"Touché." Grinning, Mahoney said, "Please go on."

"This race of 'Super Men' lost their powers by mating with mere humans. Hitler's inner circle, headed by Himmler, believed that the pure Aryan blood was being contaminated by so called 'inferior blood.' They believed it was possible to recreate this race and reclaim their powers." Adding salt and pepper to her potato, Martine looked up at her audience.

Staring at Martine with his mouth full of food, Mahoney swallowed and said, "Go on."

"Well, that was the foundation of his religion and purpose behind his evil crusade to eliminate foreign bloodlines and religions. He hated the Jews because they were God's chosen people. Right?"

"Yeah, that sounds right," Mahoney said as he cleared his throat.

Poking at her vegetables, Martine paused. "The food is great here. It's better than just hot."

"I'm glad you're enjoying your meal, I don't mean to keep interrupting your dinner, but can you continue?" Mahoney looked curious.

"As I recall, Hitler's agenda included eliminating any race that did not meet the characteristics of his Aryan Super Beings. Hitler believed he was taking out the trash, or cleaning up the garbage left in the world." Martine breathed deep, "Shall I go on?"

Without any hesitation Mahoney replied, "Please do, I'm fascinated."

"Well, Himmler took charge and instigated the search for the missing Aryan race to prove that the German people were direct descendants. I think that was accomplished in the Himalayas of Tibet, where they traced the ancestors of the Atlantian priests that escaped death during the flood. That's where, I believe, they uncovered the divine characteristics of the lost Aryan race. Himmler was convinced these priests were the descendents of God or Gods."

"When the heck did he do all that?" Mahoney interrupted.

"I think that was around 1930. He found what he was looking for. I read somewhere that he called it the Holy Grail, and with new arrogance he was going to prove that to the world through domination."

"Are you sure about that?" Jolene questioned.

"Yes, I'm very sure. They knew the characteristics of the 'True Aryan' people included; blonde hair, blue eyes, generally tall, strong body physiques, unique skeletal measurements, no Jewish ancestry, and absolutely no imperfections. To prove their superiority, Hitler's occult-driven inner circle explored many religions that could help support their madness. They then borrowed any belief that they could adapt to the Aryan cause. This was the Nazi interpretation of ancient occult law that dated back thousands of years." Martine stopped again for another bite of food.

Jolene commented, "That's really interesting. I never knew any of that about Hitler."

"Yeah, and it gets worse," she continued, "according to this German article that you just got translated, he wanted a master race with an army of these 'Super Men' to take over Europe and then the world. Hitler and his inner circle devised a program to make 'Aryan Super Men' through selective breeding programs, with Hitler as the 'High Priest' and ruler." Martine paused to eat.

Mahoney sat motionless as Martine tried to finish her meal. Watching her closely as she devoured her food, he challenged her, "I don't remember any of this. I find it interesting unless it's just your interpretation of those historical events."

Martine answered after swallowing more food, "No these are facts."

Scratching at his neck, Mahoney said, "Well there seems to be more to you than meets the eyes."

"Thank you," she said. "I think."

Mahoney signaled the waitress for a refill on his drink. "How did Hitler breed an Aryan army? How come I've never heard of this before?"

"Let me show you," Martine offered.

Reaching for the papers that didn't seem important to John Mahoney an hour ago, she turned the picture in his direction. "Look at this photo. Those men from left to right are: General Hans Frank, SA Commander Ernst Roehm, SS Commander Heinrich Himmler, Commander of the Prussian Gestapo Hermann Goering, and Himmler's Lieutenant Reinhard Heydrich. So what's unique about the picture?"

Jolene and Mahoney both answered in stereo, "I don't know."

Admiring her sister's knowledge and tact with her boss, Jolene asked, "Do you know?"

With captive skeptics listening to her, Martine continued, "These five men were very powerful during the short twelve year reign of the 3rd Reich, but they hardly got along, and they never posed for photos like this."

Jolene looked at the photo and commented, "I give up, what did the article say? I haven't read it yet."

Martine explained, "The article was announcing the introduction of RUSHA, which stands for Race and Resettlement Central Office. Basically, they're calling German women to fulfill their primary task of procreating. Thirty-million German women were asked to report to RUSHA for genetic screening. Both married and unmarried women are being called to produce racially pure children for the future of the Third Reich. They will be honored appropriately based on the number of children they give birth to. It's their patriotic duty to have four or more genetically pure offspring. They're also announcing it will be a criminal offense to terminate an unwanted pregnancy. All unwed mothers will be provided care and housing compliments of the Third Reich. Well, that is my take on the article anyways," Martine finished.

Mahoney responded, "Yep, that's about right, Martine. I pretty much got the same thing out of the script you so eloquently summarized. I'm curious how this paper could help the FBI, more than seventy years later?"

Retrieving the pages, Martine recited one of the sentences, "Fornication under the consent of King?"

Mahoney scoffed, "Yeah, and what is your point?"

Defusing Mahoney's objection, Martine explained, "That's what the origin of the word F U C K came from."

Jolene blinked in disbelief. "You're kidding, when was that?"

"Probably around fifteen-hundred-something," Martine answered.

Mahoney demonstrated doubt with a slight chuckle. "Are you sure?"

"Oh, yeah. Like snakes ready to strike, this was their big move—with no questions asked."

Shaking his head in disbelief, Mahoney questioned Martine again, "What does this have to do with our case? Do you have more than this?"

"Ummm . . .," Martine said swallowing water. "No. Not yet, but I will. I'm now even more convinced there needs to be more explored in regards to this specific missing girl's case. I know I've got a lot more questions for Della and I want to revisit all the profiles on all the missing girls. They may only appear to be random abductions."

"Martine, I'd like to go through that process with you personally tomorrow morning. Let's say eight A.M. I'll bring the gourmet coffee and Danish. I want to see what you are hedging on, or eliminate the far-fetched theory brewing in your head," Mahoney finished with a tight smile.

Jolene breathed a sigh of relief. "Alright, sir, we'll be in the office bright and early. Thank you so much for dinner." "Yes, John, thank you for dinner and your complete cooperation in getting this transcribed in English for me. I do have a few more German writings and objects to decipher . . . if you would be able to help again?"

Walking towards the restaurant door, Jolene felt liberated that the stressful meeting ended amicably. Satisfied at how her sister had managed to handle Mahoney, she was energized. Martine's services weren't to be terminated for the time being.

Anxious to be alone with Martine and get her impressions, Jolene formulated a string of questions. Inspired by her sister's boldness and tenacity she was motivated for the first time in four days. She wasn't known for being insecure—however she'd never been invited to a private dinner meeting with her boss . . . make that angry boss.

Martine was still busy checking her voice mail messages as they drove away. Testing the water when she was finished, Jolene asked, "That went well—didn't it?"

"Oh yeah, like waking up a hibernating black bear," Martine emphasized BEAR.

"What in the world does that mean?" Jolene returned.

"He's hairy, hungry, pushy, and irritable. What else could I mean? However, that is the frustration I'm accustomed to when working on a case of this complexity."

Chapter 42

Reading her journal before entering a deep sleep, Martine reflected on the last twenty-four hours. Recalling the dream from the night before, she pondered the meaning of the bear, lion, and wolf. Acquainted with the significance of these animal spirits, she prayed from her heart that she would be given the memory and recognition to correlate their meaning to the solving of this case.

Connecting the information she gathered in her prison interrogations and dinner meeting with John Mahoney was equally complex and in need of clarification. Focused on the need for more wisdom, and understanding, Martine used her faith to ask for immediate assistance from the highest realms of enlightenment. Knowing that if she didn't evoke heavenly realms of truth, love, and understanding, her human abilities would remain limited. Without help from Spirit, she would not have a greater advantage over the darkness that controlled the evil intentions behind these crimes—deplorable crimes against the innocence of young women.

Before nodding off to sleep, she asked to be placed in service to God's divine design and requested that every girl currently held in danger be protected by ministering angels. Confident that her prayers were heard, she visualized legions of angels descending from above as they zoomed in on their newly appointed wards.

Becoming visible in her spirit form, Martine found herself standing alone on a huge Mesa surrounded only by sparse foliage, unproductive land, and rocky soil. Setting down behind her was a bright orange sun that illuminated the canyon walls of a deep ravine. Looking east along the cavernous wall, she spotted the primitive cliff dwellings of an ancient people. Familiar with the adobe-style homes found in cliff walls, she realized her location was on the far side of Cliff Palace at Mesa Verde National Park.

Acting like a huge spotlight, the sun's colored rays highlighted the handmade bricks that still formed the abandoned homes of an ancient civilization housed inside a huge alcove. With her location established, Martine knew she was standing near the Four-Corners in the state of Colorado. Having frequented Mesa Verde National Park, she became instantly aware that the Colorado plateau she occupied was home to an ancestral people call Anasazi.

Anasazi is Navajo for "Ancient Ones," and considered a sacred culture, a culture that has been carefully preserved at Mesa Verde National Park. Home to the ancient Anasazi Indians, Mesa Verde's protected villages and land were suspected for guarding a multidimensional gateway to higher realms. As a child, Martine, like millions of other curious tourists, had visited Mesa Verde to explore for herself this unexplained wonder.

Hearing the shaking of beads and rhythmic chanting of a single man's voice, Martine looked up to the sky to see a primitive looking Indian walk towards her and the open star gate that separated them. Shaped like a single arched doorway, the opening became more pronounced the closer the ancient Indian came to its entrance. As the dark-skinned man stepped through the threshold of the etheric opening, she saw steps form from the clouds as he descended down to her place on the barren mesa.

Staying still in the presence of the unearthly visitor, Martine observed every possible detail in an effort to identify her new acquaintance. Diagnosing him like a forensic specialist, she surmised he was Pueblo because of his simple clothing and the location he chose to appear. He must be wise because of the props he carried and the painted symbols he wore.

"Don't you know me?" Round faced with aging wrinkles and pronounced cheek bones, the elderly man asked.

"No. I don't know you," Martine answered as she admired the stately feathers of a simple eagle headdress. "I cannot know who you truly are until you tell me what you do."

"First we pray, then I show you," he said in broken English. Dancing in a small circle, the old Indian chanted in a monotone voice and shook his rattle like a tambourine. In his native tongue he sang in a slow tempo as he performed a spiritual medicine dance.

Acquainted with Native American folklores, she knew that holy rituals required special sounds and song to invoke the healing power of spirit. Native American traditions, spanning from south-west America to the Arctic Circle, date back nearly ten-thousand years, offering a glimpse into a varied world of religious beliefs, symbols, history, and sacred objects.

Steadily shaking his rattle, the Medicine Man maintained a monotonous rhythmic pattern as he sang and used his healing stick in a circular motion around Martine's head. Having read about Shamanistic healing practices, she stayed still as he performed the ceremonial rite with his symbolic motifs.

Stopping after minutes of prayer, he continued, "It is the hope of Great Spirit to transform the *primitive predatory will* into the *will of love*." Staring at her with warm brown eyes, he reached into his sacred pouch and sprinkled the fine powder of corn pollen on Martine's head.

Considered a powerful element, Martine could receive no stronger gift than this ceremonial blessing.

"Bless you, daughter," the soft-spoken man said. "Sky dance is pathway, a passage into endeavor few can go. You have talents to sway outcomes."

Transfixed by the conviction in his voice and the sound of authority that resonated in his authentic dialect, Martine blinked with astonishment. "Me? I can sway any outcome?"

"Yes. You, Daughter of Sky," the small old man said as he waved his hand across the fading sunset's horizon.

"What do they call you?" she asked. "Your clothing is rich." Martine pointed to the buckskin skirting decorated with painted pictures, feathers, and beading.

Nodding his dark-haired head, the aborigine looking man, beautified in smatterings of white body paint on his face and arms, removed one of his necklaces. "I bring gift from other side of Sipapu."

"Sipapu?" Martine exclaimed in excitement, knowing that Sipapu was considered the revered portal from which the Hopi's ancient ancestors first emerged into this world.

"Yes," the dignified man answered in confidence. Lifting a leather necklace off his shoulders and over his chin-length hair that spiked straight-out like a porcupine, he announced, "I, Tao. I gift you powerful medicine." Placing the strap over her head, he let the necklace drop as he released his grip on the animal-hide pouch that hung from the leathery cord. "It come to pass that the old ones convey to you the way of altering dark and evil."

Touching the pouch that hung from her neck, Martine accepted the gift. "Thank you."

Raising his arms in the air, Tao made a soulful moaning sound as he once more chanted incantations in his native tongue. Taking some feathers that hung from his belted waist, he waved the plumes up and down the front of Martine's body, projecting his prayerful offering to the universe. Mumbling under his breath in a faster tempo, he kept the words secret as required in Indian ceremonies.

Watching Tao's movements, Martine deduced he was performing another ritualistic ceremony. "To what do I owe this honor?" she asked.

"Great Creator Spirit send special medicine for you, Daughter," Tao replied. "Medicine powerful, like when people walk on earth with Spirit." Changing his voice to a high-pitched falsetto, he recited his words succinctly giving emphasis to certain syllables. Like a formulated recipe, he strictly adhered to wording and procedure.

Ethereally progressing in the knowledge of Native American culture, Martine knew that combining proper prayers, plants, and animal spirits affected the procurement of each desired spirit-helping formula. Standing still for the private ceremony, she observed every unique detail that only she would be privy to.

Adorned in feathers and painted drawings of birds on his clothing, Tao's decor indicated his ability to fly. Martine understood these symbolisms represented the origins of his unearthly spiritual gifts and talents. His knowledge and guidance was deemed from another more advanced realm.

Breaking from the musical mantra, he explained the purpose of the Feather Blessing, "It a balance. When you move beyond the *primitive predatory will* to *will of love*, it natural to no longer be comfortable with predatory nature of life in realm you live in." Opening the pouch that hung around Martine's neck, the Shaman held it out for her to see inside, "This protection medicine. You move to higher existence."

Nodding, Martine acknowledged the gift and breathed deep in anticipation. Peering into the opened bag, she saw a mound of special herbs and spices. Inhaling the intoxicating scent of the earthly blend, Martine accepted the worldly properties that would serve her after the ceremony was complete. "Ummm . . .," she exhaled.

"The *will of love* ask you to love the children . . . the innocent children you can save." Gesturing with his open hand, the medicine man said, "Now I give special medicine from White Wolf."

Walking out of a pallid mist—came a magnificent white wolf. Large and majestic by every standard known to Martine, she gasped at the amazing sight. Feeling a slight tug on her arm, she glanced briefly at the Indian who gestured with his chin to a nearby campfire. "What is her name?" Martine asked her mentor as she kept pace with his steps. Drawn to the majesty and beauty of this white wolf, she kept her eyes on the animal as it accompanied them to the campsite.

"She Grace." The medicine man summoned the wolf to sit between them. "I tell story of people." He took a stick lying on the ground next to him and drew a rudimentary picture in the sand. Speaking slowly, he illustrated his tale to Martine, "This village my people. Lived in the third world. You reside in fourth," Tao paused after the correlation to finish his pictograph. Anasazi's and their Pueblo decedents were renowned for picture drawings and petroglyph carvings, left in caves throughout the southwest regions.

Pointing the tip of his stick at the largest dwelling in his sand drawing he continued, "Here home of great leader." Tao bowed his head in honor. "People dying. Medicine no cure." Tao tapped his pointer to the south. "Chief call Great Creator Spirit. All people still live in village pray with Chief." Opening the leather pouch that hung from his belt, Tao reached inside and grabbed a handful of plant herbs. Throwing them on his small fire, he spoke as a white puff of smoke formed from the dried incense. Breathing in deep the fragrant odor of pine, Tao closed his eyes as he continued, "Three day they pray."

Sketching a small child, the storyteller continued his narrative, "Little girl name Layla get sick. Mother, Father dead. Layla walk far. Want find missing mother-father. Village look for Layla. Not find her. People not leave safety of village to look more for girl. Animal danger in 'tree field' scare village people. Soon friend of Layla go to tree line and see big white wolf lying next to friend. Wolf growl— protect girl from danger. People not know wolf. Ready hurt and kill wolf . . . save girl."

Martine's mouth frowned in sadness, "This . . . this wolf?" she stammered. Looking straight into Grace's eyes, she saw the flames from Tao's fire reflected back to her like a mirror. "It can't be this wolf, can it?" Martine's face exaggerated a look of fear as she looked at Tao in the fire-lit space.

"Yes." Tao nodded affirmatively. "Chief with Shaman stop people from harming wolf. Shaman tell people White Wolf medicine sent by Great Spirit. Wolf Medicine protect child. Protect innocent sick—lost children. Wolf Medicine only come when called by crying person. He tell people White Wolf heard the cry."

Stopping his story, Tao stirred the fire with his stick. Sparks rose up like firecrackers, illuminating his distinguished face that was accentuated by numerous strands of colorful beads and stones hanging around his thick neck. Each row of the necklace bestowed the wearer with favorable attributes from the corresponding stone or relic. "White Wolf try lead small Layla back to people. Layla weak . . . fall sick to ground."

Stifling an emotional sob, Martine sniffed hard with her nose. "Please tell me Layla and this wolf did not get hurt."

Ignoring the interruption, Tao continued to weave the tale of his people, "village bring White Wolf food and water. Make friend with protector wolf. White Wolf Medicine powerful. Little Layla get up and bring wolf to village." Tossing a handful of sacred plants into the fire pit, Tao continued to speak as the smoky incense rose up, "Wolf stay till sickness gone." Petting the head of Grace, Tao looked hard at Martine and gave her a quick closed-mouth smile. "Brave brave White Wolf," he said, accepting a nuzzling from Grace.

Looking up to heaven, Martine's long hair touched the ground as she blurted out, "Thank you, God." Fixing her attention back on Tao, she released a big sigh. "Why tell me this wonderful story?"

"Not just story. I Shaman. Grace here to answer prayer from your village."

Awestruck, Martine quivered from the announcement and formulated her thoughts out loud, "Grace has heard our cries? Grace has come to help me? She brings White Wolf Medicine?"

"Yes. White Wolf hear cry. She feel much pain. She hear you howl in night." Tao stroked the magnanimous animal. "Not only White Wolf guard people with need of physical protection, Wolf Medicine weave cure for spirit trouble. You pass through dark time. Children you seek be lost like Layla." Bowing his head in nobleness, Tao addressed Martine, "You, White Wolf Woman. Time for truth. Time for balance. Follow instinct of mother—mother like you." Tao spoke with firm resolve. "Great strength needed to overcome evil way."

"What instincts do I have as a mother that will help me?" Martine asked her wise friend.

"Mother has intuition that warn of evil," he explained.

"Tell me more about the evil ways I must face."

"You face some already."

"When?"

"Today," the Shaman answered. "This why you ready now."

"In prison?" Martine questioned her confidant. "Yes," she answered herself. "I faced the evil that emerges from these criminals. Didn't I?"

"Yes. You face more than that." Using his drawing stick again, Tao drew an odd shaped S in the sand that looked like a striking lightning bolt. Parallel to it he drew another one so that together they resembled the Nazi SS insignia she had seen on Ratchet's arm. "Because you will it, Grace bring you power to *cut off snake head*."

Shifting her weight, Martine pondered his words and traced the two insignias with her right forefinger, "I faced the *predatory will* that leads to evil. But, I need to find the head of the organization. Ratchet's group."

"Grace increase your intuition and knowing. She bring answer to your concern."

"Thank you," Martine said as she rubbed Grace's head. "I will look for you in my dreams. I will listen to my intuitions."

"But why is so much attention being provided to me on this case?" Martine asked.

"Eternal law being broken. Violation to natural law of creation about to manifest, if evil not put under."

"If I can help, I will," Martine obliged.

Tao grinned as Martine conveyed her acceptance. "Follow your path, though contrary to others," he emphasized with a nod.

"But . . . ," Martine's voice trailed as her body was whisked away from Tao's campsite. Instantaneously, her soul was swept away from Mesa Verde and re-emerged into the now.

Turning over on her side, she faced the clock that read 6:04. "Figures," she said aloud. She contemplated the powerful medicine she was in possession of and surmised she could not stop searching for the missing girls. "But how?" she quizzed herself.

"Martine? Are you okay?" Jolene knocked softly on the door.

"Yeah. I'm up." Martine sat up on the side of the bed.

Opening the door, Jolene peeked in and smiled warmly. "A dream?"

"Oh yeah. A doozy," Martine mused. "Actually I think it was an allegory."

"What the heck is that?" Jolene chuckled. "Is that a legal term I should know?"

"No," Martine bit her bottom lip. "It's a story, often with animals, that presents an abstract idea to convey a whole meaning rather than just a literal fact. It represents truths or generalizations about human existence issues."

"Okay, I get it," Jolene exclaimed. "It's like a metaphorical narrative."

"Exactly," Martine agreed. "It's going to make me think really hard."

"Come on," Jolene coaxed. "You can tell me while I have my coffee on the patio."

Opening up like a flower, Martine soon shared the whole auspicious dream with her sister.

Chapter 43

John Mahoney's alarm clock buzzed loudly in his bedroom. Hearing the blaring noise, he rose from the chair in his home office and ambled to the bedroom that he had left two hours earlier. Seven A.M came faster than he wanted. The buzz stopped after he poked the "alarm off" button his forefinger. Up earlier than usual, he couldn't stop his thoughts from migrating to his encounter with Martine.

Sleep didn't go well for John after his intense evening with his new consultant. Unlocking several chambers in his mind he didn't understand if she perplexed him or enchanted him. Mesmerized by the bizarre conversation that seemed miles off the mark from his FBI investigation, he found his night's rest unsettled.

Flipping and flopping all night, like a fish out of water, he got up before the sun. Determined to be a better match today he surfed the internet for two solid hours—checking her facts. Uncomfortable with someone else controlling the knowledge throughout the entire conversation, John was intellectually challenged.

In his opinion Martine knew way too much about the topics that she successfully wove into his investigation and doubted the direction she was going in. Skeptical about her state-of-mind, or research materials, he decided he needed to be more prepared with his own sources of information.

Teddy had told Mahoney that, "power comes from knowledge." Martine appeared to be a worthy challenger, even though they were clearly on the same side of the law.

Strategizing how to verify her facts, Mahoney tried to make contact with Teddy the night before as he drove away from the restaurant. Unable to speak with his friend he rushed straight home and scoured his massive book collection on World War II history till he started to nod off in his office chair.

Upset with himself, for not readily finding answers, he went to bed but couldn't sleep soundly. Loaded with questions like—*why didn't he have a bible in his own home? How could she be so sure of herself...* kept waking him up.

Desperate to have his "game-on" today he wanted to be better prepared if this woman casually discussed World War II, or the Bible. Contemplating the Bible stories he learned as a child, he remembered the book of Genesis discussing Adam and Eve, Cain and Abel, Noah and the Ark—not sons of God mating with human women.

Anxious to debate her or Teddy on any subject, he read up on Heinrich Himmler and the Aryan Race of men. Disconcerted by what he found, he read and read until he ran out of time. Unable to thoroughly research "The Book of Genesis," he Googled the infamous book and clicked his "print" command. Hearing the printer engage, he exited his office to get ready for work.

Sprinting to the bathroom for his morning rituals, he checked himself in the mirror. This time when he looked at himself he actually imagined his face without a beard and mustache. Stroking the thick froth of facial hair, he thought, *maybe that's what I need to do to get the respect I deserve from this woman. She thinks I'm just a monkey grinder.* Out loud he pondered, "No wonder, I look like a primate."

Revved up from two hours of strong coffee and Nazi history, he began aggressively mowing all the hair off his face—well, almost all the hair. Unsure about the whole new look, he kept the mustache. Analyzing his face, he pondered; *a signature mustache would be more than suitable for an old cowboy.*

With a refined and distinguished face looking back in the mirror, Mahoney studied his new profile. Satisfied with his rugged handsomeness, he anticipated their morning meeting with renewed vigor.

Privately he declared the new look an improvement—publically he would assert too much gray was showing. Finished with the grooming—he applied aftershave cologne, pulled his boots on, parked his favorite black Stetson on his head, and gave his tall stature one last glance in the mirror. *I look younger,* he thought to himself.

Forgetting the document he printed from his home computer, John left in a rush to fetch the coffee and Danish.

Chapter 44

Inspecting every door and window to her house, Jolene verified that none of the clear scotch tapes had been disturbed. Securing a strip of tape to each operable door and window had been Martine's idea. Satisfied that security had not been breached that night, she felt reassured that everything was as it should be before leaving for work.

"Let's take your car today, Martine," Jolene said as she came in from examining the garage doors.

"Sure, I'm ready when you are," Martine replied.

Riding to the office in Martine's car gave Jolene an opportunity to speak openly, "What are the girls doing today?"

"Good question. I gave them some stuff to look up for me yesterday, but they went shopping all day with friends. Hopefully they'll remember today what I asked them to do."

"They really know how to keep busy," Jolene remarked.

"Yeah, especially when they get together," Martine agreed. "They'll find something to do as long as they have Eva's car down here. I'm hoping they will start shopping for a used SUV without me. I just don't have the time."

Curious about Martine's energy towards her boss, Jolene decided to get a pulse on her sister's impressions. Creating small talk, Jolene finessed information, "That article I read last night about Himmler was really deep."

"Yeah, I know," Martine said, placing her sunglasses on.

"I wonder what Mr. Mahoney thinks?"

Martine shrugged. "I have no idea."

"Boy, could I use a big cup of coffee. I can't believe we didn't have time for more than one cup this morning."

"I agree," Martine said adjusting her visor as she drove into the rising sun.

"How did you sleep last night?" Jolene asked.

"I think I slept okay. I mean I feel rested."

"Really? So do you think your dream had anything to do with the case?"

"Probably." Martine nodded thoughtfully. "What confuses me is all this weird Nazi stuff I dream about and read about."

"Why do you think it's happening?"

"I have no idea. I keep thinking about what I must be missing," Martine said. "Or, what could it all mean on a bigger scale?"

"No pressure. You'll figure it out," reassured Jolene.

"I suspect Mahoney will decide by the end of the day that I'm a wacko, or a dumb blonde joke that you saddled him with. I guess I'm feeling a little down and out today," Martine revealed.

"Maybe it won't be so bad," Jolene replied. "You would never give up because of one setback."

"No, I wouldn't give up unless I should—because I'm in the way, or he needs to fire me."

Jolene smiled. "He's not like that. He's really a great boss. Did I tell you he's single?"

"No, you didn't."

"He's kinda good looking—don't you think?" Jolene enticed a reaction.

"What?" Are you interested in that guy?" Martine looked bewildered. "He looks like Big Foot. Oh, and he's probably fifteen-years older than you."

"Well . . . yeah, he might be," Jolene stuttered.

"I thought you were seeing Wade for lunch," Martine sounded perplexed.

"Yeah, I'm having lunch with Wade. You're right, John Mahoney is not right for me. Plus, he's my boss. What was I thinking of?" Jolene said facetiously.

"I have no idea, Jolene," Martine said, sounding aggravated by the notion.

Realizing Martine was not catching on or reading into her insinuations, Jolene planted another one. "So, you don't like the tall, rugged, cowboy-type then?"

"You've got to be kidding. Is that where you're going with this?" Martine marveled.

"Maybe?" Jolene said cautiously.

"Jolene, did you forget that I was married and recently widowed. My husband was handsome, fun, charming, challenging, and clean shaven. John Mahoney and I are trying to tolerate each other. That would not constitute grounds for a solid relationship."

"I just think you need to get to know him better. I've never seen him look like he did last night when we got up to leave. He looked at you differently than he does any of us at work. I guess I sorta felt sorry for him."

"Don't worry about us two. I'm not interested in changing my life again. I'm just starting to adjust. I'll be fine. Really, you don't have to set me up with the first AARP bachelor you see," Martine chuckled at her own joke.

"You're right," Jolene quieted her voice in defeat.

"I think you feel like playing matchmaker because you and Wade are talking. I think you really, really like this guy," Martine said with confidence. "I'm happy for you."

Chapter 45

"Oh shit," Jolene exclaimed. "There's Levine and Hess. They're always out here smoking cigarettes before work.

"So?"

"Those are the Forensic Accountants I've had to work with on my last two assignments. They're always making blonde jokes when I'm around."

"Why would they do that, Jolene?"

"Apparently, because I'm the young rookie, and a girl. They think I get all the safe jobs."

"Well do you?"

"Jolene looked annoyed. "No. Of course not. Not really."

Martine eyed the two guys. "If you act prissy," she explained, "they're gonna let you know. You can only change and have control over the way you react to someone's behavior. You cannot change theirs."

"Well that's just great," Jolene said. "I think they've just been here so long, they think its okay. What can I possibly do different?"

"I got this one then." Martine took the lead. "These guys are mine."

Pausing next to Levine and Hess, Martine asked Jolene, "What do you call a blonde at the bottom of a swimming pool?"

Jolene, looking perplexed answered, "I don't know."

"An air bubble." Martine jabbed her sister to laugh at the joke with her. Laughing loudly, they walked into the building. "Beat them at their own game," Martine said as the door closed behind her.

Support personnel and agents were streaming into the bureau. Noticing a crowd forming in front of Mahoney's office, Jolene gave Martine a look of dread. "Oh . . . no—what's wrong now?"

"I don't know, you work here—what does it mean?"

"Could be some big change—or break through," Jolene answered. "Hopefully not about us though."

"Right." Martine pressed her lips together in contemplative thought.

"He might be making a shift in the investigation team," Jolene fretted.

Tyra, the receptionist intercepted them. Beaming with a full grin, Tyra greeted Jolene, "Hi, girl. Excuse me I have to get back to my phones. I just can't believe the change."

Jolene watched Tyra traverse her way back to the front office. Frowning she looked back to Martine. "Are we in trouble?"

"You're asking me?" Martine replied.

Holly and Bethany strolled past Jolene. Giggling, Holly said, "Wow, what made him do it?"

Nervous about the activity in front of Mahoney's office, Jolene did an about-face. Hooking Martine's arm with hers, she dragged her sister around the corner to her semi-private cubicle. "Here look at this, Martine," Jolene shoved a file into her sister's hand.

Oblivious to Jolene's job insecurities, Martine asked, "You want me to look at this file?"

"Yeah. Check that suspect out. Let me know what you think." Feeling safe for the moment, Jolene hoped they wouldn't be summoned or singled out.

Dispersing like flies under a horse's tail, the office personnel parted and Mahoney pushed through. Emerging from his office, the crowd waited for Jolene's reaction.

She did not disappoint. Frozen in shock, little words escaped Jolene, "Ah . . . Oh . . . Um . . .," was all she could muster.

Squinting at the strange man approaching, it took moments for Martine to react. Clasping her hand over her mouth, she squelched her gasp.

"Sir, good morning," Jolene finally said sheepishly. "We didn't want to interrupt you." Flustered about what to say, she stammered on, "Are we still meeting this morning?"

"Yes, of course. Let's get started right away," Mahoney said, ushering Jolene and Martine to the conference room. "I've got coffee and Danish all ready for us."

"Thank you, sir." Jolene moved swiftly into the room.

"Coming, Martine?" Mahoney asked, sporting his handsome face with a genuine grin.

Floored by the new Mahoney, Jolene glanced back at her sister who seemed to have all his attention. "Of course, Mr. Mahoney, I'm on my way," Martine replied slowly.

Chapter 46

Parking herself in a conference room chair, Martine scanned the busy-looking walls that changed on a daily basis. Apprizing each other of new files, leads, and suspects each day, was anything but routine. Staying on top of the growing case load was almost impossible for most of the agents.

Scanning the walls, Martine noticed new faces of missing girls were added within the last twenty-four hours. Mug shots of prime suspects also had expanded. Files were organized and stacked four-to-five-feet high in random locations. Having spent yesterday interrogating prisoners and sketches at the prison, Martine was experiencing her own insecurities when studying all the faces at once. Staying focused on her own deductions, was much more manageable than this alternative.

Spending yesterday with four Senior Agents, Martine counseled the interrogators while they questioned various suspects and snitches that were housed in the Arizona prison system. Desperate to catch-up with the task force that had already been briefed on the new victims, Martine was relieved Mahoney had not requested everyone attend his meeting.

So far every single lead the agents had followed up on had fizzled. Martine still felt she may be on to something with her two obscure suspects. Compelled to pursue the plight of Peter and Jules,

Martine prayed for a reason to bring them in. Without a cause in place, Martine had no authority to interview them "on the record."

Certain that Peter and Jules had information that could shed light on the eclipse shadowing this investigation—she could not stop trying to devise a way to get them in her sights. Sharing her concern with Mahoney was inevitable if she couldn't find a way soon. Timing was important—she didn't want to act prematurely, and be discredited. Likewise, waiting too long might risk another girl's life.

After offering Martine and Jolene coffee and fresh rolls, Mahoney helped himself to both. Situated comfortably, he began his meeting, "Much of the research done thus far was generated by Jolene or Carmen." looking at Martine, he continued, "Martine, I've spent a considerable amount of time, since we met last night, digesting your observations and findings. I agree we should continue to study your German writings, but only while we earnestly scrutinize every other file we've accumulated here." Nodding for approval, he added, "any objections ladies?"

"No, Mr. Mahoney, no objections," Martine affirmed. "I want to spend some time analyzing the files on all the new missing girls you've received thus far. I know I missed a lot yesterday."

"Great. Martine, I heard you did a great job yesterday with my agents. Pitch-hitting for our regular Legal Assistant was really appreciated. I don't think I thanked you last night. Actually, I overlooked the fact that you were doing us a big favor. I didn't mean to discount the work you've been doing."

"No problem," Martine obliged.

"Sir, because we have a pile of information that has not been sufficiently merged and organized I suggest we bring in Carmen to help assist in this review," Jolene suggested. "She and I haven't compared notes since yesterday morning. Together Carmen and I can summarize what we know conclusively and therefore help us avoid duplication."

"Right," Mahoney affirmed. "Having Carmen could be helpful . . . I suppose."

Paging Carmen himself, Mahoney summoned her through the inner-office paging-system.

"Carmen is the Investigative Operations Analyst that put the "F" in FBI according to, well . . . that's what her admirers say," Jolene explained. "Carmen's a little more unique than the average employee here. She's fun. You'll see."

"I might have heard about her, but I haven't met her yet," Martine acknowledged, sipping her coffee.

Jolene proceeded to introduce Martine to some new "missing persons" while they waited for Carmen to join them.

Martine cautioned Jolene about drawing any conclusions, "This is fantastic. Just try to avoid giving me your personal observations and opinions." Seeing Mahoney was still on a phone call, Martine added, "that kinda information can interfere with my own interpretations."

"Got it," Jolene affirmed.

"Great." Martine kept her voice low, "Stick to the facts, I want to be as objective as I can without running into detours."

"Got it I'll be discrete about your theories," Jolene pledged. "I got the translation done—didn't I?"

"Yes, you did," Martine acknowledged assuredly.

"Oh, here's Carmen now." Jolene turned sideways to greet her co-worker. "Let me introduce you to a brilliant criminal investigator," Jolene praised the uniquely-fashioned, fifty-something woman.

Contrasting Jolene in every way, Carmen bounced in the room with a broad smile of confidence and fun. Amazed at her bold hairstyle and clothing-fashion, Martine knew Carmen was original and spirited.

Unorthodox in appearance, Carmen wore leopard print pants with matching sandals. Trendy rhinestones—blinged brightly on the black tank top fitted tight to her large chest. Chin-length hair was colored in the latest dramatic red, and highlighted with white streaks. Punked-up with gel, Carmen's thick coif of hair made her look twenty-years younger.

Joining Jolene next to the wall of pictures, Martine compared the two opposites. Jolene's willowy figure posed in a tailored black pant suit, accented with a shimmery-cream blouse. Black pumps with two-inch heels made her tower over five-foot-three Carmen. Styled long blonde hair with brow-sweeping bangs gave Jolene the look of a runway model.

Introductions aside, Carmen briefed Mahoney and Martine on her case analysis like a seasoned CPA. Carmen explained what she and Jolene had determined so far, "As you can see we're grossly lacking forensics to devise any clear MO on a suspect." Sounding pessimistic, she added, "Frankly, it seems as if these abductions aren't even related."

Jolene swept her bangs and added her abridgment, "It's also inconclusive what kind of person or persons are responsible for these missing girls. Our profiling techniques have failed to disclose anything obvious except that most victims were young, white, and female. Since statistically a crime is within the same race, we can possibly conclude the perpetrator, or perpetrators, are also white. There probably is also some sort of ambiguity that the criminal possesses that allows him to go into the victim's world without creating suspicions."

Slouching back in his conference-style chair, Mahoney asked, "What about the new suspects. Have you finished entering all of them into your program?"

"That changes every day too," Jolene explained.

"As the new missing reports arrive, so do new suspects," Carmen added. "We input everything as quickly as possible. We haven't been able to keep up with the new arrivals."

"Law enforcement agencies are working hard gathering old cases, turning every rock over, giving us their every bottom feeder. We're even seeing petty thieves on their hit lists," Jolene said.

Looking at Martine, Mahoney said, "When they're done presenting the victims to us, let's get an update of the suspects we're tracking."

"Agreed," Martine said. "So, it looks like the rise in missing persons spiked about six-months ago, right?"

Carmen nodded. "Yes, Martine, that's what our report ultimately reveals."

"Looks like you girls proved there is an epidemic going on here," Mahoney deducted.

"Yes, sir," Jolene confirmed.

"Let's try and get through this briefing by noon. I'm meeting with the Phoenix police chief," Mahoney explained.

Checking her watch for the time, Martine saw that it was already past eleven. Wanting to stay focused, and not get distracted by every-single bad energy, she hoped they wouldn't get to all the suspects. Flying like out-of-control boomerangs, each law enforcement jurisdiction was adding every possible criminal to the investigation. No profile was being overlooked, causing a landslide of good and bad information.

Handing out the mug shot of a new suspect, Carmen described his bio, "This came yesterday afternoon from a Las Vegas detective. The guys no petty crook. He's big and organized—like Mafia. He has ties to that other crime boss they call Schultzy."

Having a reaction to the man's face, Martine expelled loudly, "Oh!"

"Do you know him?" Mahoney asked Martine.

"No. Maybe he's familiar though." Martine felt the connection. "Have you checked him out yet?"

"No. No one's even assigned to him," Jolene said.

Looking closely at the black-and-white picture, Martine felt his piercing eyes fillet through her. Muttering out loud she said, "I think he was born bad."

"Really?" Mahoney said. "We'll get everything we can on him."

Distracted with the notion she had just hit on another highly probable suspect, Martine didn't see her two daughters standing in the doorway.

"Hello there," Mahoney said when they caught his eye. "Can I help you?"

"Yes . . . yes you can," Eva replied.

Mahoney obliged before Martine could react, "Well come on in."

Perfectly timed, Eva and Alexa showed up at eleven-thirty. Accepting Mahoney's invitation they walked boldly up to Martine and Jolene. Outside the open doorway were the faces of men piling up for a closer look. Clearly the girls were a welcomed interruption for the guys filling in the hallway.

Strutting in her tight fitting jeans, Eva walked in first wearing a scarlet crocheted top. Bouncy curled hair framed her round face and bright smile. Seeing Alexa also dressed in new tight jeans with a teal camisole, Martine recognized Eva had dressed Alexa again. Long layers of hair flowed around Alexa's rosy-cheeks. Neither girl was wearing FBI issued clothing, and obviously had set off alarms in this conservative office setting that was dominated by drab attire.

"Well, who do we have here?" Mahoney grinned.

Martine rose out of her chair to introduce her daughters, "This is Eva my younger daughter who should be in school as we speak and this is Alexa my older daughter who has moved back home for awhile. We already had plans before I started working here."

Connecting immediately with Carmen, Eva socialized like they had been in a sorority together.

Gravitating to Mahoney, Alexa had employment on her mind and monopolized his attention for ten minutes.

Breaking for the restroom, Martine returned and informed her daughters they would be done meeting in twenty minutes, "Why don't you two wait at the restaurant next door. We're almost done here."

Eva said matter-of-factly, "We have some really neat research to show you. We've been working all morning on your German stuff," Eva publicized to the audience.

Embarrassed, Martine replied, "Really? Let's meet next door and talk about it when we're done here."

"Sure. We'll meet you both. You're really gonna like it." Eva beamed with pride.

Caught-off-guard by her daughters showing up unannounced, she tried to hustle them out of the meeting as quickly as possible.

"I think everyone will get more work done around here if you two wait next door," Martine whispered to her daughters.

Vacating the building caused as much commotion as when they arrived. Lost for words, Martine simply apologized, "Forgive the interruption. I know we're on a tight schedule."

Chuckling, Mahoney commented, "I've never seen you dress-up like those two, Jolene. I don't see the family resemblance."

"Yeah, I know what you mean," she replied sheepishly.

"Alright, let's give some direction to the task force based on what we have today." Mahoney got serious. "We need to set some priorities."

Bringing her attention to bear, Martine began to ponder the arsenal of information that had streamed before her during the last few hours. Voices in the room droned as her thoughts processed a theory. Rocketing past all the myriads of faces and profiles, Martine's mind began to see everything from a more vivid dimension or perspective. Combusting into a formable probability, she started to comprehend a concept that she could use to move forward, gain momentum and not stay stuck. Resting her eyes in contemplation, she waited for the whole thought-process to finish.

Suddenly, Martine calculated a course of action that she would have never thought of if her two daughters hadn't appeared and distracted the entire office.

Congealed with a formable revelation, Martine heard Carmen's voice speaking as the meeting came back into focus.

"It really does seem as if these abductions are not even related," Carmen concluded.

Recognizing that they needed to look at this case from an entirely different point of understanding, she was interiorly reminded of an incident that occurred a decade earlier with her own daughters. Martine scanned the room for the one face she needed. Springing from her chair, she moved close to the high school portrait of Lauren.

Startled by her aggressive move, Carmen stopped speaking.

Pointing to Lauren's picture, Martine interrupted, "Why did you not include this girl in your profiling?"

"Well, she's not missing—she's dead," Carmen said sadly.

Pulling the photo off the wall, Martine approached the profiler, "And does this girl not fit the profile?"

"She doesn't fit into the category of abduction, or missing person. She's also been missing longer than these other girls."

"Right, so if we want to presume all the other girls are just missing, and not dead, her death could be a clue as to why the others are alive and she is dead," Martine said as she looked at her confused audience.

"How do you mean?" Mahoney asked.

"Well, how could we possibly know those answers?" Carmen added.

"Exactly," Mahoney agreed. "What kind of a clue do you think her death can reveal that would help us find these other girls?"

"But there is something about this girl's death that can assist us." Martine looked intense.

"Like what?" Carmen quizzed.

"I would like to explore the possibility that this girl was found dead because she was a mistake or there was an error that caused her death. If we presume the others are still alive, why is she not?"

Stroking his mustache in thought, Mahoney sat back in his conference chair, "I don't know where you're going with this, Martine. How are you going to deduce that theory without talking to her or the others?"

"I would like to meet with the coroner and reexamine the body with him."

Raising his eyebrows, Mahoney shook his head. "Are you questioning his work? Are you suggesting he's missed something?"

Answering affirmatively, Martine nodded, "Yes, I do believe he has missed, or withheld something that could be extremely relevant to your investigation. Not intentionally of course."

Motioning to Carmen and Jolene, Mahoney asked, "Where is the body now and how soon can you arrange this?"

"I don't know. We'll have to make some calls and see if the family has taken possession of the remains. We thought we had what we needed," Jolene explained.

Adamant about her theory, Martine continued, "I'd like to meet with the parents of Lauren, if that can be arranged too. I'd like to actually go to their home."

"They live in Utah," Jolene volunteered. "I'll make the arrangements to visit the parents. I'd also like to accompany Martine to their home."

"Carmen can you line up the medical examination?" Mahoney directed.

Appearing confused by this rapid turn of events and this new strategy, "Sure," was all she said.

"Okay, let's get on it," Mahoney said with a nod.

Pausing at the doorway, Carmen asked, "Is there anything else I should do? I've never been to an autopsy, and I'd like to go with you."

"Of course," Martine agreed. "And there is something else you can help me with, now that I've seen what you can do," Martine flattered her. "I could really use some help on this." Martine grabbed the slim file on Sharon—the missing girl that use to be Peter's girlfriend. Handing it to Carmen, she made her request, "I'd like to have your lab do an exhaustive search to see if her body was ever found. I suspect she'll turn up as a Jane Doe."

Retrieving the file, Carmen looked inside. "There isn't any forensics to work with here. There's not much to go on that will easily match up to our Jane Doe files." Carmen looked bleak. "It could take an entire task force to find her body, assuming it is a Jane Doe."

Prepared for her objections, Martine dug in her purse for the large sized zip-lock bag that held Sharon's forensics. Handing it to Carmen she described the contents, "I managed to secure some items of hers; a hair brush, some makeup, a photo of Sharon and Peter, and a paperback book. I was hoping that we could start by lifting some prints off her personal items. I'm sure we can eventually extract some DNA from the hair brush or lipstick. I just observed how fast your department is in producing forensic evidence," Martine schmoozed Carmen. "I realize it's a long shot that Sharon's a Jane Doe, but she didn't have family looking for her and that's where most of them are until we get a lucky—rare break. Do your best Carmen.

Mahoney broke-in, "Let's get the coroner lined up for this afternoon, ASAP. When that's arranged you can begin a search for this girl." Excusing Jolene, and Carmen, Mahoney directed his attention to Martine. Clearing his throat, he got her attention, "Are you grasping at straws with this stuff? I just don't know how to take your directives. They're either awe inspiring, or crazy." Sounding flustered he continued, "You seem so sure of yourself. And where did you get that personal stuff of Sharon's? Likewise, how did your daughters become involved in this case?"

She had been expecting the confrontation, but Martine was stumped on how to answer all Mahoney's questions. Using the analogy that triggered her awareness, she tried to explain to him what made perfect sense to her, "It's actually quite simple. The girls reminded me of an incident that happened about ten years ago. We had a foster boy named Trey living with us. All three of them were going to high school together. It was a small private school and all the students knew each other, no matter what grade they were in. Anyway, I got really upset with my daughters for leaving their sandals strewn all around the house. Our little dog Chance was a puppy then, and thrived on chewing up anything he could grab, thus leaving a mess for me to pick up. So, the three of them came home from school one afternoon and . . . I let it fly. I went on and on about them leaving their thongs lying all around the house for Chance to rip and chew on. The expression on their three faces was priceless. The two girls were devastated that I'd accuse them of leaving their thongs lying around the house—and I did this in front of Trey. They argued with me to the point of demanding I describe what color they were. I answered them with an assortment of colors like orange, pink, white . . . , and while Trey stood there chuckling and smirking. He was relieved it wasn't his problem this time. Between his teachers and me the poor kid was always being corrected, disciplined, grounded, and tutored."

"Go on," Mahoney said.

"The next day Trey informed the boy's high school locker room how Alexa and Eva got yelled at for *leaving their Thongs lying around the house.* Boy did I get in trouble when the three of them came home that afternoon. It took a while to sort it out. The arguing lasted a couple hours. It turned out I did not experience what the three of them were visualizing. Like I said, it took quite awhile before we figured out what was missing. I had tarnished their honorable standing with the entire student body. Every boy now believed they wore thongs and left them discarded throughout the house. I however was referring to their flip flops. I didn't know that the thongs I wore on my feet as a child were renamed flip flops and thongs were a new type of women's underwear. Long story short, until I went to the closet and showed them the chewed flip flops, I didn't know we were missing the subject matter by miles. We weren't on the same page or any closer to solving this sorely debated case until we examined the damaged evidence together. My obsolete vocabulary and poor interpretation of the subject matter created a breakdown in our communication. The outcome was disastrous. It was a dumb, but memorable ordeal."

Mahoney let out a chuckle, "And that's what made you want to question the coroner's findings?"

"For some reason that adolescent analogy made me realize we are obligated to reevaluate our case evidence because we can . . . , and we may not have gotten it right. A typical coroner will notice the obvious. It's our job as investigators to find clues that are not obvious and make deductions. As for the rest of your questions I'd like to wait till the day is over."

"Wow," Mahoney replied. "Not what I expected. Good enough though." Checking his watch, he stood up. "Your ideas are original. Go join your daughters. We'll notify you if anything urgent gets set up."

Chapter 47

Starving for some real food, and a break from the depressing conference room, Martine moved briskly through the restaurant looking for her daughters.

"Okay, you two. What were you thinking—crashing in on us at work," Martine scolded.

"Hey, you told us to come over and get my car checked for 'devices,' didn't you?" Eva replied.

Martine frowned. "Yes, we just didn't tell you to come to our meeting."

"Did you really get in any trouble?" Alex asked.

"Of course not, but now Jolene's boss knows I took you with me to Della's," Martine warned.

"How did you get past security?" Jolene questioned.

"We showed Tyra our I.D's. Told her we had an appointment to see you and get our car checked," Eva explained.

"Boy, are you two sneaky," Jolene marveled.

"Hey," Eva declared. "She said it was fine. She could tell we were family. Oh, she gave us some really good clubs to check-out."

"Yeah, we're meeting her at her favorite bar. She's got some guy she wants to notice her there," Alexa gossiped.

"We really don't have much time. I may be leaving for an appointment," Martine said.

"I can't believe how hard you two have been working," Eva acknowledged.

"It's shaping up to be the 'Super Bowl' of investigations," Jolene commented.

"Okay, want to hear what I found?" Eva sounded excited.

"Sure," Martine answered.

Breathless, Eva went on, "Well, Alexa, asked me to see if I could make three words, from those letters you gave her . . . and I did."

"Great, what are they?" Martine questioned.

"Well, Alexa, found three words, but so did I." Looking at a piece of paper she read, 'Eleven plus two.' That's what Alexa got. I got three words also."

"Really, what'd you get?" Jolene asked.

"I got, 'Twelve plus one.' I think it's funky that they both add up to thirteen."

"Yeah, that is weird. Sounds like a confirmation within a clue," Martine mused.

"I wonder what is significant about the number thirteen, besides being unlucky," Jolene asked.

"Knew you'd ask. Here's what I found on the internet." Eva glowed with accomplishment. "I found some lore about the number thirteen."

"Let's have it," Martine said.

"Thirteen means beginning and end," Eva read from her notes. "It means birth and death. It also means change and transition. Every occurrence of the number thirteen stands in connection with rebellion, apostasy, deflection, corruption, disintegration, revolution . . . ever since Genesis," Eva finished.

"Boy," Jolene weighed-in. "Who would have thought a number could have so much significance? And from the beginning of time."

"I found some more purpose behind the Hopi dream and animal totem dream," Alexa added.

"You're kidding," Martine exclaimed. "You think they're related?"

"I do," Alexa directed her words to Martine. "Listen to this. Four of the animals, the bigger ones that faded away after they saw you, are drawn on during the Hopi pipe ceremony. Did you know that the ceremony you attended was a Sacred Hopi Pipe Ceremony?"

"No."

"Based on what you described . . . you did. Anyway, the ceremony draws from the four cardinal directions. North is guarded by the mountain lion, east is guarded by the wolf, south is guarded by the red badger, and west is guarded by the bear."

"Holy shit, Martine. What ceremony? What is Alexa talking about? When did you see those animals? What have you been doing in Durango?" Jolene sparked with alarm.

"Dreams, Jolene, dreams, that's all they were. My dreams have been memorable but not sensible," Martine explained.

"So, now can you tell us what you think is going on?" Eva asked.

"Probably not with any accuracy," Martine responded. "However, I think we need to get a bible, and read Genesis."

"What?" Jolene said.

"Yeah, and don't forget the first clue we figured out from the scrabble letters—that spelled 'Woman Hitler,' and 'Mother-In-Law,'" Alexa reminded them. "That has to mean something regarding all the Nazi stuff we saw at Della's."

"Oh, and that Hopi Pipe Ceremony, that you identified in your research, well, Della's house is very close to the Hopi reservation. Let's get a map of Arizona and a Bible," instructed Martine. "See what else you two can find out about this . . . RUSHA, it has to do with Himmler's Race and Resettlement Central Office. It was mentioned in that German newspaper article that got translated. There has to be more to it."

"Why a Bible?" Jolene inquired.

Martine shrugged, "Because I've run into the Book of Genesis twice now."

"What do you mean?" Jolene countered.

"The first time was in a dream that resembled the *Sound of Music.* In my dream Mother Superior and Maria drop a Bible open to Genesis," Martine summarized.

Jolene cocked her head slightly. "What? Did you say Maria?"

"Yeah."

"The missing girl that Wade met with me about is named Maria."

"I'm getting goose bumps." Martine shivered. "I really need to see a Bible. I can't believe you don't have one, Jolene."

"This is really getting weird," Jolene commented.

"I'm really glad you two bopped in like you did. It actually helped me figure some things out," Martine complimented her daughters.

"I wish it wasn't so hard to talk at home," Eva complained.

"Yeah, it's a good thing none of us are ever there," Alexa added.

"Since you two are going out to clubs, Jolene and I will do something too." Martine glanced at Jolene. "I have a feeling I'll be working late—late—late."

"Yeah, I don't feel like cooking," Jolene added.

"Right, we know that," Martine said sarcastically.

"It's really interesting what you do at your jobs, I'm thinking about applying for a position there. Maybe this is what I'm supposed to do down here," Alexa said. "I think I could be good at this."

Jolene smiled. "Really?"

"I'd like to help more with this case. I can do a lot of research for you. They have a job opening for an Analysts Assistant. I could apply," Alexa hinted.

"Yeah, you could. That's up to you," Jolene supported.

Interrupted by her ringing cell phone, Martine answered, "hello, Martine, here."

"Hey, Martine, it's Carmen." Excited with news, her voice was breathy, "I've got your meeting set-up with the coroner for one-thirty. He still has the body. Can you be here at one—I'll drive us there."

"Not a problem," Martine returned.

"The parents are in town right now to get Lauren's remains. I have their number. They're staying with family. Jolene can call them and set up the appointment."

"That's super, Carmen," Martine complemented her new confidant. "Is that Karma or Carmen?"

"I think it's both, Martine," Carmen returned. "Oh, regarding Sharon, I have the lab working hard on some forensics. I've got my ways."

"Yes you do, Carmen. I'll be there soon." Martine hung up her phone.

"Before you take off," Eva started, "what have you found out about Jules and Peter? Are they bad, or just weird?"

"I'm working on it," Martine said. "Haven't had enough time to get anyone to check them out for me."

"Darn," Eva replied.

"I think I know just the person to help me though," Martine said shrewdly. "I need to leave here in five-minutes."

Chapter 48

"So, tell me about this coroner I'm meeting," Martine asked as she glanced over at Carmen from the passenger seat. "What are his credentials?"

Steering her blue compact car into the right-hand lane, Carmen proceeded to describe the Doctor. "Well his name is Gus Delfore. He's conservative, middle-aged, and performed the autopsy the day he got Lauren's corpse. He does quite a bit of work for us, but I've never met him. Talked on the phone and looked over his findings. That's about it. Seems easy enough to work with and better than most when it comes to getting the forensics we need. Yah, he's okay. He seems good at his job." Carmen swung her car around the corner.

Previewing the autopsy report, Martine talked as she marked a couple areas with her pen, "How good is he at determining Time of Death?"

"On tough cases he has lots of samples sent out to the different labs and pathologists to confirm everything. When I called to request a second autopsy he complied immediately, although he felt certain he had performed a thorough exam and documented everything pertinent in his M.E. report." Searching for a parking space, Carmen added, "The guys that do work with him make fun of his Mad Professor look."

"Is that all you know?"

"Pretty much. Oh they say he cracks jokes, and sings off key—to his patients."

* * *

Listening to the echo of Carmen's sandals, Martine fell into her own thoughts while they made their way down the lonely hall to the Dr. Delfore. Knocking on the door to exam room number two, Martine heard an answer.

"Come in."

Observing a tall, average-weight, dark-haired man that looked more like a sleep-deprived artist than a Doctor, Martine asked, "Are you Dr. Delfore?"

"Yes I am. Please call me, Gus. We're not too formal down here. Get it—formal?" Gesturing to his naked patients laying on gurneys, Gus chuckled.

Carmen laughed, "Oh yeah, I get it. I'm Carmen and this is Martine. I hope you don't mind spending a little taxpayer time discussing your recent patient."

"No—not at all. I try to be thorough. This case has bothered me. So, let's see what you have in mind. I have everything about ready." Dr. Delfore ushered Martine and Carmen to the adjoining room.

Displaying a growing nervousness in the presence of the two women questioning his work, Dr. Delfore bumped into a door, counter, and cart. Martine recognized the moving disaster was out of his element with two strange women in his space. Taking control to keep him focused, Martine asked, "It's clear there was a murder here, right?"

"Yes, I'd say so, but I can't determine how, or describe a weapon."

"How about . . . time of Death?"

"Well, on paper it's almost the perfect crime. Disposing of the body in the desert can be ingenious. Wild animals normally get everything. In this case she was found early enough to probably figure something out." Removing the large sheet from Lauren's hidden body, Dr Delfore continued, "If you look here," he said gesturing to her face. "You can see dramatic signs of post-mortem

Hypostasis." Turning her head slightly, Dr. Delfore used his pen as a pointer. "See how the blood has pooled here?"

Martine responded, "Yes."

Dr. Gus spoke casually as he removed his white-coat and tied on his green surgical apron. "Did you know Dr. Chambers? He was the coroner here before I started five years ago," Gus inquired, switching on the bright overhead light. "Uh . . . no. I didn't know him. That was BC," Carmen replied with a smile.

"BC, you say?" Dr. Gus asked as he squeezed his hands into plastic gloves.

"BC stands for *Before Carmen*. I've been in Arizona a couple years now," Carmen clarified as she started the tape recorder they had brought with them.

"Well, getting back to the face, see how the accumulation of blood caused discoloration to her facial features and thighs? That is evidence that circulation ceased when she was face down. That should be an important indication what position she was in when she expired."

Martine agreed, "Right it proves she died face down—before they cut her open."

"Yep."

"Could she have been stabbed in the stomach and left face down? Did they cut her open to hide that?" Carmen asked.

"I would have seen some evidence of that by a nick on her spine, or less blood pooling in these parts of her body," Doctor Delfore explained as he fetched his portable-tray with shiny-surgical instruments.

Positioning herself on the opposite side of the gurney, Martine tried to breath-in as little as possible.

"So, Martine, what is your background with the FBI?" Dr. Gus asked nonchalantly as he selected a scalpel and began opening Lauren's sutures.

Putting on a brave face, Martine explained, "Legal—I'm mostly involved with jurisdiction matters and prosecuting."

"Really, that explains how you avoid autopsies," Gus replied as he spread-open the front of Lauren's body.

"That's right. I must say that crime photos do not do this justice," she grimaced as she continued, "and my law degree doesn't really train me for this."

"Is this too graphic?" Doctor Delfore asked politely.

"No, it shouldn't be," Martine responded.

Changing the conversation's direction, Martine asked, "Doctor, did you notice any unusual odors or marks on the body during your first exam. Maybe something that you didn't mention in your report?"

"No—not really. I can't imagine why someone would want to cut and mutilate her reproductive organs," Dr. Gus said with a dejected expression. Without hesitating, he carefully spread her cavity wide open, and proceeded in announcing his observations out loud for the benefit of the recording device, "As you can see the breasts and uterus were removed. Is that what you would consider a crime of passion, Carmen?"

"Possibly," Carmen stuttered.

Peering at Lauren's cavity, Martine gasped, "Oh!"

Carmen grabbed her mouth, suppressing the urge to throw-up. Muffled by her own hand, she spun around, walked briskly towards the exit and blurted, "Excuse me."

Contemplating Carmen's departure, Dr. Gus said, "Do we keep going or wait for her to return?"

"We keep going," Martine replied in haste.

Acknowledging her orders, Dr. Delfore commented, "Very few people can participate in an autopsy unless they are accustomed to these smells and procedures."

Nodding anxiously, Martine agreed, "I can see why."

Graphically describing the removal procedures of Lauren's organs, Dr. Gus Delfore, read his findings into the recorder.

Repulsed, Martine struggled to remain in control and sequester pertinent information, "I'm looking for the weapon that killed this girl."

"Her post-mortem exam does not show trauma or even minor injuries." Adjusting the overhead light, he directed Martine's attention. "As you can see by reconstruction of her remains we can account for all her organs except the reproductive ones. A very crude knife was used on the victim and there were no medical skills, or expertise used in the removal process." Using his tiny scalpel he examined the organs in front of Martine. "However, this type of knife would have penetrated some other organs if it had been used to murder her." Handling each body part, he demonstrated his observations. "As you can also tell, by the condition of the blood, she was dead before the cutting began." Guiding his scalpel like a pointer, he continued, "Her heart was not beating when the primitive operation was performed. The death was most likely from asphyxiation. Since there were no marks or bruising around her neck she does not appear to have been manually suffocated. She was more likely asphyxiated," Dr. Delfore concluded.

"Dr. Delfore, you say she wasn't suffocated manually, if that's true what do you think was used in the asphyxiation to cause unconsciousness and ultimately death?"

"I'm not sure. Normal screenings produced no results."

"Your report doesn't list any possibilities—not even ligature."

"Right—I know."

Studying the Doctor, Martine queried again, "Did you notice any form of restraint used to subdue the victim?"

"Now that you ask, my report did fail to mention the absence of any ligature marks or bruising around her neck. I did find that unusual in a case of brutality like this. Except for the mutilation and removal of the reproductive organs, her body lacked any trace of abuse or torture. I found no blemishes that would be consistent in a case of rape, torture or death by strangulation. Not even one defensive wound."

Martine pondered, "Did you examine the hyoid bone at the front of her neck? Was it intact?"

"I did examine her neck and found her hyoid bone—unbroken, and no sign of trauma or bruising associated with it." Gus turned to the X-rays that were backlit on the wall next to them. "Not one nick or bruise—no breaks," he announced with assurance. "I mean . . . anywhere."

"If you don't think she was strangled or restrained what could've been used to cause death?"

"Well, it wasn't chloroform or anything commonly seen here. Her lungs gave a partial residue we see from car asphyxiation cases—just not enough to kill a mouse," Dr. Gus clarified. "I presumed it was from being put in the trunk of a car."

Martine moved over to Lauren's head and bent down close to her mouth—sniffing for some type of trace odor. It was nearly impossible to completely focus on another smell when the body emitted a nasty scent, which had already successfully driven Carmen out of the room. "Have you swabbed her face for any type of foreign residues?" Martine stood back up.

"No, I guess I hadn't considered that. I did send several tissue samples to Pathology labs specializing in organs, skin, and blood analysis. What do you think we would find around her mouth that would not have been present in the lung or stomach tissue?" Dr. Gus countered.

"Doctor, I'd like to check for gasoline or some other type of crude fuel. Would it be possible to take some skin samples and tissue swabs from around her mouth and nose?"

"Of course."

"I think we need Quantico," Martine said. "If anything has been left behind they'll detect it," Martine finished.

"So, you suspect she was incapacitated by inhaling pure gasoline?" Without inhibitions, Dr. Gus moved over to Lauren's face and smelled it. Straightening up his posture, he gave a pensive reply, "I actually do smell a faint odor that could be attributed to a fuel of some sort. I'll retrieve the samples so you can have those toxicology tests run."

"Thank you, Doctor. While you're doing that I was wondering if you could elaborate on how you ruled out rape."

"There was no evidence of tears, trauma, or sperm in her vaginal area. I realize that we can't obtain positive DNA without a suspect's body fluids, but I just couldn't find anything foreign to obtain," Dr. Gus admitted dejectedly.

"Did you notice if Lauren had any medical diseases or an illness that wasn't mentioned in the report? Have you been able to absolutely rule out the prospect of her being pregnant?"

"I guess I can't say for sure she wasn't pregnant. I can say—she never delivered a baby though. I didn't do an exam that would identify every possible disease, but the normal ones that are detected in the analysis of blood, tissue and organs did not reveal anything unusual. I can honestly say I didn't run a pregnancy test. Actually, I can't say for sure if she was a virgin or not. Too much decomposition—and with the maggots and all."

"Boy, I could really use a little information like that," Martine's voice reflected her chagrin.

"Let me run one for you. I guess it's possible. If she was pregnant, her parents sure don't know about it." Silence fell in the room as Dr. Gus appeared to deliberate over this possibility. "How long was she missing?" he finally asked.

Shrugging her shoulders, Martine said, "Quite awhile."

"Oh."

"I'm curious," Martine said, "Is it possible she possessed any genetic abnormality that wouldn't have been known to her family yet?" Feeling nauseous, Martine rushed her words, "I would be curious to know if she was struggling with diabetes or seizures of some sort?"

"Martine, I'll take a closer look into that possibility, but those symptoms may not be obvious without a patient to discuss their health with."

"I understand the difficulty," Martine sympathized. "I was told you're amazing at this sort of investigating."

"Very tactful, but why, may I ask, would that be a concern? It really looks like she was a victim of foul play."

"Maybe some more samples for Quantico?" Martine urged.

"Sure."

"But—really, why do think something so specific like diabetes or seizures was involved?"

"It's just a hunch, Doctor. We're really desperate to find out more about this victim. We don't seem to have much to go on so far. Any additional forensics you uncover may be very beneficial to this case. Sure hope we can count on you," Martine solicited his cooperation.

"I'm not surprised that the FBI is involved in this case. Frankly I'm relieved. I wouldn't want to have any more patients like this in my operating room. She was so innocent, and young. I'm going to rush all these samples to Quantico for you. I have a Med School buddy who was one of the first Pathologists they hired. Now he works with over five-hundred investigators. I'll make sure everything is properly packaged—and rushed."

"Agreed. Thanks for your help. I think I have what I need for now. I'll let you finish with our victim in private. Think I'll join Carmen and get going to my next appointment." Martine picked up the tape recorder, and turned towards the door.

"I'll walk you out," Gus offered as he peeled off his gloves and joined Martine at the doorway.

Standing in the hallway on her cell phone, Carmen smiled shyly.

Rubbing his unruly hair, Gus grinned back at her. "How are you feeling?"

"I'm fine. I'll survive—that's if you two don't tell anyone."

"No problem," they said together.

"One more thing, Doctor, what do you know about the Entomology report? Have you seen it yet?" Martine inquired while breathing in the fresh air.

"Richard, from the Entomology lab called and said he's having a hard time determining time of death. Apparently he agrees the body was moved more than once and the insect evolution they studied is not very reliable. He's hoping to narrow it down within three days. Those tiny insects they're studying might tell you more than I can about this death. I know she's been dead too long for me to get this right."

"Any maggots left?" Martine quizzed.

"Yeah." Nodding Gus said, "Quantico?"

"Yep."

Shaking Dr. Delfore's hand, Martine concluded, "With your assistance, justice may be delayed, but it will not be denied."

Chapter 49

Walking to their parked car, Martine let out a big sigh. "Carmen, stop me now if you, or I, can't authorize some lab work be performed at Quantico?" Martine stipulated.

"What? You're the paid consultant. Of course you can," Carmen responded.

"Good. I'm not calling for authorization," Martine stated with determination.

"Hey, I'm so sorry I bailed." Carmen frowned.

"Not to worry. I wasn't counting on any hand-holding. This was all my doing anyway," Martine comforted her.

"Well, I would've gone back in there, but I took care of a couple things."

"Great, like what?" Martine slid into the passenger seat.

"We got some good news. First, the meeting with Lauren's parents is today—whenever you can get there," Carmen sounded like a personal secretary. "Apparently they were relieved to find out the FBI would investigate their daughter's death. They are actually anxious to meet you."

"Great," Martine exclaimed.

"Secondly, there appears to be a hit on a Jane Doe matching your Sharon's description." Carmen elaborated, "It's not conclusive—they're rushing the DNA and finger print analysis to conclude a positive identification. The samples you provided appear adequate."

Elated by the news, Martine resounded, "That's super, Carmen. You're like good luck."

"Yeah, that's me Charmin, Carmen," she kidded.

"Wasn't that a toilet paper?"

"Yep, that's me," Carmen teased back. "Tell me about the autopsy exam."

Martine waved Carmen's recorder as she replied, "Thanks to your recorder we have everything on tape. Let's get this typed up."

"So, you're not telling anyone?" Carmen implored sheepishly.

"No way," Martine affirmed. "It'll never come-up. We both toughed out the autopsy exam. Right?"

"Thanks," Carmen's voice gleaned her relief.

"We have a few more tests being run by Doctor Gus, and I have a test for you to initiate as well. I'm looking for any type of toxic fuel that may be present on these tissue samples from Lauren's nose and mouth area," Martine sneezed. "He's sending samples to Quantico. I took a couple samples with me to see what we might find first."

"Awesome, I love it," Carmen cheered. "While I was in the hallway I contacted the guys in Internal Investigations to begin tracking down the two boys you have an interest in."

"How did you get on that so fast?" Martine quizzed her new friend.

"Jolene told me."

"Let's remember how sensitive the case is," Martine cautioned. "We don't want anyone, to know that we're investigating multiple disappearances."

"Yes . . . yes of course," Carmen promised.

"Any slip in our conversations may lead a doctor or parent to reach out to the media for answers," Martine reiterated.

"Definitely," Carmen agreed.

Chapter 50

Jolene programmed the Olson's temporary address into Martine's navigation system. Driving Martine's car was considered wiser than taking hers—since the transponder was still planted in her car. Jolene turned her phone off so that there was no chance she'd be followed.

"I'm so glad I'm going with you, Martine. I just can't stand being stuck with all those files. I don't feel like I'm getting anything done."

"You are. Don't even think that it doesn't help."

"I don't know how you get people to go along with your theories," Jolene sequestered her sister while they were alone. "I've never seen anything like it in our office."

Martine sighed. "Let's get the information we need. I have to get something from these parents that fits—or, should I say doesn't fit the profile. I can't bear the thought that I could waste anybody's time right now."

* * *

Greeted by the grieving parent's of Lauren Olson, both Martine and Jolene paid their respects.

"Come in," Anna Olson invited. "We are both so pleased you contacted us. We had no idea the FBI would consider this case. We're really so grateful."

"Please sit down ladies," Bill Olson offered. "I don't think I'll rest until you find out who did this. Have you apprehended anyone yet?"

"No, sir," Jolene said.

"This is my single life's ambition now . . . to find out who killed our only child," Bill vowed.

Distraught, with tears beginning to form in her eyes, Mrs. Olson lost all her composure. Relying completely on her husband's strength, she insisted on cooperating in the interview. Mr. Olson had no success in removing her from the process.

Skilled at interviewing victims, Jolene felt confident in her ability to adequately dialogue with this couple through this sensitive topic.

"May I speak frankly?" Jolene began. "Anything you share with us may be very beneficial to the arrest and conviction of the party responsible for this crime."

"Yes—yes, of course," he answered for both of them.

Familiar with Martine's questions, Jolene started her interview, "Let's just begin with Lauren's health?"

"Certainly," Mr. Olson responded.

"Do you know of any health problems Lauren may have had?"

"No. She was very healthy and athletic. She performed in the Color Guard squad at school and was an excellent student," Mr. Olsen finished with satisfaction.

"I hear Lauren was an only child. Have either of you had any other children?" Jolene asked with as much sensitively as possible.

"No. Positively not. We would've if we could," Mr. Olsen answered with a heavy heart.

"I'm sorry, why is that? Why couldn't you have more children?" Jolene probed.

"Well, I guess it doesn't matter anymore if our secret is out. Lauren is adopted. We never could have any children," Mr. Olsen revealed their secret. "We were married almost twenty years before we adopted Lauren. Neither one of us has ever been married before."

"I see," Jolene nodded encouragement. "Why didn't you tell the police that in the original interview? I mean the adoption part?" Jolene questioned.

"Because she was our child in every way," returned Mr. Olson. "Lauren never knew she was adopted. We believed she'd return home. We didn't want her to find out in some news story that she was adopted." Mr. Olson comforted his wife while she sniffled. "We've seen the effect that has on a family when a child discovers they're adopted. The reality of such news creates a void, or feeling of abandonment in an adolescent. They're not ready, as teenagers, to deal with the notion that their birth parents rejected them. Plus nobody can answer all the questions that would inevitably come up about the birth parents."

"I see." Jolene noted their response on her note pad.

"What could it possibly matter if she was adopted?" Mr. Olsen asked.

"We don't know yet," Jolene answered back.

"What do you know about the birth parents?" Martine delicately asked.

"We used Lutheran Adoption Services. It was a very professional and discrete process. Everything was extremely confidential. We knew nothing about the parents and they would in turn know nothing about us or our location. They guaranteed everyone's privacy," Mr. Olsen advocated the arrangement.

"Can you think of anything that may have inadvertently been made known to you about the daughter you adopted? Anything? Like the name of one of her parents? Or what religion or nationality they were," Martine requisitioned for any added information.

"No. We never saw that type of information," Mr. Olson answered emphatically. "Do you think the birth parents have anything to do with her death?"

"No, I'm sure they didn't," Martine reassured.

"Wait, Bill," Anna Olson spoke up. "Remember how excited we got when the agent told us that she was of Swedish heritage, like we were. She certainly looked Swedish as she grew up. Everyone thought she was our daughter in every way."

- 265 -

"You're right, dear," he concurred as he looked back at Martine and Jolene.

"We chose the Lutheran Adoption Services because we would have a greater chance of getting a child that came from Swedish or German parentage. We did ultimately want a child that would resemble others in our large family. Actually, we're more like a clan. There's so many Olsen's. It's just that once we saw her it didn't matter. She could have had red hair and freckles. We would've taken her home no questions asked," Bill reminded his wife as he gazed into her forlorn face.

"Just a couple more questions if you please," Jolene resumed her questioning. "Is there any chance Lauren ever had a boyfriend?"

"No, absolutely no boyfriend. We didn't allow dating. She was only sixteen," Mr. Olson was emphatic.

"Maybe he wasn't a boyfriend to her. He may have been more like a stalker," Jolene asked deftly.

"No. No one ever did anything like that. Her friends and journals didn't turn up anything that pointed to a boy. Reuben, the police detective, who interviewed everyone, was looking for a scorned boyfriend. I think he spoke to 200 people. He never turned up a single thing," Mr. Olsen validated with Mrs. Olsen nodding in agreement.

"Are you sure she was in perfect health," Jolene asked again. "Can you think of any episodes that may have been health related?"

"No, nothing like that," Mrs. Olson joined in again.

"Any chance she may have hid something from you?" Jolene pried carefully.

"No!" Mrs. Olson said in defiance. "Are you suggesting she had anorexia, or some sexually-transmitted disease? Something we would keep a secret?"

"No. Nothing like that," Jolene promised.

"Are you implying incest?" Mr. Olsen snapped impatiently.

"No. Nothing like that at all," Martine jumped in. "We're just checking to see if Lauren was suffering from the beginnings of anything like diabetes, or blue baby syndrome."

Jolene also tried to smooth the emotions, "we're just trying to rule out the possibility of natural death."

Mr. Olson looked shocked. "Are you saying they don't know how she died?"

"They're not sure," Jolene said truthfully. "Right now it's inconclusive." Jolene hated to imply something was wrong with their daughter, which was a mere speculation on Martine's part.

"What Jolene and I were wondering is if Lauren ever had any dizzy spells that weren't easily explained," Martine pried again. "Or maybe she had some moments of forgetfulness. Or possibly she complained about déjà vu's happening to her. Any ordeal that went unanswered may be relevant and helpful as to why this was done to such a beautiful innocent girl," Martine simplified the sensitive nature of the request.

"Well, since you put it that way, she was taking vitamins and iron pills," Mrs. Olson volunteered.

"Really, why is that?" Jolene quizzed.

"Because she said she was feeling weak and light headed," Mrs. Olson explained. "It was getting in the way of her Color Guard activities. I thought she was probably a little anemic because her periods where really heavy and irregular. It seemed like a normal deficiency for a very overactive adolescent girl. It didn't sound too serious, and we never went to the doctor. Her coach told her about the vitamins and iron pills. Maybe it was worse than I thought. I only went by what she told me. Lauren was not a complainer. That's really all I can tell you."

Holding back reaction, Jolene nodded slowly, "Good. That might be of some importance."

"Do you know something about her you're not sharing Ladies?" Mr. Olsen inquired.

"No. We're just considering every possibility as to why she was found the way she was," Jolene tried to pacify the emotional reactions that were generated as a result of sensitive questioning.

Mr. Olson's face appeared more drawn. "If you find anything more out about our daughter we expect you to tell us the truth. We'll eventually sleep better when we know the whole truth. We already realize it will never be the same. We would prefer the facts to not be hidden from us. Our faith has told us 'The truth will set you free.' We really believe that with our whole hearts. You're welcome to contact us at any time. We don't want to be a burden, but we do wish to help and remain informed," Mr. Olson pleaded.

Ending the visit with goodbyes and hugs, Jolene and Martine departed from the brokenhearted couple.

Chapter 51

Merging into the rush hour traffic on freeway 101, Martine and Jolene checked their cell phones for messages. Martine was so ready to decompress in a quiet restaurant, she asked Jolene to select her favorite place.

"I know exactly where we should go," Jolene said with a grin.

"Wait," Martine exclaimed. "I have a text. It says . . . dinner tonight," Martine touted. "It's signed JM. Who's that?"

"Duh!" Jolene shot back. "Our boss?"

"Oh. So no quiet dinner," Martine muttered.

"Nope, don't think so," Jolene supposed.

"Check your phone," Martine requested. "See if you're going too."

"Doesn't look like it, but Wade called. Do you care if I meet with him instead?"

"Of course not," Martine said positively. "I'll get done sooner if you're not there too," she justified.

"Well, it's as good a time as any to tell him what we know. Maybe he's got something to tell me," Martine said in a hopeful voice. "I'll text him that I'm on my way."

Jolene offered a sympathetic smile, "It'll be fine."

"Better have Wade pick you up. I'll need my car," Martine arranged.

* * *

Seated in his regular booth, Mahoney waved at Martine like an expected friend. She thought how different he looked from the night before. After greeting him she realized he even felt different. Something had changed.

Martine sat across from him. "Oh, excuse me, its Eva calling me," Martine explained the telephone interruption.

"Hello, Eva."

"Hey, mom, just want you to know that we are leaving now for the club. We're eating with Tyra and her friends. She wants a good table by the dance floor."

"Okay, have a good time. Bye."

"My daughters are out with Tyra and her friends."

"Well, they're in good hands with her. No one messes with that little pistol."

"Right, I noticed."

"I know it's late, but I thought I'd get an update and dinner at the same time," he said clumsily.

"No, its fine. Jolene and the girls all had plans and I'm so hungry I'm ready to eat a box of Bisquick," Martine said hurriedly.

Laughing, he said, "Well then I'm glad you came."

"Yes, thank you," she picked up the menu lying in front of her.

"Let's order so we can get down to some business," Mahoney cut to the chase.

"Yep, I'm ready when you are."

Martine ordered first, and Mahoney followed. Handing their menus to the waitress, Mahoney started, "Was anything accomplished by your need to broaden the search for detailed information on Lauren Olson?"

"Yes, I think so."

Mahoney looked surprised. "Tell me what you got."

"The autopsy did generate more questions that are being followed up on. I hope that the tests being performed by Quantico and the M.E.'s lab generate some forensics. He seemed curious enough to review his own work too. The interview with Lauren's parents was definitely enlightening. We did discover she was adopted and may have been showing the signs of some illness, or disorder, that hadn't been disclosed to the family physician prior to her disappearance. Oh, she also is most likely of Norwegian descent."

"Is that important?"

"Yeah, I think it might be. However, without knowing more about the real birth parents, that can't be confirmed."

"What would you like to know about the birth parents?"

"I'd like to know heritage, and drug history. If one of the birth parents *used* they could have passed on epilepsy, seizer disorders, mental illness, etc."

"Alright, let me see what I can do to get some information on the real birth parents. You said you're having the samples sent to Quantico?"

"Yeah, don't be upset with Carmen, it was my idea."

"No, I was going to suggest that they have the ability to do some DNA genetic profiling."

"Really?" Martine flashed. "But more to the point, Lauren didn't know she was adopted and believed she was Swedish."

Before John Mahoney could respond Martine's cell phone rang again.

"Martine, this is Carmen. I took your advice and just left Dr. Gus's lab. I'm calling you from the phone in his office. He just verified that Lauren was most probably pregnant prior to her death. Also, he did find some evidence showing the beginnings of diabetes. He wants to know how you knew to look for that. I want to know how you knew. It also looks like the residue around her mouth and nose was unleaded gas. What does this all mean?" Carmen took a deep breath. "What did you learn about her at the parent's house?"

Carmen would have kept rambling, but Martine stopped her, "Good work. I just can't talk right now."

"Hey, Martine, I'm glad I came back over here to see you-know-who," Carmen whispered. "Don't worry, he knows everything is confidential."

"Good, that's really good. So I'll talk to you tomorrow," Martine hung up.

"That sounded interesting," Mahoney presumed.

"It certainly was. Carmen went back to the coroner's. I told you he was curious. Anyway, it does appear that Lauren was pregnant at the time of death. It also appears she was developing diabetes. It sounds like she may have been asphyxiated with gasoline."

"Huh," Mahoney sounded bewildered. "Sounds like a second exam was needed on our girl. What does this all mean?" He asked.

"That's what I'll work on next."

"Well it looks like you got answers to all your questions today. Can we figure out how this helps locate the growing number of abductions," Mahoney said with a facetious grin.

"Sadly, Mr. Mahoney, I don't have all the answers but I do expect this will help us. And what do you mean growing number of abductions?"

"Please stop calling me, Mr. Mahoney. It's, John."

"Okay, I didn't feel I knew you well enough to do that yet."

"You do. Anyway, it seems that while you were out and about all day, more missing girls were identified as 'suspicious missing persons,' instead of mere runaways."

"Oh—no," Martine moaned.

"That's right. With the local police departments in four states forwarding volumes of documentation to us, we're being deluged with everything from hookers—leaving their johns, to missing canines in heat. I'm contemplating the notion this may be an epidemic in all fifty states. And I don't see how the information you acquired today on this girl can be helpful if this is a national crisis." Mahoney shook his head in desperation.

"What? Are you kidding?"

"No, I'm not," he said flatly.

"Oh, shit."

"Yeah, we can't even process the reports fast enough. I'm being bombarded and can't even delegate a file before another one lands. All because some enthusiastic detective notified the police departments of our involvement in a "Human Trafficking" investigation—being headed by me."

"Wow. I can't believe this. I could tell you were irritated. Now I know why."

"The mass e-mails and faxes have created hysteria. You've no idea how much some answers would mean at this point."

Martine gulped, "Yes I can."

"Jolene has two dozen more cases sitting on her desk as of this afternoon. You know—your sister thinks you're some kinda savant," Mahoney said as he glanced at her.

Feeling like a parking meter Martine sat motionless. "Wow! I assure you we're getting somewhere," Martine stated positively.

"How can you possibly say that with nothing more than flimsy medical test results?" Mahoney vented.

"I strongly suggest that the other victims that have been abducted against their wills may still be alive. I don't believe they're going to be murdered at random. I realize we're fighting against time. I pray that Lauren will be the only fatality," Martine reiterated her position.

"Alright, Ms. Martine—other than processing files, what would you suggest next?" Mahoney languished.

Cringing at proposing another off-the-wall-request, Martine seized the moment. "I was hoping that we could locate Peter Jules.

"Why?"

"When Carmen and I spoke earlier she mentioned a possible hit on Sharon. Did I mention that when I was at Peter's house, I found a gas can, with gas, stored in his dungeon?" Martine shared.

"No, you didn't. I just don't see how these two individuals, and a gas can theory, could possibly account for abductions of this magnitude. They couldn't cover the area by themselves." Mahoney twisted his napkin like a rope. "Plus, these two kids couldn't conceal that many women. And why would they?" Mahoney refuted.

"Frankly, it's always better to have all possible scenarios presented up front. Documentation available early on, versus discovering crucial information mid-trial is always preferred. For instance, I propose that if your staff does find merit in most of these new, and existing cases, Peter and Jules are only a small part of a bigger group. Therefore, we'd never want to approach them like the petty criminals they probably are. Right?" Martine wagered her logical deductions for the answer she wanted.

"What are you getting at?"

"We should get to know them. You're correct, John Mahoney, this very well may be a far and wide reaching case." Martine nodded slowly. "That's why I'd like to meet with the German translator as soon as possible. I'll meet him anytime he can see me." Martine redirected her efforts to continue on a path she felt more confident pursuing.

"You certainly are persistent. I need results though. The clock is ticking, and girls keep going missing. I'll arrange for you and him to meet tomorrow evening. Do you play poker?" Mahoney inquired with a twinge of humor.

"Yes, I do. Dealer's Choice or Texas Hold'm?" Martine asked with poise.

"I guess you've played poker. Well, my friend loves it. It's his hidden vice." Mahoney chuckled.

"John, I know we're all feeling a bit helpless and overwhelmed. My experience has proved a goodnight's sleep will help us all to process the information that was downloaded today. I absolutely know it'll help. I'll get you that smoking gun you're waiting for," Martine promised as she stood up to depart.

Mahoney slid out of the booth and walked Martine to her car. "I need results. I need everyone pulling their weight. I just can't believe our best agents have turned up nothing."

"I understand," Martine reassured him. "Hey, even the best Doctor needs a needle to find a vein. Maybe that's why you hired me."

"Yes, I see your point."

"Hey, that was funny." Martine smiled. "Oh, I got a little plan that might help us. I'm still working on it," Martine said mysteriously.

Chapter 52

Martine went to bed thinking about her hopeless circumstances surrounding the case. Compelled to find meaning in the clues and information she had gathered together so far, she asked for assistance and clarification while her eyelids lay heavy and ready to shut down for a night's sleep. Martine busted out a simple request in a rapid burst, "I call on St. Michael the Archangel, God the Father Almighty, and all my heavenly guides and saints to assist me in receiving all the divine illuminated truths that I can access at this time."

Martine drifted into a deep slumber that spiraled her higher consciousness into another etheric realm.

"Who are you," she heard a young man's voice yell.

Turning around to see the person addressing her, she saw an Indian Warrior jump down from a rock ledge. Armed with a large tomahawk, the Indian Brave raised his weapon and charged her.

Camouflaged in the wilderness of trees and shadows were his friends, ready to ambush her. "Stop!" Martine shouted. Stretching her arm out like a traffic cop, her voice brimmed with apprehension, "What have I done?" Seeing her own hand glowing with golden light, she kept it raised like a force field.

Braking in midstride, the Indian Brave halted his assault and lowered his weapon. "Who do you fight for?" he ordered, his voice stern.

"I come in peace. Who do you defend?"

"I defend no one. I fight for land. This *my* hunting ground. You leave now or fight me."

Seeing nowhere to run, Martine choked on her words, "Then you must fight me. Because I cannot leave."

"I not fight squaw that wears dress," he spoke angrily.

Startled by his comment, Martine looked down at her attire and saw that she was wearing a beautiful palomino-colored deerskin dress with a dark-clay-colored mantel. Long fringes, in shades of brown and green, hung thick around the base of the mantel and the three-quarter length sleeves. Stretching across her chest, and down each arm, was a multi-shaded band of blue beading. Four intermittent black-beaded crosses were placed inside the band of blue beading. Small elk teeth lined both sides of the intricate work. Twelve–inch sprays of fringe hung lightly from many of the ivory teeth. Narrow bands of white beading wrapped around the circumference of her hip and knee area. More long strands of fringes, colored like the deerskin dress, hung every few inches from the white bands. Large V-shaped designs were painted brown around the bottom of the dress. Outlining the peaks and valleys of the mountainous scene was more blue beading. Brown and green fringes completed the bottom of the dress where the mountains touched the ground. Elaborate to perfection, the garment was gorgeous. Touching thick-black hair that hung down to her waist on each side of her face, she realized that she must be a Native American. Pointing her right foot out in front of her dress, she saw a knee-high moccasin that was fringed up-and-down the side with dangling strands of beads and feathers.

Jolted back to her circumstances by the noise of the Indian boy's friends approaching her, Martine's eyes widened as she found herself outnumbered and surrounded. "Why do you not fight me? What will you do instead?"

"You squaw," he answered in defiance. "Not good enough to fight. You lose," shaking with fury, the Indian Brave spat on the ground. "You die slower death like slave."

Realizing a worse fate lie ahead if he had his way, she mustered strong words that could alter the course she was stuck in, "You are filled with darkness and cannot harm me," Martine saw her hand glow brighter as the words flew out of her mouth.

Agitated by her insolence against him, he seethed, "You no power here. Mine greater." Thumping his breast with a firm fist, he signaled his hostility.

Feeling energized by the golden light, Martine continued to challenge the Brave, "You do not have to destroy me. I will come with you to your Medicine Man and let him decide my fate. I will be judged by higher beings than you. They will not be wrong."

"You come with us. We bring you to Wise One," the young Indian nodded conceitedly.

Marched to the Indian village like a prisoner, Martine felt like a lamb going to slaughter as they aggressively prodded her along. Saying nothing to her captors, she felt increasingly uncomfortable as she was led through a deep wilderness land inhabited by wild horses and untamed beasts.

Paraded through the Indian village that was peppered with hundreds of teepees, Martine marveled at the sight of a different world. Tightly bound and out of her element, she couldn't comprehend a plan of escape or what to do next.

Causing a ruckus as she was marched to the center of the tribal community, Martine felt shame as Black Hawk and his band of followers hooped and hollered at their new found fame.

Pushed to her knees in front of the biggest teepee, Black Hawk called for the wisest man in the village.

"Lion Spirit, we bring enemy."

Throwing back the flap of his teepee, the Medicine Man known as Lion Spirit emerged wearing a feathery headdress. Small colorful bird feathers created a rich bonnet that blended down into the Shaman's thick black hair. Like the top of a tropical pineapple an array of large bird feathers spiked upwards at the crown of his headdress. Dressed in loosely woven primitive attire, he looked more intimidating than astute. Standing taller than her and the boy warriors, he scoped Martine's body like a lion sizing a prey.

Supported by his eight-foot wooden staff, he strolled up to Martine and motioned her to rise.

Black Hawk and one of his companions grabbed her arms and awkwardly jerked her up from her kneeling position. Still tied at the wrists, she remained a vulnerable captive inside the Indian fortress.

While using his free hand to touch and examine the fine bead-work and feathers she wore on her elegant clothing, Lion Spirit sniffed the air around her as if he was taking in the essence of her aura. Directing his attention to Black Hawk, he asked, "Why you bring me, her?"

"She enemy. She say only Wise Man judge fate. I kill woman if Lion Spirit say. She be slave and die."

"Why you kill woman?" The old Shaman spoke in a steady monotone voice.

Black Hawk's voice projected loudly for his audience, "She enemy. I kill for you."

Lion Spirit walked around Martine's nervous body and scrutinized every inch. "How you know she enemy?"

"She on my hunting land." Black Hawk fisted his hand and struck the center of his chest again. "She not ours. Not leave. She say I with darkness and not harm her."

"Ah," Lion spirit replied. "Her bravery bring more light. See no weapon." Lion Spirit eyed Martine closely. "Because her Spirit seek help, she find it. She overcome darkness. Arrogance bring your demise, Black Hawk. Your darkness devour you."

Black Hawk sounded angrier, "I not see her power. I capture her and bring to you. This our way."

"No," Lion Spirit rebuked sharply. "That your way. I say *she* bring you to me. She not fight with tomahawk. She not fight with words, like foolish boy."

Black Hawk grunted disgust, "I great warrior. I many weapons," he seethed at Martine as he spoke.

"She greater," Lion Spirit corrected him. "You not leave this realm because you only compatible here. You not enter higher world until you abide by our laws and become attuned to enlightened way. You not have own hunting ground, Black Hawk. You repeat same mistakes."

"This wrong," Black Hawk argued. "I famous Brave who kill enemy and hunt wild beast. She nothing but foolish woman who not know our ways. She not dress like us. She lost, not me."

"No," Lion Spirit disagreed again. "She better dress. She come from better place. She not say she lost."

"Good. If she not lost, I will go there," Black Hawk scoffed. "She take me there. I bring back gifts to Lion Spirit."

Shaking his head negatively, Lion Spirit retorted, "No. You not go there. You not make good choice. You take what not for you."

Arguing, Black Hawk crossed his arms and stood as tall as he could, "It hard to make good choice here. I go another place."

"No. You first make good choice here. You listen to Great Spirit. Learn lesson like she."

"My lesson too hard. Her lesson not hard."

Lion Spirit used his tall staff to demonstrate the strength of a wooden-post support. Forcing the staff's base into the ground till it stood erect, he explained on, "Lesson different like teepee." He let go of the staff that was now standing straight on its own. "Some big strong and complicated." He gestured to his staff that stood firmly planted in the earth. "Every size, every shape, many color."

"Who need teepee? I live where I want. I go where I want. I use father's teepee."

Frowning at the young man, Lion Spirit said, "Time for you to make own way. Build good life—strong teepee. Not use other tepee." Pointing towards the myriads of Indian lodgings, he added, "Look. Pick teepee Black Hawk can 'brave' on own."

Black Hawk walked over to shortest and smallest teepee in the village and claimed it. "This *my* teepee. This be enough."

"Yes, Black Hawk," the Medicine Man said. "You chose wisely for impatient Indian. You do every time. That your teepee. That been your teepee. You pick same teepee and repeat same path. You not seek knowledge, skill, or understanding. You not seek wise way, or Spirit help. More help come when you chose to be *like* Great Spirit Guide."

Enraged at the insult, Black Hawk scowled and crossed his arms defensively. "What you do with prisoner I bring you? She not one of us. She no have teepee."

"Why you bring me her? Not need prisoner, I seek wise way."

Fiery-eyed, Black Hawk grabbed Martine's hair and demeaningly pulled her head back so that everyone could see her face. "She ask see Medicine Man," he touted.

Turning to face Martine, Lion Spirit addressed her, "Why you seek Medicine Man?"

"I seek help from Great Spirit," she said humbly. "I need someone I can trust in difficult lesson."

"Daughter, we help you. You honor us with your finest dress, you seek our wisdom, you come in peace, and respect our way. You could destroy Black Hawk and warrior friends with your power of light. You not enemy. I give you gifts you seek. Come."

Perplexed by this turn of events, Martine quantified his proclamation, "How do you know this?"

Solemn faced, Lion Spirit said, "You are of Mother Earth. Your dress of many color show your way." Moving closer he stroked the front of her clay-colored mantel. Looking up, he spoke to his people, "Brown for fertile soil, and green for new growth." Nodding with approval, he brushed the back of his hand across an array of delicate feathers that hung from her neckline. "Feathers from pigeon, hawk, quail, and dove mark spiritual growth. Exotic plumes from parrot turkey and macaw indicate status." Looking down past her waist, he pointed to her two white bands of beading. "Many journey made on straight and narrow path."

Reaching slowly for her sleeve, he used his aged fingers to trace the wide band of blue, as if translating a message in Braille. "You walk under light of sky." Studying the four beaded crosses strategically spaced inside the blue band that stretched across her breast, he pointed his shaky finger, "You, daughter, have gone many direction. Seek truth." Lifting up one of the ivory teeth that bordered the blue band, he examined the artifact. "Tooth of wild elk show stamina to do what you must."

Glancing down towards the bottom of her garment, he added, "Many mountains to climb in journey on earth. Sky over peaks and valleys show Great Spirit blessing along path." With an admiring nod, he gently stroked the batch of eagle feathers that gracefully hung from her belt. "You soar free with Spirit."

Angered by the notion that this stranger carried more gifts than he, Black Hawk's tongue could not contain his jealousy, "Her feathers are not great like mine. I have feather of hunter." Pulling his friend closer, Black Hawk said, "Running Elk have ivory of great buck."

Lion Spirit turned from Martine to confront Black Hawk's tirade. "It not what feather you wear on journey, Black Hawk, it how many. You could learn much from this Wise One."

Visibly irritated by Lion Spirits proclamation, Black Hawk pushed his friend aside so he could leave the scene.

Pulling his staff out of the ground, Lion Spirit ignored Black Hawks tantrum and rejoined Martine. Freeing her hands, he beckoned her, "Come."

Leading the way, he brought Martine and his entourage to a Spirit Lodge with a primitive shrine inside a structural lean-to. Stopping, in front of the rock-constructed altar, the wise Shaman motioned Martine to stand next to him. "You are twelfth generation to our people," he said. "I know your thought." Turning to face her, he continued, "I give you medicine of Mountain Lion."

"Mountain Lion Medicine?" Martine repeated reverently.

"Yes, daughter." Lifting a necklace off of the surface of the rudimentary looking altar, he held up an amulet that hung from a leather cord. Carved from bone and inlaid with bright abalone shell, the unique form resembled two cloths-pins stuck together top-to-top. Each open-end depicted the face of a roaring lion. Centered between the two lion heads was a human figure with long hair.

Displaying the amulet for his people to see, the Shaman bestowed his blessing, "Out of lion's den you find new friend." The Medicine Man nodded his affirmation as he slipped the leather cord over Martine's head. "Lion Medicine give you power to lead. Remember, daughter, the qualities of true leader not insist that all follow. You follow your heart. Show other people good way. Balanced leader seek truth and follow difficult path." Gesturing towards the defiant Black Hawk who had stormed away, he added, "Not path of selfish serving heart."

Moving away from the shrine, Lion Spirit led Martine and his crowd of people to the edge of a vast pasture land where he pointed to a herd of Indian horses. "You need speed for journey. Mount your pony."

Puzzled, she scouted the enormous band of Indian ponies for one that she would recognize. "I don't know," Martine admitted.

"Which one please you?" The Medicine Man asked.

The question startled her. *How could she possibly choose*, she thought. Using her hand like a visor, she scoured the herd again. "The strongest and fastest," she decided.

"Which one can that be?"

Lowering her hand, she looked at Lion Spirit. "The stallion. The one in charge."

"Good. His name Sun Dance. He white like sun and dance with his heart."

Martine grinned widely as she easily identified which one he was. "He's beautiful."

"And wild," Lion Spirit added. "Can you tame him?"

"I don't see how." Martine studied the herd in bewilderment.

"We honor our animal like guide and teacher," Lion Spirit instructed her. "We learn much from their way. Can you?"

"I don't know how to tame the big stallion."

"Call him like you call to Great Spirit. Show my people how to speak from heart."

Martine closed her eyes and visualized her invitation to Sun Dance. Seeing herself seated on the powerful white horse as they galloped through the endless meadow, she used her mind and her heart to call his name, *Sun Dance, ride with me.*

Rearing on his hind legs, the stallion pawed the air with his fronts while letting out a long whinny. Dropping to the ground, he spun around to face Martine, neighing as he galloped towards her. Parking himself in front of her petite frame, he nickered softly and bent his head for her touch.

"He will lead you safe on journey."

Charmed by each other, Martine hugged the thick neck of the proud stallion. Sensing the horse's approval she hiked her dress up slightly and mounted the magnificent animal like she had done in childhood dreams. Connecting as one, she stayed on the horse as he galloped across the field until they were almost airborne.

Chapter 53

Most of the investigative personnel chose to work Saturday morning. Deciding they needed the extra hours to review the avalanche of files received on Friday, the dedicated team rallied at nine in the morning. Martine and Jolene were no exception to the arrangement.

Commencing with a nine A.M. briefing, Mahoney announced that early mistakes found in most of the "missing girl" files complicated the FBI's efforts. Local police departments that were the first responders initially treated the majority of the cases as runaway's. Mahoney also reported that no two cases had the same investigator. Team leader Helm added that; *most of the reports look like traffic citations—brief and innocuous.*

Anticipating how her time would best be spent, Martine adjourned to her temporary desk with the Maria Danielson file and the Osborn file.

Phones were quiet, and the absence of the administrative personnel made the whole building feel peaceful. Pehaps it was the sporty attire they were all wearing. Everyone was sharing their personal plans for the afternoon as they intercepted each other at the coffee station.

Concentrating on her work was easier when unproductive chaos was absent. Martine was not accustomed to this Bureaus work environment, nor a difficult case that continued to escalate.

Determined to accomplish something before the morning was finished, Martine went to Director Mahoney's office.

Standing up when she entered his office, Mahoney eagerly greeted her, "Hey, Martine, I meant to thank you for coming in with the rest of the team."

"No problem," she answered as she sat down in the guest seating across from him. "I'm not going to stay all day. I absolutely have to help Eva get a four-wheel-drive vehicle before she goes back to school."

"Certainly, I completely understand," Mahoney gave a warm smile.

"You weren't exaggerating about the work piling up here." Martine shared her own smile along with her witty comment, "Actually, it looks like a piñata exploded."

"Yeah," Mahoney concurred. "I wasn't exaggerating last night."

"No you weren't. I just left Carmen and she mentioned that you have the files on Peter and Jules."

"That's right. After hearing you imply they could be the needle I'm looking for, I thought I should see for myself what has you so suspicious."

"You wouldn't be able to find those files in this paper-detonation . . . would you?" Martine asked with a hint of humor.

"My, aren't we in a clever mood today. And yes, I have your files right here. What I want to know before I hand them over to you is what your big plan is. I'm not going to allow any unnecessary risks. These may very well be dangerous guys if they're involved. Their friends may even be worse," Mahoney cautioned.

"Yes, that has already occurred to me. Can I take a look-see? I'll come up with a strategy we both agree on. I just don't see how I can be useful until I dig into their backgrounds more," Martine proposed.

"Alright, take a look. I think you'll be disappointed though," Mahoney said as he handed two very thin files to Martine.

After reviewing them like a seasoned attorney, she raised her disappointed face. "They can't possibly be boy scouts. Just because there's no criminal records on file doesn't mean they haven't broken the law. It just means they haven't been caught," Martine contemplated out loud.

Slowly Mahoney nodded in agreement, "I thought you might say that. I've clearly picked up on your need to check these two out. Short of you convincing them to come in here for lie detector tests, finger printing, mug shots, and DNA samples, we don't have a plan that will break them. I also can't possibly waste any manpower right now on tracking either one of them. We've got a reasonably long list of criminals, sex offenders, pornography leaders, drug lords, and johns hanging on the wall in the war room—we can't seem to investigate properly. There're too many suspects that already present a clear danger to the population. From what you've told me, the only crime these two have committed is extremely bad housekeeping," Mahoney rebuffed with a fastidious stab at humor.

"Finger printing? Did you say finger printing?" Martine made a quizzical expression.

"Yeah," Mahoney said.

"You reminded me of something," Martine's eyes scanned the ceiling as she contemplated her revelation. "I really thought something better would have turned up in their background checks. I didn't expect to resort to this. I'm a little embarrassed to show you."

"Whatever you've got let me see it."

"Desperate times call for desperate measures. I'll be right back."

Rushing out of Mahoney's office, Martine grabbed her big purse and hurried back to finish her conversation, "Here," she said, reaching in her purse.

"What do you have there?" Mahoney studied the see-through package dangling from her hand.

Martine revealed her primitively preserved photographs, marijuana butts, and fingerprint-lifts from the Della Avery's root cellar. Setting the Ziploc down on Mahoney's desk, she continued, "You see, when Eva, Alexa and I were at the Avery's home I took it upon myself to lift some prints off the inside of the root cellar door—the door that only these guys had access too. I assumed the prints would have to be theirs on the door since they had to push it to close it tight. Della was certain that no one, not even herself, had ever been aware of the cellars location. The photos she gave me are their high school pictures. I know it's a stretch, but I'd like to run these prints and see if anything new surfaces. Remember, just because they don't have mug shots and prints on file, doesn't mean they haven't broke the law. It just means they're better criminals than most, and they've found a way to avoid the law," Martine reasoned.

Laughing, Mahoney said, "Fair enough."

"I can't say my lifts will produce satisfactory prints, but I was hoping you'd try. Can we move on this now? I hope you'll put these at the front of the line," Martine pleaded.

"How 'bout right now. Will that be soon enough?" Mahoney asked with questioning tone. Using his interoffice paging system, Mahoney called for the Senior Laboratory Analyst that had also come in on Saturday, "Thomas, please come to my office."

"While I'm here can I set up a time to meet with your translator?" Martine looked at her watch as she tried to finesse more than she dared to ask.

"I wasn't kidding about poker," Mahoney called her bluff. "You can meet him tonight. It's our poker night. Can you make it?" Mahoney casually invited her.

Surprised by the expedient response to her request, Martine mustered a jubilant, "You betcha."

Dressed in casual jeans and a blue polo shirt, Thomas interrupted their conversation as he walked in Mahoney's office—like he was expected. Noticing Thomas was well groomed, at least fifty years old, and without a wedding ring, she imagined he was a better housekeeper than her.

Handing Thomas the Ziploc containing wrapping tape, joints, and photos, Mahoney instructed his Senior Laboratory Analyst to *rush the results.*

Witnessing the expression on Thomas's face was priceless. Martine cringed with embarrassment when Thomas accepted the Ziploc and held it up in the air with two fingers.

Ignoring Martine, he repeated his orders, "You say you want me to lift prints off this bundle of tape? And you want some DNA off this drug paraphernalia?" Thomas said in a tone laden with apprehension.

"Yes, Thomas, that's all I want," Mahoney tried to keep a straight face. "And when you're done, run them through the system for a match."

"With these photos—I presume?" Thomas skeptically eyed Mahoney.

"That's right." Mahoney maintained a cordial smile. "And quickly. It's a rush."

Acting put-out, Thomas held the package gingerly in the air as he exited the office.

Dialing the phone to speak with his friend, Teddy, Mahoney kept his eyes on Martine, "Hello, TW, it's, John. Calling to confirm we'll be there at six-o'clock tonight."

After terminating the call, Mahoney confirmed the final arrangements, "Done. I'll pick you up at Jolene's if you can be ready at five-thirty. Oh I have a little something here for you to try out." Mahoney opened his desk drawer and retrieved a modern looking device. Handing it to Martine he explained, "This is your new secure phone. If you're going to be out of the office so much, we need to be able to contact you."

Accepting the strange looking technology, she examined its unusual features. "Is this the 'Crackberry' everyone's been talking about?" Martine asked as she touched one of the tiny buttons. "How do you close it?"

"Crackberry?" Mahoney blurted. "We call it the Blackberry."

"Yeah," Martine ran her fingers over the screen and keypad. "This has a keyboard for typing e-mails in real-time. They say it is as addicting as crack cocaine. It's the new smart phone. I know my daughters both want one."

Rubbing his chin, Mahoney shook his head in disbelief, "Well, I think you got me on that one. The Crackberry. I won't forget that."

Looking confused, Martine replied, "You want me to learn how to use this? I will probably need a class."

"No you won't. Go see the tech kids. They'll show you what you need to know and get it activated. They'll program everything for you. We can stay in touch as long as you have a signal."

Reluctantly, Martine took the technically advanced phone and left Mahoney's office. Feeling less than tech-savvy, she headed back to her desk to wrap up her day before finding one of the computer geeks that would train her in.

Chapter 54

Preparing to leave for the afternoon, Martine put one more thought into action. Curious if enough time had gone by for Thomas to lift a print, she headed down the hallway to find the lab.

Martine found Thomas absorbed in crafting a print off of her crudely fashioned packing tape. Observing his diligence in lifting a print, she hesitated before approaching him.

Anticipating a cool reception, Martine walked up casually and greeted him.

Acting invisible, he ignored her.

Touching him on his shoulder, Thomas jerked from surprise, causing his earphones to fall out.

"I'm sorry," Martine apologized.

Clearing his throat, Thomas gulped, "I didn't see you."

Stepping up beside him, Martine asked, "Are you having any success."

"Yes," Thomas said formally.

"I know the technique is a little unorthodox."

"Hmmm . . .," Thomas said in a low pitch.

"When can you tell me what you've got?"

"Hmmm," Thomas uttered again.

Realizing she was going to get as much out of him as road kill, Martine moved away.

Deflected away by his lack of interaction, she moved toward the adjoining room that was lit up bright. Snooping where she probably didn't belong, Martine saw a young man working intently on a computer monitor. Surrounded by shelves of hardware devices, she walked up to the young man and introduced herself, "Hello, I'm Martine."

"I'm Brandon."

"Boy, are you tucked-away in your own world back here," she commented.

"Yeah," he agreed. "Pretty cool, huh?"

Noticing manuals and technical devices strewn in every direction around him, she joked, "This looks like customer service."

Laughing with her, Brandon said, "That's good."

Brandon reminded her of her older-cousin . . . uneasy with people, but completely comfortable with electronic devices. Confident she'd get along with him too, Martine asked, "Are you the one that can show me how to use this phone? And what else can I get in here with this snappy security pass?"

"Well, I can give you a crash course on the phone, and I can see what we have that fits your needs," Brandon offered like a salesman. After leading Martine through her phone briefing session, Brandon picked up his own phone and directed Martine to conduct a test, "Now, just type me a message and send it to brandon83@hotmail.com."

"Okay," Martine said as she sent Brandon a message which read, *need tracking and surveillance devices that can be easily installed.*

After he received her mail, Brandon wrote back, "I definitely have something like that."

Reading the reply, Martine looked up at Brandon and said, "Why don't you demonstrate your personal favorites?"

Jumping up from his stool, Brandon signaled Martine to follow him.

Loving this boy's enthusiasm and synergy, Martine confided in him about monitoring her suspects. She added a couple more stipulations. "If I set a trap with these guys, what can you do to make sure I'm not in any danger?"

"Don't you worry, Martine, I got your back," he boasted. "Me and Craig oversee all the remote monitoring on the weekends. We switch tapes and check the transmissions twenty-four-seven." Pointing to another secure room, Brandon directed Martine's attention to the surveillance equipment he maintained. "We can even be contacted if an agent needs protection while undercover. We have visual and audible tracking capabilities," he bragged.

"Wow, I guess you could hook me up with some really sweet stuff."

"Oh—yeah."

"Okay, here's what I think I need . . ."

Martine and Brandon filled a bag up with bugging equipment and instructions. Thanking him profusely, she exchanged phone numbers and said goodbye.

Passing next to Thomas on her way out, she waved goodbye.

To her amazement, Thomas spoke, "Well I believe there's a lift. I just don't know if it's merely a partial or a whole one. I doubt if it is a single unblemished—unblended print though."

"I hear you're an artist, Thomas. I need a Picasso print. If we can't retrieve a solid lift, or two, I'll have to go back to the source with your professional fingerprint kit. I'm attempting an emergency shortcut and didn't mean to frustrate you," Martine explained apologetically.

Chapter 55

Confining all case-related conversations to the bedrooms or patio, Martine chose to meet the girls outside and initiate a plan that both her daughters were anxious to partake in.

Excited about all the fantastic technology she acquired from Brandon, Martine huffed her breath—unable to catch up to the adrenalin rush she was on. "Okay, girls, you're right, you may be the only way I'm going to get to run surveillance on these guys," Martine paced the patio area. "I just don't know how to do it yet. Just need to figure out a way for me to get close enough to them or their vehicles. We can show you how to tail them, but we need to do it at sundown, which is when I think they're operating. Then I can swoop in and plant a device."

"No way. I can't stay up all night chasing derelicts around," Eva objected boldly. "There has to be a better way."

"She's right," Alexa agreed. "Mom, I've heard you say, 'If you hear the sound of horse hooves, you don't go looking for race cars.'"

"What does that mean, Alexa?" Eva asked.

"It means we need to get closer and hang out where they do. Go undercover . . . be like—focused on just them and not what they do all night."

"Ish, Alexa, you're not serious? There's got to be another way."

"There is," Martine agreed. "We have you tail one of them so you can accidently talk to him and distract him long enough for me to plant this stuff."

"Maybe," Eva said guardedly.

"That could work," Martine sounded anxious. "We need to track down Peter or his cousin," she went on, "they're probably accomplices to something much bigger. We just need one of them to feel comfortable enough to confide in you and invite you into a car or home. Remember we don't have time to waste. Eva you need to be . . . be . . . be . . ."

Alexa smirked at her sister. "Devastatingly beautiful?"

"No"! Martine said shaking her head. "I was going for riveting. Let's figure out how we can use you without casting any ambiance of distrust."

Filing a chipped fingernail, Eva nonchalantly offered, "I'm ready whenever you two are. It's not going to be hard to out-think those guys."

"I think not." Martine paced on the concrete pavers. "It's mandatory you stay safe and avoid posing any threat to yourself. You're way too classy and attractive to be genuinely interested in either one of these guys."

"No kidding, Eva, did you see the other guy—Jules?" Alexa cringed, "He looks like he drives around with bodies in his trunk."

Martine sat on the lawn chair, "This whole charade has to be believable or you could find yourself alone and in danger. We have to devise a way for one of them to become infatuated or comfortable with you. You'll need some kind of a diversion. No wait," Martine stopped briefly, "a disguise."

Eva objected, "I do not need a disguise."

Martine was adamant, "If you really want to get involved and be a part of this operation, you'll follow my directions. There's no way you're going to be allowed in a precarious situation that you can't get out of. You're talented and have always had a flair for acting. You've spent the better part of your life practicing on your dad and me. Lord knows you're not shy or lacking confidence. I'm also aware I can count on your resourcefulness and big smile to get you out of most jams. This time I want you to . . . no wait," Martine corrected herself, "I insist you change-up your appearance—for your own safety. We can create a different identity, a minor deception for your protection. Eva, please work with me on creating a theme that plays into snagging one of these guys attention."

"Yeah, Eva," Alexa chimed in. "Try and find a topic that will generate dialogue. Find his passions and relate as quickly as you can—and I don't mean STARBUCKS! Try dogs, cats, guns, drugs, or bars."

Frowning at her sister, Eva replied sarcastically, "Sure. I'll have plenty in common with these guys."

"Oh, I got it," Alexa waved her hands for attention. "You gotta do one of these with them." Using both her hands she pretended to straighten out a small piece of paper. Taking her forefinger and thumb she pinched something out of an imaginary bag. Sprinkling the smidgen onto her phony-paper, like airborne confetti, she rolled it up and twisted it like a tootsie roll. Inserting the invisible hand-rolled joint in the corner of her mouth, she pretended to light it and take a deep drag—holding her breath till she nearly suffocated.

"Damn it, Alexa, that's not funny, what are you now—a mime?"

"Oh please, you're such a drag," Alexa snickered. "Get it? I said you're such a drag."

"Yeah, I get it," Eva said disgustingly.

"I got it! I got it, girls! Astrology."

"Astrology?" They harmonized.

"You bet. Eva, when we find a way for you to run into Peter you'll notice his eyes and tell him, 'you must be a Pisces.' That should impress him. He'll want to know how you know. You'll explain to him it's his eyes—that they're a dead give-away. Then you can ask him to guess what you are. He'll need to know you better to do that—and study a little astrology, which you can help him with—at a book store."

"How do you know for sure he's a Pisces?" Alexa pondered.

"Hello . . . , Alexa, she has his driving record for sure," Eva triumphed.

"Oh yeah," Alex conceded. "I knew that. That's good."

Exhibiting confidence, Eva agreed, "That will be easy. I can do that."

"Great!" Martine resounded. "We'll target Peter, and Jolene and I will be very near when you socially encounter him." Martine nodded confidently. "Are you ready to lose the college prep look then?"

Indignant, Eva scoffed, "What college prep look?"

Chuckling, Martine elaborated, "Your skirts and shorts are too small for a fairy."

Defending her minuscule clothing, Eva retorted, "What? They're not that small. Everyone dresses like this."

"Your wardrobe is so small and tight I'm afraid you'll get stuck in one of those outfits," Martine frowned. "I really mean it. You need clothes that don't say 'look-at-me I'm a princess.'"

Giggling, Alexa butted-in, "If Eva's a princess—you know what that makes you, mom?"

"Yes I do, Alexa. That makes me a queen, and I got some rules that we're going to abide by here." Martine led the girls over to the patio door where they could clearly observe their reflections as she gathered Eva's long hair into a temporary ponytail. Examining her daughter's appearance without the professional hair cut gave her an idea. By holding the precision-cut layers and colored highlights away from Eva's face, Martine illustrated her plan. "Do you see that? You already look different." While both girls analyzed Eva's reflection in the patio-glass mirror, Martine explained, "That definitely changes things up a bit. We need to lose the designer hair style and give you an undercover makeover."

"Please," Eva protested. "I'm not cutting my hair."

"Focus, girls, I got a great idea. Alexa, you're going to the library to check-out a book on astrology, the older and more used the better? Eva, remember Nanny Angie?"

"Nanny Angie," they said in chorus.

"Exactly! Who wanted to look like Nanny Angie when they were little girls?"

"We did!" Eva sounded apprehensive.

Alexa glanced at her mother. "Do you want Eva to look like Angie?"

"That's right, Alexa. Angie had long auburn hair, loose hippy looking clothes, a tattoo on her cheek, crystal necklaces, a ring watch, and floppy hats. She was like a seventy's flower child."

Alexa scrutinized the connection, "Where are you going to get that kind of stuff?"

"That my dear would be a thrift shop." Martine folded her arms with pride.

"She would make me go shopping there," Eva whined.

"That's right, now you can see where your clothes will end up when you stop wearing them."

Eva projected her notorious glare. "You can't be serious."

"Eva, what we're doing is very unorthodox. We need to do something unconventional and that means thinking outside the FBI box. If we don't come up with a fantastic plan you won't be able to get close enough to plant a couple devices, and you could put yourself in big danger . . . and that's not happening on my watch. If we're on the right track we are dealing with potentially volatile and distorted personalities. Likewise, what we learn from this guy's patterns and behaviors could prove exculpatory for him. Therefore comma if you don't do this yourself, I'll pick out your wig and new wardrobe myself—period."

"Fine." Eva relented.

Chapter 56

"**H**ow do I look, Alexa?"

"Wow, you look like a plant."

"What?"

"You're so green. Does your lime-colored shirt really say, 'Get it Here' on the front, and 'Hanks Bar' on the back?"

"Seriously, what do you think? Check this out." Removing a hairy mass from the shopping bag, Eva dangled a long haired wig in front of her sister.

"Wow, put it on."

Positioning the new "Do" on her head, Eva flipped the hair forward over her right shoulder. The waist-length hair dramatically flowed next to her face and over her chest. "Do I look like Angie now?"

"Yeah, Eva, you do look like Angie. Nobody would recognize you." Alexa blinked, raising her eyebrows simultaneously. "It's amazing."

"I know," Eva said victoriously. "I feel like I'm going pimping. Do I really look different? I feel like someone else."

"Well, let's just say I like it." Alexa admired the creation reflected in the mirror.

"It really makes me feel different," Eva replied.

Alexa was enthralled with the process of molding Eva into another person. Recognizing that her sister was definitely in character, she saw how that could protect her and make her more equipped than ever to handle this undercover operation. Validating the success of the make-over, she reassured Eva, "You don't look persnickety now." Still adjusting to her sister's transformation, Alexa couldn't take her eyes off her. "I didn't know you could look so funky."

"Funky? You think I look funky? I put the F U in funky." Eva snapped her fingers.

"Nice. You are really convincing. You don't look or sound like Eva—the Diva."

"Eva—the Diva? Where did that come from? Yeah know, I wonder how this would work if we went bar hopping?"

"Eva, dating is not a recognized job."

"Not dating . . . working undercover with the FBI." Remaining serious, Alexa cautioned her, "You still really need to be careful. Curiosity killed the cat."

Shimmying her shoulders, Eva said, "Satisfaction brought him back."

Turning one last time in front of the mirror, Eva evaluated her extreme make-over that included a very long light-brown hair wig pulled back in a pony tail, big hoop-style earrings, a large book on astrology, a desert-style-military cap, several necklaces, a lime-green tank top, cargo pants in a jungle camouflage fabric, and brown-commando-style boots.

"Okay, let's show mom."

Chapter 57

"Wade's here," Martine yelled from the kitchen. "He's got flowers."

Almost ready for her Saturday night date, Jolene peeked out her bedroom window when she heard Wade pull-up. "I'm almost ready, Martine. Get the door."

Jolene listened as Martine greeted Wade at the door and introduced herself, "I'm the big sister. It's nice to finally meet you. Come in. Jolene's almost ready."

"I can't believe the family resemblance." Wade reached his arm out for a formal hand shake.

"I'm glad we can finally meet." Martine returned a firm grasp. "I heard you're quite the detective, Wade."

"Hi, Wade," Jolene interrupted, as she joined them in the kitchen. "Have you met the girls yet?"

"No," he answered. "Just Martine. Where are those nieces I've heard so much about?" Walking up close to Jolene, he kissed her on the cheek. "These are for you." Handing her the bundle of red roses, he added, "Sorry I'm a little late. I did make reservations for seven."

"I'll take these for you," Martine offered. "I'll put them in a vase so you can get going. You can meet the girls another time." Martine took the bouquet from Jolene. "Alexa and Eva are very busy getting ready for some dance club."

Waving goodbye to Martine, Jolene said, "Have fun winning JM's money. I'm counting on you getting it all."

"Right," Martine said sarcastically. "Don't bet on it."

Jolene's stomach flitted with nervousness as she walked down her driveway with Wade's arm wrapped around her shoulders. "Thank you for the flowers. I didn't expect them." Stopping for him to open the car door, she gave him a quick peck on the cheek.

"I hope there's more where that came from," Wade joshed.

"We'll see," she teased. "The flowers really helped."

Laughing, Wade said, "Well, then I'm glad I got you something else."

"What?" Her reply was squelched when he shut her door.

Jolene waited for Wade to slide into the driver's seat. "What did you get me," she giggled coyly.

"You'll have to wait till dessert." Wade raised his eyebrows when he grinned. "I know how you like presents."

Dinner was formal and perfect in every way. Jolene felt proud to be with Wade, even though she wasn't completely ready to forgive and trust after the break-up she had endured. Still unsure if he had the same feelings for her she kept her guard up, making him flirt even harder all through dinner.

"Here," he said, handing her a small gift box. Grinning like a Cheshire cat, he added, "I hope you're a good sport like me."

Scared that he was getting back at her, she held the box and wouldn't open it. "I don't think I want to see what's inside."

"Come on," he goaded. "Chicken?"

Closing her eyes, she lifted the top off the bright pink box. Sparkling like a star in the sky was a diamond pendant necklace. "Wade, it's beautiful," she exclaimed. "Why would you get me such a special gift?"

"Because I'm sorry and I miss you."

"I'm sorry too." Jolene started to cry. "What made you think of a necklace like this? It's so amazing."

"You're like a faceted diamond, Jolene. I know you're perfect in every way. Maybe a little too perfect," he paused. "And, hard on me.

But, I probably deserved it. I can't just let you walk away though." Wade reached for her hand.

Charging the atmosphere with emotional sparks, Jolene whimmpered, "Why, didn't you call? You didn't even e-mail, or text. You cut me out." Exasperated, she added, "I thought you hated me."

"How else am I supposed to get your attention? I shouldn't have to hunt you down. You insulted me," Wade defended his hurt. "But, I never could hate you."

Bantering back and forth over whose fault caused their falling out, lasted minutes until Jolene's stubbornness relented. "I don't want to fight about it anymore. You think I overreacted when you hated the birthday present I made you." Like a magnet, she drew his gaze to her eyes, "You think it's my fault we stopped seeing each other."

"I'm not judging what you did." Wade offered a contrite smile.

Softening her tone, she replied, "Yes you are."

"No," Wade lowered his voice and tried to console her, "I'm not good enough to judge you. I just don't agree. It pissed me off. I don't see myself as an ego maniac."

"I don't want to fight about it. I don't want to fight at all." Jolene wiped her tears.

"What's wrong with a little fight anyway?" Wade smiled charismatically. "My mother said it's good to have arguments."

"How's that?" Jolene fidgeted with her napkin as she listened to Wade explain his mother's reasoning.

"Making-up can be so good," he finished.

"Well we wouldn't know about that."

"No we don't. Not yet anyways. You haven't even told me how you like the other little gift I left you with."

Surprised, she sat up straight, "You left me a little gift?"

"Yeah, you know," he said. "I just wanted to see how it's going. You haven't even mentioned it all week."

Completely caught off guard, Jolene shrugged her shoulders. "Why didn't you just ask?"

"You didn't really act like you wanted to talk about anything except the case your on," Wade answered.

"That's no excuse for bugging my house."

"Jolene, what are you talking about?"

Looking around the crowded restaurant, she shushed him, "Lower your voice. My house. Why did you bug my house?"

"Your house? I haven't bugged your house."

"What gift did you leave me? What are you talking about?"

"I'm talking about the dog I gave you. I want to know how it's doing. You still have the dog don't you?"

"Of course. I thought you were talking about something else. I thought you put bugging equipment in my house."

"You better start at the top. I have no idea what is going on here."

"Alright. I guess I didn't tell you about the surveillance around my house. Somebody bugged my house. So we added our own security precautions."

"Explain," Wade demanded. "What surveillance? Who's surveillance?"

"We don't know. It's pretty high tech. Any ideas who'd do that? You know a lot about that stuff."

"No. I have no idea. Nobody I know would be involved in that unless you were into drugs, or espionage," Wade wagered.

"I'm getting worried because we've done reverse surveillance for a week and nothing has been set off. No unidentified vehicles. No prowlers. No reentry. Nada."

"Why didn't you say something sooner?" Wade shook his head in disbelief.

"I didn't think I'd have to."

"Describe it to me."

Detailing the location and type of devices found inside her home and car, Jolene added, "Worst part is we dusted my car and computer. No prints. None, except a few of mine. Everything was wiped extra clean. So far it's a ghost."

"Jolene, who's at your house right now?"

"Nobody. Martine's at a meeting with Mahoney. Eva and Alexa are hanging out with Tyra. Actually, they're staying at Tyra's house tonight, with the dog."

"Let me guess, they're planning to drink," Wade chuckled.
"Right. As much as they can."
"I got an idea," Wade stood up. "Are you done eating?"
"Sure. Are we leaving?"
"Oh yeah. Come 'on," Wade said.

Chapter 58

Answering Jolene's doorbell, Martine was greeted by John Mahoney thrusting a file folder into her hands. Stepping outside for privacy, she shut the door behind her.

"Is that fast enough?" He asked.

Opening the folder for a glimpse of its contents, she heaved a sigh. "You found an address. How?"

"Apparently, Peter's unregistered and uninsured car was recently reported stolen. And, that's not all," Mahoney gloated.

"What do you mean?" Martine questioned. "There's more?"

"Some unique DNA results on Lauren. A rare DNA marker."

"Rare like what?" She asked.

"It's an anomaly."

"What kind of anomaly?" Martine tried to listen and read at the same time.

"It's too early to know what the DNA profile is." Mahoney shrugged. "They'll need a few more days to complete it, but it does indicate on the first sample they started that an unusual marker has been identified."

Martine glanced up. "Did they elaborate on what it could mean?"

"You've met Thomas." Mahoney shook his head. "He doesn't speculate."

"Right," Martine sounded perplexed.

"He did say it's a genetic marker dominant in some people of Scandinavian descent."

"So, it's an ethnic marker," Martine deduced.

Mahoney shrugged. "I believe so."

"Does it tell us anything about physical characteristics?"

"Nope, not yet." Mahoney took Peter's file out of her hand. "Thomas made it very clear that more information is days away and the samples will have to be compared to thousands of DNA profiles in multiple databases. After he isolates that marker he is going to have it sent out to a lab that specializes in ancestral profiling. He said that with a little math they can get some discerning signatures and clues from that unique DNA."

"Thank you," she said. "This is very interesting."

"I thought you might say that."

"You know what we need to do?" Martine asked firmly.

"You want DNA from all the missing girls checked."

"Yep."

Mahoney gave a quick laugh, "We'll see. Ready? Did you remember all your money for the buy-in?"

"Depends, how much do I need?" Martine looked in her wallet.

"A couple Jacksons will do it."

"I'm good," she said. Opening the front door, she set the file inside the home.

"All right," Mahoney returned. "Let's get going."

* * *

Six-o'clock sharp Mahoney introduced Martine to Frye Manor. Impressed with the size of the sprawling estate, Martine felt a rush of intrigue as Mahoney nosed his car through the security gate. Accompanying her boss up the flagstone sidewalk to an ornate display of architecture, she couldn't help but look perplexed.

Sporting a debonair smile, Mahoney said, "I thought this might floor you."

"Dang," Martine gasped. "This is so amazing. It's like going back in time."

"Wait till you see the rest," Mahoney's voice hinted intrigue.

Answering the door himself was Teddy Frye. Welcoming them into his home, like a maître d', he charmed Martine's heart. Captivated with every aesthetic detail, she could hardly remember why she came. Truly his home was an experience for anyone with appreciation for art history.

Teddy conducted a brief tour of his unique residence. Older than almost every other mansion in the Phoenix area, it was in dire need of renovating.

Feasting her eyes on massive oil paintings that hung randomly throughout the residence, Martine remarked, "Teddy, if this wasn't your home, it would be a museum."

"Thank you, madam," Teddy's English accent was prominent and distinctive. "This art has been in my family for centuries."

Escorting them down a long hallway with an arched brick ceiling, Martine passed alcoves adorned with precious southwest art. Lit for added drama, each artist's piece held a place of importance. "I see you're a local collector as well."

"Yes, yes I am," he said proudly. "These are my additions to the family's art collection."

Arriving at a single room with twelve-foot walls lined with shelved-books and movable-ladders, Martine exclaimed, "A library."

Dumbfounded, she sped over to one of the walls and pushed the ladder to prove it was real. "Darn, this is fine. It's like finding Bruce Wayne's Manor in Gotham City." Turning to Mahoney, she commented, "I thought I was meeting your poker buddy who teaches at the University—not royalty."

"So, you say you're impressed," Mahoney teased.

"Come, now, let's see what we can find in this library to help you," Teddy offered.

"Speak for yourself," Mahoney injected.

"Oh, you're going to help alright," Teddy's voice warned.

Settling into burgundy velvet game table chairs, the three of them joined together around a mahogany wood table.

Martine wanted answers and couldn't wait to hook up with this man's intelligence. Enamored with his good fortune, Martine inquired, "How did you amass such a monstrous collection of books and writings?"

"Mostly, inherited. My family roots can be traced back to the Tudor family in England. Of course I do my own collecting too."

"It's marvelous." Martine smiled at the Englishman. "Hey, Teddy, I believe you're my new best friend," she winked at the man she would be focusing on tonight.

Teddy might be years older than her, but he was suave and original. A sexy English accent made him all the more dashing.

"Well, Martine is a history buff like I told you on the phone the other day," Mahoney explained. "She's anxious to get some more of your assistance. Then she wants us to take all her money in some 'Texas Hold'm Tournament.' Right, Martine?" Mahoney finished jokingly.

"Definitely. I was wondering if you can explain more about the German language used predominantly in the documents I found. I know the stuff I submitted is a little odd, being crudely photographed and all, but I do not own it yet," Martine explained in as vague a fashion as she could muster up.

"Yes, funny you should mention that. I'm very curious as to how you came across such unique items. You see the Germanic language used is called Frisian."

Martine asked quickly, "Did you say Frisian? Like the horse?"

"Yes, I suppose so, I don't know too much about horse breeds, but if the Frisian horse dates back . . . back before the Middle Ages, and from around the North Sea, that's where it got its name then. Anyways, this German dialect came from the Germanic tribe that inhabited a chain of islands and a land called Friesland. The islands extended along the Netherlands, West Germany, and Denmark. The language closely relates to English. I, being from England recognized it immediately. I would be very interested in purchasing the documents you are evaluating. Are you a buyer too, Ms. Martine?"

"Yes, I'm considering the purchase, although the prize writings and artifacts may have a more appropriate resting place here with you. I don't think they're current residence is fitting. I'll keep you in mind if I pass on this deal."

Glancing at Mahoney for validation on the credibility of her find, Martine said, "I think I'll show them to John first."

Alerted by the mere mention of his name, Mahoney engaged in the conversation, "Yes, I'd be happy to look at them with you." Sitting back in his chair with his arms folded, he resumed his silence.

Organizing her numerous photocopies on the table, Martine began asking questions and referencing her pictures. "Can you tell me anything about what this document means?" Passing a photo of a very old looking certificate, she waited till he held it up for close examination. "All I was able to read and translate in the library, was the word Decree, and the word 'ficken' which in English means . . . you know what it means."

"Yes, I suppose I do," Teddy concurred fastidiously.

"Well I don't," Mahoney piped in. "What does 'ficken' mean?"

"It has to do with our English slang word . . . here let me just show you," Martine said as she reconstructed the four letters exactly as she had seen them in her *Sound of Music* dream. Displaying 'F.U.C.K.' the way it appeared in her vision, she turned the writing tablet around for Mahoney to see. "I prefer not to say the letters out loud, though I'm thinking the four letters individually have a deeper meaning that grew into an acronym. Like in law school we learned they meant 'unlawful carnal knowledge.' Carnal knowledge is always unlawful unless it's between a married man and his wife." Chasing the voice in her head, Martine sequestered her host, "Basically, it was a crime in ancient England during the middle ages. Is there a more historic translation you could help me with?" Martine paused for an answer.

"Yes, I see. You want a more authentic explanation or meaning?"

"Yes, please," Martine answered. "If you look here at this poor photo image, the German written document constitutes a legal decree. It references 'Ficken' in a bolder typeset. In the library's dictionary that translated to that same word," Martine motioned to her four-letter acronym. "I just can't read the hand written order."

Mahoney leaned forward to preview the four letters in question before Teddy rotated the note pad for his own viewing. Studying Martine's documentation for about a second, Teddy flashed,

"Yes, I have a thought." Leaving the table, he went to his desk and rummaged through a couple drawers. "Ah-ha," look what we have here?" Returning with a thick magnifying glass, Teddy plunked himself down in his chair and scrutinized the document like a mad scientist. "Yes. Yes, here it is," he exclaimed in excitedly. "I believe that in England it meant 'Fornication Under Consent of King' which is what it also says in the hand written portion." Leaping up from the table again, he excused himself, "Sorry let me grab my favorite resources. Hold-on a minute, I'll be right back."

Martine got her next question prepared. Ready to have all her questions answered before the poker game, Martine wished he'd get back—right now.

Armed with a load of special publications, Teddy returned to the table. "I have it here. It's actually a very old Germanic word. It's been around England and Germany since the fifteen-hundreds. It basically started in Germany and means . . . you know, that legal definition you gave us. Appears its most likely origin is from the North Sea Germanic inhabitants." Teddy muttered softly, "Hum . . . it says these invading kings that came to Christianized Anglo-Saxon Britain, would require their troops to rape the women in a common demoralization procedure. The rapists were given legal permission to go against the religious laws."

"Then it *wasn't* a crime," Mahoney weighed-in.

"Correct, and no one could be prosecuted," Teddy added.

"Teddy, you're like a historical compass," Martine flattered him.

"What does this have to do with all the German things you found?" Mahoney asked Martine.

"I can't be sure, but it appears this decree was signed by the leaders of the Third Reich."

"Teddy, can you find a date?"

"Yes, Martine, I believe you might be correct. The year is nineteen-thirty-two."

Handing him another photo that claimed the front cover of an ornately bound journal, she said, "This one has no type setting. It must be the oldest of them all."

"Yes, I see that too. What is this other thing next to it?"

"Oh, that is a very old Ouija Board. I mean really old. It was signed in 1892."

"Who signed it?" Teddy sounded most intrigued.

Scrounging through her papers, Martine handed Teddy another sheet. "Here is a better photo of the board. As I recall it's signed by E.C. Reiche."

Using his reference book and magnifying glass, Teddy agreed, "Yes it is. It actually reads, 'to my friend Olaf and his beautiful daughter Freida.'"

"You probably think it could be worth plenty as a collector's item," Martine theorized.

"Yes. Yes. I do. Don't you?" Teddy admitted.

"No. I think it is without a doubt a divination tool that is used for no good." Martine was frank, "I think it will end up costing you more than it could ever be worth as an antiquity."

"Sounds like you know a little bit about this item," Mahoney chimed in.

"I know enough to not want it. I know it is more than a mass-produced game board with a plastic pointer. I know it can be used to tap into the user's subconscious and ruin their life."

"Wow," Mahoney exclaimed. "Why do you believe that?"

"It may have been patented in the late 1800's as a parlor game, but its origins go back to ancient times in Rome, Greece, China, and Egypt. It was never a children's game. It was an alphabet board used by mediums to communicate with spirits. It's just not the toy many believe it to be."

"Well," Mahoney responded to her indignation. "Why wasn't it dangerous for mediums?"

"Because they knew how to protect themselves and were well versed in the banishing rituals," Martine knowingly defended her beliefs.

"Yeah," Teddy agreed. "Philosopher P. Celsus says here, 'don't call up that which you cannot put down.' It also says here that morbid curiosity with these board games has caused unexplained hauntings with the owners of the game," Teddy closed his resource book. "I see. I guess I'll pass on this item when it comes up for bidding. I too thought it was just a game."

"There is no way it is just a game," Martine replied.

"So, back to the handwritten journal," Teddy examined it closely. "It says it's . . . it's, oh, this is a diary by a girl named Gretel."

"Gretel?" Martine's voice pitched.

"Yes, Martine," Teddy confirmed. Reacting to the loud chime of his door bell, he excused himself, "Let me check on dinner. I think it has arrived. I'll be back in a few minutes."

Chapter 59

With the radio turned-up, Eva moved to the beat of her music as she applied make-up and packed clothes for their overnight stay with Tyra. To avoid a lecture from Martine, she stayed busy in the bathroom till she heard the front door close and Mahoney's car drive away.

"Alexa," Eva summoned her sister into the bathroom they shared. "Did you hear what Mr. Mahoney just gave mom?"

"A folder I think," Alexa said nonchalantly as she started styling her hair.

"Not just any folder," Eva corrected her. "I heard everything they said through our window. I heard him say, 'Is this fast enough for you? Here's an address for one of the punks you want.'"

Alexa's face froze. "Wow. Let's look at it."

"I am," Eva whispered excitedly. "It says that this Peter kid just had his car stolen and he made a police report. The police report has an address for him."

Alexa supposed, "Oh my God, we could find him tomorrow."

Nodding in agreement, Eva added details, "Exactly. It also says where he works. We don't have to wait, we can go right now."

"Heck no," Alexa retorted loudly. "We're not going anywhere without mom. We need to call her."

Eva's mischievous smile said she disagreed, "Yes we are." Eva closed the bathroom door tightly. "She's out tonight playing poker or something, and Jolene is out with that Wade guy. We're supposed to stay out of the house anyway. Remember, we're going out with Tyra. We can track down Peter and find out what he's driving now and plant a device. Do you know how important that would be?"

"It's too dangerous," Alexa argued.

"Alexa, mom is gone and you know what we have to do." Eva smiled confidently. "I've been thinking how I can turn this into an extra credit report for that technology class I'm taking. I was going to do it on the Blackberry phone mom got, but this is better," Eva reasoned.

"What?" Alexa expelled loudly. "Are you nuts?"

"No. We have to find Peter or Jules and get this tracking device planted in the car or she isn't going to know if they're really involved."

Alexa waved Eva's proposal off like a pesky fly. "Well maybe they aren't anyway."

"When has she ever been wrong?" Eva asked with knowing in her voice.

"You heard her say that the FBI will never waste the money and manpower to track these two guys down." Eva yanked on Alexa's arm. "And frankly, she's never gonna have the time. We can do it without her."

"You're right," Alexa relented. "We can't let her break the law, and Jolene said they need to do everything by the book."

"Right." Eva smiled with admiration. "But we can do it and no one will know."

"Who do we know at the Bureau that can help us," Alexa pondered out loud, "just in case you can't get away from him?"

"Tyra," they said in unison.

Eva pulled her wig out of the bag, "We're staying at her place tonight anyways. She can find some back-up."

Hurrying to get Eva's disguise back on, the two worked feverishly to duplicate every last detail.

Alexa started organizing the operation as she styled Eva's faux hair, "Let's take mom's car with the navigation. We can find both places in no time."

"Make sure all the stuff we need is still in her car."

* * *

Faded house numbers painted on the curb outside a rundown building identified Peter's most current address. Eva pulled over to the side of the street and turned the auto off. Slumped low in the front seat of the car she and Alexa took turns spying on the building. Recognizing him from the photos at his grandmothers, she soon watched an older version of his high school picture exit the dilapidated building. Jabbing her texting sister, tension rose in her voice, "Look look look! It's him."

Excited that they had tracked him down at the right address, Eva instructed Alexa, "We need to follow him now."

Tucked in the shadows of the adjacent street, Eva saw Peter enter a used white-van with no plates. "He's leaving. Can't lose him now."

"I'll text Tyra," Alexa said hurriedly.

Eva relayed instructions, "He's heading south on twenty-fourth." Studying the navigation screen, Eva added, "The next big intersection we're going through is Palm Avenue. Let's try and catch up to him before the light."

Tailing the white van like undercover cops, Eva stayed close for the next few miles. Turning off the main street, Eva followed Peter's van into a large gas station.

Frantic to concoct a diversion to meet him, Eva yelled, "I'm getting out here. You drive and park in front of his van while he fills his car."

"Are you sure?" Alexa questioned nervously.

"Definitely," Eva replied.

Rummaging through the glove compartment, Eva searched for an Arizona map. Armed with her gaudy purse, an old map, an astrology book and a crazy costume, she jumped out of the car.

Seeing Tyra cruising into the gas station, she nodded slowly at her friend who stared back in disbelief. Walking briskly up to Peter, Eva flashed her undeniable smile of confidence, "Excuse me, I'm lost. Do you live around here?"

"Yeah, I don't live too far anyway."

"My friend said that there's a party around here." Eva smiled innocently. "Do you know anything about a party?"

Coughing a couple low guttural bursts, Peter cleared his voice to answer, "Probably. Do you know the address?"

Acting like a naive adolescent, she giggled sweetly, "No, I forgot it at home, but I heard it was near this corner." Eva pointed to an intersection on the map, "I don't have my own car. Now I'm stuck out here all alone."

Looking at the map of the Phoenix area, Peter coughed again, "You're not at this intersection. That intersection is way up here. It's a little confusing in this part of town."

"You mean I have to walk way up there?"

"Yeah," he said as he struggled with the persistent cough. "Do you need a lift?"

"For sure. I should have come down yesterday with my friend, but I couldn't. Too much homework. I just got down here from Flagstaff. I hitched a ride, and this is where they dropped me off. I thought this was the right place."

"Cough. Cough." Peter suggested, "Call someone and get the address."

"Well, I'm not late, so my friend is probably way up there waiting for me. I'm just at the wrong place. She doesn't have a phone. I just need to hitch a ride up further."

"Do you want me to give you a lift? I'm going up that way myself."

Standing next to Peter while he gassed up the van, Eva tried more small talk, "That might be okay. What kinda parties do you like to go to?"

"I don't go to parties."

"Do you go to clubs?"

"No."

"Do you work around here?"

"No."

Getting nowhere with her conversation, Eva tried her technique one more time, "Is this your van?"

"No."

Striking-out, Eva used her mother's suggestion to propel the conversation forward, "You must be a Pisces."

"What?" Peter looked up from the nozzle of the gas pump. "How'd you know that?"

"Easy, it's your eyes. They're a dead giveaway."

"You can tell by my eyes that I'm a Pisces?"

"Absolutely. I bet you don't have a nine-to-five job either."

"You're right. That's amazing."

"My horoscope said I would meet a very creative and sensitive person today. That's you . . . isn't it?"

"I guess it is. How do you know all that?"

"You're probably an artist," Eva probed again. "No . . ., I know, you're a model."

"Nope," Peter laughed it off sheepishly. "I'm not an artist or model."

"I . . ., I know . . . you're a musician or an actor."

"No. Wrong again. I did just get a new job though."

"I bet you work at night."

"How'd you know that?"

"You hate discipline," Eva stated with confidence. "And you like to try new things."

"Exactly. Are you a psychic?"

"No, but I bet you are," Eva answered with charm. "Pisces are like really strong psychics. You want to find your soul mate. You don't want to just hang out with any good-looking girl. You need your spiritual companion."

Peter looked at Eva carefully, "That's remarkable. I feel like we've met before."

"Maybe we have," Eva said flirtatiously.

"Wish I didn't have to work right now."

"Tell me about your new job," Eva moved in closer to Peter's comfort zone.

"First tell me about what's so great about this party?"

"Well, after you pay for your gas, why don't I show you?"

"No can do. I work tonight."

"I was right. You do work at night," she exclaimed.

"Yeah, that's right. I'll be right back. Go ahead and get in." Peter left Eva alone while he went inside to pay the cashier.

Hoisting herself up into the front seat of the van, Eva settled in quickly and rummaged through the big purse for the GPS tracking device. Placing it under the passenger seat of the van, she moved it around till it magnetized to the metal frame under the seat. Satisfied she had installed it securely, she found the listening device her mother had thrown in the purse. Using the Velcro strips Martine had "jerry-rigged" for attaching the device, she peeled off the protective strip that covered the adhesive side and pushed it tight to the bottom-side of the seat. Scrambling to put everything back in her purse, she looked up to see her sister backup tighter to the front of the van as Tyra's car nosed in tight behind it, blocking the van. Squeezed in by the two vehicles, Eva jerked nervously as Peter popped into the driver's seat. "Guess what?" Eva asked breathlessly, blood draining from her face.

"What?"

"I really need a big bottle of water." Digging in her purse for money, Eva handed him a five. "Can you get me a bag of chips too?"

Alone in the van again while Peter ran her errands, Eva called her sister, "Keep me boxed in. I'm almost done. Don't let him pull out. And honk when you see him coming." Hanging up the phone she used her camera feature to see in the back of the van.

Curious about how much more time she had, Eva glanced in the side view mirror to spy on Peter's whereabouts. Relieved that he was still shopping for her chips, she turned her focus back to the contents stored in the van.

Eyeing a large plastic bag behind the driver's seat she used her free hand to remove contents and disperse them for some candid camera shots. Feeling a ball of hair at the bottom of the bag, she pulled it out and held it up for examination.

Feeling her phone vibrate, she dropped the frock of hair and answered. "What."

"Register. He's at the register," Alexa shouted.

Pressured for time, she snapped at her sister, "Delay. I need a diversion." Peeking through her window, she saw Alexa jump out of her vehicle and run into the store.

Looking in her side mirror again, she glimpsed the commotion flaring up inside the store. Satisfied with the ensuing interference devised by her sister, she regrouped and resumed her espionage work.

Aided by the intense lighting in the filling station's bay, she eyed a bunch of smoked cigarettes in the van's ashtray. Duplicating her mother's recent actions, she snatched a few and tossed them in her bag.

Seeing Peter accept change from the cashier, she snapped a picture of the wig and pulled a few hairs out. Stuffing everything back in the bag, she sat up straight in her seat and collected her composure at the exact moment Peter opened the driver's door.

"My friend is here. Look. That's her." Hailing her sister in the car parked in front of her, Eva opened the passenger door to exit. "Thanks, Peter." Excited and desperate to escape, Eva talked fast, "Why don't you give me your phone number?

"Yeah. Can I take you out? I mean, if you don't have a boyfriend?"

"Sure you can." Eva wrote a fake number on a piece of paper and handed it to Peter. "Maybe we can get together next time I come down here."

Getting into Alexa's car, Eva exploded, "Alexa, move it. Gun it. Go."

"How bad was it?"

"Yuck."

"What'd you think? What's he like? I couldn't see his face. What's he look like?"

"Let's just say he's not the hottest log on the fire."

Chapter 60

Returning to the Library, Teddy resumed his role as translator of Gretel's diary. "It says here that her mother was Freida and she gave her this journal. Oh my goodness. Listen to this, *'Yesterday the soldiers came to our town and killed every resident. They leveled the town and ate a picnic in the park. They saved a few of us girls that had some kind of special blood. They said we were 'good Nazis' who were lucky to be saved so we could make babies for the Fuhrer. They killed my whole family.'"* Teddy paused, "I can't read the rest of this page. There's water damage."

"That's horrible," Martine called out. Borrowing the magnifying glass, she looked through it herself, "I think her tears bled on that page."

"Here's another entry," Teddy continued. *"'The bombings were so great last night that the black-out has not ended. More people are starving and have no home to go to. Today my friend Brigitte was taken away. I heard she will be a slave because the Doctors say her blood is not good enough.'"*

"What kind of slave would her friend be?" Mahoney questioned.

"I don't know," Martine mused.

"Her next entry says, *'It has been a week since Brigitte left. She has not written and I don't know where she is. Today ten new girls from Norway arrived. They say they were kidnapped when they were hired to be models. I want to be friends with them. They hate me because I'm German.'"*

"What is going on?" Mahoney leaned into the circle.

Teddy went on, "Listen to this entry, *'Last night was a big party with important German soldiers. I met a Kommandant that is with the SS. He said he will be back tomorrow.'"*

Gripped in fascination, Martine urged Teddy, "What happens next?"

"It says, *'The soldier came back to see me and is going to hire me to be his typist. I will have a good job with high ranking men.'"*

"Is there more," Martine asked.

"Her next entry says, *'I have been told by Nurse Frau Schneider that the soldier that hired me was born to die for Germany. I must do what he wants before he dies. I am to have his baby.'"*

Martine interrupted, "I think I know what this is about. She is going to be a Lebensborn mother. She will procreate for the German race."

"Explain that to me," Teddy said.

"This girl Gretel is going to be a breeder for the Third Reich. Nazis had the same policies for people as for art. They destroyed the unacceptable and promoted the Germanic. They wanted global domination. This was part of their international plan. They didn't just exterminate. They bred German blood."

"I can't believe you found a diary from a . . ., what did you call it?" Teddy scratched his neck.

"Lebensborn girl," Martine clarified.

"Can you skip over nine months and see what happens?" Mahoney asked.

"No," Teddy replied. "There is only one more entry photographed here. It says, *'I hope I have a baby girl. I will name her Ada. Her father is an elite soldier, I cannot say his name. He said we will have more beautiful children.'"*

"So, Freida was her mother, who was killed in a massacre. Gretel is kidnapped and produces a high-ranking soldier's baby. Is that about right?" Martine summed up the writings.

Teddy nodded, "Yes. They probably bred more than one."

"This is unfathomable," Mahoney concurred. You weren't kidding the other night when you told me about Hitler's plan to make an Aryan race."

"No I wasn't," Martine tapped her pen in contemplation. "It was such an embarrassment that it got covered up. It was never publicized. The Third Reich was an extreme example of ideology run amok."

"I personally never realized how important the concept of Germanization was to the Nazis," Mahoney shook his head in disgust. "I must say I'm a little surprised how sophisticated their whole plan was."

"Well, they did plan to have a thousand-year reign," Teddy confirmed.

"Right, it's obvious from this diary that the degree of German blood a child possessed determined their fate," Martine said. "I researched RUSHA and learned that the German Lebensborn mothers with children were basically unidentifiable when the war ended. The secret held, and they blended into the rest of the refugee population. The breeding records were destroyed to cover-up the heresy. The program dissolved when they lost the war."

"What about the rest? The kids without mothers?" Teddy asked.

Revealing her recent research, Martine captivated her audience, "The children without mothers ended up in institutions and orphanages. They were considered shameful."

"This diary started when she was only fifteen years old." Teddy's excitement grew. "She had that baby when she was fifteen or sixteen. She was brainwashed, and working for Hitler. This has to be read."

Seeing Gretel's girlish handwriting though the magnifying glass, Martine reflected on the revolutionizing content, "I only took a few pictures of this journal. I had no idea what it was about. It is the thickness of a book. I'll try and borrow it, Teddy."

"Yes, do."

"How about a look at this? It has something to do with this family too. It's called the Mutter-Kreuz. The library translated it to mean The Mother's Cross. I don't have anything else on it. I can't tell you what the antiquity stands for."

"Yes. This is a rare find," Teddy said as he set down the photo and started reading the library article Martine had found. "It means the mother had four or more children for the Fuhrer. Wait, this is a golden one. That means she had eight or more."

"Eight or more children for the Fuhrer?" Mahoney said. "Martine, are you thinking this stuff has something to do with the case? Is that what all that bible stuff you were talking about meant to you?"

"What bible stuff?" she said absentmindedly as she studied at the photo again.

"Genesis? Remember?" Mahoney said decisively.

Reminded that she wanted read it herself, she asked, "Oh. Teddy, do you have a bible?"

"Of course. There's more history in there than this whole library."

"Where have I heard that before?" Mahoney chuckled.

Opening the bible to Genesis, she skimmed through the first few chapters till she hit number six. Slowing down, she scanned till she stopped. "Listen to this, *'At the time the Nephilim appeared on the earth, after the sons of heaven had intercourse with the daughters of man, who bore them sons. They were the heroes of old, the men of renown.'*"

"What were Nephilim?" Teddy asked.

"They were the prehistoric giants of Palestine that were the result of marriages between daughters of humans and the fallen angels." Finishing her explanation, Martine realized she had read verse four—6:04. Suddenly she knew she was on the right track.

"This is what you believe Hitler was trying to do? Recreate the God races that were on earth before the flood?"

Unwavering, Martine stated, "That's not what I believe, that's exactly what he was trying to do."

"Dear, Lady, I most certainly wish we didn't have a big poker tournament arranged for your evening. I had no idea this was going to be so entertaining. I promise to assist you in your further research. I trust you and my friend John will fill me in on what this is really all about."

"Of course we will, old friend," Mahoney obliged.

"Okay then, that should clear things up for now on that. How 'bout we look at some of these scripts?" Martine motioned to a few pages of Germanic writings. "I just have a few more to go over with you, Teddy."

"No problem, I'm thoroughly enjoying my time with the both of you. Please allow my server to bring in some dinner. I often eat in here alone. I was wondering if you'd like to dine right here so we can keep going. That will give Big John something to do in case he finds our History Trivia game boring," Teddy nodded at John in the most dignified and gracious manner.

"It's unanimous, we eat here," Mahoney accommodated the researchers.

"How long have you practiced law, Martine," Teddy asked.

"Almost twenty-years."

"That's impressive," he commented. "Did you hear this one? The Attorney said to the witness; *Are you sexually active?*"

Martine grinned. "No, I haven't heard that one."

"The witness answered; *No, I just lie there.*" Teddy laughed at his joke.

Joining with his light heartedness, Martine joshed back, "I suppose you think I like lawyer jokes?" Grinning with mischief, she answered her own question, "Well I do. The Attorney says to the witness: *All your responses need to be oral, okay? So, what school are you from?* Witness answers; *Oral?*"

Laughter echoed in Teddy's private library as Martine joined the men in their fun. Feeling alive inside for the first time in many months, Martine savored the moment. What odd friends they make she thought, there has to be a story here. "Well let's check out this candlestick and the inscription on it," Martine requested.

"Oh my, have you found one of these?" Teddy inquired.

"Actually I believe there are two. I pulled what I could find in the library but can't understand its origin or purpose." Martine was holding her breath a little on this one. "I want to verify our translation. I don't want to find out it really says 'Merry Christmas and Happy New Year.'"

"Yes, well I see, the inscription on the candle stick holder says: *'You are only a link in the clan's endless chain.'* The page from the resource book you printed says *'If a mother produces more than four Lebensborn children she receives a silver candlestick with an inscription.'* Down here it says *'Show that you are ready, through your faith in the Fuehrer and for the sake of the life of our blood and people, to regenerate life for Germany just as bravely as you know how to fight and die for Germany.'* That's some heavy stuff," Teddy commented.

Teddy's server came in with a large platter full of oriental cuisine. After the plates and utensils were handed out everyone dished up as much food as they desired.

"What a feast, Teddy, thank you for your hospitality." Martine lightly inhaled the aroma.

"You're welcome, I love the company. Let's see what else you have here, Martine."

"Here's a photo of a blue-and-white Byzantine cross with a swastika in the center. The bale on the top indicates to me it was worn around the neck. I don't think men ever wore their medals around their necks," Martine theorized. This is another photo of a similar cross I found in the local Library."

Utilizing his magnifying glass, Teddy studied the photos like a lab technician. "I must say, Martine, your find is original. I've never seen artifacts like these before. This cross appears to be a medal of honor. No wait," he stopped. "This medal is for the child-rich mother that has four or more children." Reading the library article, he went on to say, "Bronze for four-children, silver for six-children, and gold for eight-children. This is a medal of honor for German women. Looks like you have all three in this photo," Teddy scrutinized. "That means this mother had at least eight children. Oh, see the inscription around the swastika says, *'Of the German Mother.'* There isn't much written here about it, but it says these mothers had children for the cause of the master race. These women were apparently called to duty for this cause," Teddy finished his interpretation.

"Goodness," Martine said. Momentarily reminded of Sky Warriors tiled-letters that spelled 'Woman-Hitler,' she tried to cover-up her reaction. "I mean, I wonder how many children one mother could have? Actually, I wonder who the father was?"

"What have we here?" Teddy picked up the last photo copy. Studying the typed page, he hemmed and hawed, "this document highlights the concepts of Germanization throughout the world, reproducing Germanic blood, suppression of all religions, and patriotic duty to colonize the Aryan race."

Pensive, Mahoney remarked, "Did you really find all this stuff in one place?"

"I really did," Martine replied sheepishly. "Just think what these people could do with the DNA knowledge we have discovered in the last decade."

"This is turning out to be a real story of something or other. I just don't see what we're going to do with it right now," Mahoney motioned towards the voluminous records of research.

"It's like a perfect storm," Martine barely finished her words when she remembered the dream that replicated the *Wizard of Oz* events, most importantly the tornado. Then she recalled the DNA test with an unusual marker relating to a specific heritage. Martine knew she must continue to unravel this family's secret.

Chapter 61

Parking his car in his driveway, Wade clicked his remote to open his garage. "Stay here. I'll be right back." Unbuckling his seatbelt, he exited his auto and ducked into his garage as the door slowly opened up.

Brightness from Wade's headlamps shone into his garage, providing the light he needed. Rummaging through miscellaneous items strewn around inside the garage, he appeared to be searching for something specific.

Seated in the idling car, Jolene watched as he located a black duffle bag. Snatching the bag that bulged from its' mysterious contents, Wade checked inside the zippered carrier before nodding at Jolene.

Proving to be satisfied with his find, he returned to his GTO and tossed the bulky bag into the backseat. Entering through his driver's door, Wade slid back into his car and sped out of his driveway. "I found what we need. Let's have some fun."

"What are you up to?" Jolene questioned. "What's with the bag?"

"Babe, I've got stuff here that nobody's supposed to know about."

Hatching a plan while they drove to Jolene's, Wade talked faster than a cassette on fast-forward, "This will disable any electronic device. We'll disrupt the signal, and cause a backwash effect."

"What does the backwash do?"

"It's a clash with their frequency. It's electrostatic or magnetic." Excited, Wade rambled, "I don't know exactly, but a current is created that will raise havoc with all the connected equipment. Let's just say, we're gonna be jammin.'"

"Are you saying big or small, we're sabotaging their home base operation?" Jolene summarized her understanding of the optimal affect.

"Yep." Waded accelerated the gas again. "It's gonna be like throwing a smoke grenade into their house."

"How do you know this concoction's gonna work?" she asked.

"Well, we'll find out soon enough. If they're organized and professional, they'll be right over."

Concerned about jeopardizing her boss's plan she debated with Wade, "We should call this in to our guys."

"Why? If they're doing their jobs they'll show up too. That's if anything goes down."

"Oh . . ., don't worry, if anything goes down the FBI will be here. They'll be here before your buddies."

"We'll see about that, little girl."

Challenged by Wade's nonchalant behavior, Jolene took the dare. Braver by his side, it actually sounded fun.

"Okay, your car is in the garage, all the surveillance is in operating condition, and we don't want to set off any of the FBI devices. Right?" Wade organized the sting. "That means we go in the house and plant this little gadget by their camera/mic equipment. Make sure FBI equipment is at least ten feet away."

"Then what?"

"We hide."

"What does this thing do to our equipment?"

"Nothing, I hope, but we'll find out soon enough. Your stuff should be activated if someone breaks in."

Locating the audio and video device planted in her living area, Wade worked in the dark to position his apparatus next to the others. Whispering to Jolene, he said, "This ought to wake someone up if they're really monitoring you."

Forty minutes passed before Jolene heard a noise outside her home. Elbowing Wade, she pointed to the back yard. "Look, someone's opening my back gate."

"Keep down. Can you see if there's more than one guy?" Wade asked.

"Only see one," Jolene whispered.

Wade cautioned Jolene, "Don't move he'll probably have a flashlight for when he gets inside."

"Right." she nodded eagerly.

"Well." Wade looked intense. "You know they weren't too close to your house."

Responding with a doubting-grin, Jolene shuddered, "Yeah, but they weren't too far either."

Listening to the perpetrator gain access into her residence, Jolene's heart raced from the inevitable danger.

"He just entered through my overhead garage door. That's the only door that doesn't trigger the outside alarms."

"Sounds like they're on to you already. How 'bout the garage door that comes into the house?" Wade inquired hastily.

Looking out from behind her hiding place, Jolene listened down the hallway leading to her garage door. "That will definitely set off some loud noise in here."

Pulling her back, Wade said, "What about the horns?"

Jolene pondered the question, "Only if they break-in through the windows or outside doors."

Unable to hear more, the inside alarm started blaring in the home. Pandemonium ensued as Wade leapt up and took off after the intruder. Lunging at the confused criminal, Wade tackled him down like an All Star Wrestler.

Losing his grip on the home-invader, Wade yelled, "Door, Jolene."

Rushing for the front door, Jolene tried to head him off. Turning to face him, she pulled out her 9mm pistol and pointed the gun at him. "Stop or I'll shoot."

Charging her like a human battering-ram, the mammoth-sized man smashed his shoulder into her small frame. Caught off guard by the huge blow to her chest, Jolene crumpled to the ground.

Jolene grabbed for his moving leg as it passed over her body, holding tight to the pant leg as he proceeded to dragged her to the door.

Bending down, he backhanded her face has hard as he could, causing her to drop her hold and fall back.

Wade scrambled to his feet and bolted after the menacing man. Swerving around Jolene's fallen body, he yelled at her, "Stay here, I've got this."

"Not a chance," Jolene said as she regained her composure, scrambled to her feet, and lit off after the two of them. Sprinting down the residential street with only a moon for lighting, she saw Wade duck into the shadow of a large mesquite tree.

Duplicating Wade's steps with her gun clutched between her hands, she traversed through the tract-home yards in her subdivision. Zigzagging around prickly cacti, thorny shrubs, and towering palm trees, she stayed close on his heels.

Tracking the suspect to a closed-in yard, Jolene caught up with Wade as he hiked himself over a four-foot privacy wall. Panting from the fast run, she stopped to catch her breath and holster her gun. Hoisting herself up on the wall, she came over the top and hit the ground running.

Cornering the intruder inside the homeowner's yard, Wade bolted at him before the criminal could scale another wall.

Trapped by an eight-foot high stucco partition, the man dressed in black turned to confront Wade. Instigating a brawl, the unlawful stranger swung at Wade—hitting him hard with gloved knuckles.

Clenching his fists for a fight, Wade matched his opponent's aggression and jabbed at the perpetrator's jaw.

Dodging Wade's advances, the man ducked and weaved before throwing a second punch.

Wade's quick serpentine dodge spared him the blow so he could pack a right-cross. Boxing like a pro, Wade knocked him hard, but not down.

Swinging low, the giant-sized man sucker punched Wade in the stomach. Moaning from the wind being knocked out of his body, Wade gasped a loud, "Son of a bitch."

Watching helplessly, Jolene didn't know how to stop the skirmish. Dogs from nearby homes started barking at the ruckus. Afraid to use her gun while Wade was in the way, she looked for a weapon to hit his challenger with. Finding a piece of driftwood, she grabbed it and threw herself into the fight.

Smacking the intruder on the head, Jolene screamed, "FBI."

The stranger nailed Wade's weakened body with a knock-out blow to the head. Fighting like a machine, he turned and socked Jolene in the face again.

Jolene landed on the ground next to Wade's comatose body. "Wade. Wade. Are you alright?" Hearing no answer, she felt for his beating pulse. Satisfied he was okay—Jolene forced her disoriented body to stand up again.

Searching the yard for her assailant, she saw his long legs hurdle a short retaining wall before slowing down for a tall stone privacy partition. With one momentous chin-up, the stranger catapulted over the barrier. He was one of the largest men Jolene had ever seen.

Pursuing him with all the strength she had, she shimmied over the tall barricade and chased after him into the natural drainage wash that divided the long block of home sites.

Hunting him down the ravine, she heard the outbreak of snorting javelinas. White tusks gleamed in the moon's light as the hog-like animals clicked incessantly. Disrupting the wild pack of wiry-haired beasts brought on another round of barking from dogs. Trailing the sounds of noisy animals, Jolene located her suspect as he jumped into another homeowner's yard.

Climbing onto a short concrete wall that was topped with a wrought iron fence made Jolene slowdown briefly until she could maneuver herself over the spiked detour. Once she was free from the iron divider, she leapt from the wall. Landing on the ground in a squatting position, she took out her semi-automatic gun and gripped it with two hands. Scanning the perimeter of the illuminated yard, she saw her adversary making haste for the adjacent wall.

Separated by a lighted swimming pool, Jolene's breathless voice yelled at her enemy, "FBI. Stop or I'll shoot."

Ignoring the threat, the villain reached for the bars of the metal fencing.

Planting her feet in a shooter's stance, Jolene steadied her heaving body and yelled again, "Freeze. You're under arrest."

With his back to her, the ninja dressed man took something out of his waistband.

"Drop it," Jolene ordered.

Slowly rotating to face her, he exposed his face for the first time.

Unable to discern what he was holding in his gloved hands, she yelled again, "Drop it, I said."

Raising his hand like a gunman, he aimed at her.

Taking no more chances with the violent predator, she fired.

Hit in the leg with one shot, he slumped to his knees. Lifting his hand again, she saw the gun clearly. Cloaked in darkness till now, Jolene's wounded menace could not escape the submerged pool lighting that washed over his kneeling body.

Reacting to the sight of his automatic gun, she dropped and rolled sideways. Hearing a shot fired from his gun, she crouched behind a BBQ grill.

"Damn," she muttered. Taking a deep breath, she held her gun tight with both hands and rolled out from behind the metal protector. In a prostrate position, she shot him square in the chest.

Falling face first, the assailant belly flopped on the concrete like a stiffened nutcracker.

Amazed and shocked, Jolene gasped to catch her breath.

"I called 911. Are you okay," a homeowner shouted as he peeked out his patio door.

"Yes. I'm fine."

Hearing the crescendo of police sirens confirmed his report. Alone in a stranger's backyard, she looked around at all the people converging on her.

"Jolene. Jolene," she heard Wade's voice call.

"Wade?"

"Are you alright?" Wade hollered as he entered the yard with a squadron of uniformed men. "Holy shit, Jolene. You took him down?"

Police Sergeant Dahlstrom trotted up to Jolene and Wade, "What happened here? Why'd you chase and shoot this guy?"

"Because he broke into her home, plowed us both down, and ran like a cheetah," Wade replied sarcastically.

"Is this a domestic?" The officer asked.

"No." Wade flashed his credentials. "And she's FBI."

Aided by landscape lights encircling the homeowner's pool, Jolene's eyes zoomed in on the intruder's exposed arm. Partially hidden by his short-sleeved t-shirt was a distinct looking tattoo.

Curious, Jolene moved close and inspected the slain man. Lifting his eyelid for signs of life, she couldn't help but notice the intensity of his blue eyes. Sliding his left sleeve up, she saw a set of black-inked lightning bolts with a number three on the right-hand side. She recognized the unique insignia from one of Martine's photos. "What's this?" she questioned. "What does this tattoo mean?"

"I have no idea." Wade scratched his head. "Looks like a Nazi gang symbol."

"Sorry. No identification," a local police officer reported.

Thad Reese walked up to Jolene. "Who's the muscle?" Signaling his crime scene investigator, he looked the dead man up and down. "Run his prints tonight," he directed. "Find out who this guy is." Looking at the first responding police officers, he assumed authority, "We'll secure this scene." Taking Jolene's weapon from her, he added, "We'll do your debriefing here. Both of you wait." Thad pointed to a patio table and chairs.

"Yes, sir," Jolene said as she turned to Wade. "Do you think that's enough fighting for one day?"

Chapter 62

Arriving back at his crappy apartment by three-thirty in the morning, Peter rushed inside and closed the door as fast as he could. Haunted by the job he just performed, caused uncontrollable nausea. Desperate to escape the negative feelings brewing inside, he lit up a big joint and sat on the edge of his bed.

With each deep drag, he tried to smoke out the memories of four different girls—one of them Eva. Just thinking about her made him cough sporadically, causing an escalating urge to vomit. He knew she would probably be the perfect victim if he told Jules about her. He also became agitated at the thought of Jules and the people he worked for ever getting their hands on the beautiful Eva.

With her consuming his thoughts, Peter tried to relax and fantasize about being with her. However, with his mind swirling from the high, his paranoia soared uncontrollably as he was called to remember the past events that got him to this place.

Distorted memories flooded his brain as he recalled the falling-out he had with God and his family. Barely eight-years old when he confronted his abusive stepfather, Peter thought he was doing the honorable thing when he avenged his mother's death. As a result of harboring the painful memories, his character was indelibly scarred.

Fourteen years later, he still doesn't seem to be able to control and suppress the events without some help. The kind you buy on the streets.

Meeting Eva seemed to provoke the reoccurring nightmarish thoughts. "Why," he muttered. "Why does *she* do this to me?"

Unable to stop obsessing over her, he opened his eyes wide as he realized it was because she was so like his friend Sharon. Accepting the magnitude of this implication, Peter started to shake and cough till he consciously decided to ask for control over his life. Tired of feeling punished for being alive, Peter thought of Della's soft comforting words, "Only you can punish yourself, unless you break the law. And don't forget God has laws, eternal laws. Always do what's right, and you will be protected and guided for eternity." Reminiscing about the woman that raised him helped calm the fears that pulsed through him.

Little did he know that his life would change after this emotional plea for help. Asking was all that was needed to help him find a way out of the impossible circumstances he had engaged himself in.

Chapter 63

Martine tucked herself in bed. Asking God for further assistance, she closed her nightly prayers with a litany of thanks for all the heavenly support.

Confident that questions were being answered and guides were being supplied, she asked for clarification on the suspicions she harbored for Peter. Accepting the depth of the lessons she was learning, she called for the Archangel Michael and asked for his aid in revealing the truth. Adding her usual request for Alexa, Eva, Jolene, and all the missing girl's protection she fell asleep in her earthly bed.

Tumbling down a twisting-earthen-shaft, Martine hit the bottom of a cosmic-fall, like *Alice in Wonderland*. Picking herself up off the ground, she squinted to see down the darkened corridor leading to her right. Inside the only open doorway she saw what resembled a medieval chamber.

Moving in for a closer look, she witnessed a conflict arise between a group of fetish-dressed women and a man that looked remarkably like a pimp. Appearing to be prostitutes, the three risqué females were shouting in anger. Distressed about something, the animated whores talked over each other's voices.

Crouching behind a massive pillar, Martine was able to hide inside the primitive room that housed the agitated She-Devils.

"Peter is mine," the red-haired Imp shouted. Pacing wildly, her fair porcelain-white body that was clothed like a porn star commanded everyone's attention in the room.

"Yes, Anora, Peter is yours," the black-haired vixen's irritated voice agreed. Olive-skinned wearing a red-bustier with plunging neckline, the provocative-looking friend stomped her exotic-heeled shoe.

"Shut up, Raven, this is not about what you think," the warlock snapped. "This is about Anora ruining our plan." Spinning around to face the sultry looking girls, the cloaked man let his hood fall off his head.

"Get rid of that vile girl. She will spoil everything. Even her name is like Eve's," Raven screeched as she stepped forward in her black-fishnet stockings.

"I found him first—he's mine. He's done everything I've asked. Just get rid of the blonde Eve girl," Anora pushed as she strutted in her gartered-black-thigh-high nylons.

"You're jealous." Seizing Anora by the corset, the warlock pulled her close to his body and lewdly licked her throat.

A tall black-skinned wench who watched with her arms crossed spoke up, "I'm out of here. You better get this right, Darvon." Storming away, she kicked a dog that crossed her path. Her long legs wrapped high in leather ties rivaled an Amazon woman. Ashen hair hung long and full around her dark face. Unique in her black vinyl jumpsuit, the naughty-looking giant resembled a kinky model.

"Where are you going, Hellith? I command you to return. The three of you are going to fix this," Darvon's raspy voice echoed.

"This is not my fault. That Eve girl showed up and changed Peter. We have to get rid of her. We need your magic, Master," unfurling and flicking her long tongue, Anora pleaded.

"It's your job to torment men. You find a way to cause him anguish. I have no power over an innocent human soul. There is no weakness in this girl." Darvon grabbed for his drinking goblet.

"You must be able to do something, Darvon," Raven urged as she crisscrossed the room with Anora.

"I can only read your male's thoughts—not change his heart. He was vulnerable—the Eve girl changed that." Darvon gulped his drink.

"She's despicable," bellowed Anora. "Something must be done."

"She's despicable—save me," mocked Hellith. "You are worthless now, Anora. Give him to me. It's my turn to have his seeds." Stalking the red-haired femme fatale, Hellith provoked her old friend.

"Never," insisted Anora cracking her whip in the air. "I have done all the work," she scowled with her deep-red lips.

"You have had all the pleasure." Stretching her long clawed fingers, Hellith hissed back.

"Come here, My Pets," Darvon beckoned. "Together we will find pain for the female named Eva."

Purring like kittens the threesome huddled up to Darvon. The black one named Hellith said, "Let me have his babies. I'm a better seducer than Anora. Give her another male."

"No. I like this ignorant one. He suits our cause. He's mine forever." Anora glared, exuding possessiveness. "Get your own human, Hellith, you . . ., greedy Nymph." Pulling back from the coven, Anora hissed her words, "He will choose me." Winged like a bat, Anora took flight. Soaring in a circle over the group, she threatened Hellith, "You may not have Peter. You do not know what he likes. I will own his soul. Stay away. I know what hurts you."

Darvon bellowed, "This is not about one man's seed. This is about millions of babies for the master's reign."

Careful not to be seen, Martine stayed behind the thirty-foot pillar located at the back of the gothic-looking room. Certain she had witnessed the exchange of dark-cult members, Martine presumed to be privy to the arguing of sexual vampires.

Scanning the rest of the quarters, she saw piles and piles of people's possessions. Knowing she was in the presence of evil spirits, Martine figured she entered the realm below the surface of earth that was inhabited by the "trashy and selfish." Primary sins consisted of not loving, not trusting, and not caring about others. Uncharitable and lacking any interest in God, they preferred to be trapped in this dominion and become thieves of the race they envied. The ultimate prize for this assembly of crazed entities was a human soul. Nuisances in every way, they hide behind their ambiguity.

Wanting to exit the forbidding domicile, Martine searched for an egress. Seeing an adorable white bunny hopping out in the hall-way, she quietly slid out the doorway to catch the fluffy-looking puff. Dreading that the soft little bundle could become their next sacrifice, she snatched it in her arms. Proving her love and bravery in saving an innocent creature, Martine was whisked out of the cavernous world.

Back safely in Jolene's home she couldn't wait to check on her two daughters.

Chapter 64

"Jolene, we have to talk." Martine cornered her ailing sister who was pouring a cup of coffee. "I know you're swollen and miserable today, but we need to discuss what I found out last night while you were hunting down Bigfoot."

"That's really cute," Jolene's puffy face tried to muster a laugh as she sat down at her kitchen table. "What could you possibly find at a poker game that's more important than what I tracked down?"

"Well, I think if we pull together what I've documented in my dreams, and the research that we've done so far we should be able to zoom in a little closer on who's abducting girls. More importantly . . ., why."

"Seriously?" Jolene's bloated face made her eyes look like slits. "You think you've got that much?"

"Look at this." Martine spread out her crude chart of genealogy. "I really think I do. I've been up since five working on this."

"What time is it now?" Jolene asked

"Noon."

"Noon? Where is everyone?"

"The girls haven't come back from Tyra's yet, and Wade said he'd be back later to see you."

"Alright. Let's see what you have. I don't feel like doing anything anyways."

"When I was at Teddy's last night he spent almost three hours translating the stuff I couldn't understand."

Hearing the front door open up, Martine was interrupted.

"Hello? Hello? We're home," Eva's cheerful voice rang through the home as she and Alexa barged in.

"We're in here," Martine answered from the kitchen. "You two must have had a good time last night."

"Wait till we tell you what Eva did," Alex blurted as they entered Jolene's kitchen.

Reacting to Jolene's battered face—Eva cupped her hand over her mouth and squealed, "Eeeoouu." Dropping her hand, she winced. "What happened?"

"Everything happened last night," Martine returned.

"Oh my gosh," Alexa gushed as she rushed up to Jolene. "Are you alright?"

"I'm okay. I'm okay now."

"Tell us what happened." Eva moved Jolene's bangs and examined her black-and-blue eye. "I can't believe this," Eva said as she sat next to Jolene. "Were you in an accident?"

"No. Not exactly." After relaying the whole sordid sequence of the last night's events, Jolene finished her story, "So, no more secret surveillance in the house anymore." Addressing Eva, she continued, "Why are you wearing that ridiculous outfit. Yesterday you were dissing your mother about it."

"I guess we sorta used it last night to meet that Peter kid," Eva batted her eyes with satisfaction.

"You what?" Surprised, Martine glared at her daughter in disbelief.

"Yep. We really did it," Alexa boasted. "Don't worry he didn't suspect anything. You won't believe what Eva did. She got all the tracking devices inside his van and got evidence."

"What van?" Martine bellowed. "You two have some real explaining to do."

"I'll let Eva tell you everything," Alexa walked over to the refrigerator. "I'm going to make us breakfast. We're starving."

Relaying her evening of intrigue took Eva a good twenty minutes. At the end, she exalted, "It wasn't hard at all. I think he really likes me too. He wasn't really scary. Actually, he's like a pansy that smells like skunkweed." Shaking her head in disgust, she continued, "He's still a pot head."

"They say Ted Bundy, and Dahmer were pansy's too," Martine rebuffed her daughters flippant comment, "you had no business doing that without backup. You didn't tell anyone?"

"Of course we told someone. We told Tyra. She was there. She even helped. It's fine. It wasn't hard at all. Water under the bridge."

Angry with her daughter, Martine argued, "Tyra is a receptionist. I just don't understand why you did this last night?"

Alexa defended Eva, "Because we believed you. You're never wrong, and we wanted to help you and Jolene."

"Really?" Martine said sarcastically. "I never taught you two to take unnecessary risks."

Alexa set down plates of eggs, toast, and bacon, "Let's eat before its cold. I think Eva was really brave. She submarined him. He never knew what happened."

"You're right," Martine conceded. "I'm just amazed, and protective. That was a really dangerous thing you did. I need your promise that you'll never do something like that again."

"Fine! I promise never to see Peter again." Eva grimaced, "he's not my type of fish anyway. Get it? Pisces? The sign of the fish?"

"Yes. We get it. Funny, I mean good," Jolene agreed. "Because, we're not going to fill you in on anything else if you continue to dive into dangerous waters where you don't belong."

"We'll never do that again," Eva promised. "Just so you know I didn't even cause a ripple."

"Don't worry, we don't want to get in hot water with the FBI," Alexa laughed.

"Enough with the water metaphors." Martine shook her head and frowned. "Thanks, Alexa. Let's eat."

"Hey, now that your stuff isn't bugged anymore, can I use your computer to look at the pictures I took inside of Peter's van?" Eva asked. "I want to see what kind of shit he had in the back of his new wheels."

"Sure. We can do anything we want in here now," Jolene reassured them.

Devouring her hot breakfast, Martine listened to her daughters and Jolene as they each revealed more details about their bravery in the face of mortal enemies. Unwilling to concede that Peter was less dangerous than the giant Jolene took down the night before, she sat silent contemplating what to do with all the information.

"Martine, what are we going to do next?" Jolene asked as she handed Alexa her empty plate.

"Funny you should ask. I've been sorting out what all the clues could mean if I put them together."

"Oh, that's right. You were going to tell me what you learned at that professor's house last night. What did he tell you?" Jolene queried.

"I think you'll find it pretty fascinating." Getting up from the table she fetched her journal, and stash of loose leaf papers. "Here, look at this," she said pointing to the hand-written pages of Gretel's diary. "This belongs to a German girl who had eight children for the Nazi party. One of these children may be called Ada. I either have to get the diary, or speak to someone that knows more about this family." Looking up at her audience, Martine continued, "I think you know who I mean."

"Della?" Eva suggested. "What did you read about in this diary?" Jolene asked.

Martine repeated the controversial story of Gretel's life in Nazi Germany. Sharing the evidence presented in the photos of candelabras and medals, she elaborated, "Almost every dream I've documented in my journal points to some mystery tied in with Della's German paraphernalia."

"We need to go back there," Eva stated.

"No. I need to go back there," Martine corrected her daughter.

"We're going too," Eva snapped.

"You two have helped enough. Besides, Eva, you need to head back to school tonight or tomorrow morning."

"Then let's go today," Eva countered.

Martine shook her head. "Della's working today. I called her last night and left a message. She called back this morning and said she was not working tomorrow. I'm going to see her first thing. Today we need to look for your four-wheel-drive vehicle. It's getting really late. We need to get going if we're going to check out the ones you have your eye on."

"Do you want to come with, Jolene?"

"No," Jolene moaned as she got up from the table. "I'm sore all over. I mean my toenails hurt. I feel like my whole body got beat up last night."

"Go lay down on the sofa while we clean up the kitchen," Martine sympathized with her sister.

Alexa removed Martine's dirty plate. "Why are your dreams so full of animals, demons and creepy places?"

"Because they're teaching me how to discern and gain knowledge." Carrying the dirty glasses from the table, Martine set them next to the sink.

Alexa started rinsing the dishes. "why can't they just tell you what you want to know?"

"Spirit Guides won't help us with the day to day things in life. They can and do act as teachers, providing us with spiritual wisdom through dreams, prayer, and meditation but, only if we invite them into our lives and ask. We must choose to accept assistance. They will never impose on our Divinely appointed gift of Free-Will."

Eva took her last bite and brought her plate over. "Why doesn't the dead girl Lauren just talk to you?"

Martine took the dirty frying pan off the stove, and brought it over to the sink. "Normally when we die our soul moves on and goes into the light. Even though it looks like she died a tragic death, we don't know how she passed on, or her faith in God. It appears like her end was violent and sudden, but since I have had no contact with her spirit—I assume she went into the light immediately."

Alexa took the pan and rinsed it, "I guess that makes sense, but I don't understand why some people don't go into the light when they die. Especially if it wasn't a good death."

"Because some people who die suddenly or violently don't even know they're dead," Martine tried to make her knowledge understandable. "Others are too attracted to the dark things this world has to offer. They liked drugs, alcohol, violence, sinister music, and bad company. They don't want to let go of that . . . that stuff, no matter what. Or, they have enough conscience to fear going into the light because they know they'll be going down—not up. I don't know how Lauren died yet, but I'm not so sure it was violent."

Eva looked confused, "why do we have to ask God and our guides to help? How are we supposed to know when we need help? Isn't that what they're for?"

Martine smiled. "how are they supposed to know when you need help? How can they help when your own Free-Will supersedes their efforts? Your own Will trumps everything. They cannot interfere with the actions of even the most hardened criminals. They can lead us to the answers—if that's what we ask for."

"So that's what they're doing?" Alexa asked.

"Right," Martine replied. "The Guides are my friends. My allies. They become active in life-saving situations, or times of need. Like last night. I think all three of you experienced some life-changing events."

Eva started loading the dishwasher. "Are they always available to help?"

"Yeah, they're on stand-by. Most of them are unemployed these days because no one calls on them for guidance and aid. But, not yours," Martine chuckled.

Alexa put the silverware in the dishwasher and shut the door. "How many do you have?"

"Apparently a lot." Martine wiped the counters around the sink area.

Eva took the rag from her mother and wiped the table down. "Why do you have Indian Guides? You're not Indian."

"Most likely they're part of my ancestry. And, they're part of a culture I've come to know and understand. My respect for their ways has created great friendships. My awareness of their many sacrifices has connected me to them as a Nation. Their Medicine

Men have befriended me over the years and are considered spiritually advanced."

Shaking crumbs into the garbage can, Eva persisted, "I still don't understand why these Guides or Angels can't give you more information."

"They can't do my job for me. Spiritual advancements rely on the teachings and learning's of wisdom. They teach the concept through lessons. Words spoken are not lessons. Being human is considered an honor. We are honored with the opportunity to live our lessons and progress our beings into more evolved states of divinity and closeness to God."

Alexa raised her voice as she ran the disposal, "So what can these dreams of yours really tell us? They're so dark and cryptic. They don't seem to be helping a lot."

"I think they're showing me that we're dealing with a lot of destructive bad energy, and it's probably ancestral. If the chain isn't broken, it will repeat through future generations. When we study dreams we will find meaning in the form of a concept—and understanding that can be communicated through symbolism . . . symbolism that we must interpret ourselves. They cannot be a true guide if they tell us what something means and what to do."

Impatient, Eva threw her rag down "why not?"

"Dark entities use their spiritual know-how to do this. They manipulate humans through their abilities to communicate like a spirit guide. They can even pretend and mimic loved ones. They can disguise their true demonic personas by impersonating whoever they want."

Alexa faced her mother. "How can you tell the difference?"

"It's our job to discern. We must use and develop this skill, like an athlete perfecting a tennis or baseball swing. That's the only way to know with clarity the difference between Supreme light and the darkness of the false light. And never let yourself listen to the wrong advice. Or, do what most people do."

"What's that?" Alexa questioned. "What do most people do?"

"Ignore everything. They just ignore all the signs, and all the right advice. Remember if you don't stand for something . . . you'll fall for anything."

Jolene lifted her head off the sofa pillow, "How do you know if it's the wrong advice?"

"Good advice will be harder to follow. Matthew 7:15 states: *'You will recognize them by their fruits.'* It also says: *'So, every healthy tree bears good fruit, but the diseased tree bears bad fruit. A healthy tree cannot bear bad fruit, nor can a diseased tree bear good fruit.'* I always look for the truth, the good intentions, the righteous advice, and the lesson to be learned. Expect a more difficult road. We didn't come here to be rewarded. We came here to gain knowledge through experience. Angels can't do our job and deny us the opportunity to discover truths on our own. We came to comprehend what God wants us to know."

"Give me an example," Eva said. "You make it sound so natural."

Addressing her eager student, Martine described her latest revelation, "Remember when I described the vision I had of the lion, bear, and wolf defending me in the underground cavern? The small animals had multiplied ten-fold from the first dream I had with them." Grabbing a piece of paper from her menagerie of research, she read, "Matthew 12:43 'The Return of the Unclean Spirit' says; *'When an unclean spirit goes out of a person it roams through arid regions searching for rest but finds none. Then it says, I will return to my home from which I came. But upon returning, it finds it empty, swept clean, and put in order. Then it goes and brings back with itself seven other spirits more evil than itself, and they move in and dwell there; and the last condition of that person is worse than the first. Thus it will be with this evil generation.'* I believe I've been shown how extreme the corruption has evolved with a person, or more probably a group of persons. We can't battle the enemy without first getting inside the masterminds head—that will help us track them down. Also, the badger was not with me, but against me. The badger presented itself as a vicious force, displaying connotations of hatred. The Badger totem describes them as dictators that are very negative and self-serving."

"I can see that," Jolene agreed. "Tell us about another one."

"Okay, we all know I love scrabble. It was ingenious for the Thunder Being to use letter tiles for several clues. I would have to go out of my way to sort out the words and meanings or, engage some help, which I did. You two proved the tiles spell out both words and concepts. As of last night I know that there's a woman's diary that describes a life as a Lebensborn mother for Hitler's elite Third Reich. I also know her legacy in some way lived on because her family's relics are housed in Della's basement."

"Well," Jolene began, "you might need this bit of information. "I just remembered that the big guy I tangled with last night had a Nazi tattoo of a SS insignia."

"See," Martine perked up. "I keep finding more connections to my dreams every day. It is a symbol of the SS soldier Regiment for the Fuhrer. It has to mean something. Right?" Martine's hands gestured her frustration.

Alexa patted her mother on the back. "It's really neat how you're sharing your dreams with us. You've never done that. Why?"

"Well, you were too young to understand the real reasons for keeping these things to myself. They're a gift and a curse. Once people know about it, you can never put the Genie back in the bottle."

"Why would you have to do that? Why would you have to take it back?" Eva questioned.

"When I was in college I wasn't careful and people found out. Suddenly boys wanted to date me for sports scores, and girls couldn't trust me because they thought I had no scruples. I was accused of cheating on tests, and stealing boyfriends. I was thought to have an unfair advantage for anything I wanted. People got hurt and blamed me."

"How did it get out?" Eva probed.

"A close friend had a sister go missing. She fell apart and was dropping out of school. I tried to console her and offered to help find the girl."

"Did you?" Alexa pulled her mother into the living room.

"I did. But, the price was great." Martine sat down in the living room chair. "I loved being able to help the family. The girl was found.

She was a runaway. That's when everything began to change, basically my friends would rather avoid me than be associated with me. By the end of the semester I had to transfer to another college. I just wanted to disappear."

Eva consoled her mother, "it worked out okay. You met dad there. I like learning about your dreams. They're like stories."

"While we're on that, I better tell you about a dream I just had. After what you told me about your adventures last night, I believe it involves Eva," Martine said thoughtfully.

"What?" Eva sparked.

After carefully relaying the entire dream she had with Anora, Hellith, Raven, and Darvon, that was still a fresh impression, Martine paused, "okay, that's about it. I'm guessing it is the result of you meeting Peter. It makes more sense now that I know you have had an encounter with him."

"What are you saying?" Eva demanded.

"Okay, I think the girl you made jealous is not a girl."

"Eeeoouu," Eva whined. "You mean it's a transvestite? Is that why he had a wig in his van?"

"No. Have you ever heard of a succubus?"

Eva answered, "No. Is that like a witch?"

"No. I think it might be worse." Martine's face flinched.

"Okay, what's worse than that?" Jolene rolled over on her side to face Martine.

"She's a temptress. She torments men."

"How can you call that sexy girl a tormentor?" Jolene quizzed her sister. "She might be a call-girl, or a hooker."

"She did look ravishing. Visually, her voluptuous body was definitely squeezed into a tight leather bodice." Martine shook her head. "But, no, sadly she wasn't some hot girl that likes Peter."

"Yeah, and you said she had a whip," Eva added. "Peter had weird shit in his van. He probably knows a dominatrix."

"Right, but what I didn't mention was the bat wings she can fly with."

Eva's jaw dropped, "What? That is really gross."

"No kidding," Martine wasn't laughing. "What do you know about a succubus?"

Alexa shrugged. "Nothing. What do you know?"

"According to legend, Adam had a first wife, her name was Lilith. Adam and Lilith were both created from the dust of the earth and there was equal dominance. Not balance, but total identicalness. Lilith didn't like Adam to dominate the sexual positions and Adam wouldn't let her dominate at all. She insisted on equal dominance and it caused constant friction between them, so she left. She is said to have gone to hang out with the demons. She became Satan's lover. She's considered a sexual monster."

"Why is she upset with Eva?" Jolene asked.

"I think she's possessed Peter. She's probably in love with him now. A devoted succubus can have fits of jealousy, especially if her male lover starts paying attention to a human woman."

"I wasn't that close with Peter. I'm definitely not interested in him," Eva explained.

"Only she and Peter know how Peter felt about you."

"Are you really sure about this?" Alexa took Eva's hand to comfort her.

"I can only tell you what I saw, and what others have seen or experienced. I don't know if the legend is completely accurate. It's a very old writing that dates back to the time of ancient Judaism. It helps explain why Genesis actually has two creation stories. It doesn't say much in the bible about Lilith. This writing that did exist was left out. Now it's just a legend, a legend with a lot of mystery."

"Do you think this succubus has anything to do with the case?" Jolene frowned with concern.

"Actually I do. It makes sense because the legends of Lilith stem from ancient Jewish, American Indian, and German folklore. Oh, and the Ouija Board would easily have conjured up a warlock or two, and the warlocks use the succubus to manipulate weak men, or should I say, men with weak wills. The succubus is basically a demonic prostitute. If Peter was messing around with the board he would have opened up a doorway for a warlock . . . at a minimum."

"So, she sleeps with men to seduce them into what?" Alexa asked.

"So, that she can make more demon children, and control a man's mind. Ultimately she wants to possess his soul."

Eva shivered. "Why would anything want to end up like that? A devil prostitute?"

"I don't know." Martine shrugged. "Winston Churchill said, 'If you're going to go to hell—keep going.'"

"So, there's no hope if you're that bad," Eva surmised. "I want to know more about Lilith."

"Good idea." Alexa shook her head in disgust.

Chapter 65

Returning to Jolene's home for some dinner and relaxation was exactly what Martine had planned when she finished shopping for Eva's four-wheel drive vehicle. After walking through several parking lots full of used automobiles, Martine was more flustered than ever when Eva and she couldn't agree on the same car.

Hungry and tired, Martine was relieved when they arrived home to see Alexa cooking away in the Kitchen. "How did you know what we wanted for dinner?" Martine teased.

"Wow, this is great," Eva exclaimed as she crunched on a chip.

"It's all ready and Jolene's starving." Lifting a stack of plates out of the cupboard, Alexa grinned at her mother and hollered, "Jolene, they're home."

Joining together in the kitchen, the group of four dished up the homemade meal. "Let's talk about anything except cars," Eva started.

"Right on," Martine agreed.

"Right on?" Alexa dipped her nacho chip in her spicy salsa, "Okay, here is what else I found out about those succubi." Snatching a tablet of paper from the nearby counter, she revealed her findings, "The tale of Lilith does originate from a medieval work called The Alphabet of Ben-Sira. They're like warlock pets." Shuddering from the notion, she shared more, "This is definitely part of Jewish mythology. But, in the bible, Isaiah lists Lilith among the beasts of prey which will devastate the land."

"So, Lilith is mentioned in the bible?" Martine asked like an eager student. "I thought so."

"Right," Alexa responded. "Isaiah speaks of the 'night hag,' who dwells in the wilderness with wild beasts and hyenas."

"Did you find more?" Martine probed.

Alexa looked at her computer print outs, "Yes, according to a Midrash, Lilith was the first Eve who disputed with Adam because she was unwilling to forego her equality." Running her finger down the page she read another highlight, "The Zohar, describes Lilith as the harlot, the wicked, the false, and the black."

"Yuck!" Eva blurted in revulsion.

"That's not all I found," Alexa flipped to another page. "She looks for men sleeping alone, seduces them and uses their seeds to make demon babies."

"Well, you were right again, mom," Eva tossed her head back in disgust. "If I wasn't so hungry, I would've lost my appetite."

Alexa tisked her sister, "But, here is what is interesting about that. They say she is a vengeful mother. A horrible *Mother-in-law*. The mother to be feared." Pausing for a reaction, she went on, "Medieval Germany studied mystical Jewish teaching."

"Oh no!" Martine reeled at the information.

"Exactly," Alexa confirmed the connection Martine had made. "German's had believed in Lilith and her succubus stuff. Lilith was a Queen to them."

"Right." Martine hastily swallowed a mouthful of food. "So, Peter probably was exposed to the negative energy of a pagan belief that manifested in Gretel's German ancestry."

"Do you mean that only German's are haunted by Succubi?" Jolene asked.

"No, not at all. They just didn't have any problem accepting it," Martine clarified. "Because they already believed it possible, the door . . . the wrong door was easily opened. Or, they maybe didn't fear or reject the nasty spirits of Lilith's progeny. That family may have revered Lilith."

"Does Peter know he is with a succubus at night?"

"Doubtful he doesn't suspect something by now. It's like bed wetting."

"What?" Jolene gulped.

"You weren't awake when it happened," Martine said. "But, who else could have done that deed in your bed? So, if he didn't know before, he most likely will now."

"How come?" Alexa asked.

"Eva just turned the heat up. I think the succubus will do something desperate," Martine explained. "Based on my dream, Peter doesn't know he is being seduced by a powerful succubus. He is being used. And she and her friends are fighting over him," Martine interpreted her vision.

"Yeah," Eva agreed. "He's not a renegade. He doesn't even know he's being manipulated by a satanic-type warlock that owns succubi. I could tell Peter is really a wuss."

"All he has to do is consent repeatedly," Martine countered. "And she will eventually own him—own his soul. It won't matter how naïve he is."

"Are you sure?" Eva looked perplexed.

"Yes," Martine affirmed. "His sexual appetite will be his demise."

"Oh, Martine, Teddy called here," Jolene interrupted. "He gave me his number so you could call him."

"Great," Martine sounded puzzled. "Any idea what he wants?"

"Nope."

"Excuse me girls." Dialing Teddy Frye's number, Martine cupped her cell phone's mouth piece, and whispered to her family, "I gotta see what's up?"

"No problem," Jolene responded.

Connecting with Teddy, Martine addressed her new friend, "Hey, Teddy. It's, Martine."

Excited, Teddy returned the greeting, "Martine, I've been doing a little research on the information we discussed last night."

"Really?" Intrigue registered in her voice.

"My goodness yes. The more I looked, the more I found. Lots of information on that internet."

"Like what? I've been preoccupied all day and haven't had a minute to do any of my own searching. I do, however, have an appointment tomorrow to go see the diary again."

"Excellent," Teddy said. "Listen, do you have time to meet me tonight then?"

"Sure. Just finished eating," Martine said.

"Great. We can meet at a little coffee shop on Scottsdale Road," Teddy dictated the address.

Chapter 66

Martine walked briskly up to the glass door and pushed it open into the coziest little coffee shop. Seated in the back corner was Teddy. Sporting a plaid tam hat on his head and a dark brown tweed jacket, he resembled a sixties movie star.

Standing up to acknowledge her, Teddy appeared debonair and sounded distinguished when he greeted her with his authentic English accent, "Martine, you are so beautiful tonight. Thank you for joining me at this late hour," Teddy formally tipped his hat. "Sit, sit down. Please join me," he graciously invited her as he placed his sporty hat back on his head.

"Thank you. I can't wait to hear what you've got." Martine felt invigorated in the presence of this brilliant man who proudly wore England's coat of arms on the lapel of his handsome jacket. "A lion," Martine remarked, reacting to the notion that Teddy might be the *friend from the lion's den*. "Britain's **Royal Coat of Arms** has a lion," she pondered aloud.

"Yes," Teddy looked down and sideways to acknowledge the badge of honor. "Curious you should notice."

Scrutinizing the emblem, she remarked, "I just find it a coincidence."

"You do. Please tell me," Teddy inquired.

"Huh . . . a fortune cookie said 'out of a lion's den, you will make a new friend,'" Martine bent the truth slightly.

"Well, most intriguing," Teddy commented cheerfully. "I do believe in good fortune. Speaking of fortunes, you've certainly stumbled on some very unique paraphernalia."

"Tell me," Martine said.

"I just don't know where to start. I haven't taken a break since early this morning. I kept finding more and more information," Teddy rambled.

"Well, start where you started this morning," Martine suggested.

Beginning with a slight stutter, Teddy relayed his day, "I . . . I researched the Lebensborn program that our girl, Gretel, was introduced to. Based on the year she was moved to the girl's home, she would have been one of the first and most senior of all the women. It also has been proven that the breeding program was Heinrich Himmler's baby," chuckling softly, Teddy said, "No pun intended."

"None taken," Martine responded.

"It was Himmler's dreaded SS soldiers that set up these Lebensborn homes and cared for these women." Teddy paused. "I mean girls."

"Right," Martine acknowledged. "How young?"

"Fifteen and up," Teddy stated. "That's what's published."

"That young?" Martine bit on her lip. "Go on."

"The girls who were anointed as one the Fuhrer's 'racially pure' were forced to help populate the new German Empire that was deemed to conquer Europe and rule the world for the life of the thousand-year Reich." Teddy sipped his tea. "Racially pure characteristics were established by none other than Himmler."

"Ask me what they were," Teddy said.

"What were they, Teddy," Martine humored him.

"Norwegians, Viking blood. The Master Race had racial features that included blue eyes, blonde hair, no Jewish ancestry, and perfect health. Attractive and strong. No blemishes of any kind." Teddy tapped his tooth. "Not even one filling. The racially pure came from places like Sweden, Norway, Denmark, and other Baltic and North Sea lands. Most Germans didn't qualify. Hitler didn't qualify." Teddy's eyes narrowed in on Martine. "You're from Scandinavian descent, aren't you?"

"Yes, I'm Swedish," Martine confirmed. "You're scaring me."

"Martine, you might have been abducted yourself if it was 1935. You just had to be Aryan looking to be snatched." Swallowing hard, Teddy continued, "They sought the physically perfect and beautiful women." Pointing at her nose, he continued, "Your straight nose, fair skin, and thick blond hair would have turned every soldier on." Raising his voice he said, "They stole these gorgeous women and reduced them to sex slaves, especially if they were Scandinavian."

"You say Scandinavian?" Martine's mind flashed some of her recent dreams.

"Yes!" Teddy raised his voice a decibel. "Preferably Swedish. Himmler believed that Swedes had the purest Aryan blood on the planet," he finished with an affirmative nod.

"Whoa," Martine said.

"The files," Teddy went on, "were all destroyed. No one knows who the Lebensborn children are, or what became of them. Supposedly the birth records were burned or dumped in the Isar River during the 1945 invasion of US Troops." Sitting back in his chair, Teddy reflected out loud, "You were very fortunate to locate a diary like that."

"Not unless it helps me solve a big case I'm consulting on," Martine confided in Teddy.

"Do you think a diary can?" Teddy quizzed.

"For some reason," Martine confessed, "I think it can. That's why I'm so grateful to you for the help you've given me."

"Okay then. Let's get going on this," Teddy rallied for progress. "Wait till you hear what else I've found out?"

"Go on," Martine said enthusiastically.

"Since Nazi's were successful abducting racially suitable females, they only needed to find select German men who qualified for the Aryan breeding program." Teddy slid his papers around till he found a tiny black and white photo. "Guess who the big breeder was?"

Martine sounded shocked, "Himmler? That piece of shit."

"I see you're a fan. You are good, young lady. How could you have known that?"

"Just a feeling," Martine smiled affirmatively. "And the fact that he thought Hitler was the Messiah."

"Well, let's see how good you really are," Teddy challenged her like a contestant. "Who fathered many of the children at the Steinhoring home for Lebensborn mothers?"

Scrolling her memory, Martine shouted her answer like a game show contender, "Himmler!"

"Right again," Teddy cheered. "You win a Volkswagen."

"I don't feel like a winner," Martine refused to be humored. "I need to know why all that crap is haunting me."

Serious, like a melodrama mask, Teddy leaned in, "I think I know. Bear with me."

Startled by the notion that Teddy could really help, Martine went crazy, "What? Spill."

"Gretel was a high ranking soldier's secretary. Right?" Teddy waited to hear his fact validated.

"Yes."

"Gretel became a high ranking Lebensborn mother. Right?"

"Yes," Martine played along.

"It was Himmler's idea to create a kingdom of Super-people."

"I suppose."

"Himmler actually started the breeding program before Hitler became Chancellor. Right?"

"Yes. That's probably true I guess."

"Himmler was a teacher and chicken breeder before he was a Nazi. Right?"

"Right?"

"Himmler thought women were broodmares, and sex slaves. Right?"

"Absolutely."

"Only a few German women were enticed into his breeding scheme. Right?"

"Probably."

"Well, Gretel was photographed at Steinhoring with Himmler. Right?"

Martine hesitated, "She was?"

"Yes. I went back and re-translated the article you had Mahoney give me. There was another photo with the article and based on the information we have now, that woman in the picture with Himmler was Gretel. I'll bet Himmler was the father to her eight children. I'll bet the ledger-looking journals you photographed, are the covers of Lebensborn birth records from the ten homes established in Germany before the Third Reich fell. You found the genealogy documentations that were carefully hidden from the world."

"Yes," Martine pondered the revelation. "Hidden underground," she said under her breath. "Oh my God. What if the children born in the Lebensborn homes have been tracked down by a new Nazi group that wants to continue the breeding? Maybe the children being abducted are the offspring of racially-engineered Aryan parents. If the girls were targeted based on that type of profile, they would be missing from all over the world. Primarily Europe." Martine had a hunch, "The rest are abducted based on their Aryan qualities. Yes, that makes sense. And these parents probably wouldn't even know if they were progeny of the Lebensborn breeding program."

"What do you think?" Teddy asked.

"I think the most evil incarnation of a man found a way to reproduce. What am I saying?" She paused, "How can he even be considered a man when he had such disregard for human life? He was put in charge of the Final Solution and extermination."

Teddy agreed, "Martine, it was most likely his idea. He also was the backbone behind the notion of creating a new Nordic master race . . . that he planned to be in charge of. He believed that the Nordic race came directly from God. It did not evolve. He believed it had to be bred. He was so delusional that he thought they would get their God like powers back if he bred these bloodlines."

"Well, you're confirming what I've suspected," Martine said.

"Martine, in 1943 Himmler gave a speech and said," Teddy glanced down at his notes and read, "'I think it is our duty to take these children even if we have to rob or steal them. Either we recover this superior blood and use it ourselves or we must destroy it.' See what I mean?" Teddy asked.

Martine let her guard down, "The stuff I read about him in the library was really chilling too. Survivors called him cold blooded, and detached. Oh, he was called the Fuhrer's *evil spirit.*" Martine added excitedly. "Actually he was the one that betrayed Hitler when he tried to seek peace with America and Britain so he could save his own life. That would make him a coward and a traitor too."

"I think I know where you're going with this," Teddy hinted.

"Do you?" she blinked. "Did you tell John any of this?" Martine changed the subject.

"I tried. Let's just say he'd didn't get into it," Teddy hedged.

"Be specific. I'm already walking on eggshells around the big guy," Martine pressed.

"I think he said something about you writing another book after he solves the case for you."

"Oh, did he now?"

"I'm sure it sounded nicer when he said it," Teddy looked dismayed. "Sorry."

"Did he mention the Amazon man that my sister took down last night?" Martine asked.

"No. You mean while *you* were playing poker?" Teddy joshed. "The rest of us were just giving *you* our money."

"Very funny, Teddy," Martine grinned with satisfaction. "While we were dealing each other cards last night my sister hunted down an intruder that was about 6'5", blond, blue eyed, and better looking than an Abercrombie model."

"Who was he?" Teddy asked.

Shrugging, Martine answered, "No ID of any kind. Finger prints haven't turned up anything either. There was a tattoo though. It resembled the SS insignia worn by Hitler's SS soldiers. It had a number three added. I had already researched the symbol because I'd seen it before and found that it was used by *Der Fuhrer Regiment* soldiers."

"Where did you see it before?" quizzed Teddy.

"Prison. I recently interviewed a convict that had the same tattoo."

"So," Martine said. "If Gretel is a co-conspirator of a Nazi enclave, she would have brainwashed her own children. And, we know her offspring survived. Gretel would have been actively involved in the sorting and murder of girls that did not pass the vetting process."

"Yes," Teddy nodded. "She definitely would have helped create the social experiment that lasted thirteen years," wagered Teddy.

"And that's why it was legal to procreate children out of wedlock. And be a criminal if you aborted a baby. Women were being forcibly raped and then prosecuted if they tried to terminate the pregnancy."

"Exactly."

Martine dropped her fist on the table, "We know that because her heirs moved these records to a basement in Arizona. Don't we?"

Teddy grinned. "I do believe we do, madam."

Chapter 67

Departing from Teddy at ten-thirty meant Martine didn't get back to Jolene's home until well after eleven. With everyone already in bed for the night, she went straight to her room.

Restless in mind and spirit, she tossed and turned while she mulled over all the information that seemed to be downloading into her being at warp speed. With all her recent impressions being funneled into her like a data processor, she had no choice but to flail around with insomnia.

Desperate for assistance and a yearning for heavenly insights, she called on humanities special protector against demons, assaults, and stratagems—Archangel Michael. Educated as a child, and believing as an adult, Martine knew the significance of Archangel Michael's place with God. Pure in Spirit, and high in importance, he is mentioned in many religious Scriptures and is clearly recognized as an opposer to Lucifer and his evil followers.

With rhythmic breath she prayed from the depth of her heart-center, raising her vibration and reaching a higher level of consciousness. "Through the office of Christ, I call upon St. Michael the Archangel to assist me. With your magnificent sword, cut away all the psychic debris and let me fly free. Take me to the highest heavenly realm I may attain at this time. Let me return with memory and recognition."

Without continuation of additional invocations, Martine's physical body fell sound asleep while her higher consciousness activated, connecting her with another divine destination.

Embodying on top of a large Mesa, she looked around for identifiable landmarks. Scanning the northeast horizon, she recognized the undeniable contours of the Sleeping Ute Mountain range. With her bearings confirmed, she knew her location was on Indian reservation land in Southwest Colorado. On the barren looking ground in front of her, four deer peacefully grazed on grass.

Suddenly, dozens of twirling feathers floated down from above, somewhat obstructing her vision. Overhead she saw a single eagle fly by and land in a lone pinion tree that shaded the little herd of mule deer. She instantly recognized the connection between the eagle and Archangel Michael. Eagle being the most powerful and noble earthly sky creature, fittingly symbolizes the heavenly powerhouse that is St. Michael. Renowned for leaving clever gifts and calling cards, God's winged messenger instantly responded to her, as he always does to one of his own.

Now that she had reached a higher state of being, she was able to distinguish who the eagle and deer from her first dream symbolized. The two does and two fawns represented herself, Jolene, Alexa, and Eva. The eagle obviously represented her own winged-warrior guide, Archangel Michael. Because he had left numerous identifying signs for her, she knew he had been there all through her life guiding and protecting her—ever since asking for his help after the loss of her sister Michaela.

Raised Catholic, she was taught in catechism that St. Michael was the greatest messenger of God. Learning that the name Michael is Hebrew for "He who is like God," and the name Archangel Michael means, "The Greatest Messenger who is like God," Martine immediately gravitated to him for assistance.

Without her sister Michaela in her life, Martine drew closer to St. Michael and relied on his protection and guidance. Martine's constant prayers for Michael's intercession may be the single reason for her clairvoyant experiences. Faith-filled and completely responsive to heavenly guidance, Martine's veil between the worlds became thinner and thinner as her insights began to expand and her spiritualist abilities became more defined.

Martine accepted that the Commander-n-Chief of all the Archangels and legions of heavenly forces was always available to serve God's creation. Representing the power and Divine Will of God, as well as the powers of protection and truth, he is depicted as a Nordic-looking warrior slaying a dragon.

After linking the vision of the deer and eagle to her family and St. Michael the Archangel, Martine witnessed the treed eagle spread its wings for flight—simultaneously manifesting into a human-shaped winged-warrior holding a shield and sword.

Ethereally relating to the right-hand general of God's armies, Martine could clearly understand his words as he relayed the importance of his coming.

"Original sin is; transmitted through the seeds of the seven deadly sins, is implanted through repetition, is cultivated by tolerance, and grows through the mass of humanity's ignorance." Stretching his sword of truth up high, he flicked the pointed end in the sky seven times—revealing the name of each deadly sin—*pride, greed, envy, anger, lust, gluttony, and sloth.*

Martine examined each word as it materialized boldly in the air.

Archangel Michael spoke again, "Original sin can only be transformed through the seeds of the seven heavenly virtues, implanted through repeated good choice, cultivated by discernment, and grown through the singular awareness of an individual soul. Each person is responsible for their own transformation, but only together can humanity be transformed."

Using his sword again he struck the air seven times till the corresponding words for the seven heavenly virtues—*humility, hope, love, courage, temperance, prudence,* and *justice* appeared in the atmosphere.

Feeling overwhelmed, Martine looked questioningly at Michael's glowing-angelic being. "Why do you tell me this?"

"You have a soul that has awareness. Stop the seeds of evil miscreation that are manifesting on the earth. I give you *your* sword of truth to slay the evil doers." Bestowing the magnificent double edged sword to Martine, he dissipated into vapor.

Now in possession of the powerful weapon, her eyes beheld its glistening path as she practiced slicing through the air like a warring Jedi with a laser of light. Wielding the mighty blade like the biblical famed Archangel gave her renewed confidence and strength. "You see through my eyes like open doors," she said in awe.

Invisible to her eyes, the Captain of the heavenly armies departing voice responded, "You will physically be called to put down evil in a day's time. Stay your course."

"Wait," she shouted. Startled by her own voice, Martine was awakened at 6:04 to a new day. Filled with conviction, she sprang out of bed.

Chapter 68

Arriving at Della's was exciting this time. Reuniting with the mild mannered woman was comfortable in comparison to the apprehensive encounter they all experienced the first time. Riddled with curiosity, Martine couldn't wait to learn more about the treasure trove of historical memories buried in her primitive basement.

With plans in place to purchase a new vehicle for Eva, She had reluctantly agreed to let them accompany her to Della's.

Greeting her hostess, Martine smiled like an old friend, "Hello, Della. Thanks for seeing us again."

"Hi, girls. It's so good to see your pretty faces. What do you have to show me that's so important you drove all the way out here?"

"It's a little complicated. Can we sit down?"

"Yes, of course. Please come in." Della stepped back so Eva, Alexa, and Martine could enter. "Let's go sit in the living room. You make yourselves comfortable." Della shut her door and followed. "I made lemonade for you."

Making her way to the sitting room, Martine admired Della's huge house plants that filtered the sunny rays of light entering the windows. "Have you heard from Peter lately?"

"No. You . . . didn't come to tell me something's . . . wrong, did you?" Della's pained voice stuttered.

"No. Absolutely not. Actually, I wanted you to know that he hasn't committed any crimes, or been picked up for anything. He must be doing okay. I was just wondering if he has been back, or if he might be staying with you?"

"No, Martine. Peter hasn't visited for a long time. I'm so relieved that he's not in any trouble. How about Sharon? Have you found her?"

"No. We haven't found Sharon," Martine lied. Seating herself on the sofa, Martine continued, "I did a little research on some of the items that are stored in your basement. Are you familiar with the German documents that are down there?"

"No. I didn't really know that there was old stuff like that in my basement. They must belong to Jules and his family. I've never really seen what's in there." Ready with lemonade, Della poured everyone a glass.

"Can you tell me about his family? There's a girl's diary that I'd like to look at again. Would it be okay if Eva and Alexa went back in your basement to get it? I'd like to show it to you. We even brought a flashlight this time," Martine laughed lightly.

"Why yes. Of course they can. Whose diary is it?" Della set the pitcher of lemonade down.

"It's a girl named Gretel. Have you ever heard of her?" Martine sipped the refreshing drink.

"Yes. I think I've heard of her."

"Really? What can you tell us about her?" Eva asked as she set down her glass. "Wow. This tastes like its fresh squeezed."

"It is, dear." Della smiled bright. "Let's see . . . Gretel was born in Germany in the early nineteen-hundreds. It's quite a story I hear. She would have been the great grandmother of my son's first wife."

"Let's see," Della searched for old recollections. "Her name was Laura. Her family was German. I mean really German. They all spoke German."

"How did Dan meet Laura then?"

"Laura spoke pretty good English and was here because of a summer exchange program that was run by our Lutheran Church."

"Is Gretel still alive?" Alexa probed as she took a paper out of her purse.

Turning to Alexa, Della tisked, "I heard she committed suicide when World War II ended."

"Is this her?" Alexa opened up the folded paper and showed Della.

Taking the picture, Della smoothed the crumpled document. "Yes, I suppose it is." Moving her finger across the page, she remarked, "There are eight children in this photo. That must be her."

"What did you know about Gretel?" Martine questioned.

Still scrutinizing the photo, Della shared her memories, "Supposedly, she was an orphan that married a German soldier."

"Who did she marry?" Eva asked.

"Nobody seems to know his name. Or, at least I don't know."

"Why's that?" Eva asked.

"I heard he died young and they hid his identity because of the eight children he left behind." Della looked down in shame. "It sounded like he was a bad Nazi. I couldn't get Laura to talk about her family."

"What happened to the children?" Martine pushed Della's recall.

"We don't know what happened to all of them, but her daughter Ada ended up in an orphanage after the war. She lived there until she was seventeen. She met Heinrich Schultz and married him. He was much older than her."

"Where is Ada now?" Alexa took the photo back and refolded it.

"Ada lives in Europe somewhere. One of her sons' is Jules father."

"Della, can you think of anything else you've heard about Gretel and Ada?" Martine tried to guard her suspicions while quizzing Della. "There just has to be a lot more to the story." Diagramming a rudimentary family tree, Martine was ready to reconstruct the flow of ancestry. "Tell me again how your family is related to this family?"

"Well. My son Dan was twenty-one years old when he met Laura. They got married, but it only lasted a couple years. Laura died of ovarian cancer when she was only twenty." Grieving from the tragedy, Della sniffled, "I know that's when my poor boy got angry and started drinking. Anyway, Laura's mom was Elsa. Elsa's mom was Ada. Ada's mother was Gretel. Ada had a daughter and a son named Bernhard."

"Did you know Elsa and her brother . . .?" Writing down the new names, Martine paused.

"Bernhard," Della said pensively.

"That's right. Bernhard," Della perked up. "Thank you. I remember him now."

"Bernard and his son Jules moved here from Germany when Dan married Laura. Laura's dad William came with them."

"What did you say his name was?"

"His name was William Mann. I mean Osborn. He changed his name to Osborn when he moved here permanently."

"Why did he do that?"

"Well, I think he said he wanted a famous name."

"Did he ever tell you anything about Ada?"

"No. But I visited with Bernard at Laura's funeral and he told me the story of Ada's life."

Making notes, Martine pried for every detail. "Tell me what you remember hearing about Ada."

"Ada was born around nineteen-thirty." Counting with her fingers, Della continued, "Yes. Ada was born before the German war. She was raised in elegance. She had a magical childhood of privilege and wealth. Her mother Gretel was very important. High-ranking military men were always visiting the big house they lived in. Her mother was always dressed up in the best cloths. Ada's mother Gretel was so busy that a nurse called . . . called, let me see, what was her name?" Della searched the air for the answer. "She wrote us after the funeral. Oh, her name is Frau Schneider. Frau Schneider cared for all Gretel's children. When World War II ended Gretel was never seen again. They say she committed suicide. Ada was about fourteen or fifteen when she lost her mother. She was taken to an orphanage. Well, Bernhard said that when Ada was seventeen, Nurse Schneider found her and took her into her home.

Nurse Schneider had saved all Gretel's personal possessions. The jewels and silver valuables had all been taken."

"Then what happened to her?" Alexa grinned excitedly. "This is quite a saga."

"It's so *Gone with the Wind*," Eva remarked.

"Ada was introduced to Heinrich Schultz. She was a very young girl and he was an old ex-Kommandant from Buchenwald." Della mused, "It was probably an arranged marriage." Shaking her head from sadness, she continued Ada's story, "They had two children before he died. No one knows where he got all his wealth. But when he passed away, Ada, Elsa, and Bernhard were very rich."

"What happened to Elsa?" Eva asked with concern.

"Elsa died of cancer, just like her daughter Laura. I never met her."

Fueled with curiosity, Martine wanted more information, "What's Ada like?"

"I've never met her either, but they say she is a cold-hearted woman. Very secretive. Probably in her late seventies now. She doesn't speak any English. Bernhard said she will never live here because of our language."

"What else have you heard about her?" Enthralled, Martine kept writing.

"She's very ruthless, and very wealthy."

Alexa cleared her throat, "how do you know that?"

"She set up her son and son-in-law in business here, but when the Indian's didn't renew the mining permits the way she wanted, she pulled out and permanently shut down their operations."

"Which mining operations?" Eva inquired.

"They mined the silica sand for the oil digging."

"Oh, yeah." Eva said, "Isn't that where your son Dan worked?" Fetching the framed picture of Dan and Peter, Eva set it down in front of Della.

"Exactly. Dan was the manager."

Martine used her pen and tapped Della's framed picture of Dan and Peter sitting on a huge trackhoe. "What happened to the mining operation after that?"

"It's been abandoned."

"Why is it abandoned?" Eva passed the framed picture to Alexa. "Why isn't someone else mining there?"

Dismay painted over Della's face. "Because Ada's son built the entire facility, and no one can use any of their structures without their permission. She won't let anyone use her stuff, and I don't suppose the Indians want to try that again with another bunch of white people. My boy and everyone else lost their jobs."

"So, everything is exactly the way they left it about ten years ago?" Martine supposed.

"Far as I know."

Eva shook her head in disgust. "She sounds so vindictive and calculating."

"They say she is. When the Indians decided to let her have her way it was too late. She wouldn't even consider leasing their land again. Instead she tied it up by controlling who could buy or lease the buildings she had constructed."

"That sounds so mean," Alexa agreed.

"The rumors around here described her as very manipulative and greedy. Nobody liked working for them."

Martine's prying persisted, "How did you end up with all that stuff of her families?"

"I guess Dan let Bernhard and William put it in our basement when they shut the plant down and left."

"Where's William now?"

"Vegas. He has a casino, and still runs oil wells."

"Where's Bernard?"

"Bernard died of a heart attack."

"What else do you know about Ada?" Martine asked. "Any endearing qualities?"

"She isn't afraid of anything. As far as I know. Oh, I heard my boy Dan say, 'on a good day she warms to the temperature of an ice cube.' I know Laura didn't like her own family. She probably married Dan so she could stay here."

"Another question, Della. There weren't any keys down in the basement. Is it possible you still have your son Dan's keys to that mining plant?"

"Maybe," Della answered. "We can look in the old key box. What do you want inside that old mining place?"

"Well, the artifacts you have may be worth a lot of money to some collectors I know. There are many pages torn out of some of the journals. I'd like to see if I can find them for you before we tell anyone what you have. It could be an answer to your prayers. Legally, they abandoned the stuff on your property and it is deemed yours."

"Really?" Della said excitedly as she walked to kitchen. "Do you think it's worth money?" she yelled from the doorway.

"I do, Della. I'll do what I can."

Dangling a ring of keys, Della said, "These were Dan's. If he had keys to that facility, they're on here." Rummaging around further, she grabbed a small padlock key, "I'll help you open the cellar door."

Chapter 69

Maria sat cross legged on her cot paging through another old magazine. Fearing what her captures would do with her next, she imagined escape routes that would lead to her freedom. Sober, now that the drugging was worn off, Maria felt the full effects of a helpless victim.

Hearing the mechanical tumblers turn with obnoxious clanking, Maria looked up to see Steve enter her cell.

"Sorry I couldn't make it back yesterday. Doc got real busy and didn't have time for you. He does now though."

"I don't want to see Doc." Maria sat frozen to her bed.

"Not up to you. He said if you don't take his little pain pills, I can stick you with this needle."

"Don't even try," Maria said defiantly.

"He said it's for your own good."

Maria tightened her hidden fist. "I'm not going to let you drug me again."

"Yes you are. Doc said I can't watch if I don't do my job here."

"Oh, okay. I'll pretend I'm drugged and then you can watch. What do you get to watch?"

"Don't you want to be surprised?"

"No. I wouldn't say I want to be surprised. Where's your German goon?"

"Jacob?"

"Yeah, that guy," Maria sassed.

"He's busy. I told him I could take care of you."

"Good idea. If the Doc isn't going to kill me, we could hang out together when he's done. Right? That is if I'm not drugged and all."

"Maybe we could," Steve said. "You have to act real sleepy so he'll know you took your pills."

"I can do that," Maria said flirtatiously.

"Okay, lean on me while I get you in your wheelchair," Steve smirked. "We'll practice your acting."

"Sure," Maria obliged. Moving slowly towards Steve, she sat down in the wheelchair.

Wheeled down a long concrete-walled hallway gave Maria the first glimpse of the type of facility she was locked-up in. It was anything but a hospital or nice medical building. Realizing how crude and primitive the place really was, she knew there would be no normal route to escape a building that was constructed like a prison. "Where are we, Steve?"

"Down under."

"What does that mean? Australia?"

"Not exactly. Here's the Doc's headquarters. Don't talk."

"Hello, young lady."

Maria garbled her words slightly, "Hi. Who are you?"

"I'm your new doctor. Are you ready to get started?"

"Sure. What are we going to do?" Maria tried to sound drunk and happy.

"You're in a good mood," he commented. "That's perfect. We're going to start a little exam. Do you like needles?"

"No."

"That's too bad. Good thing you took your pills. They should be working really well in a few more minutes."

"What Kind of doctor are you . . .?" Maria deliberately slurred her sentence.

"I'm a Gynecologist."

"Why do I need a Gynecologist?"

"Is your name Maria Danielson?"

"Yes." Maria acted intoxicated and belligerent. "So what?"

"Maria, if your mother and father didn't adopt a sister, or a brother, who did they adopt?"

"That's a stupid question. They didn't adopt anyone," Maria laughed at her own answer—sure that she outsmarted the creepy doctor.

"Wrong, my dear, they adopted you."

Chapter 70

66 **I**'m leaving now to check out that silica sand plant," Martine announced as they drove away from Della's home. I'm really haunted by the fact that it keeps sounding like a place that I see in my dreams."

"I'm coming with," Eva sounded supportive.

"Me too," said Alexa.

"How about I drop you two off somewhere while I check it out?"

Eva shook her head. "No, we'll all go together."

"I think I know right where it is," Martine said. "It's near Indian Hopi land. But, I think it's on the Navajo reservation."

Anxious to get going, Martine grabbed the directions that Della prepared for her and sped off with her small posse.

Following detailed directions, Martine left the freeway and exited off to the east. Dirt rose up like face-powder as they neared the property. "This soil is getting finer," she commented. "Hope we don't get stuck out here in the middle of nowhere."

What is this dusty stuff?" Eva complained.

"Very fine sand. Used for oil drilling," Martine responded. "This is nasty to drive on. We must be very near the plant."

Hurrying to the location of the abandoned facility, Martine stepped on the gas till she got a good glimpse. "That's it."

"Where? I don't see anything," Eva said, looking up from her phone. Dejected, she added, "There's never a signal on these reservations."

"See those silos way back there?"

"Oh yah," Eva answered back. "Not even one bar," she griped.

Alone on the loamy-sand road, the three passengers sped closer. Turning left onto a smaller one-lane road, Martine mumbled, "This looks traveled, I see tracks."

Slamming on the brakes, Martine shouted, "Damn."

"What's wrong?" Eva jerked from the abrupt stop.

"Security. Big time." Martine's face tightened as she scanned her surroundings.

Alexa, sitting in the back seat leaned forward to look out the windshield. "How can you tell? It's just a fence."

Pointing out the window, Martine said, "That sign, the one that says 'Security No Trespassing Beyond This Point.'"

"That's nothing," Eva declared. "Everyone has one of those. They never put the systems in though. Even if they do put one in, they never turn'em on."

"True, but they don't have *that* security sign," Martine annunciated. "It's *Sicurit*. They provide State-of-the-Art Perimeter Security for military and nuclear facilities," Martine explained. "We can't go in there." Straining to hear, her heightened awareness detected a monotonous low-pitched buzz. "Hear that? That humming noise?" Martine shushed her daughters, "Listen. Do you hear that?"

Shrugging, Alexa conceded, "Yeah. I sorta hear that. Sounds like one of those big power lines. What does it mean? What will happen if we do try and get in?"

"That big chain-linked fence is loaded with alarm mechanisms and tamper alerts. If we get near it we set off warnings." Martine contemplated her own words. Remembering her first dream with all the animals and the annoying hum, she knew she was on to something. She had found the source of the hum.

"How do you know that?" Eva interrupted her mother's thoughts.

Dejected, Martine's wondering mind slowed her response, "The government uses this stuff for prisons and compounds. Financial institutions use it too."

"There're no guards or vehicles, who's going to know? I don't see anyone around," Eva rationalized her own observations.

Martine continued the debate, "These guys sell microwave and infrared security systems that have almost no false alarms. This system can probably detect and localize any disturbance within one-hundred yards of the fence—on either side. It's designed to keep people in and out. It can tell the difference between a dog and a person. It can tell the difference between a bird and a helicopter. We're not getting in there on foot or in a vehicle."

"Sounds like the Great Wall of China," Alexa deduced.

"Worse, it can measure the location and the size of the intruder—instantly," Martine explained.

"Will loud alarms go off if we get inside?" Eva asked.

"No, I'm sure it is monitored remotely. What good would sirens do way out here? Who would even respond?" Turning to face the backseat, Martine stretched her arm and pointed to the back of her car. "Alexa, can you hand me my camera bag? It should be behind you in the hatch area."

Rotating, Alexa searched in the back of the SUV. "Good idea—we can photograph this stuff and show the FBI."

"Not exactly, I need my telephoto zoom," Martine explained.

Eva handed her the camera bag. "Here you go."

Taking the camera case from her daughter, Martine removed the 35mm digital camera and attached the high powered telephoto zoom lens that James had given her for Christmas. Exiting the car for a thorough examination of the property, Martine held the camera-viewer up to her eye and aimed it at the tallest building.

Eva and Alexa joined her outside and watched as Martine used the camera like binoculars. Surveying the landscape around the structures, she reported, "This chain fencing goes as far as I can see. Looks like it stays twenty-feet high all the way around."

Adjusting the powerful-scope till the distant buildings were in her face, Martine yelped, "Oh shit." Snapping multitudes of pictures, she reasoned out-loud, "They got the cameras on the main building, and the transmitter is on the ground—it's on. There Is no way to disarm this system. They're using fiber optics."

"Any other way in?" Alexa asked anxiously.

"Not really. You couldn't parachute in without being detected."

Eva disagreed, "There has to be another road, this place is huge."

Frustrated, Martine answered, "I didn't see one."

Eva grabbed the bulky camera and previewed Martine's work. "Wow, did you get close up with this camera. I've never taken photos like this. You can see every detail. I could see in the windows—if there were any."

"Right," Martine mollified. "Pictures of that building aren't much good to us now though."

Alexa balked, "Why would you think it's safe for us to go in there if we could?"

Frowning, Martine answered, "Well nobody has any idea where we are, and this place is empty right now."

Shooting a few pictures of her own, Eva made mention of her own findings, "Hey, did you see all the deer back there? How did those guys get inside? They can't jump a fence this high, and they didn't set off any alarms."

Martine took the camera and looked at Eva's photos. "I don't know, but there's a whole herd that migrated in there." Distilling her thoughts, Martine went on, "They must be coming and going, there's no water in sight."

"Well, maybe the alarms aren't really on. I told you, people fake security systems with bogus signs," Eva defended her theory.

"No," Martine said flatly. "This system discriminates between animal movement, and vegetation blowing. That does not mean the systems off, it means it was probably at least a million dollar investment."

"How do you know all this?" Eva inquired.

"Prosecuting a big case," Martine explained.

"Oh . . . that makes sense," said Eva.

Taking the camera, Alexa stated, "They must be guarding something very important."

Looking at each other Eva said, "I got an idea. Let's go."

Chapter 71

"**L**isten to me, Peter, you . . . , fucking lab rat." Glaring at his passenger, Jules pushed his agenda on Peter like a bully on the playground. "You're gonna do what I say. You took this job . . . no questions asked. If you don't want to get caught you'll do what I say. Now put this on."

Peter's head spun fast from the effects of his favorite drug. Delighted by the euphoric sensations saturating his consciousness, he blinked his eyes and fought the desire to zone-out. "Tell me again what I have to do." Shaking his head slightly, he let the indifference of his new mindset takeover. Barely alert, Peter grinned at Jules and conceded to his demands, "I know you know best."

"Damn right I do, good buddy." Jules tossed the shopping bag at Peter. "Just put this on. It's for your own protection. How else are we gonna make a hit in broad daylight and not get caught?" Patting Peter on the face, Jules imitated a Mafia crime boss. "Let's go. We're on the clock."

"Sure, Jules. You're the man." Climbing into the back of the van, Peter mumbled, "I'm gonna do it just like before. Right?"

"Right," Jules sighed. "Don't forget your wig." Reaching behind the passenger seat, he nabbed the long blonde hair piece and handed it to Peter, "get back up here as soon as you're ready."

"Whatever," Peter chuckled like a drunk.

Despite the limitations of his passive personality, Peter had become extremely important in Jules's perfect plan of corruption. Disguised like a working female police officer, Peter created the ideal deception for abducting their victims. Agreeable to the arrangement, Peter utilized his wimpy demeanor to dress like an attractive woman, while numbing his conscience with the habitual use of drugs. Finishing touches to his costume included earrings, a badge, holster, gun, and hat. Peter's transformation was complete before he slid himself back into the van's passenger seat.

Answering his phone on the first ring, Jules pushed the speaker button and greeted the caller, "Jules, here."

"Jules," a thickly accented female German voice snapped.

"Yeah?" Jules answered.

"Abbreche deine mission," ordered the commanding voice.

"Did you say abort our mission?" Jules asked abruptly. "Are you cancelling our job, Olga?"

"Du hast dein tarnung aufgegeben," replied the German woman.

"What do you mean we've blown our cover?" Jules huffed. "That's not possible. We have a contract with you. We need to get paid. Don't you try and get out of it. I'm calling my uncle."

"Dein auftrag ist fertig," Olga said in a gruff tone.

"What?" Jules pulled over and stopped the van. "Speak some English. Did you just say my contract is done?"

"Yes," Olga said with defiance. "Deine stellung ist nicht mehr sicher," her stiff foreign voice blared. "I mean, your location is no longer secure. Do you understand that?"

"Yes," Jules returned sarcastically. "We want to get paid. How will you pay us?"

"Ziehe deine ware nach sudden ab," Olga instructed.

"What? Move the cargo south?" Jules sounded panicked as he repeated every word for Peter to hear. All of it? By ourselves? Are you insane?"

"Der transport ist arrangeird," Olga explained.

"Who arranged for transportation?" Jules appeared annoyed as he probed deeper, "where are we going?"

"Mexico," Olga stated firmly.

Looking perplexed, Jules asked, "Now?"

"Now," Olga repeated.

"We're leaving now," Jules obliged as he disconnected the call.

Glancing at his watch, Jules snapped at Peter, "Change your cloths. We're out of here. You heard our new orders."

Losing his buzz, Peter's skepticism returned. Yanking the hat and wig off his head, he stared out the windshield as his thoughts ran deep. Reflecting on the manic phone call, he felt fear and vulnerability ebb its way through his gut.

"That was intense," Jules exclaimed. "Ever been to Mexico, Pete?"

"No. I don't even have a passport."

"Don't need one for there yet," Jules reassured him. "Need that driver's license you're so proud of though."

"What's up with that Olga?" Peter asked. "Who is she?"

"The coldest bitch I've ever known," Jules beat his fist on the steering wheel as he drove through the heavy traffic. "Damn it! Move out of the way, you asshole," he cussed.

"It's going to take hours to get up there during this time of day," Peter surmised. "Are we in trouble? What just happened?" Peter sounded shaky as more questions burst forth, "How do you know we're going to be safe if we go up there now?"

"Think about it, Pete. There's no way anyone can get in there. It's a fortress. Just make sure no one's following us. That's your job."

"Some job," Peter whined. "You said I'd never get caught if I just did what you said. Now we're already in trouble. So, who's Olga?"

"Olga's my Uncle William's partner. I think she ran a concentration camp."

Chapter 72

"I can't believe we just rented three dude horses," Martine said to Alexa as she watched Eva pay the weather-worn cowboy for the steeds.

Alexa agreed, "Yeah, but look at it this way, we have a way in now—hopefully." Looking back down at Martine's FBI smartphone, Alexa changed the subject, "Check it out, 'Google Earth' came up. I don't believe it."

"What? You got a connection?" Martine looked impressed.

"Oh, you might need your reading glasses," Alexa cautioned her.

Shocked that Alexa succeeded in obtaining a cell phone signal, Martine joined her daughter and studied the miniature map uploaded on the FBI's phone.

"This is awesome. Keep zooming," Martine urged.

Focused on the small screen, Martine studied the terrain on the backside of the remote facility. "Zoom a little more," she said.

"Do you see what I see?" Alexa asked.

"Yeah, we can get in here," Martine said, using the phone like a map. "If we circle around on this high ridge, we can drop down in the ravine at this spot. Looks like the horses can follow this deer trail, and then ride down in the canyon floor till about here." Using her finger nail she traced the route. "About here, we climb out. Hopefully, no fencing—no security."

"Then what?"

"When we get in, we stay on that side of the property—away from all the cameras. If the system isn't picking up on the animals roaming around there now, it won't detect us on our horses. Anything bigger or faster than a large buck or bull-elk would probably signal an alert," Martine explained.

"Check out Eva, looks like they have the horses ready," Alexa commented. "Let's get going—we're at least three miles away from the ridge."

"Come on, you guys, the horses are ready." Eva beckoned with her hand.

Entering the corral, Martine commented, "I can't believe you talked this guy into renting us these horses."

"It's a riding stable," Eva said nonchalantly. "This guy rents his horses out to people all day long."

Martine exaggerated a frown, "I know that. But, he uses them for guided trail rides," she pointed to the big highway sign that said "One hour ride $40.00." Smiling at Eva, Martine went on, "they don't let people take the horses off the property on a joy-ride."

"Well," Eva answered coolly. "I might have told him we are looking to buy some horses. I told him we'd be back by dark. He's fine."

"Can we really get there and back before dark?" Alexa questioned.

"If these three can move faster than a walk," Eva replied while patting her new horse's neck. "I picked out the youngest and best looking ones, unless one of you wants to ride old Goliath. He might not pass as a deer though." Eva laughed at Alexa's expression when she looked at the huge draft horse with hooves the size of plates.

"Ummm…No, I think I'll stick with this buckskin," Alexa replied.

"Which one do you want, mom?" Eva unhitched the reins of a white horse. "This one okay?"

Remembering her white Indian pony dream from a few nights ago, she walked over and retrieved the reins with confidence. "I believe I do want this one. What's his name?"

"They call him Sundance Kid," Eva answered proudly. "I knew he was for you."

Martine's jaw dropped slightly, "You say his name is Sundance Kid?"

"Yep," Eva replied with a nod. Leading her horse up next to Martine and Alexa, she added, "He used to be their stallion until they gelded him."

"Really," Martine mused. "He seems familiar somehow."

"Using 'Google Earth,' to zoom in was brilliant, girls. I'm sure the imaging is old and out of date, but who cares, nobody's done any development around that area since the plant went in forty years ago." Martine exchanged a grateful smile with her daughters. "It also proves that the fencing is new. Not in place when they actually mined the sand. The buildings and silos are the same though," Martine guessed.

Securing the saddle bag that tied to the back of her seat, Alexa said, "I hope you're right. I packed the camera, flashlight, and water."

Martine looked pleased, "Good thinking. Thank goodness we remembered to get a flashlight before going to Della's house."

"You got that right," Alex agreed. "I wouldn't forget to pack it in here after being in a basement like Della's."

"I just realized something about that map we just looked at." Martine shared her revelation, "The reservation land we're going to be riding on is Navajo. This part of their reservation boarders the Hopi Reservation. Hopi land is surrounded by the Navajo land. That explains the contact I've been receiving from the two very different Indian cultures."

Mounting up like a posse, Martine led the way out of the corral. "Is that old cowboy still watching us?"

"Of course. He's still shaking his head too. Who buys dude horses? I'm so embarrassed," Alexa sighed in disgust. "Eva, you'll ride anything with four shoes, a tail and a mane."

Eva changed the subject, "Whatever, let's ride." Kicking her horse she peeled out in a fast trot.

Alexa copied her sister and followed. "How do we get them to run?" Alexa's voice reverberated from the bouncy trot she was stuck in, "I need spurs."

"Hold on," Eva's voice vibrated from the fast trot she was stuck in."

"Eva, no galloping," Martine cautioned as she urged her horse to keep up. "These horses aren't thoroughbreds, or ours."

"They're fine—I'll keep it under fifty-miles-an-hour." Gathering up her long-thick-leather reins, Eva used the extra length to whack her horse's ass as hard as she could. "Hee-yaw!" Bucking his hind legs in the air, Eva's horse took off at a gallop. "Wee," she yelled.

"Hee-yaw!" Alexa yelled, coaxing her horse to follow.

Martine clucked at her horse and kicked it again. Breaking into a gallop the three horses charged towards the ridge. Excited about the chance to race away from the confinement of the stables, the three horses eagerly bore-down into a very fast run with their tails waving high in the air.

* * *

Reaching the area identified on the satellite map that Alexa downloaded, Martine looked down into the ravine that edged the backside of the large silica plant. Scanning the trail system used by the wildlife, she saw a way down that lead across the bottom towards the entrance to a cave.

"My God," Martine exclaimed. "This is really proverbial. I've seen this place before." Troubled at the sight of a steep ravine, leading up to the entrance of a cave, her mind swirled with multiple recollections. Like jello forming in a mold, her psychic impressions solidified. "This is it. This is where we go in."

Chapter 73

Dismounting their horses outside the entrance to a cave, Martine and her daughters tied the three horses up to a gnarly tree. Cautious, and suspicious of what lay ahead inside the dark space, Martine dug inside the saddlebag for the flashlight they had packed. "You stay here," she instructed Alexa and Eva. "Let me see where this goes." Checking her cell phone for a signal, she frowned, "If I'm not back in fifteen, ride out till you get a signal and call Jolene and 911."

"We're not letting you go in alone," Eva's face reddened as she defied her mother's command. "I'll go with and Alexa can watch for us."

"You're not trained to go in here and check it out."

Eva disagreed, "Neither are you."

"Fine," Martine relented. "We can't waste anymore time arguing. It's getting late. We're just gonna see what it's like in here and get out. Give us twenty minutes, Alexa. If one of us isn't back, ride out and call 911 and then Jolene."

Walking about twelve feet into the dark opening they encountered a barrier. Constructed of metal, the solid-steel door and jamb resembled a commercial-rated fire door. Hinged on the inside, the only possible way to penetrate the obstacle was with a key. Baffled by its existence, Martine tried to turn the knob. Without success, she said out loud to Eva, "Key . . . we need a key. Let's try the keys we got from Della."

"What is it," Eva asked as she used the flashlight to scan around the huge clunky obstruction.

"It's either a door rated for testing explosives or, part of the intense security system. I hope it's for security."

Eva shined the light on her mother. "Is it really locked?"

"Yep. I hope one of the keys works this door." Digging deep into her jean pocket, she pulled out the wad of keys. After trying several that didn't work, Martine finally looked pleased. "I got it," she said, and slowly opened the big door. After blocking it open and moving through the threshold, she huffed in relief, "Stay here Eva," Martine ordered. "Let me go ahead and check it out."

"No," Eva corrected her. "I'm going with."

Taking the flashlight from her daughter, she searched inside the tunnel with the wimpy source of light. "I don't see any security sensors blinking. I hope we didn't trigger an alarm. It's so far away from the building ahead they probably didn't plan on anyone finding this entrance." Using the light like a wand, she inspected the ceiling and walls. "No lights or electricity here either."

"They probably wanted to secure the area after they abandoned the place," Eva theorized.

"It's could be the fire exit," Martine whispered. "Or, they didn't want anything to get out," she added. "Let's go. We need to be really quiet. I don't know if we're going to be alone or not."

Sneaking down a long, curved, underground hallway, the two moved in tandem with Martine in front. Guided by the rays of the flashlight, Martine used the device until she saw the faint glow of another light source ahead. Switching the light off, she stopped. "I don't think we're alone." Directing Eva's attention to the stairs on the right, she pointed to the hint of light leaking out at the landing's threshold. "Someone might be there."

Tiptoeing together they crept-up to the steps and found the door partially ajar. Stalling at the foot of the stairs, they listened through the loosely hung door.

"Olga, what's our next move?" A man's voice echoed into the space where Martine and Eva hid. "Jacob and I can't move all these girls with those two guys."

"You do what I say," thick-sounding German words shouted at the man. "I have much to take care of," the woman spoke in broken English. "Do what I tell," she ordered.

"Just because some chick that Olaf targeted busted our security—that is no reason to shut all this down. We're not ready."

Anger seethed in Olga's voice, "Not just bust surveillance, kill my favorite."

Alarmed, Martine looked at Eva and mouthed an order, "Go back."

Eva vehemently shook her head to the contrary and pointed to her watch, indicating she had fifteen more minutes.

"What went wrong?" Jules asked as he entered the room. "What do you want us to do?"

"Olaf's Swedish girlfriend killed him last night, and someone showed up at the gate today," Steve replied. "They snooped around, but they're gone. That's more than you need to know. We don't need you to do anything except help move these girls out of here." Arrogant sounding, he added, "And try not to think. Don't want you in my way, or screwing anything up. I'm not here to take care of you."

Jules answered sarcastically, "Good, cause you're not my type and I ain't letting you take care of me."

Olga butted in, "Shut-up, stupid boy." Directing her attention to Jules, she gave a condescending look, "Do your job. Transport be here soon."

"You still haven't told us what to do," Jules remained obstinate.

"You wear security uniform," Olga barked. "You move girls to new location. Now! You do what Steve and Jacob say."

Peter nervously cleared his throat, "whose Jacob?"

"Jacob and Steve your new boss," Olga authorized.

"What?" Peter exclaimed.

"You don't like new boss, we leave you here," Olga's cold voice froze in the air.

Sounding shaky and scared, Peter replied, "I don't want to do this. I don't want to move any more girls. Let's get out of here, Jules."

"Yes," Jacob said. Coming out of darkest part of the room, he walked up to Peter. The German hoodlum confronted the young man, "But, you not leave like you come."

"What does that mean?" Jules flexed his upper body.

Steve moved in and shoved Jules hard, "I must be hearing things. Did you hear what I just heard?" Smarting off, he rammed his palm into Jules chest.

"Knock it off, shit-head," Jules pushed him back. "I don't think I heard anything, except you need our help."

"Just do what you're told," Steve's conceited voice cracked like a whip.

"Don't touch me again, creep," Jules seethed. "You got more issues that the evening news."

Calmer, Steve confronted Peter, "see, we just need your help. That's what you're both going to do. Don't even think about taking a walk on us. I want you to do what we tell you or Jacob here is going to rearrange your knees."

Banging a metal rod on the concrete floor, Jacob threatened Jules and Peter with the gang-style weapon, "after I fix kneecaps you be stuck here . . . alone. No walk. No crawl. You still want stay?"

"No," Jules answered. "We're in."

"Good," Olga replied. "Get ready. Dispose of all this things. We destroy with fire."

Hearing footsteps move away and doors slam, Martine kept eavesdropping. Straining to hear every sound, she stayed silent in the darkened hallway as her eyes adjusted to the dimness. Not sure if her adversaries had all left the area, she leaned towards the doorway to see if there were silhouettes moving in the adjacent room. Seeing shadowy movement on the ground, she signaled Eva to stay quiet.

"What's going on Jules?" Peter's concerned voice whined. "Listen, I didn't sign on for this kinda stuff."

"Just don't ask, Peter," Jules dodged his fears. "You don't want to mess around with any of these people."

"How are we going to move girls? We can't use gas and rags on a bunch of girls. How many girls?"

"Drugs," Jules said. "We'll use drugs."

"Something is wrong. Something is wrong with these freaky German people," Peter panicked. "What do they want with a lot of girls? You said they were going to be given back to their real families. I thought we were bounty hunters or something."

"Don't be getting a conscience now, Peter," Jules sounded annoyed. "We gotta do what they say if we want to get out of here alive."

"I don't know, man. I'm nervous, and don't trust these guys," Peter's voice quivered. "How we gonna destroy all this stuff in here?"

Eva shook Martine's arm and mouthed a message, "That's Peter."

Nodding in agreement, Martine used her forefinger to shush her daughter.

"We'll use the gas to torch this place," Jules continued his planning. "Go get your gas can out of the van," Jules ordered. "Don't mess around, Peter. You needed the money, now we've gotta finish the job and not get caught. We do what they tell us or they'll probably kill us."

At that moment chaos resumed.

"Why aren't you boys ready," Olga yelled. "Osborn is here. Truck be here soon. I leave for airport."

Commotion intensified when Steve returned with Mr. Osborn, who was in a foul mood. Addressing Peter and Jules, he hollered, "Are you girls ready? If you're not all in, we'll leave yah here."

"Can we talk?" Jules asked his boss.

"You want to talk? You think we have time to talk after I flew in here for this emergency. You go to hell, Jules," Osborn berated his nephew. "You, and your boy Peter, do the job we hired you for." Scolding Peter like a ten year old, he said under his breath, "Don't you give me any trouble, Peter. You're not part of this family, and I don't care what happens to you now."

Martine let out a gasp. Turning to Eva, she whispered, "I need a diversion. I'll stay here and think of something. You and Alexa need to call for help. Go. Get on those horses and ride. It's already getting dark."

"Okay," Eva nodded. "I have an idea." Eva took off, running down the hallway back to her sister.

Alone in the tunnel, Martine studied her surroundings. Desperate for a way to find the girls, she looked for some sort of weapon. Seeing nothing but an old shovel left behind from the earlier mining days, she slowly crept over to the abandoned tool. Stuffing the flashlight into the back of her jeans, she snatched the shovel and made her way up the stairs.

Sensing everyone was finally out of the room, she peeked through the one-inch crack to confirm her hopes. Because nothing was in the room except computers and monitors, she figured the room housed the high-tech security system they had installed on the perimeter of the grounds.

Sneaking into the room like a cat burglar, she tiptoed up to the ceiling light fixture and smashed the bulb with the end of the shovel. Accustomed to seeing in the dark, she prowled around the room for a layout of the facility. Glancing at the first active monitor, she saw a long interior hallway with several doors.

Pondering how to access the rooms, she looked at the next monitor. Darkly imaged, like the night outside, she could barely make out a white van and sports car parked outside. Noticing movement around the van, Martine realized Eva had ridden her horse up the ravine and into the property.

Martine felt panic as she watched her daughter ride up to the fancy car and drop a heavy rock on the driver's window—setting off the car's security alarm. Seconds felt like minutes as she watched Eva and her nervous horse gallop up to the building. As Eva pitched another rock into the security device, she instantly realized that a diversion had been created.

"Shit," Martine swore as the rock assault set off another noisy alarm.

Springing into action, Martine ran out of the room towards the primitive corridor she saw on the computers monitor. Dead ended by a locked security door, she huffed with desperation, "One of these better work." Digging into her jean pocket, she pulled out Dan's wad of keys. After trying two that didn't work, Martine found the one that relaxed the door knob.

Once inside the lighted passageway, she overheard the sound of running footsteps on the level above her. Wishing she was invisible, Martine took her trusty shovel and smashed each exposed light bulb as she moved down the narrow hallway. Searching for the first door, she used the shovel and cloak of darkness as her only defense.

Desperate to find them before she too was discovered, her anxious heart beat like a time bomb as she opened the first door. Inside she found a group of terrified girls, all dressed in hospital gowns, huddled together in the corner. Standing in the doorway with her rusty staff, Martine called out, "Come on girls, we need to move it now."

"Who are you?" a girl's voice called out.

"FBI," Martine answered. "We don't have much time." Waving for the girls to move out of the room, she questioned the first one, "What's your name?"

"Maria," the young girl introduced herself.

"Maria?" Martine repeated.

"Yes."

"Are there more girls here?"

"We think so," Maria acted as the spokesperson. "We don't know."

"I need to keep the lights off." Martine switched off their ceiling light. "It's really dark down there, but you must get going." Taking the flashlight out of her jeans, she handed the device to Maria. "Take this. You go first. Get out and don't come back."

Pointing in the direction she came from, Martine gave her rapid directions to go back down into the underground tunnel and hide in the ravine. "If something happens to me keep walking to your right down the ravine. My daughters are out there waiting to help."

"Come with us," Maria begged. "Please help us get out of here."

"I can't. I think there are more girls. Run. Now." Martine rushed the frightened girls back towards the tunnel she entered from.

Knowing there could easily be more adolescents in danger, she went to the next door. Inside another group of pajama clad girls were gathered in fright. Martine repeated the same commands to them. "Hurry, you can catch up to the other girls."

With only one light bulb left in the ceiling, the corridor was nearly pitch-black. Hearing the girls start to cry and whimper as they searched for an escape, Martine gripped her shovel like the mighty weapon her Archangel Michael ethereally gave her while she slept the night before. She knew she would soon encounter her enemies, if she didn't turn back herself. If the worse happened the shovel would be her only defense.

As she neared a turn in the corridor, Martine was met by a large male figure. Abruptly tackled to the ground by brute force, Martine let out a loud moan as she crashed hard on her back. Looking up, she made out the outline of a thuggish-looking man as he lifted himself off of her.

"Stand," Jacob's German voice demanded.

Gathering her faculties in the dark hall, she hurriedly gripped the shaft of her shovel and jabbed the handle into the man's stomach. Knocking the wind out of him, she rolled away as he dropped his gun and clutched his gut in pain.

Scrambling to get up from the ground, she got to her knees, and warded off his partner as he charged her. Using her shovel again, she swung hard as if she was brandishing a heavenly weapon. Hitting his kneecap with the steel blade delayed his attack.

"Bitch," Steve yelled. Pulling a gun out from the front of his pants, he threatened Martine, "You'll pay for that."

Martine swung the other way and struck his second kneecap, collapsing him to the ground. With the help of her shovel she pulled herself back on her feet and stunned him with a swift blow from the tool's metal end.

"Jacob," the fallen man yelled. "Get help."

"Nein," the German answered. "I get her, Steve." Recovering from the blow to his abdomen, Jacob came stomping after Martine.

Rushing over to where she knocked his gun, Martine turned to face Jacob and tried to wield her shovel again, but he blocked the blow and pulled the tool out of her hand. "Uh," she uttered as he disarmed her.

"No good," he warned Martine as he kicked the gun away and grabbed for her.

Suddenly a spotlight illuminated the disgusting face of her attacker. Barely ducking his grasp, she hastily backed away.

"Mom," Eva's voice called out.

"Eva?" Martine turned to see her daughter pointing the gun at the assailant. Next to Eva was Maria—blinding the man with the flashlight she had given the girl to use in her escape.

Picking up the HK45 handgun that lay on the ground, she joined the two girls. With Eva's help she forced the two men into the room that had jailed Maria and the other girls. Shutting the door, Martine knew they weren't going anywhere. "Let's go," she said to Eva and Maria.

Their exit strategy was immediately compromised. Dressed in their security uniforms, Peter and Jules initially appeared to be police officers.

"Don't shoot," Martine cried out when Jules drew his gun. "FBI. Don't add *murder in cold blood* to your crimes. The police are on their way. No one will be leaving."

Blinding Jules with the flashlight, Maria said, "These are the guys that took me."

Pointing the semi-automatic Glock she absconded from Jacob, Eva yelled out, "That's Peter." Directing her two-handed aim at him, she added, "Still want to take me out? Get in this room, or I'll be taking you out. And I don't mean to a party."

Martine's motherly instincts took over, "I'm not going to 'talk' anyone down. Drop the gun or I'll shoot you with cause."

Martine watched Jules drop his gun. Making a careful approach, she faced Jules and kicked the gun over towards Eva. After checking them for more weapons, she directed them into another room that had imprisoned young girls. "I think you saved my life," she said to Eva and Maria. Securing the self-locking door, she turned to leave with the two girls. "Where are the others?"

"They're fine," Eva answered. "Alexa has them hidden until the police get here."

Martine took Jules' gun from Eva, "Thank God you girls grew up hunting with your dad." Martine congealed her recent visions and experiences like a film editor as she stuffed one of the guns in the back of her pants, "Now where's that Olga and Osborn?"

"How did you find us?" a German man's voice echoed.

Startled by the quick response, Martine raised her gun and pointed it into the dark recesses of the passageway. Exposed by Maria directing the flashlight's rays on the advancing stranger, Martine watched the unarmed man walk towards her. Skeptical, she kept her gun targeted at his chest, "Are you surrendering?"

"I asked how you found us?" he said again.

"What does that matter?" Martine answered. "Now put your hands in the air."

Standing alone, he raised his hands over his head, "Nobody would have ever known what we were doing. How did you? No one, I mean no one had a clue—or would have ever located this facility. I gotta know how you did it."

"Now turn around and face the wall," Martine said as she walked up behind him, "Well, sir, for me you were about as subtle as a battleship in the Arizona desert."

"Not to anyone else."

Martine kicked his right calf, "spread your legs and keep your hands behind your head." Frisking him for keys and weapons, she asked, "Why don't you tell me *why*?" Martine pried sarcastically. "Money? Power? Greed?"

"Of course. All of that, and good old fashion world peace."

Finding nothing but car keys, she poked him in the back with the gun, "You're going in here with your friends. I'll let the authorities read you your rights for the last time."

Motor sounds closed in on the compound. Outside, the girls and Martine could see helicopter lights oscillating as they searched the ground and lit the way for rescue vehicles.

Pulling into the silica plant like a presidential motorcade was a stream of law enforcement and rescue vehicles. Standing outside with her white horse and little posse, Martine smiled as the first responders came out of their vehicles with guns drawn. "It's okay, officers, we're unarmed."

"Are you okay," the officer holstered his weapon. "Do you need anything?"

"A horse trailer?" Eva winked at the cop.

Mahoney jumped out of a helicopter and jogged up to Martine. "Are you okay?"

"We are now."

"I cannot believe what I've heard," he said. "Jolene and Wade filled me in as much as they could. They'll be here any moment." Pointing at Osborn and his thugs, he added, "You were without a doubt the wild card they hadn't planned on, Martine."

Martine glanced at Eva, "I wonder how that happened?"

"They never played poker with you," Mahoney said with wink.

Chapter 74

The next afternoon, Martine joined Ken Harmon outside the interview room where Jules was being held.

"Thanks for coming down here on such short notice," Ken said. "John told me about how keen you were on these two kids." Looking serious, he added, "I'm curious why and what kind of hunches you had that led you to these two."

Feeling physically drained after the harrowing events from the night before, Martine explained, "I'm still trying to figure that out myself, Ken." Puffy in the face from being knocked-around, Martine had to force a smile, "Let's find out together." Preferring to avoid discussing any supernatural details that brought her to the capture of Jules and Peter, Martine relied on her professionalism. "I'll let you take the lead on this interview."

"Jump in when I need you, Martine." Ken smiled warmly. "I see you feel terrible today. This is going to be our third attempt to get this guy to talk. Reese and Dwyer tried first and got nothing. Meyers and Helm just left and got nothing. The other kid isn't talking either."

"Of course I'll do what I can," Martine reassured him. "If we hit a dead-end here have you got Peter close by?"

"You bet we do," Ken affirmed with a nod. "Do you want to talk to him first?"

"No. It doesn't matter," Martine said confidently.

"Alright then," he chuckled. "Let's go get'em, tiger."

Opening the door for Martine, Ken let her enter first.

"Well, Jules," Ken started the interrogation. "Looks like you and your friend Peter have some explaining to do." Ken tapped his pen on the table. "I'm Ken and this is Martine. Thought you might want to tell us your side of things."

"Not a chance." folding his arms, he flaunted his insolence.

"We can find out from Peter what we need," Ken countered Jules response. "It may help if you cooperate now. Waiting too long may mean we don't need your testimony," Ken paused. "Down the road, we may be busy prosecuting you."

"Let's just start with what you were going to do with all those girls," Ken sounded firm.

"I don't need to talk to you. I said I'm waiting for my lawyer. Don't you remember reading me my rights?" Jules chuckled at his own wit.

"Sure," Ken said. "We read you your rights so that everything is by the book. We're here to do you a favor. Either cooperate, or get the book thrown at you." Ken looked strict. "You're old enough to know what that could mean."

"You can't prove I did anything wrong. I was just there by mistake," Jules smirked. "Those girls never saw me before."

"Really," Ken replied. "None of those girls ever saw you? Are you sure?"

"Damn right I'm sure," Jules smarted off. "You can't prove I had anything to do with those girls being in that place."

"Jules, buddy, I plan to prove that, even if I have to find your finger prints somewhere in that building. Or, maybe I'll find one of their prints in that white van."

"Good luck," Jules answered smugly. "Let me know how that goes for you."

Ken opened up the little file he had on Jules. "There isn't too much in here. Don't you want to keep it that way? All you have to do is cooperate. Start answering my questions."

"I'm not talking to you, or anybody except a lawyer," Jules said coyly. "When I have a lawyer you can talk to him."

Martine couldn't take it anymore, "I'm a lawyer, Jules. Why don't you talk to me?"

Glaring at her face, Jules made a slow smirk. "You're the broad that got us arrested last night. Why would I talk to you?"

"I might have been there," Martine responded. "Got a couple questions though. Let's not talk about last night, let's talk about Sharon."

"Who's Sharon?" Jules looked suspiciously at Martine. "Is she one of those girls you found hiding out in that place?"

Martine shook her head once and gave Ken the look she knew he'd been waiting for. Unable to conceal her Swedish temper she took over the interview like a blood-seeking mosquito, "No, you idiot," she said in disgust. "That was a friend of yours and Peter's. Seems she was found murdered. Seems she might have been murdered like a girl named Lauren. Seems like there are forensic similarities. Seems like we're going to be able to connect you to both girls." Pausing for a reaction, Martine glared at Jules. Making him uncomfortable, he squirmed in his chair till she broke silence, "But the good news is, as they say in the old west, 'it's better to be tried by twelve than carried by six,' so, answer this, are you going to give us some answers or am I going to talk to Peter?"

"Peter? I don't have anything to say about Peter, except don't believe anything he has to say." Tisking, Jules added, "Peter is delusional. He's psychotic. I tried to stop him from getting himself into trouble. I think he might be a big nut-job. He has a problem with drugs and hanging out with the wrong people."

"Is that right," Martine acknowledged. "You say Peter has a drug problem?"

"Yeah. That's what I'm saying," Jules stated emphatically. "You need to drug test him. If it's not too late."

Fed-up with Jules cocky disposition, Martine rose out of her chair, "Well, Jules, let me know how this works for you. You're being arrested for the murders of Sharon and Lauren. See you in court."

Jules started to capitulate, "wait . . . wait a minute."

Walking towards the door, Martine said, "I'd rather let Peter turn states evidence than see you go free?" Without turning back, Martine left Ken with Jules.

Chapter 75

Martine requested several evidence bags before she joined Ken for Peter's interrogation. Already advised that he hadn't given up any useful information, she threw a few more things in the box.

Setting the large box down on the table, she greeted Peter and took the lid off before sitting down across from him. "Here, Peter," Martine said. Reaching inside the box, she retrieved his smokes and an ashtray. "We want you to be comfortable and tell us your side of the story. Seems like a lot of things are being blamed on you."

"Me?" Peter grabbed for his cigarettes and nervously lit one as fast as he could.

"Yeah, you," Martine answered. Knowing it's far easier to know what's right than to live it, she was ready to make Peter very miserable in order to get good information. "Peter, I know your Grandmother. I called her."

"You what?" Peter's cough resurrected.

"I called her," Martine repeated her words. "She's coming down to see you. I'm going to let her watch when we interview you, that is," she paused, "if you don't cooperate."

"Don't do that," Peter looked ashamed.

Martine finessed her interrogation strategy like a champion poker player, "She won't be here for an hour. Let's see what we can get done before she arrives." Figuring most criminals would rather give up information than be exposed to someone they love and respect, Martine kept the pressure on, "We'll ask some basic questions. All you do is answer."

With his hands clasped behind his back, Ken paced behind Martine. "Why don't you start with why you have a wig in your van?" Ken cocked his head with a curious nod.

Looking panicked, Peter answered with a stammer, "I . . . I guess it was sorta a disguise."

"Are you gay or did you dress-up like a girl cop?" Martine questioned Peter as gracefully as she could.

"I'm not gay," Peter coughed. "Am I in a lot of trouble?"

"I don't know," Martine answered slowly. "Cooperating and providing valuable information may make you a witness. Do you understand how that will help you?"

"Yeah," Peter nodded sheepishly. "I think I do."

"Okay then," Ken continued. "How do you know Jules?"

"He's sorta my cousin," Peter's involuntary cough picked-up.

Observing Peter's body language, Martine asked, "What were the uniforms for?"

"Jules and I worked in security." Peter took a long drag on the cigarette. "I just started the job."

"Why did you wear a wig?" Ken asked.

"My job was to get close to some girls."

"How many girls?" en asked.

"We got close to a few," Peter cleared his throat. "I didn't know all those girls were in that place." Peter took another long drag and blew the smoke out the side of his mouth.

Ken planted both fists down on the table and leaned in, "How did you pick the girls out?" Ken kept the interview moving fast, "explain your role."

"Someone gave us the name and location. We just had to pick them up and leave the van in a disclosed location. I never saw where they took the girls, or who picked them up."

With doubt written on his face, Ken said dubiously, "I see . . . until last night?"

"Yeah," Peter said.

Ken shot his next question, "Why were those girls targeted?"

Peter coughed twice, "I have no idea."

"So the uniform and wig was a disguise to lure these girls into trusting you," Martine summarized. "Is that correct?"

"Basically," Peter fought to suppress another cough.

"And then what," Ken probed.

"Jules used a rag with gas on it to make them pass-out," Peter snuffed the cigarette out in the ashtray. "It was Jules' plan. I just did what he told me. I never hurt anyone."

"Why in the world did you go along with this, Peter?" Martine's bewildered look was shared with Ken.

Signaling Martine back with a confident nod, Ken added, "What was in it for you?"

"Money," Peter fidgeted in his chair as he lit another cigarette. "I needed the money. My car got stolen and I had a shitty job. I couldn't even pay my rent. I needed the money."

Martine opened Peter's skimpy file, and made a note while asking him her next question, "Peter, you needed money because you wanted wheels . . . and drugs. Your blood work shows a cocktail of drug favorites. Are you coughing because you're finally sober?"

Peter set his cigarette down and rubbed his down-turned head with both hands, letting out several guttural coughs, "I don't know. I don't know. You're confusing me."

"Okay, Peter," Martine continued. "Do you still trust Jules to do the right thing? Or, is he in the next room blaming everything on you?"

Resuming his chain smoking, Peter whimpered between puffs, "I don't know. I don't know. I had no idea all those girls were in that place. Jules told me we were paid to get girls back to their legal guardians. He said they were taken illegally by one of the parents. I really believed him. He said we were like bounty hunters."

"Who were those other men that were arrested with you?" Ken raised his eyebrows and backed away from the table.

"I don't know," Peter wiped his nose with the back of his hand. "That was the first time I was ever in there."

"Peter, what can you tell us about Sharon?" Martine changed the subject for another reaction.

"Sharon?" Peter looked surprised. "How do you know Sharon?"

"We're asking the questions," Martine reminded Peter. "Why don't you tell me what happened to Sharon."

"What has she got to do with anything?" Peter shook his head in disbelief. "Don't try and pin anything to do with her on me. I haven't even heard from her in years."

Martine looked perplexed, "She hasn't done anything wrong. Someone wronged her."

"What? I don't get it," Peter replied. "Who wronged her? How?"

"Your grandmother told me about your friendship with Sharon," Martine revealed. "I know she went missing. I'm wondering what you would know about that."

"Why don't you ask her?" Looking irritated, he added, "I have no idea why she took off."

Ken walked behind Peter. "We can ask her, but I don't think she's gonna answer. She's been found dead."

Trying to suppress a cough, Peter's voice cracked from the shock, "What?"

"Just tell us what happened to Sharon," Ken ordered.

Peter waned for a moment and then launched into a litany of recollections he had regarding Sharon's disappearance. Directing the blame towards Jules, Peter finished with, "Jules might have been the last person to see her."

"What were they doing together?" Martine asked.

"She liked to get high smelling gas."

"Peter, she may have died from smelling that gas." Martine pulled an evidence bag out of the box, displaying the contents to Peter. "Here are some of her personal effects that your grandmother found. Della found her backpack. She may have met with foul play at your home." Martine frowned and paused for a reaction before continuing, "Peter, don't you know how deadly that practice is? I'm serious. Too much sniffing will kill. Were you there or not?"

"We knew what we were doing," Peter said. Agitated, he aggressively tapped the ashes off his cigarette. "Jules wouldn't let her get too much."

"What if he did?" Ken injected himself in the conversation. "Would he tell you? Sniffing gas could end someone's life accidently, or deliberately."

Martine used both her elbows to lean into the table. "Peter, maybe Jules thought she was getting what was coming to her. Your grandmother seems to think Jules didn't really like her around."

Visibly shaken, Peter cried out, "I didn't have anything to do with Sharon's death. I loved her. I'm not an evil person."

Reacting to his last statement, Martine's curiosity delved into the origins of Peter's cough, "Peter, explain to me when you got this cough reflex? Do you have some type of nervous disorder?"

"Of course not," Peter sounded more irked.

Pulling a file out of the evidence box, Martine set it down between her and Peter as she proceeded, "There's a saying—perhaps you've heard it. 'All it takes for evil to succeed is for good people to say it doesn't exist, or it's none of my business.' Have you ever done that?"

"Whatever," Peter deflected the insight Martine tried to impart. Putting out his cigarette, he tried to avoid eye contact.

"Peter, this is the investigator's report regarding your mother and stepfather's murder-suicide." Proving her point, she opened the file to reveal the old memory. "I'll re-open this case." Martine stayed sedentary. "I think I know what really happened that day."

Peter grabbed for the pack of cigarettes, and pulled one out, "How could you?" Lighting up his smoke, he tried to dodge Martine's look.

"Easy." Martine continued to berate him, "You came home and found your mother murdered by your stepfather. It's obvious he strangled her. But no way does a creep like that kill himself. I think you know the difference between good and evil and you took your stepfather's gun and shot him. I think you stood up to the evil. Peter, that doesn't make you evil. You were defending yourself and your mother. You live with this cough because of what you had to do when you were a little boy."

"How could you tell that from an old file?" Peter asked.

"Because of the trajectory of the bullet. It is a perfect aim if the shooter is about eight years old. We're a little more sophisticated with this type of forensics than they were in a one-sheriff town."

Peter's eyes began to water as he finally made eye contact with Martine, "What are you going to do about it?"

Martine felt sorry for Peter, more than she expected to. "Nothing. There obviously isn't a crime scene anymore, and based on what I've heard, you did what you did in self-defense. I just have a few more questions." Removing the Ouija board from the box, she asked, "Did you three play with this board?"

Confused by the absurd question, Peter responded, "Yeah. What about it? We didn't steal it. It belonged to somebody from Jules's family. Sharon liked to play with it."

Knowing that the board was probably the source of Peter's succubus and more, Martine tried to be discrete around Ken. Noticing Ken was on the phone again she asked Peter, "Have you experienced any unusual visitors at night?"

"Maybe?" Peter glanced back at Martine suspiciously.

"You might want to banish that illusionary visitor before more harm comes to you."

Accepting Martine's nuance, Peter nodded slowly, "Can I?"

Hearing Ken answer a phone call, she whispered, "It's easy if you verbally send it away."

Peter nervously responded, "Does it have a name?"

"Yes," Martine answered. "Better not to use it though."

Terminating the phone call, Ken joined in again, "Do you acknowledge that these girls were taken against their will?"

"Yeah," Peter said dejectedly.

Ken directed his focus to Martine, "That was Quantico. Lauren's forensic samples prove she was pregnant prior to death. Appears she was very diabetic and probably suffered from seizures."

"What do you know about a girl named Lauren, Peter?" Martine snapped.

"Nothing. I swear." Peter fiercely shook his head. "Jules said the girls had to be in perfect condition when they were delivered, or we don't get paid. I never hurt anyone."

Because her suspicions were right and Lauren's death may have been accidental, she believed Peter. Likewise, if her pregnancy was deliberately terminated she felt certain Peter was not involved during that period of time. "Good," Martine said. "You will make a good witness if you answer the rest of this agent's questions. Ken can be trusted to help you more than anyone else in your life."

Certain that they had acquired Peter's complete cooperation, Martine excused her from the room, "I need to leave now. When you're done with your statement you can see your Grandmother. She'll be here soon."

Chapter 76

"Come on, girls," Martine hollered. "Let's load the cars up before breakfast." Rolling her suitcase down her sister's hallway, she paused next to the bathroom door. "Hey, did you hear me with that hair blower going?"

"Yes, we heard you," Eva answered for them. "I wish we didn't have to leave today."

"I know, but you've already missed too much school. Let's get you graduated."

Eva spoke over the noisy hair dryer, "I know."

Martine called back as she moved on, "I'll meet you in the kitchen."

Martine loaded her bags in the jeep and breathed in the warm Arizona air.

"Breakfast is ready," Jolene announced through the screen door.

"Coming," Martine answered.

Meeting Martine at the doorway, Jolene opened the door for her. "Before you take off today do you want to call Director Mahoney? He really wants to know if you would consider another case and he doesn't understand why you won't make any statements to the press."

"Jolene, I'm sure he knows I'm still thinking about doing another consulting job for him. And why would I want my name in the paper? I like being under the radar. Right now I just want to get back to Colorado. I can call him from there."

"I know. I guess I'm the one that wants to know what you've decided. I'm not ready for you guys to go."

"We don't want to leave you either, but last night I started getting really homesick for my little place in the mountains. I'm ready to get back. I only packed for a long weekend. Not a permanent stay. I can't keep wearing the same clothes every day."

Walking back to the kitchen together, Jolene snapped her fingers. "Oh, Teddy sent you an e-mail this morning. He said it's a little present. There's an attachment."

Martine stopped, "Okay. Do I have time to look at it now?"

"Probably not," Jolene said. "I mean it's a pretty big file and you won't have time to read it all now. Just push print if you want it. I also forwarded the e-mail to your personal e-mail address. So, you'll be able to have it when you get home."

"Thanks," Martine said, walking over to Jolene's computer.

"No problem," Jolene returned.

Sitting down at Jolene's computer, Martine checked-out the e-mail. "I can't believe it!" she exclaimed. "It's Gretel's diary. Teddy said he will return the diary to Della, or purchase it from her for a handsome price. He has read it and oversaw the translation. How could anyone translate that whole diary in two days?" Martine tossed her head in disbelief. "Oh, it says that Teddy's class translated it for a college competition," Martine kept talking out loud as she read the entire e-mail message. "Wow. I had no idea I'd ever read the rest of Gretel's story."

Hearing the commotion of her girls as they wheeled their suitcases to the front door made her quit reading and hit the print button. Joined together at the dining room table, Martine listened to Alexa, Eva, and Jolene chatter like chimps as they each dished up pancakes and eggs.

"I can't believe the four of us solved the biggest case your department ever handled," Eva bragged. "And all those guys you work with thought we were like handicapped."

"We couldn't have done it without your mother." Jolene beamed with admiration.

"Actually, it really did take all four of us. Remember how Eva and Alexa tracked down Peter, bugged his van, and found his wig," Martine reminisced. "Nobody would have ever found us if that bug and tracking device wasn't in that van."

"Yeah," Jolene chimed in. "How 'bout the interview your mother insisted on with Lauren's parents? Mahoney really thought she was strange for insisting on that. We could never have explained her death if you hadn't figured out she was adopted, and diabetic."

"At least we know it wasn't premeditated murder," Martine sighed. "She probably did die of complications resulting from an abnormal pregnancy."

"They still caused her death," Jolene added.

"That they did," Martine concluded. "I know that isn't really very much consolation for the family."

"Right, how about when mom dragged us down to Della's basement and made us get joints, finger prints, and pictures," Eva recapped.

"Oh, how 'bout Alexa and me using Jolene's scrabble tiles to solve word puzzles from your dream," Alexa recounted.

"And what about some of those dreams," Eva said teasingly. "The wicked succubi and evil warlock?"

"Augh." Jolene cringed. "Lions, bears, wolves, rodents, and skunks. Did I miss anything?"

"Who were the skunks?" Jolene asked.

"Peter and Jules," Eva shouted. "They weren't getting along when we showed up and found all those girls."

"Eva's right," Martine agreed. "It took me a while to figure out that Jules and Peter were definitely the skunks." Martine elaborated, "As kids, they used a crude method of drugging themselves by using pure gasoline to get high. Jules probably got high with Sharon and didn't get her off the gas can in time. I think she died accidently and he couldn't admit it to Peter. I think that's why Jules hatched the plan that he could easily abduct girls by using gas. He knew its' effect."

"So, sniffing gas can kill?" Alexa questioned Martine.

"Absolutely," she replied.

Alexa's face showed disgust. "How dumb and dangerous."

"Don't forget the Spirit Guides," Martine reminded them. "Thunder Beings, Hopi's, Navajo's, and Anasazi's."

"And the key. How many clues were there about that key? The key we found at Della's house," Alexa shouted.

"The Bible," Eva cried out. "Genesis, Chapter 6, Verse 4. How long did it take mom to figure out her alarm clock was giving her clues?" Eva flipped her hand up in the air.

"And the land I kept seeing in my dreams," Martine collaborated. "Desolate uninhabitable reservation land. Land that has been in the possession of Native American Indians for eons. Who would have thought these ghoulish crimes were being hidden from everyone on remote innocent Indian reservation land?"

Jolene rubbed her temple, "And the lion. The lion that would be your new friend turned out to be Mahoney's best friend, Teddy," Jolene mused. "If he only knew."

Martine shrugged. "Hellish realms, Nazi soldiers, demented demons, and traitors. Could there be more?"

"Hardly," Jolene answered. "It seems all your visions were relevant, Martine."

"Yeah," she agreed. "Why when we talk to God, and his heavenly hierarchy, do we call it praying? But, when they talk to us, we're crazy?" Martine said as she looked at her audience. "I'm really glad I listened. I'm really glad I listened to you, Jolene."

Jolene furrowed her eyebrows. "What do you mean?"

"Your life was being monitored. That big guy you took-out was planning on abducting you. Your own heritage is what he saw. It had nothing to do with the FBI. You trusted me to help when you sensed something was very wrong. You called me when you didn't know who to confide in."

"Yeah, she's right," Eva agreed.

"We heard them talk about it when we were hiding in that tunnel," Eva confirmed the fact. "That big guy picked you as his target."

"Just because of my heritage?"

"Your name, your characteristics, your ancestry, and your age," Martine confirmed. "You were in danger. That's a big enough concern to have a call for assistance go out to all the helping guides that follow our family lineage," Martine explained. "Jolene, that shows you have awareness. You called me, remember?"

"So, who's the traitor?" Eva blurted.

"Is it Peter or Jules?"

"That's right." Martine sat back. "Someone is the traitor. I'm not sure who or how. I don't know if it is important at this point."

"No kidding," Jolene agreed. "It could be that 'Terminator' guy that wanted to take me."

"Exactly," Eva said. "We figured everything else out, didn't we?"

Jolene did a high-five with Eva, "I think so. Your mother even figured out that legal stuff. You know what I mean. The F.U.C.K. thing."

"Sorta," Martine hesitated. "I never figured out why all the dreams . . . or, clues, didn't all make sense to me. I thought some would shake out after the FBI arrested all those people and started their investigation."

"Like what?" Alexa asked. "It's only been like a couple days."

"Well, the puzzle words you and Eva figured out have me a little confused. I assumed the clue 'Woman-Hitler' had to do with Gretel."

"Right," Jolene said. "Who else?"

"I don't know. Because the clue 'Mother-in-law' didn't make sense then. And the clue, which had a double meaning, would pertain to the same person. And I assumed it was important. And it would point to someone that would be a criminal."

Eva shrugged, "Is that all?"

"No. Not entirely. I don't think I know exactly what the double meaning of 'thirteen' and twelve + one stands for. And who's the badger?"

"It's no big deal." Jolene stacked her empty plate on Eva's. "They may still find more things out. It's probably going to make more sense when they're prosecuted."

Martine stacked her plate on Alexa's. "I just don't like loose ends."

Eva stood up to remove the tableware. "They're probably just incidental things. You know what I mean?"

"Traitor is a big one, folks. Technically a traitor is like the worst offense. That wouldn't be incidental."

"How can that be?" Jolene passed Eva some dishes. "I thought murder was the worst offense."

"Traitors—betray," Martine stated. Rolling her thoughts like a bingo cage, she closed her eyes and searched her mind for the legal definition. Reciting from memory, Martine described the enemy she hadn't found, "Traitors betray or deceive someone that trusted them or loved them. It's deliberate," she started counting the characteristics with her fingers. "Premeditated. Calculating. Treacherous," pausing for more memory, she took her last bite of breakfast. "Oh, an immoral violation of trust or confidence. Someone who misleads in a relationship."

"It's not murder?" Jolene questioned again. "Wouldn't murder be worse, wouldn't it?"

"It can involve murder, or cause murder. It's just worse because the victim morally and psychologically trusted someone who . . . deliberately destroyed them. Like King Henry VIII did to most of his wives, Benedict Arnold did to America, Brutus did to Julius Caesar, Rasputin did to Emperor Nicolas, and Himmler did to Hitler."

"Sheesh," Eva said. "Like Judas Iscariot did to Jesus."

"Exactly, Eva," Martine affirmed.

"Sounds like a sociopath," Alexa added. "My psychology class paper was on that disorder. They are nasty people."

"Traitors probably are sociopaths. Judas could have easily been a sociopath."

"What are sociopaths' like?" Eva questioned.

"No conscience," Alexa answered. "Spoiled. Blame their failures on others." Searching the air with her eyes she pondered the definition's depth. "Isolated personalities. They harbor grudges." Closing her eyes briefly, she exclaimed, "Oh, they like to get even. Really poor losers that are socially handicapped." Directing her attention back to her listening audience she concluded, "They are pouters. They are unable to love or be loved. Rarely have a mate."

"Oh my God," Martine shouted. "Where's my brief case."

"What is it?" Alexa demanded.

"I'll get it," Eva offered. "It's by the door."

Eva moved briskly to fetch Martine's briefcase. "Got it." Jogging back to the table she presented it to Martine. "What is it?"

"My journal. I need my journal," she repeated. Martine stretched her hand out to accept her satchel from Eva. Pulling out her journal, she flipped through her hand written pages, "Where is it?" Skimming like a speed reader, she complained out loud, "I know it's here. It's at the beginning. Where is it?"

Confused by the commotion, Eva, Alexa, and Jolene stared at each other as Martine frantically scanned through her journal.

"I got it. Listen to this," she took a deep breath.

"The truth is hidden—the story deep,
It's only there for those who seek,
To pass the test and lessons learned,
Find the meaning in two double words,
Never forget your guides are near,
There is no need for human fear,
Narrow minded you are not,
Find the things that time forgot,
So much is there for us to show,
With time and wisdom you will know,
Look among the letters sublime,
To see how man offends the divine."

"Yeah," Alexa said. "I remember that's the dream with the Indian guide and letters we made into words."

"Correct. But listen, the first line says, *the truth is hidden—the story deep.* Whose story?"

"I don't know. Peter's?" Eva suggested.

"No. Not Peter's. We have a real story. In German. We need to finish reading the story."

"What story?" Alexa asked.

"Gretel's diary. A diary is a real life story. We have it. It's on Jolene's printer. I just printed it."

Alexa jumped up. "I'll get it." Returning back to the group, she said, "It's a typed manuscript. Wow, who did this?"

Jolene pulled her chair next to Alexa's. "Teddy sent it this morning for your mother." Fanning the pages she added, "Martine, this is a book. What are you going to find in it? Plus we solved the case. We found the girls and caught the bad guys. I don't think any of them are going to get off. We'll find the rest of them if there are any more. They're certainly not going to be named in this old diary."

"It'll be fine, mom. You saved the day. You solved the case. It's over. Right?" Eva reassured.

"No, I don't think so. Not until we find the hidden truth in the story. Remember? *It's only there for those who seek.*" Studying her own notes, she said, "Ah ha. It says here, *find the things that you forgot. With time and wisdom you will know. Look among the letters sublime,*" stalling, she looked up with a blank expression. "Look for an entry in that diary of Gretel's for December first or January twelfth. Find *twelve plus one*, or *one plus twelve.*"

"Cool," Alexa said. "Every entry in here is clearly dated in the margin, just like a diary. It's' so formal."

Turning over page after page, Alexa examined each left margin for the number's 12-1 or 1-12. "I got it. Here it is, 12-1." Paging forward, Alexa counted the pages left in Gretel's book. "This is close to the end of her story."

"Just read it, Alexa," Eva said excitedly.

"Okay, here is 12-1," Alexa started. "'*The year has been prosperous and exciting. We begin preparing celebrations for the Winter Solstice and Christmas season. My children only think about stories and presents. All, except for my daughter Ada. Ada and her twin brother Harold turned fifteen on December first. Their father sent special gifts and promised to come in January. The birthday party was spectacular. The girls all dressed in the finest clothing and the boys wore uniforms fit for the elite. Harold came home from his boarding school wearing a new uniform. Harold showed off his medals of honor from the military academy he attended. My son was handsome like a man and captured the attention of all his brothers and sisters. Ada's girlfriends stared and giggled when he walked by.*

Harold resembled me, but took charge, like his high-ranking father. At the birthday extravaganza the most popular musicians played as everyone danced. Harold looked like a prince when he danced with the girls. Everyone admired my beautiful son as he twirled young women on the dance floor. I'm so proud of my confident and talented son. He will be famous. Because he is quick-witted, outspoken, and intelligent, he will be a great leader like he was raised to be.'" Alexa crinkled her nose, "Is this helping?"

Impatient, Martine answered, "Yes, yes. Keep going."

"Okay," Alexa continued, "*'Ada got in a fight with her brother Harold. Ada was angry that all her friends wanted to be with Harold and ignored her. She wasn't asked to dance and blamed Harold. Ada said she was teased that if she looked more like her brother, she might be pretty. Ada was insulted and ran away from the birthday party. Ada has a jealous mind that makes her mean to others. She is not kind to her brothers and sisters. She said she will run away.'"* Alexa stopped reading to comment, "What a brat."

"Yeah, yeah," Martine agreed. "Keep going. Don't stop."

"Next entry is 12-27," Alexa announced. "*'The holidays were a wonderful time. Harold will leave for school in two days. He waits for his father who is now the Commander and Chief for the Fuhrer. Ada has stayed in her room and pouted for weeks. She found out that she will marry a special soldier and be an important wife. Ada does not want to marry any soldier. Ada wants to be a soldier like her brother. Ada hates her brother because he can do what he wants to do. He will be famous and she will not. Ada screamed at her brother that she wished he would die.'"*

"She's a bitch," Eva remarked.

"Here's the 1-12 entry," Alexa went on. "*'Today we received word that the enemy soldiers are advancing. My children are not safe. Their father does not trust the Fuhrer. He fears we are all in danger from American and British soldiers. He has promised to negotiate safety for all of us. Ada, my oldest daughter guards us and is a soldier like her father. Ada refuses to hide with her brothers and sisters. She fights for Hitler. Ada loves the Fuhrer. She will do anything for him.'"*

"Read on," Martine said.

"1-15," Alexa continued. *"Ada's future husband was killed in bombing. Ada will not stay with us anymore. She dressed in Harold's uniform and left to fight for Fuhrer."*

"Last entry was 5-2, 1945," Alexa announced. *"'Intercepted message that Heinrich was captured by British forces.'"*

"Oh my gosh," Martine took the diary back and looked at the last entry. "Their father was Himmler. For sure."

"How do you know?" Jolene asked.

"In January 1945 Himmler was Commander-in-Chief and was successful in pushing back the Americans and French. Hitler was so impressed with his loyal comrade that he gave him another army to fight the Soviets with. He put Himmler in charge of stopping the Soviets from taking Berlin. In the end, Himmler ultimately sold out Hitler to save himself."

Like the walls of Jericho, Martine's mind blew open wide and the mental blocks that held her in limitation came tumbling down, shattering into shards. Memories of her recent encounters began fitting together like a finished gig-saw-puzzle. "I got it. I know what happened."

Digging in her purse for her cell phone, she surveyed Eva, Alexa, and Jolene. "I'm not crazy." Speed dialing John Mahoney, she continued as her phone rang, "I'm getting to the bottom of this today."

Visibly perplexed, Eva said, "We're not leaving?"

"Not yet." Turning away from the trio, Martine couldn't contain the speed of her thoughts, "John, where is Osborn? I need to see him."

"He's right where you left him. In jail."

"Has he talked? Get anything out of him yet?"

"Not a thing. He's lawyered up."

"Meet me there?"

"Right," he said with a chuckle. "I should be used to this by now, shouldn't I, Martine." Hearing no answer, he got serious, "Is everything okay? I thought you were leaving today."

"I'm not leaving quite yet. I need you to bring a few things with."

"Okay," Mahoney said. "Are you going to tell me what this is all about?"

"I will when I see you."

Chapter 77

"**W**ell, are you going to tell us what this is all about?" Mahoney asked Martine as they stood outside the interview room.

"Absolutely," she answered. "Did you bring everything?"

Ken answered, "Yeah. I think we got everything. We are waiting for feedback from Interpol. Their clocks are different over there. The time change had them eating dinner when I called. They're getting on it as we speak." Ken handed off the items he was holding.

Martine took the bundle of objects that Ken handed her. "Let me know as soon as you get something."

"Of course," Ken replied. "Where are you going with this stuff?"

"In there. Alone." Martine looked through the one-way mirrored window at the man she had busted just days earlier.

Ken chuckled, "That's not what I mean."

"You're not interrogating him alone," Mahoney took her arm to stop her. "He won't talk without his fancy lawyers."

Martine, feeling indignant, shook her arm free, "This guy is mine. I need to do this. I need to try."

Ken interrupted, "Let her go, John. She'll be fine. This will probably be really good to watch." Escorting her to the locked door, he wished her good luck.

"Osborn, look who's here to see you," Ken announced as he opened the door to the interview room. "She wants to say goodbye."

Entering the room alone, Martine faced the criminal that tried to have her killed. "Good afternoon, William. Do you have time for a chat?" Throwing down the pack of cigarettes Ken had given her, she pushed them towards him. "I hear you like these."

William Osborn admired the pack and picked them up. "I don't think we have anything else to talk about." Opening up the brand he favored, he smirked, "Cheap tricks aren't going to work on me."

"Yes we do have something to talk about, and you guessed right, it's a little tricky. I'll start. Tell me again what you were going to do with all those girls?"

"I told you, modeling."

"Right," she said sarcastically. "What kind of modeling?"

"The girls were going to model bathing suits."

"That's fine. Tell me who they were going to model for?"

"Guys. Guys like that kinda stuff," he smarted-off.

"Who are you really working for? Who paid for this operation? I'm sorry, William, you're just not bright enough to organize a racket like this."

"Don't bother insulting me, it won't work. I'm not telling you anything else. I'm already going down hard according to your boss. That's as good as it's going to get for you."

"Tell me about Ada Schultz."

"Don't know her." William Osborn took out a cigarette.

"Yes you do, William. She's your mother-in-law. Isn't she?"

Lighting his cigarette, he arrogantly blew out the match. "No she's not."

"You don't think Ada Schultz is your mother-in-law?"

"Nope. She must be someone else's."

"No. I say she's yours," Martine persisted.

Leaning in towards Martine, he blew smoke in her face, "You're crazy. I don't even know where my parents are much less my mother-in-law."

"I think I'm right," Martine continued. "But I don't need to find her to prove it."

"Lady, how are you going to prove that someone I don't know is my mother-in-law?"

"I have DNA," Martine set down a dirty ashtray with a snuffed out cigarette in it.

"Whose is that? I don't smoke butts. It must be someone else's."

"You're right. It's not yours. It's your nephew Jules'. We got his DNA all over the place. Actually, we already ran it." Shoving Jules DNA results across the table, she added, "seems we've turned up some unique ancestry gene in his profile." Martine elaborated, "A very unique German ancestry gene."

"I don't have a nephew," he argued. "You're wrong again. Having a bad day, counselor?"

"No. I'm not having a bad day. You are."

"This interview is over. You can't prove any of this."

"This isn't an interview, or interrogation. It's your last chance to talk and make it easier for you and Jules."

"Easier than what? Who told you that Jules was my nephew?"

Martine set a hand held tape recorder on the table and clicked it on, *'Think about it Pete. There's no way anyone can get in there. It's a fortress. Just make sure no one's following us. That's your job.'*

'Some job. You said I'd never get caught if I just did what you said. Now we're already in trouble. So, who's Olga?'

'Olga's my Uncle William's partner. I think she ran a concentration camp.'

Stopping the tape recorder, Martine looked down at William Osborn, "That was Peter and Jules. Oh, there is a lot more where that came from."

Osborn's jaw slacked. "So what's the big deal if Jules is my nephew?"

"It means you were both working for a vicious woman that has evaded criminal prosecution for decades. It means you know where she is. It means your real name is William Mann, and you were married to Ada Schultz's daughter, and your other alias is Schultzy."

Shocked at her wild conclusion, William got defensive. "You'll never find out that kind of information from me or anyone."

"We can now. We just needed her DNA to prove who she really was."

"You don't know what you're talking about. How are you going to prove Jules is related to whoever you're looking for?"

"With a little forensics' help, and Jules DNA, we will prove who she really is."

"I'm not going to help you," William's obstinate voice echoed in the cell-type room.

"Helping the FBI is easier than being extradited back to Germany—that is when we're done with you."

Alarm spread across William's face. "What does Germany have to do with this? What are you talking about?"

"Well, I have this journal." She dropped Gretel's diary on the table for William to see. "And this baby book with a lock of your mother-in-law's newborn hair. Carefully opening the ancient looking book, she started, "Oh," pausing she tossed a World War II hat on the table, "and this hat that will probably have the DNA of Ada's father."

Opening the book up to the page with hair clippings, Martine explained, "This journal belonged to Gretel, the mother of your mother-in-law. Gretel kept a lock of hair from all of her children, including Ada and Ada's twin brother Harold. Who, was apparently murdered by your own mother-in-law, Ada. Gretel's memoirs are as dramatic as a daytime soap opera. Ada did a good job hiding you here. That is until you got caught."

"Is that all you got?" William said smugly. "So what if she's my mother-in-law?"

"You're mother-in-law hired you to round up these girls for her. She had plans for them, not you."

"I don't know anything about that," he smirked. "Why would I round up girls for some mother-in-law. I'm not even married."

Martine rapped her knuckles on the table, "You're not married now. But you were. You were married to Elsa. You came here when Laura married a boy named Dan. Remember him? The thing is you changed your name and stayed here after Laura died. You are a wanted criminal. Just tell me when I'm wrong."

Showing displeasure, he yelled as he jerked his shackled leg, "This is bullshit. Why would I ever go in business with some old mother-in-law?"

Pleased at his reaction, Martine pressed him, "Blackmail."

Bewildered at her statement, Oswald denied it, "Why would I blackmail my mother-in-law? That is laughable and you're a joke."

"You weren't blackmailing her," she continued pressuring him. "She was blackmailing you. You've been a fugitive. You are a wanted man. I'm guessing it was pretty bad. Or, maybe you just didn't want to be married to her daughter Elsa and hid out here until Ada found you. Either way, you're caught."

Defying her allegations, Oswald spouted louder, "You are out of your mind. If you think you can make me talk. Guess again."

"Excuse me." Martine answered her ringing phone. Opening it up, she saw that a text had been sent. Previewing the miniature screen, she scrolled through the document. "You want to see what you looked liked twenty years ago?" Martine leaned over and quickly flashed William Osborn his old rap sheet. Walking back to her side of the table, she said, "You look the same to me. After we enhance it and blow it up to actual size, it will be you." Hearing another chime from her phone, she watched her phone display another rap sheet. "Here's the one I've been waiting for. Want to see it?"

"No. I don't have to," Osborn rebuked Martine's newest transmission."

"So," she started, "you do know that Ada has been wanted for murder. Make that murder and war crimes. Blending into an orphanage after the war was a great cover till now. I think we can prove that when your friend Olga leads us to Ada." Martine softly clucked her tongue as she nodded positively. "You might think she got away, but that's not exactly true," Martine said mysteriously.

Visibly alarmed, Osborn rambled, "I wasn't going to hurt anyone, and I certainly didn't murder anyone."

"Really?" Martine moved in closer. "Maybe you should tell me what you know, because I think Ada murdered her family to get what she wanted and to protect someone else's identity."

"Whose?"

Pleased that she finally solicited his interest, Martine fired back her response, "Her father's."

"And why would she do that?"

"Because she believed in his cause and wanted to fulfill his legacy." Anxious to keep him engaged, she tried to ignite his curiosity with more shocking news, "She murdered her own brother out of jealousy, and the rest of her family to gain power in her father's world. She believed in his cause and carried on his crimes against humanity. Did you really know what she was up to?"

"I don't know what you're talking about."

"Let me read something to you," Martine picked up Gretel's typed memoirs. "2-4. *'Ada has not returned since her Brother Harold's death. She left after his death to join her father's Secret Service Action Guards. She dressed herself in Harold's uniform and said she looked better as a man.'*"

Martine continued, "3-9. *'I found a secret letter in Nurse Schneider's room. She communicates with Ada. Ada has successfully impersonated her brother Harold and has become a soldier. She told Nurse Schneider that I am a spy and cannot be trusted. Ada said we must be moved to protect the cause.'*"

Martine glanced up to see if William was listening. "4-11. *'The memories of fancy balls, beautiful women, military banquets, and victory celebrations are fading fast. Bombings are constant and enemy soldiers are getting closer. I want to fight for the cause, but I still have six young children that need to be protected. If we lose the house we will have no food or shelter. German Resistance Fighters have told us to move by tomorrow. Frau Schneider said we are in danger if we stay. Frau Schneider has found a safe house to move to. Only some possessions are allowed. I must move important information for the Fuhrer. I have no one else to trust.'*"

Before proceeding, Martine noticed this next entry added up to thirteen too, "I wonder if you knew about this. 4-9. *'We are living in basement of small house. I fear we will be captured and this will be my last time to write. The children's father has not sent communication for months. BBC radio reports that Heinrich is negotiating* with Western Allies and Soviets are three-hundred meters from the Chancellery. Frau Schneider brings Ada to us. Ada says Heinrich is captured and we are not safe. She says we must protect the Fuhrer's cause. She is right, our magnificent idea is finished. With everything beautiful, admirable, noble, and good that I have in my life being destroyed there will be nothing left for us. I must do what's right and obey. The world that will come after the Fuhrer and National Social-ism is not worth living in for me and my children. Ada brought poison for all of us. Ada warns me not to fall into the enemy's hands. The Third Reich must be saved, and we will be tortured by its enemies if we are found.'" Martine set the manuscript down. "How many more did she deceive, betray, destroy and murder so that she and her father's legacy could survive?"

"What does that have to do with anything? What would she want with a bunch of young girls?" Osborn produced a menacing smile.

"I wager," Martine answered, "if she were as diabolical as her own father, it's plenty. I mean plenty. Crimes against Humanity ring any bells? Want me to explain?"

Osborn smirked, "Maybe she just wanted the world to be a bet-ter place. It sure isn't being run very well right now."

Martine objected vehemently, "Don't you mean dominance? You did this to re-create a God–centric race, didn't you?"

"Yeah that's right. What's wrong with cleaning up the human race? Don't you think your God would want this mess cleaned up before he returns? Why wouldn't we want to breed better people who are qualified to take care of this planet? Smarter, stronger, better-looking, healthier people," Osborn preached.

"Are you crazy?" Martine's brow furrowed.

Provoked by insult, Osborn began a tirade, "It's the only way to purge this world." Osborn's face creased with agitation. "And get rid of drug addicts, welfare, illegal aliens, criminals, homeless, unwanted breeding, and mentally ill. Seventy percent of the popu-lation has something wrong with them and they're draining the resources. The world won't go on much longer like this. They're depleting the planet and our checkbooks."

Martine felt the poignancy of the moment and pelted her words back at him like a machine gun, "So you feel inconvenienced? And this is your solution? Well guess what . . .? You're one of the criminals and mentally ill."

"You don't know me at all," his bitter voice rang. "I'm more . . . more than any of you will ever know."

Martine shuddered, "You're right about that, you're a Hun, Neo-Nazi, troll, retrogresser, and who knows what else."

"Shut up," William blurted, "you, little bitch."

"Excuse me?"

"Lady, you don't know who you're dealing with. We're the creators of the new world. A perfect world."

"Hell no!" her anger swelled. "It does not say God on your driver's license. Heck, I don't even know what name you use on your driver's license. But, I know exactly why you shouldn't be doing what you were about to do."

"Oh, Yeah," sarcasm swept his face. "You probably think you can help the poor by destroying the wealthy."

"No, actually I don't. *'You can't strengthen the weak by weakening the strong. You can't bring about prosperity by discouraging wealth,'*" Martine paused. "Abraham Lincoln also said, *'you cannot further the brotherhood of man by inciting class hatred.* He also said *'you cannot build character and courage by taking away people's initiative and independence, or help people by doing for them what they should do for themselves.'*"

"Abraham Lincoln. I care nothing about this man. I only answer to God's cause," the belligerent man scoffed. "And we need to get back to what God created."

"Really. Then let me help you with that. God won't ask you about the quality of your neighbors, or if they were good enough to live on your side of the planet—He'll want to know how good of a neighbor you were. God won't want to know if your neighbor has a great job—he'll want to know if you worked well with others. God won't ask what nationality your neighbor was—he'll ask how you treated all nations. Sir, you got it all wrong."

"Really—how would you stop all the countries from fighting, stealing, and blowing each other up?"

"Mr. Osborn, just when the caterpillar thought the world was over—it became a butterfly."

"That's your solution, lady? Let nature take its course? Let them kill each other, and us? Let women and dictators keep trying to run our world? What good has that done?"

"Well take this with you when you go back to your cell. 'There is only one good—*knowledge*, and one evil—*ignorance*,' Socrates."

"Bullshit. You are full of bullshit, lady."

"Do you see where world domination got you, sir? You were arrested by women."

Osborn sneered, "This is not over. You cannot stop regenerating the race we created. We will find a way to breed and rise-up."

"I want to clarify something. You and Ada activated an obsolete plan that already had failed once, and you think it will find a way to succeed. Is that right?"

"Of course it will. You can't stop it."

"Einstein once said, '*The definition of insanity is doing the same thing over and over again and expecting different results*.' I say, you, by definition, are insane, and have made the same mistake." Martine stopped briefly, "What do you say now?"

"I say I'm going to need a better lawyer."

"I say you start talking, turn states evidence, or you get to face the death penalty. Lucky for us Arizona is a capital punishment state. You were better off in Germany."

"I didn't murder anyone. Those girls were all found alive."

"Two girls are dead," Martine challenged Williams's innocence. "Sharon and Lauren will need justice. And, now that we have the 'Proof of Life' needed on Ada, which our Asian neighbors have been looking for, you and Jules can go down as accomplices to her sociopathic indiscretions."

"I don't know what you are talking about," William's distorted smile broadened on his face.

"Based on what I've learned over the last couple weeks, Ada is a self-centered, egotistical, baby-farming monster, with a God complex. When she was shunned by society she let her insatiable scorn become justified."

Certain she had identified the epicenter of the storm—Martine stared into her phone, searching for something that had caught her eye when Oswald's rap sheet was displayed on her screen. Shoving her chair back in a sudden thrust she stood up tall, towering over Oswald. Walking around the steel grey table she had been sitting at, she stopped next to him and showed him the communication. "So, you're e-mail is bager2@alltel.com.

Pausing momentarily, Martine asked her final question, "What do you know about badgers?"

"That's a stupid question," Osborn muttered.

"You're right. It's not what you know that matters. It's what I know. Let me enlighten you," Martine paused and walked back to her side of the table. "They're a member of the weasel family. They're bold and unsociable animals. They are remarkable diggers with ties to the underworld, and they have a great deal of trouble relating to others. Expressing themselves in a balanced way is one of their greatest challenges. You are a badger, and I bet Ada is badger1@alltel.com."

Satisfied she had found a conclusion that fit all her clues, Martine left the room and joined Jolene, Mahoney and Ken who observed the confrontation.

Ken spoke first, "What do you call that?"

Martine grinned at Ken, "That's what I call *cutting off the head of the snake.*"

Mahoney looked at her and asked, "How the *hell* did you figure all that out?"

Still smiling with satisfaction, she looked skyward, "*Hell* had nothing to do with it.